Brilliantly written and emotionally gripping, Ancient Secrets is a must-read for anyone who loves action packed adventures." **– Ali Whelan**

"I couldn't put it down – a gripping thriller that kept me on the edge of my seat until the very end and made me question many of the mysteries of our universe." **– Camilla Bateman**

"A fast-paced action-packed novel that takes you on an adventure into other worlds. I can't wait to see what Sam Kini does next." **– Harrison Lloyd**

ANCIENT SECRETS

The Uroboros Key

Copyright ©2024 Sam Kini

Apart from any fair dealing for the purposes of criticism or review, as permitted under Copyright, Design and Patents Acts 1998, this publication may only be reproduced, stored or transmitted, in any form or by any means, with prior permission in writing of the publishers, or in any case of the reprographic reproduction in accordance with the terms of licences issued by the Copyright Licensing Agency. Enquiries concerning reproduction outside these terms should be sent to the publishers.

PublishU Ltd.

www.PublishU.com

All rights reserved.

For Anna, who inspired me to start it.
For Seb and Elliot who inspired me to finish it.
For Jonathan and my parents who gave me the belief I had this book in me and the confidence to think I could actually do it.

Preface

I became interested in the myth and history of countries and was struck by how many things we still don't really understand about the universe around us, the mysteries of our past and the huge gaps that there are in our understanding of things. I travelled to Machu Picchu and the Amazon in Peru, Angkor Wat in Cambodia, Borneo, Bali, Thailand, Laos, India, Rwanda and Uganda (amongst others) and gained an understanding of different cultures and belief systems.

I realised that the earliest stories ever written were always attempts to explain the things that baffled humans; ways to make sense of the mysteries in the world around us.

So I decided that I wanted to write a book that was about just that: many of the secrets and mysteries of our universe in a fast-paced action-packed plot, a book that would be about growing up and trying to make sense of the world, in a very real sense.

The result was Ancient Secrets: a story set in the present day about a fourteen-year-old boy named Max who discovers a series of startling secrets. The story takes place over nine days. It's nine days that change Max's life forever and force him to question everything that he knows: about his life, his past and the very fabric of the universe.

'Try and penetrate with our limited means the secrets of nature and you will find that, behind all the discernible concatenations, there remains something subtle, intangible and inexplicable.'

– Albert Einstein

Chapters

Chapter 1:   The Visitors in the Night

Chapter 2:   The Plan

Chapter 3:   The Forbidden Door

Chapter 4:   The Mysterious Disk

Chapter 5:   The Other Crowd

Chapter 6:   The Unexpected News

Chapter 7:   The Elders

Chapter 8:   The Unusual Invitation

Chapter 9:   The Overheard Conversation

Chapter 10:   The Ancient Council

Chapter 11:   The Weird and Wonderful Shop

Chapter 12:   The Covenant

Chapter 13:   The Burden of Guilt

Chapter 14:   The Map

Chapter 15:   The Escape

Chapter 16:   The Journey Back

Chapter 17:   The Hidden People

Chapter 18:   The Rocky Start

Chapter 19: The Book of Travel Charts

Chapter 20: The Search Begins

Chapter 21: The Temple of Fangs

Chapter 22: The Room with No Exit

Chapter 23: The Second Key

Chapter 24: The Clue

Chapter 25: The Near Miss

Chapter 26: The Standing Stones

Chapter 27: The Veiled Woman

Chapter 28: The Secret Chamber

Chapter 29: The Uroborologs

Chapter 30: The Hooded Man

Chapter 31: The Return

Chapter 1
The Visitors in the Night

Max woke with a jolt. His eyes flickered open in the darkness. For a moment, he lay completely still, lying on his back, his head resting on the pillow.

He blinked. A pale sliver of moonlight was shining through the gap in his bedroom curtains casting a weak grey light through the room. His limbs felt heavy, his head felt fuzzy, his body was telling him that it was the middle of the night.

So why had he woken?

He listened hard. The sycamore tree, outside his open bedroom window, was rustling gently in the summer night air. Everything seemed quiet.

Maybe he was mistaken, he thought. Except that something had woken him. But, what?

Then the sound came again. Hushed voices drifted up from downstairs and a creak from below, as though someone was moving about in the kitchen.

He tensed immediately, then rolled over and peered at the alarm clock glowing beside his bed. 3:32 am.

Perhaps it was just his Grandad, he reasoned. But he knew that it probably wasn't. Knew that it couldn't be really. His Grandad was in bed by 10 pm every night. Why would he be up this late? Besides there was more than one voice downstairs.

A soft thud drifted up from the kitchen below.

Max felt his stomach clench with fear and then after a moment, almost without thinking, he slowly eased the covers back, slipped out of bed and crept silently across the room towards the door. The door was ajar and he paused, his hand resting on the cool metal door handle. He could feel the rapid thud of his own heartbeat. For a moment everything was quiet and then it came again; the hushed murmur of a woman's whispering voice. 'Definitely the kitchen,' he thought.

Filled with misgiving, Max eased his bedroom door open and peered across the landing. Moonlight was pouring through the landing window casting a cool milky light across the carpet. Trying to ignore the sudden trembling in his stomach, Max carefully edged his way along the landing.

Another sound drifted up from the kitchen, more distinct this time; the low, deep rumble of a man's voice. A man's voice that was not his grandad's.

Clutching the banister tightly in his sweating palm, Max held his breath and cautiously peered down into the lounge below. The kitchen door was ajar; a vertical slat of yellow light glowed through the gap casting a shaft of light across the purple patterned carpet.

Max glanced quickly around the room; he could see the phone at the far side of the lounge on the table by the kitchen door. What was he doing? What did he think he could do, even if someone had broken into the house? He was only fourteen.

A tall dark shadow flitted across the crack in the door, momentarily blocking out the light.

Max took a sharp intake of breath then quickly shrank back out of sight, his stomach twisting into a tight knot of fear. He waited for a moment – then slowly, silently, he leant forwards again and peered down into the lounge.

The woman's voice came first in a low urgent whisper, 'We came as quickly as we could; we thought you should know.'

'There have been rumours for years of course,' a man's voice came next in a low gravelly whisper, 'We've tried to keep track of him, as you know...but it's always proved impossible.' The man hesitated, 'But now we know, it was definitely him. I saw him myself.'

Someone sighed deeply.

Max hovered on the staircase, confused. Who were these people? What on earth was going on?

'We have to view this as a potentially very serious threat, Quinn.' The woman's voice continued in an anxious whisper, 'The rumours that we've started to pick up... of what he's been doing...' Her voice trailed away.

It took Max a couple of seconds to register the fact that he had just heard the woman say his grandad's name — Quinn. A million questions immediately surfaced in Max's mind. These weren't burglars — it was his grandad. His grandad never had visitors; he didn't really have any friends. In fact, in as long as Max could remember, he had never really known anyone to visit his grandad. So why was his grandad having whispered conversations with strange visitors in the middle of the night?

He slowly became aware that he was gripping the banister very tightly. Glancing down, he saw that the skin over his knuckles had turned bone-white. Max blew out a long breath, then he let go of the banister and sat down at the top of the stairs with a soft bump; his eyes flashing a deep silvery grey in the darkness.

The gruff man muttered something, but Max couldn't quite catch the words.

'So it's true...after all this time...' Quinn whispered in return.

'You know what this means...' said the woman. 'The significance of this — you realise what he has done...'

Quinn sighed heavily. 'Of course I know what it means.'

There was a long pause.

Max folded his arms across his chest, suddenly aware that he was only wearing pyjama bottoms and that he was actually quite cold.

'If we're right,' the man whispered gruffly, 'and Xegan has broken the Covenant, then he will be the first person in centuries.'

'If we're right...' the woman hesitated. 'Oh Quinn, if he has told them, then who else has he told? The ramifications of this not just for us, but for the whole of the Five Kingdoms...' her voice faltered, 'I can't even begin to imagine...'

There was a taut silence.

Max felt a sudden surge of uneasiness. There was genuine fear in the woman's voice.

'It may be a while before we come again now Quinn,' the woman whispered, 'we've brought you extra money this time, in case we can't get back...'

'We'll manage,' said Quinn.

The gruff man muttered something in a low voice, indistinct.

More questions flooded into Max's mind. What on earth was going on here?

'How are you really doing in this strange place, Quinn?' the woman asked suddenly, she sounded troubled.

'We're doing okay...' Quinn said wearily, 'it's not easy...'

'Do you think you'll ever come back home?' the woman asked gently, apprehensively.

There was a long pause and then Max heard his grandad cough quietly, 'I don't know Imeda, I just don't know.'

Home? Max shifted uneasily on the staircase, his mind racing. Surely this was his home. What on earth were they talking about?

The gruff man muttered something and then suddenly, there was the sound of chairs scraping back on the tiled kitchen floor and he was startled from his thoughts.

Realising that they must be leaving, Max quickly rose to his feet and slipped silently back across the landing to his room. He eased the bedroom door closed and crept noiselessly back into bed.

His heart hammered in his chest, Max rolled over and stared at the ceiling. What was going on? His Grandad never had visitors. *Never.* In fact, in the nine years since they had moved here, Max couldn't once remember anyone ever having visited them. Now strange people were visiting his grandad in the middle of the night and bringing them money. Why?

There was a noise downstairs, which sounded like the gentle click of the backdoor being carefully closed.

Breathing hard, Max stared into the darkness

of his room and tried to make sense of what he'd heard. He was sure that there had only been two other voices besides his grandad: a man with a deep gruff voice and a woman. The woman had been called Imeda – Max was almost sure of it – but he didn't remember the man's name being mentioned.

So, who were they? His grandad had obviously known them both well. Yet Max was positive that he had never met neither of them, nor that his grandad had ever mentioned them to him. But why? Why was he keeping it secret?

Then there was the other person they had discussed; the person called 'Xegan.' They'd said that they'd been searching for him for years, but that now he'd come back. They'd seemed worried – frightened even. But what did any of this have to do with his grandad? And why were they asking him if they were ever going home? Wasn't this their home?

Max knew that they had lived somewhere else before they had moved here. But then there had been the accident. Max didn't remember very much about it but he understood that there had been a terrible tragedy at their home. His mum and dad and his grandmother had all perished in a fire, but by some strange twist of fate, Max and his grandad were the only ones that had survived. Max had immediately gone to live with his grandad and then soon afterwards, they had moved here. But that was all he knew. All he had ever really been told. And that had been almost nine years ago.

In the nine years since they had moved here, Max couldn't once remember anyone ever having visited them. Max had always thought that it was a bit strange that they didn't seem to have any kind of contact with their old life; that his grandad seemed to have completely cut off from it. They'd never even gone back to visit. For a long time, Max had never really questioned any of it, but recently he'd started to think more about it. There were so many things that didn't quite make sense. Max had questioned his grandad about it of course. But whenever Max had asked his grandad anything about his parents or where they used to live, he had never wanted to talk about it or he got angry and Max would eventually drop the subject. Now there was this tonight. Tonight was a big deal, Max recognised that. There was definitely something that his grandad wasn't telling him. But what? Max didn't know. What he was sure of was that his grandad was keeping some secrets.

Big secrets.

The soft tread of his grandad's footsteps on the landing, distracted him from his thoughts. Max rolled over on to his side with his back to the door and pulled the covers up to his chin. The footsteps paused outside Max's bedroom door for a moment, before softly continuing along the landing. Max listened to them pass, then he rolled on to his back again and stared back up at the ceiling. His eyes scratched with tiredness, but his mind was spinning with questions.

Max lay there for a long time, frowning into the darkness and turning everything he had heard over in his mind. His head filled with strange thoughts of criminal gangs, Police Witness Protection Programmes and things he had seen on TV. Much, much, later he fell into an uneasy, restless sleep.

He slept fitfully after that and woke early the next morning. For a moment he lay under the warmth of his bedcovers, his eyes shut, the night's events flooding back. He was sick of secrets. He needed answers and it was time to talk to his grandad.

He washed and dressed quickly; glancing at his reflection in the bathroom mirror. He noticed that the black-haired, blue-eyed teenager staring back at him looked very tousled and weary this morning. His face was creased from lack of sleep and his eyes were puffy from tiredness. He did his best to quickly flatten his thick, dark, unruly hair, with a comb and a splash of water, then set off downstairs in search of breakfast.

His grandad was already in the kitchen, sitting at the table hunched over his paper. Max noticed immediately that he also looked tired and strained; his grey hair was dishevelled and his normally bright blue eyes looked shadowed, and his face looked drawn. No wonder, thought Max, glancing around the room and eyeing the three freshly washed cups on the draining board.

The radio was on a local news station and the opening notes of music chimed, heralding the 8 o'clock morning news.

'Are you not saying hello this morning?' Quinn glanced at him over his newspaper.

'Hello,' Max replied, with more indignation in his tone than he had intended.

Quinn eyed him narrowly for a moment then looked back at his paper, 'There's toast already made, if you want some.'

'No, I'll have cereal thanks,' said Max, grabbing the box from the cupboard, along with a bowl and spoon, before plonking himself onto a seat at the table, opposite his grandad.

Max stared at the cereal box in front of him, he wasn't ready to meet his grandad's gaze. He wasn't actually sure what he was about to say, now that it came down to it. He had dozens of questions spinning through his mind and he didn't really know where to start. He hadn't even decided whether to come clean and tell him what he'd overheard the previous night. Perhaps not, he decided. Better not to get him angry that he'd been eavesdropping on him before he even had chance to get his questions out.

'Grandad?' he said trying to sound casual as he poured some cereal into his bowl.

'Umm,' said Quinn, taking a bite of his toast and glancing up momentarily from his paper, before turning the next page.

'Tell me about where we used to live before we lived here.'

Quinn sighed and put down his newspaper wearily, 'But I've told you Max about a hundred times.'

'No, you haven't and anyway, what's wrong with wanting to know about where we used to live?'

Quinn contemplated him for a moment – a slight frown played about his blue eyes.

He cleared his throat, 'Well,' he began, 'we lived in a different city, it was quite a long way from here... and obviously there was the fire and... well I don't know what you want me to say Max – you know what happened. Then, we moved here.'

Max looked at him across the table and realised that this was exactly what always happened. His Grandad would be vague and then he would change the subject. Well not this time, Max thought determinedly.

'But what was it like?' he pressed. 'I mean, you know, the place and the people. What were they like?'

Quinn looked at him carefully for a moment, as though weighing how much to say.

'Well, it was nice, the people were nice,' he said evasively. 'But it was hard and we needed a fresh start after everything that had happened.'

'But what was it called though, the place where we lived?' Max persevered.

'Umm...' Quinn paused, he reddened visibly and shifted in his seat, his eyes flicking towards the clock on the wall, 'Cassini, but its miles from here.'

'Cassini, I've never heard of that place before. It sounds Italian. Could we go sometime?' Max studied his Grandad's face carefully, looking for any indication of the conversations he had overheard the night before. His face, however, was as unreadable as ever.

'Maybe...' he said carefully, 'but like I said, it's a long way from here and there's nothing really there for us now.'

Quinn returned to his paper and turned the next page, obviously believing the conversation to be over.

Max fell silent. He stared down at his cereal bowl, a tight knot of angry frustration growing inside him. Why were things always so difficult? Why couldn't he just tell him the truth?

'But are you still in touch with people, from there... from Cassini?' Max asked carefully.

Quinn didn't answer for a moment. 'A little, but not much really now,' he said taking another bite of his toast.

'But don't you miss them; everyone you used to know?' Max persevered.

Quinn slowly finished chewing his toast, his blue eyes regarded Max over his paper as though he were considering carefully what to say.

'I miss lots of things,' he said heavily. 'I miss your parents and your grandmother very much. That's why we're here Max. There's no point living there anymore.'

Max glanced down at his grandad's hands which were on top of the newspaper and watched him twist his ring around his finger. It was an unusual ring now that Max studied it properly – a dull silver grey colour and on the top was etched a large circle, with a smaller circle inside it, touching one edge. He didn't wear it on his wedding finger, but instead on the middle finger of his right hand. Max had no idea what it meant or why his grandad wore the ring but he'd had it for as long as he could remember. Another thing that he didn't know about, Max thought.

Max bit his lip and considered what to do next. 'But was that it... the only reason why we left?' he said after a moment.

It came out wrong with hindsight. He didn't mean that it was a small reason that his mother, father and grandmother had all died in the fire. He knew that it was a big deal. But he was still shocked with the wrath of what came next.

Abruptly the smile left Quinn's eyes and his mouth became a hard line. 'Max, how dare you! You will not diminish their deaths like that. You have no idea what this family has been through!' Quinn shouted, his eyes suddenly a very steely grey, 'You will drop this now!'

Max watched as his grandad's eyes changed colour from bright blue to a deep silver grey. He knew what it meant when his eyes changed like that. It was the same as when his eyes changed colour – it meant he was angry. Very angry.

Another strange thing that his grandad had never really explained to him, Max thought bitterly, the knot of angry resentment growing inside him.

'I'll tell you why!' Max roared. He felt his face flush with anger and imagined his eyes also turning grey. He knew that he should stop but he couldn't help himself now. He felt all of the questions, all of his uncertainty and frustration bubbling up inside. 'The only reason I've got no idea what this family has been through is because you don't tell me anything!' He stared at his grandad, the blood pounding in his ears. 'Secret visitors in the night, people giving us money... I'm sick of it!'

The words were out of his mouth almost before he really had a chance to decide whether or not he was going to mention it. Max watched Quinn's face change from wide-eyed shock to narrow-eyed rage.

A tense silence stretched between them for a moment.

'How dare you spy on me!' Quinn's voice was dangerously quiet.

Max glared at him across the table. His arms crossed, cereal forgotten. Fearful, but too angry to stop himself. 'You treat me like a child, but I'm not... It's my life and you don't tell me anything about it.' He pushed his chair away from the table with a jolt, keen to leave the room now.

'–and finally...' the newsreader on the Radio said, '...last night, local farmer – Ned Matthews of Grains Farm, Normington – reports that a new crop circle has again appeared in his fields. This is the tenth crop circle to appear in Ned Matthew's fields in recent years, making his farm one of the most frequent farms for crop circle sightings in the whole of Wiltshire. And next the weather – over to you Pam...'

Max stomped from the kitchen without giving his grandad a chance to reply. He grabbed his school bag from the hall and stormed out of the front door, slamming it behind him, surprising even himself with how angry he felt. It was almost as though all of the questions that had built up over the years, all of the suspicions and uneasiness that had lurked at the back of his mind for months had suddenly burst forth – and something inside him had snapped.

SAM KINI

Chapter 2
The Plan

Max had walked to the bottom of the street before he even noticed where he was, and then past the corner shop before he realised with a sinking feeling that he'd forgotten his gym kit for school. There was no way he was going back for it now, he decided. He definitely didn't want to face his grandad; he'd just have to deal with the consequences at school.

He kicked a stone down the street, his anger and resentment subsiding slightly. He just didn't understand it. Why wouldn't his grandad tell him anything? What could be so bad that he had to keep all of these secrets from him?

What caused people to have secret visitors in the middle of the night that brought them money? And why would they bring news of a person they were obviously afraid of, a person who sounded as though he came from the place where Max and his grandad used to live?

Max didn't know. What he was now absolutely certain of, was that his Grandad was keeping some pretty huge secrets. The conversation this morning had just confirmed it. If his grandad wasn't going to tell him the truth, then he would just have to find out for himself.

He wandered along the road to school, his brain buzzing with a million questions. However, by the time he had reached the school gates, the glimmerings of an idea had begun to form in his mind. Max knew that his best chance of getting any answers to his questions lay behind his grandad's locked study door.

Realising that he was still almost forty minutes early for school and having not eaten any of his breakfast, that he was actually really quite hungry, he decided to go to the corner shop to get a snack and then plan how he could get into the study. Rebelliously, he bought a chocolate bar, knowing that his grandad wouldn't approve, and then found a bench on the far side of the small square across from the school and settled himself, ready to make plans.

Quinn had always been extremely secretive about certain things and the study had been out of bounds for as long as Max could remember. He had once returned home from the shops and found Max sitting in the study. The door had actually been left open and Max had just wandered in for a look around, but Quinn had been more furious than Max could ever remember him being. That night he had asked him all sorts of odd questions and then, seeming satisfied that Max hadn't seen anything of consequence, he had finally dropped the subject. However, Max had noticed that he had been much more careful about locking the door ever since then. Max had never really understood why. Now after last night, Max felt sure somehow that it could be connected.

Luckily Max thought he knew where the key was kept. He'd watched from the landing as Quinn had put something in the drawer of his bedside table one evening just after he'd left the study. It shouldn't be too tricky to check.

Max turned the plan over his in mind. If he was right and the key was there, Max realised that he would have to make sure that he took the key at a point in the evening when he was certain that his grandad wouldn't go back into the study again. Max felt the slow burn of excitement start to build. The idea that he might actually be able to find out something – anything – that might help him understand what was really going on and where he was actually from, made him feel hugely better. In any case, he couldn't carry on like this, he decided firmly. There were just too many secrets.

He was still busy thinking this through when Bigsy and his friends rounded the corner.

'Well, look whom we have here,' Bigsy sneered, a triumphant smile spreading across his face.

Max's heart sank. 'Bigsy' – whose real name was Henry Bigson – was the class thug. He wasn't bright, but he was big for his age. He had very short brown, tightly curled hair, a freckly red face, blue eyes that were as hard as flint, big arms and loved nothing more than to taunt Max.

'Not in school now, freak boy!' Bigsy smirked. He glanced around at his three spotty friends, who laughed back.

'Why don't you make your eyes change colour again – you total freak!'

Max felt his face flush with anger, but he bit his lip and said nothing.

'What's wrong with you freak boy? Got no friends?' A triumphant smile spread across Bigsy's smug face.

There was a titter of laughter from Bigsy's friends.

Max stared at his hands trying to control his temper. This was what always happened. Bigsy would taunt him until it happened. His eyes were his cross – they always betrayed him. Hating himself for not being able to control it, Max stared at his hands and willed it not to happen.

'Oooh, scared of us, are you? Is 'ittle' weird, freak boy scared?'

Before he even had chance to respond, Bigsy had lunged for him. Max dived off the bench and out of the way of Bigsy's right fist, just as the school bell rang across the yard. He stood just out of reach of him and stared defiantly into Bigsy's hard blue eyes.

'Saved by the bell!' Bigsy sneered. 'Just you wait until later, freak boy!'

'Leave me alone Bigsy! I'm not scared of you and your stupid friends!' said Max with more confidence than he actually felt. Then he turned and marched across the square towards the school yard.

A sudden sharp pain slammed into the small of Max's back. Winded, he took a sharp intake of breath, then his knees folded from under him, his hands and then chin hit the ground.

'You should be scared!' Bigsy's voice sneered from behind him.

A cackle of laughter erupted from the group. Then they sauntered past him across the square towards school, one of the boys aiming a sharp kick at his school bag as he passed. The contents of Max's bag scattered – everywhere.

For a moment Max didn't move. Shocked, he lay sprawled across the ground. He could taste a coppery trickle of blood on his lip, his hands stung with grit. Out of the corner of his eye Max could see the exploded contents of his bag; his pens and lunch money rolling away from him across the yard.

Slowly, his cheeks burning with a mixture of anger and embarrassment, Max got up and gathered his things together. He hated Bigsy and his friends.

Max's day continued as well as it had started.

Predictably his gym teacher, Mr. Bagson, did not believe his genuine mistake of having left his gym kit at home, having accidentally-on-purpose forgotten it on two previous occasions that term already to avoid having to play football with Bigsy and his thugs. It earned him a detention.

In Geography, Mr. Crawlie rambled on about soil and earth samples, causing Max to start daydreaming about how he was going to get into the study that night and miss a question that he was directly asked about soil types in the Outer Hebrides in North West Scotland.

'Not listening again Max!' exclaimed Mr. Crawlie, his moustache and beard twitching furiously and looking as they always did, as though they were about to dive off his face and scurry across the floor like huge brown hairy caterpillars.

'I,...' Max's voice faltered, he hadn't actually been listening. So much so that he didn't even remember enough of the question to be able to hazard a guess that he was sure would sound even half relevant.

'Yeeesss, Max?' said Crawlie, the corners of his lips twitching into a satisfied smile. He knew that he had caught Max out and he was enjoying it.

Max watched the smug look on Mr. Crawlie's face and decided that Mr. Crawlie was his least favourite teacher.

Somebody giggled at the back of the class.

Max's mind went blank. How could he listen to someone drone on for hours and not think of a single thing he could say? Not a single thing.

There was a long silence that seemed to stretch for an eternity.

Crawlie said nothing. He simply let the silence endure and waited for Max to crack.

There was a ripple of laughter at the back of the class.

Max stared at the desk and felt himself reddening.

'Acid,' he said finally. 'Acidity,' he added, trying to sound more convincing. He could feel the heat rising in his face and he suspected that his eyes would have changed again.

'Acid what?' said Crawlie, his bristly eyebrows rose.

Max felt himself squirm. You're acid, he thought, staring at his desk.

'I'm waiting...'

Another bubble of laughter erupted at the back of the class, louder this time.

'Errrm...' Max stalled, he realized that he actually couldn't think of a single thing to say. His mind had gone completely blank. Surely Crawlie was going to give him a break at any moment and move on to the next topic in the lesson or ask someone else. But he didn't.

'Acid what?' Crawlie persisted.

'I don't know,' Max muttered finally, he kept his head down.

'Right! Detention then! That should teach you to listen next time!' Crawlie announced looking extremely satisfied.

Mute with frustration and too scared to react in case Crawlie saw his eyes, Max folded his arms across his chest and stared at his desk. He'd just earned his second detention of the day, the third in two days and a letter home to his grandad. This was a disaster; a record, even by his standards.

Max left school quickly that evening as usual. He wandered back via the long route as he didn't particularly want to get home to his grandad and the moody atmosphere that would probably await him at home. He also really, really wanted to avoid Bigsy and his horrible friends, and any further trouble for that day. He meandered through the park and the Wilmsley Housing estate, trying to avoid anyone from his class and trying to finalise his plans for that evening.

He was definitely getting into that study tonight, he decided firmly. He'd had enough of not knowing what was really going on. Quinn hardly ever went out, so Max knew that his best option was to try to get into the study late at night, when his grandad was asleep. Judging by his tired demeanour that morning, Max was guessing that he probably stood his best chance of getting in without disturbing him tonight.

He checked his watch. 16:25. He then decided to wander around for another fifteen minutes before going home. Max knew that he was just putting off the moment when he would have to face his grandad. He didn't really want to deal with the fallout from that morning. He'd never seen his grandad so angry.

He wandered around the block for a second time and then after loitering around for another couple of minutes and rearranging the gravel on next doors driveway with his feet, Max decided that he had been putting it off for as long as he could and reluctantly set off up the driveway to the front door. An inviting smell of food greeted him as he stepped into the porch. He could see though into the kitchen and hear his grandad clattering around and humming to the radio. Max took a deep breath, plonked his school bag on the floor and then headed in the direction of the smell of food.

'Erm, hi...' he said hesitantly, entering the room. He eyed his grandad's bent back, as he stooped over the stove from the opposite side of the room and tried to decide how angry he still was.

'Hi,' said Quinn, he turned and gave Max a broad smile but Max noticed that the smile didn't quite reach his eyes.

'Stew!' Quinn added expectantly. 'You know that beef, vegetable and tomato one you like.'

Stews were a staple diet at 41 Greyeville Crescent, Normington, but this one they only had on special occasions.

'It's got dumplings,' Quinn added.

Max gave his grandad a smile. He felt a pang of guilt, knowing his grandad would never admit it, but he was trying to apologise. Max also knew that he would be furious if he had any idea what Max was planning for that night. The study was his grandad's private domain, containing his most secret and personal things. It was strictly off limits for Max.

The evening passed uneventfully. At about 8:30pm, when Max saw his Grandad starting to nod off in his chair, he put phase one of his plan into operation. Slipping out of the lounge and up the stairs, he made his way across the landing towards his grandad's bedroom.

Max carefully eased Quinn's bedroom door open and apprehensively peered into the room. It was June and although it was almost 9pm, late evening sunlight streamed through the window, flooding the little room with a warm golden glow.

Max paused and hovered in the doorway for a

moment, straining to listen for any sounds of movement from downstairs. Then, satisfied that he could still hear the soft deep breath of Quinn sleeping in his chair in front of the TV downstairs, Max slipped silently across the room towards his bedside table.

Slowly, carefully, Max eased the bedside cabinet drawer open and peered inside. There was a notebook, a handkerchief, his grandad's watch and some lozenges that looked as though they had been in the drawer for a very long time. He quickly slid the notebook to one side. Max's heart sank. Nothing.

Disappointed, he pulled the drawer out as far as it would extend and lent down on his knees to take a better look. Still nothing. Max gave a weary sigh. He should have known that it wouldn't be that easy.

He was just about to straighten back up when something caught his eye. A thin dark shape, not exactly in the drawer but attached to the underside of the cupboard lid.

Max held his breath and slowly slid his fingers along the underside of the cupboard. The rough wood dragged gently on his fingertips. His fingers hit a long thin lump. He quickly ran his fingertips over it, feeling something smooth and plastic with a hard serrated edge... Something had been very carefully taped to the underside of the cupboard lid.

Max quickly ran his nail over the edge and peeled the tape away, the cool hard shape of something small and metal fell into the palm of his hand. The key! Max felt his pulse begin to quicken. He quickly withdrew his hand and peered at the small grey key in the palm of his hand. Then he carefully repositioned the notebook, took one last look at the drawer to make sure that it didn't look as though anything had been disturbed and then eased the drawer closed, jubilantly placing the key in his pocket.

Mission accomplished, he thought to himself. Well, at least the first part of his plan.

He left the room, quietly shutting the door behind him and then paused at the top of the stairs, peering over the banister and down into the lounge below. The finishing credits had just begun for the programme they had been watching and his grandad's eyes flickered open with the sudden change in tempo and music. Slipping downstairs unnoticed was now impossible, so Max strolled downstairs, trying to look casual.

'Just been to the loo,' he lied as he wandered over and plonked himself back down on the couch.

'Good programme, I enjoyed that,' Quinn said, rubbing his eyes. He glanced towards Max and gave him a sleepy smile.

'U-huh,' Max muttered in agreement. He ran his hand over his hip, feeling the slender hard shape of the key in his pocket and then glanced quickly at Quinn, feeling a tiny pang of guilt. He didn't like lying, but if his grandad wasn't going to tell him what was really going on, then what else could he do? There was definitely something – some kind of secret. Max was certain of it. The fact that Max had just found the key taped to the underside of the cupboard – *taped* – had just made Max even more sure.

What was his grandad doing taping keys to the underside of cupboards? This was *his grandad* after all. What could he possibly be hiding?

No. Max told himself firmly; a wave of conviction swept over him. He was doing the right thing. There was definitely something and if his Grandad wasn't going to tell him, then he was leaving him with no choice.

The rest of the evening passed uneventfully. At 9pm, they watched the evening news. The last feature was about crop circles, and a farmer named Ned Matthews who lived in Normington was being interviewed and was explaining how crop circles had mysteriously appeared on his farm on a reasonably regular basis over the last five years or more. On the screen was a picture of a huge elaborate crop circle[1] that had miraculously appeared in one of his fields the previous evening.

Max felt a spark of recognition. He was sure that he recalled hearing the same news story on the radio that morning, but that had been a local radio station. This was the national evening news.

'Grandad?' he asked, 'That's in Normington. Isn't it that farm quite near here?'

'What? Erm... I'm not sure... I think so...' Quinn said vaguely.

'But it must be, mustn't it? If it's in Normington, isn't it that little farm just down the road?'

'I really don't know Max, I can't remember.' Quinn gave the clock on the mantelpiece a furtive look, then added, 'Come on Max, I think it's time for you to go to bed.'

'Okay,' said Max. He was eager to begin his investigation of the study so for once, Max decided not to argue.

'Okay!?' said Quinn quizzically. 'Are you unwell?'

---

[1] Did you know that the term Crop Circle was first created in the 1980s by Colin Andrews to describe strange circular flattened crop formations that were being found in fields? The unusual formations usually appeared overnight although some are thought to appear during the day and can be very extravagant patterns. There has been little scientific study of crop circles or why they appear. There are many theories about what creates them including alien theories. Other ideas are that they are a hoax created by people.

'Just really tired tonight,' Max shrugged, 'Goodnight, Grandad.'

He quickly made his way upstairs to bed and after hastily washing his face and cleaning his teeth, he changed into his pyjama bottoms, and eagerly dived into bed. He wondered how long it would be before his grandad came upstairs and then when he did, how long he should leave it to make sure that his grandad was fast asleep?

The study was located at the opposite end of the landing close to Quinn's bedroom. To get there, Max would have to pass by Quinn's bedroom, which meant that there was the risk of him hearing Max if he was still awake reading or hadn't yet fallen into a deep enough sleep.

He glanced at the clock. 21:52. Too early for him to come to bed yet.

Max pulled the key out from under his pillow and slowly turned it over in his fingers, carefully examining it in the fading light. It was a normal key; grey, metal and medium sized, the kind that usually locked inside doors. It was entirely unremarkable, hard to imagine that it might hold the answer to so many questions.

What would he find? he wondered. Maybe nothing. But what would he do if he did find out that they were on some kind of Witness Protection Programme, just like he'd seen on TV? What if his grandad had somehow accidentally seen the Mafia commit some brutal murder and the police had made him go to court to give crucial evidence, without which the Mafia leader would walk free? And that maybe the Mafia leader had gone to prison for life, forcing them to go into hiding and... maybe his name wasn't actually Max at all, maybe it was—

A sound on the stairs distracted him from the alarming thoughts that were skittering around in his mind.

The floorboards creaked softly as his Grandad walked along the landing and passed by his bedroom door. Max listened to the sound of Quinn going into the bathroom and then a few minutes later quietly retreating into his bedroom. The door clicked softly shut.

Max's stomach gave a tiny nervous jolt. 22:16.

He rolled over and stared at his alarm clock glowing beside his bed and wondered how long he should wait. At least half an hour, he decided. He had to be certain that his grandad would be asleep.

He lay watching the shadows in his bedroom slowly increase as darkness fell. How slow time passed when you wanted it to go fast, he thought glumly, remembering Mr. Crawlie's Geography classes and then remembering that he would have to tell his grandad about his detentions in the morning.

Restless, Max rolled over, then rolled over again. He glanced at the alarm clock.

Only thirty minutes had passed since his grandad had closed his bedroom door, but it felt like an eternity. He wondered if his grandad would be asleep by now. Deciding to wait another fifteen minutes and then make his move, Max rolled over and lay on his side and watched the red glowing numbers on the alarm clock slowly change ten times.

22:57.

It was time.

Without a sound Max carefully slipped out of bed, reached for a t-shirt that he'd left discarded on a nearby chair and pulled it over his head. Then with a tiny surge of nervous excitement, he slipped silently across the room towards the door. Clutching the key in one hand and gripping the door handle tightly in the other; he carefully eased the door open and peered out on to the landing.

SAM KINI

Chapter 3
The Forbidden Door

A pale sliver of moonlight shone through the landing window casting a cool grey light across the purple patterned carpet. Max glanced quickly towards his grandad's bedroom, eyeing the narrow gap that stretched along the bottom of the door. He was relieved to see that it looked to be in darkness. Max blew out a long breath, then he slowly stepped out on to the landing and gently pulled his bedroom door to a close.

He crept silently across the landing carpet, then paused outside his grandad's bedroom door; he hesitated, listening into the tiny crack of the door frame, then reassured that he could only hear the muffled sound of rumbling snores, he turned and took a quick step towards the study door.

Taking a deep breath, Max placed the key in the lock. It gave a soft click and Max felt a tiny shiver of excitement. He reached out, turned the handle, and Max found himself staring into his grandad's tiny study – a room that he had only ever visited once before in his life.

It seemed strange to him now that he thought about it, that in this house – *his home* – that was so familiar to him in every other way, there could be a room that was so completely unknown to him. He hovered apprehensively in the doorway for a moment and then quickly stepped inside carefully pushing the door to a close.

The room was even smaller than he remembered, but then the last time he had been inside the room had been about five years ago. To his left a bright yellow window of light spilled into the room from the street lamp outside the window, bathing the room in a soft yellowy, grey glow.

Max looked around the room, wondering where to start. Across from the door, stood against the wall, was a large heavy dark wooden desk with three deep drawers on each side. On the top of the desk was a pile of papers and a small elaborately carved, dark, wooden box. To the left of the desk was the curtainless window, through which he could see out onto the deserted street and the streetlight on the corner. To the right of the desk was a narrow bookcase, crammed high with books.

He wandered over to the bookcase scanning the titles on some of the old leather bound volumes: 'Leading the People', 'The Ancient Council – 1997 Yearly Review', 'Lucem life', 'The Hidden History of the Hidden People Revealed,' 'I Win, You Win – Great Negotiating Tactics for dealing with the Wokulo', 'Great Sea Navigators of the Worlds'...

Max paused, his gaze hovering over the books for a moment, confused. Hidden People? Wokulo?

Worlds?

He decided that he should definitely look through the books in more detail, but for now, he would take a quick look at everything in the room and then decide what to really focus his attention on.

He turned and wandered over to the desk. He reached for the handle on the top right drawer and gave it a tug. It refused to budge. Swallowing down his disappointment, Max glanced around the room and decided that the key was probably in here somewhere. It was unlikely that his grandad would have gone to the trouble of hiding the key anywhere else in the house. He was bound to stumble on it as part of his search, he decided.

A quick check of the other side of the desk revealed that these drawers were also locked, so he moved on to the paperwork sitting in a neat pile on top. The pile contained mostly bills and a letter from Wiltshire Council about a change to the day when the bins would be emptied. No huge secrets revealed so far. So he moved his attention to the elaborately carved wooden box sitting in the middle of the desk. It was a small box, made from dark polished wood, and carved all over with an intricate swirling design. The base of the box was balanced on top of four tiny, clawed feet.

Max carefully lifted the lid. Just as he did, there was a loud click on the landing. Startled, he jumped and dropped the lid; it hit the box with a dull clunk.

Max froze, his breath caught in his chest. He listened to the heavy-footed padding of his grandad's sleepy footsteps slowly tread past the door as he headed towards the bathroom. The bathroom door gave a soft click. It suddenly occurred to him that perhaps he should have locked the study door or that maybe he should have made some effort to make his bed look as though he was sleeping in it – padded it out with clothes and cushions or something. It was too late now. He waited, rooted to the spot, until he heard the sound of the toilet flush and his grandad slowly pad back across the landing and pass by the door. The bedroom door clicked quietly shut.

Max blew out a long breath, then silently slipped back across the room and locked the study door.

Returning to the desk, Max regarded the small intricately carved wooden box for a second time, then reaching out, he carefully lifted the lid. Max felt a small jolt of excitement. There, nestling in the deep red velvet interior were two tiny keys. He regarded the keys thoughtfully, turning them over in his fingers. He was surprised to see that they were entirely different. One was medium sized and quite ordinary looking, whilst the other was much smaller and had a tiny design on the handle. As Max peered at the key he realised that the handle was in the shape of a tiny snake coiled into a circle and with its tail in its mouth.

He regarded the keys thoughtfully, turning

them over in his fingers, then placed the first more ordinary key into the lock above the drawers in the desk and turned it. It immediately clicked open. In the first drawer, Max found a series of diaries; however, it was immediately apparent that his grandad was not a big diary keeper who spent hours writing down his deepest thoughts. The diaries contained reminders and events and typically, for his grandad who rarely went out and had no friends to speak of, there were very few diary entries. However, as Max flicked through the diary for that year, he noticed as the diary fell open for that week, that an entry was in the diary for the previous evening.

There in his grandads looping scrawl was clearly printed one word: 'Imeda.'

The night the visitors had come.

Max stared at the word, then quickly flicked back through the diary. There was nothing for weeks apart from a dentist appointment and then just less than two months earlier – the exact same word – Imeda.

Max flicked further back through the diary and again this time on 15 February, exactly two months earlier again, the same entry once more – Imeda. Max quickly picked up the previous year's diary and immediately found two months to the day on 15 December another entry, this time an abbreviation 'I & C visit'.

Max considered the diary for a moment. 'I' he

decided was probably Imeda, but then who was 'C'? Could 'C' be the man with gruff voice who had visited his grandad with Imeda on the previous night? Max wasn't sure.

What was clear to Max, was that whoever 'Imeda', the gruff man and 'C' were, his grandad seemed to have a visit from someone approximately every two months. In fact, these mysterious visitors appeared to visit his grandad exactly every two months to the day, with the exception of this month, when they had suddenly arrived five days early.

Yet Max had never met any of them and his grandad had never, ever mentioned it. Not on any of the occasions. But why?

Max thought back to the conversation he had overheard the previous evening. He remembered the comment 'Imeda' had made about money. Did this mean that they were visiting every two months to bring them money?

Puzzled, Max placed the diaries neatly back in the drawer and after a final glance; he carefully pushed the drawer shut.

In the next drawer, Max found a pile of old papers and manuscripts, which he quickly set about unfolding. It took a moment for him to realise that he was staring at a series of very old maps. There looked to be about ten in total, all hand drawn in colour, with beautiful, detailed illustrations. Not at all like the kind that his grandad used when they decided to take a rare trip out together or the kind of atlases or maps that he had seen in class at school. In fact, not at all like anything Max had ever seen before.

The main body of each map was dominated by two large circles, which were drawn neatly side by side. The two circles appeared to show the two sides of each world, each meticulously detailing every landmass, island and sea. Set to one side of each map were two smaller circles which showed a bird's eye view of the north and south poles.

On many of the landmasses, Max noticed that there were frequently tiny drawings of strange frightening monsters and in the seas, spiny, sharp-toothed fish and ferocious sea creatures lurked in the choppy waters, alongside elegant ships bearing tall masts and white billowing sails.

Max carefully flicked through the maps, the first five appeared to be grouped together and he set about inspecting these first. Neatly written in small spiky handwriting at the top of the first map was the word 'Lucem'.

He carefully peered at each of the circles in turn and then frowning slightly, slowly set the map to one side and began to look at the next. This map was headed 'The Shadowlands' and again he looked at the circles, the furrow between his eyes deepening. The third map was entitled 'Hyperborea', the fourth 'Arcadia' and the fifth 'Naburu'.

Puzzled, Max stared at the maps for a

moment, uncertain what exactly he was looking at. Everything, he realised, was entirely unfamiliar to him. The landmasses, islands and seas all looked completely different to Earth.

Perhaps these were imaginary lands, he decided, perhaps his grandad liked to collect old, hand-drawn maps of strange, make-believe worlds. But if he did, he'd never mentioned it or shown any of them to Max. Why would he hide them from him and keep them in here?

Max spread the five maps out in front of him, noticing that each had a matching blue border that ran around the edge. Then with a jolt, Max noticed something that he had missed before. At the top of each map was written three words – The Five Kingdoms. Max felt a sudden spark of recognition. He realised that he'd heard of the Five Kingdoms. Imeda had mentioned the Five Kingdoms to his Grandad the night before. She had said that the Five Kingdoms were in danger.

Feeling increasingly confused, Max shifted his attention to the second group of maps and began to flick through them more quickly. A map headed 'The Forbidden Lands' immediately caught his attention. Huge landmasses covered in deserts, jagged mountain ranges and volcanoes dominated much of the map. An area to the North called The Lost Ridge depicted a glacier of ice covered in tiny intricate drawings of fierce monsters and bears and to the south was a dark shaded area where the drawing on the map suddenly petered out and a single word had been handwritten in red ink. Danger.

Wondering curiously what it really meant and why someone had simply stopped drawing the map, Max hesitantly set it to one side and then shifted his attention to the next map in the pile. It took him a moment to register that he was looking at a series of landmasses very familiar to him – Earth. Although on this map, it was entitled 'Earthe'.

Max's eyes quickly scanned over the map. All of the countries were mapped out in painstaking detail and looked from Max's recollection as though they were all in the right places. A few neat little old-fashioned ships adorned the seas along with a drawing of a whale and a few dolphins off the coast of South Africa. A ferocious looking tiger prowled across one of the landmasses that looked like it might be India.

Satisfied that everything looked quite normal, Max set it aside and picked up the last map.

The last map was completely different. It was double sided and appeared to be a detailed map of two areas within Lucem. One side was entitled Cassini and appeared to show a series of jagged mountains and dense jungle to the East and a large town or city which was located along the banks of a large river which stretched out towards the sea in the west. The other side of the map was entitled Mimas and depicted a vast flat valley flanked on both sides by a series of steep mountain ranges and a dense forest.

Cassini.

Max felt an immediate spark of recognition, he stared at the map for a moment; the streets and roads that ran through both cities and the trails and pathways that weaved and wound their way through the jungles and forest. He remembered back to what his grandad had said that morning. So was this really where he was from? And if it was, then what were all of these other maps supposed to be?

An uneasy feeling settled over him. Max gazed at the maps that were spread out in front of him. He felt as though he was missing something; something that connected all these strange things that he had found. Something that would answer his questions.

Deeply confused, he carefully folded the maps back up again, before moving onto the next drawer, a steady thrum of questions streaming through his mind.

The next drawer contained almost every Christmas and Birthday card that Max had ever sent to his grandad but yielded no further surprises. He moved quickly around to the other side of the desk and opened the next set of drawers. There inside, filling almost the entire drawer, sat another wooden box. It was made from a dark richly polished wood and inlaid into the lid carved out of a dull, heavy, grey metal was a strange ornate snake coiled into a circle, its tail in its mouth. Just like the key, Max thought. He eased the box out of the drawer and placed it on the desk in front of him, taking care not to knock the heavy wood against the desk for fear of waking Quinn.

Max gazed apprehensively at the box for a moment, then he reached out and tried to lift the lid. Just as he had expected the box was locked, so he picked up the tiny snake key and firmly placed it in the keyhole on the front of the box. The lock gave a soft, firm click.

Max's heart gave a tiny leap of excitement. He lifted the lid and there nestling inside the blue velvet interior was what looked like a strangely patterned stone disk. It was covered in spiky hieroglyphs and symbols and was the size of the palm of one hand.

Puzzled, Max stared at it for a moment, realising that he had absolutely no idea what he was looking at. The symbols reminded him of the ancient Egyptian hieroglyphs he had seen on the museum visit with school, but these were interspersed with strange spiky letters that he didn't recognise.

Max turned the disk over in his hands. As he studied it more closely, he realised that it was actually made up of a series of concentric circles or rings each of which moved separately to each other, to the right or left rather like dials. Engraved around each of the first three rings was a series of strange, spiky symbols and hieroglyphs. The innermost fourth ring was – just like the key and the lid of the box – a serpent coiled around with its tail in its mouth.

A thin ridge-like crest came out of the serpent's head and flicked back up in a slim point stretching over the three dials and reaching towards the outer most edge of the disk, giving the effect that you could line up the hieroglyphs with the crest. A tear-shaped, smoky blue gem sat in place of the serpent's eye which was the only thing on the strange mysterious disk that did not appear to be made from stone.

Max stared at the disk mesmerised for a moment. He had never seen anything remotely like it before in his life. He didn't know why, but something told him that this was what he had been searching for. This – if only he could work out what on earth it was – would somehow hold the answers to his questions.

Max turned the disk over in his hands again, enthralled by its shape and the strange cold hard stone. He slowly ran his fingers around each of the dials, tracing the tiny ridges and grooves of the curious symbols and hieroglyphs beneath his fingertips. It felt weighty and solid and there was something very pleasing about the feel of it in his hands.

What could it possibly be for? he wondered. It couldn't simply be decorative.

Intrigued, he gently clicked the innermost dial two symbols to the right, then thinking better of it, he quickly returned it back to its original position.

That was when it happened.

There was a soft click as the original symbol slipped back into place. It was followed, a second later, by a dull clink, as though an ancient mechanism was suddenly triggered from somewhere deep inside the disk.

Max held his breath and stared at the disk, a slow burn of excitement beginning. Something was happening; he was sure of it.

Suddenly, the snake's pale blue eye began to glow softly, moments later a soft grinding sound began to emanate from the centre of the disk. Without warning, the snake began to slowly revolve around the centre of the disk.

Max's heart skipped a beat. He stared at the disk transfixed. With a sense of mounting excitement, Max held the disk gingerly between his fingers, feeling the gentle vibration as the snake slowly coiled and wound its way around.

Then suddenly, Max felt a sharp jolt from somewhere deep in the pit of his stomach, he lurched forward and his feet abruptly left the ground.

SAM KINI

Chapter 4
The Mysterious Disk

Max felt a blast of ice-cold air, the wind howled past his ears, and he felt himself spiralling upwards at great speed. Higher and higher and higher, he swirled. His eyes stung as raw freezing wind whipped his face and hair.

Squinting, he caught a fleeting glimpse of sharp white lights twisting and swirling around him, before he closed his eyes. After that, he lost all sense of direction. Then suddenly he became aware that he was very quickly spiralling downwards, moments later his feet slammed to the ground, his legs buckled from under him and he fell, landing flat on his back, winded.

Max coughed and lay still for a moment. Tears stung in his eyes. Something green and blue interspersed with beads of light glittered and swam somewhere in the distance above him.

He blinked, the bright white lights gradually dissipating. He blinked again. With a jolt, Max realised that he was lying staring up at the green canopy of a tree. Sunlight and blue sky were shimmering through the foliage, turning the leaves a bright intense green.

Max sat up with a start, realising to his utter astonishment that he was no longer in the study and that it was no longer night-time. Instead, he appeared to be sitting on a large patch of flattened grass, on the edge of some kind of woodland glade. Shards of sunlight streamed through the leaves, casting mottled shadows across the grassy floor. Birds chattered in the trees around him and he could hear the gentle bubble of running water hidden from view, somewhere in the surrounding vegetation. In the distance through the trees, he could just make out a tall grey stone building with a tall pyramid-like roof.

Rigid with shock, Max gazed around in open-mouthed, stunned, disbelief. For a few seconds, he couldn't move – he could hardly breathe – as waves of shock broke over his head.

Then, very slowly he reached out and gingerly ran his fingertips through the grass. It felt fresh and spiky and slightly damp. It felt real.

And yet how could it be? Just moments ago – it had been night-time – he'd been at home, in his grandad's study.

A gentle breeze blew through the glade, whispering through the trees. Max felt the goose bumps rise on his arms.

How can I possibly be here? he wondered. This cannot be happening.

This isn't possible.

Then a thought occurred to him. He definitely

was here, wasn't he? This wasn't a dream.

He pondered the idea for a moment and then pinched himself hard on the forearm. He felt an immediate sharp twinge of pain then watched incredulous as the small pink nail indentations slowly dissolved, fading away into his skin and his arm resumed its normal colour. He glanced around. Nothing had changed – he was definitely here and that had definitely hurt.

But how? How can this be happening? he wondered. How could someone possibly go from being inside a locked study to sitting in the middle of a wood in broad daylight? The last thing he remembered was that he had been crouched in his grandads study inspecting the strange stone disk.

The disk! Max gave a start. Glancing around, he immediately spotted it lying a few feet away, upside down on the flattened grass. He eyed it warily for a moment, remembering how it had moved, and then cautiously reached out, flipping it over. The serpent was still again, the pale blue eye dull.

Had he imagined it?

Straight-backed, Max gazed around the glade again, a fresh wave of shock washing over him, the enormity of what he could see before him, slowly settling in his mind.

Max wasn't sure how long he sat on the grass, but after a while he slowly became aware that he needed to find out where he was and realising that he wasn't going to find out anything more by continuing to sit in the middle of the clearing, he slowly, dazedly gathered himself together and stood up.

He immediately noticed that he had been sitting in the centre of a relatively wide expanse of flattened grass. The flattened area stretched out evenly around him and appeared to form a neat circle.

Deciding to investigate further, Max wandered over to the edge of the circle and bent down. The broken stems stopped abruptly and perfectly at what appeared to be the edge of the circle, where they immediately resumed their natural upright stance and were proudly swaying about in the balmy afternoon breeze. This grass, bizarrely and quite abruptly, seemed entirely unaffected by whatever flattening force Max appeared to have arrived with.

Even more mystified, Max reached down to touch a broken blade of grass, noticing that every stem folded over at exactly the same point and in exactly the same direction. Things were becoming stranger and stranger, he decided.

He wandered around for a few minutes, and then decided to head towards the sound of bubbling water. He quickly found a small narrow brook meandering between the trees, bouncing over boulders and stones and splashing gently onto the bank. Then, finding nothing more than a small bright green bird that he startled from its worm, he decided to head back towards the glade.

Still feeling slightly stunned, he hovered on the patch of flattened grass and wondered what to do next. I think I must be in shock, he thought dazedly. His thoughts were fuzzy and he noticed vaguely that he felt a strange tingle running through his body, as though every hair follicle and cell in his body had been energized and was gently vibrating. He shook himself and glanced around. He needed a plan. He needed to decide what to do.

He spotted the grey stone building through the trees. It was a three-storey building with large, curtained windows and a very tall, peaked roof. It looked, although Max couldn't be sure, as though it might be a large house.

Max eyed the building uncertainly and wondered what to do. He imagined that wherever he was, someone arriving at the door in their pyjamas and claiming that they had just flown into the back garden, when five minutes ago they had been in Wiltshire in the dead of night, was probably enough to get you locked up or carted away. But if he didn't go down to the house, then what else was he going to do? How else was he going to find out anything? He would just go and take a quick look, he decided. He would stay out of sight and see if he could find out anything.

So, with a final glance at the woodland glade,

Max nervously set off towards the house. The woodland quickly petered out, the trees thinned and almost without noticing, Max realised that he had left the wood behind and was wandering through a wide expanse of garden. The sudden openness unnerved him, and he quickly stepped back behind a tree, peering cautiously at the house before him. The large windows were in darkness, everything was still. Just take a quick look, he silently repeated to himself.

Taking care to remain out of sight, Max cautiously edged his way through the garden, his heart beginning to pound. As he neared the house, a large expanse of lawn opened out in front of him. Unwilling to risk exposure and make the move across the lawn, Max hovered behind a group of prickly shrubs, wondering what to do next.

Just as he had decided that the risk probably wasn't that great after all and he was about to step out across the lawn and make for the safety of a small shrub close to the house, the door suddenly banged open with an energetic clatter and a young blonde-haired girl bounced out of the house and jumped down the steps.

Max took a sharp intake of breath and then hurriedly stepped back into the shrubs where the prickles immediately attached themselves to the fabric of his t-shirt and pyjama's. He held his breath and waited for a moment, then slowly eased a branch out of the way and peered through the leaves.

The girl looked to be of a similar age to Max around fourteen years old. Her hair was a blond-brown and was cut into a chin length bob. She had big brown eyes and her gangly legs and arms that protruded from her blue short-sleeved dress were tanned a light coffee colour.

'Anna,' the sound of a woman's voice emanated from the open door, 'You have one hour and that's it!' The voice had a musical, motherly, no arguments quality to it.

'Okay, okay,' the girl muttered sulkily, kicking a stone across the grass.

Max watched her wander around the lawn for a moment, wondering what to do. Perhaps he should say hello, he thought. Maybe she could tell him where he was. Maybe she could explain how he'd got here.

What he saw next however, changed his mind completely.

A loud thump echoed from the direction of the house. The girl glanced up. 'Lokie!' she exclaimed, her face brightening.

Max followed the direction of her gaze. As he did, he saw something that stopped him dead. Undoubtedly, the strangest creature that he had ever seen, appeared in the open doorway.

Standing upright on its back legs, the creature was less than a foot tall and covered in rusty, orange coloured fuzzy fur; its legs were short and stumpy, and its body round, giving it an almost bear-like appearance, except that it had huge brown eyes, a small button brown nose and huge, oversized, green, droopy ears. It waddled out of the doorway and then upon reaching the stone steps, and having such short, stumpy legs, it sat down on the top step and began quickly shuffling itself forward and down to the step below.

'Where have you been? I've been looking for you everywhere!' said the girl. She wandered over to the creature and scooped it up into her arms. The creature murmured something indistinguishable to the girl. The girl gave a loud laugh and then set off wandering through the garden.

Taking care to remain out of sight, Max peered through the branches of the shrub and watched them stroll around the lawn. He stared at the strange orange creature with its huge green ears; he had never seen anything like it before in his life. Where on the heck am I? he wondered.

At that moment, the girl changed direction and began to wander towards the shrubs where Max was hiding.

Max's heart began to pound. He knew that from a distance he was well hidden, but if someone walked close by, he wasn't so sure. 'Walk away,' he silently urged. 'Turn around and walk away.'

But she didn't. Instead, she continued to walk steadily towards the shrubs where Max was hiding

– steadily towards him.

Hardly daring to exhale, Max shrank back into the shrub, feeling the sharp retaliation of the thorns as they pressed through his clothes, snagging his pyjamas and digging into his skin. There was a soft crunch as a twig snapped under his foot. Max froze mid-step.

Heart pounding, he waited for a moment and then slowly leant forward and peered through the branches. To his horror he saw that the creature's enormous green ears had shot vertically up into the air and it was murmuring agitatedly to the girl. The girl halted and frowned.

'What?' questioned the girl, her wide brown eyes peering curiously at the creature, 'You want to get down?'

Max's heart sank. Hoping desperately that his hiding place was not about to be revealed by this little orange ball of fluff, he clenched his teeth and retreated as far as the spiky branches would allow.

The girl stopped walking, 'Okay,' she said hesitantly. She frowned and bent down.

The creature jumped from the girl's hands and to Max's utter horror, immediately scurried directly towards the shrub where Max was hiding.

Max felt hot beads of nervous sweat start out on his forehead. Glancing down, he spotted a stone on the ground and hoping to distract the creature, hastily kicked it to his right. The stone bounced out of the shrub and rolled across the grass. But the strange orange creature was not to be deflected; it gave the stone a quick sideways glance and then continued to waddle directly towards Max.

Glancing around desperately, Max quickly weighed his options; but he could see no way out of it. He realised that whether he liked it or not, he was about to be unceremoniously announced by this strange little, orange creature. Feeling oddly as though his legs had just turned to lead, Max took a deep breath and then slowly extracted himself from the shrub. There was a soft ripping sound, as the thorns reluctantly released his pyjamas.

He stepped out on to the grass and gave the girl an awkward smile.

The girl didn't smile back; her dark brown eyes widened with shock. She stared warily at Max, taking in every detail of his torn pyjama's and barefoot, dishevelled appearance.

Max's mouth went dry. A mental image of how he must look flashed fleeting through his mind and he immediately felt himself redden with embarrassment. He glanced around awkwardly, realising that he had absolutely no idea what to do next. Deciding that perhaps he should probably at least say hello, he glanced back at the girl. But the words died in his mouth. The girl was no longer looking at him; instead, she was staring at the strange disk that he was clutching in his hand.

She gazed at it; a look of surprised recognition flashed across her face. Her eyes narrowed. Then suddenly she bent down, snatched the little creature up into her arms and charged straight back across the lawn, shouting at the top of her voice.

Max felt fear flood every nerve and cell in his body.

He turned and ran.

He charged through the garden, plunging through the trees and shrubs and back towards the woodland. He didn't stop until he reached the strange circle of flattened grass where he skidded to a halt. He cast his eyes desperately around the glade; he needed to find somewhere safe, somewhere he could think and fast.

A voice shouted in the trees behind him.

Panicking, Max set off running again, flinging himself through the trees. He found the little brook and attempted to jump it in one leap, but his foot found a boulder, slick with moss and he slipped, slopping into the water, soaking his feet and the bottom of his pyjamas. Chest heaving, he scrambled out of the stream and set off running again.

He stumbled through a thicket of brambles, snagging his clothes and scratching his arms. He ran on, his eyes darting frantically around the wood. He was searching for somewhere –

anywhere – he could hide.

Then suddenly he spotted a dense group of shrubs over to his right and he dived towards them, pushing himself through the leafy branches. Thankful that it appeared to be slightly less aggressive than the last, he crouched inside his heart racing.

Moments later, he heard the sound of voices shouting, then faint splashes. Max froze. They were at the stream.

They'd come after him.

Max shrank back into the shadowy foliage of the shrub, his stomach twisting into a tight ball of fear.

There was a crunch and rustle of branches moving nearby. The rustle drew nearer then halted a few paces away from the shrub. Someone coughed.

Rigid with fear, Max crouched in the dense foliage, a thin trickle of sweat slid slowly down his spine.

'Well, he seems to have gone now,' a man's voice muttered.

Max heard the soft crunch of a twig snapping close by. With every breath, he expected a hand to suddenly reach in and drag him out.

'He must have used the key,' said a woman in

a quiet worried voice, 'He could be anywhere by now, we might never find him...'

Another crunch. Further away this time.

'Come on, we'd better go back. Cade will want to know what's going on,' said the man.

Max listened to them move away; their voices dying away into the distance. An intense stillness descended on the wood.

Minutes passed and he crouched rigidly in the dense foliage, straining for sounds. The silence intensified. Eventually he realised that the voices had faded away and his heartbeat gradually slowed. A bird chirruped in a nearby tree.

Feeling almost sick with relief, Max took a deep breath and forced himself to focus. He needed to think. He needed to get back home.

Home. With a pang, Max thought of Grandad Quinn and what he would say when he found out. He'd only planned to go snooping in the office for an hour; he didn't think that his grandad would ever need to know. Then with a growing sense of dread he had an even worse thought. What if he couldn't get back at all?

Max realised that he had been so intent on trying to find out what was going on, that he hadn't really considered how he was going to get back. In the back of his mind, ever since he had arrived in the wood, he'd had the vague notion that if this disk belonged to his grandad then it had to be safe. That no matter what, he would always be able to get home. He'd just assumed it was possible. Now he wasn't so sure.

To his utter horror Max realised suddenly that he had absolutely no idea where he was or how he had managed to get here. And if he didn't know that, then how on earth was he going to get back?

Gulping down a wave of panic, Max shook himself and tried to think. His memory skittered back over what had happened in his grandad's study. The last thing he remembered was that he had been holding the disk, the serpent's eye had glowed, then it had started to revolve and then somehow something had happened and he had found himself here. It had to be to do with this disk, he decided.

His thoughts racing, Max picked up the disk and started to turn it over in his hands. He remembered holding it and tracing the shapes of the symbols with his fingers, then he'd moved the outermost dial two symbols to the right and then back again. Then – it had happened.

His heart hammering in his chest, Max clutched the disk firmly between his fingers then twisted the inner dial two symbols to the right; he waited for a moment and then carefully swung it back again. There was a soft clunk, as the original symbol slowly slipped back into place. A moment later, just as before, Max became aware of a faint grinding whir from somewhere deep within the disk and the serpents smoky pale blue eye began to glow.

Max held his breath and stared at the snake, silently willing it to move.

But it didn't. Abruptly the soft grinding sound stopped, the luminous pale blue eye dimmed.

Max stared at the disk. A fresh wave of panic rose inside him. What had he done?

Panicking, he ran his fingers around the dials. But that was it – that was all he had done – he was sure of it.

Max went hot, then cold with fear. An unthinkable thought began to settle in his mind. What if he was actually stuck here?

Wherever *here* was.

He decided to try again and quickly swung the dial to the right then back again. Again the pale blue eye began to glow. And again it stopped.

He stared at the disk.

What now? he thought desperately.

Anxiety and fear blinded his concentration and for a moment Max just sat, crouched in the shrubs, turning the disk over and over in his fingers and staring at it blankly, a blur of frantic thoughts churning through his mind. The disk slipped from his fingers and fell to the ground. It bounced off a rock with a loud chink.

The sound jolted Max to his senses. Glancing down, he noticed that the disk had landed upside down. He reached down to pick it up; as he did, something on the back of the disk caught his attention.

Max peered at the disk. Close to the centre, on the back of the dials was a small, pale stone button. Slowly, cautiously, Max ran his fingernail over the stone ridge and then gently but firmly clicked it to one side. The stone slid sideways with a soft click.

Just as before, Max felt a gentle clunk as though an ancient mechanism were suddenly triggered from somewhere deep within the disk. Flipping it over, he saw to his relief that the serpents luminous pale blue stone had once again begun to glow.

Max stared at the disk, his breath caught in his chest; a faint glimmer of hope began to grow inside him.

For a moment nothing happened. Then, there was a soft grinding sound from somewhere deep within the disk and the snake slowly began to move.

Hoping desperately that the next thing he would see would be his grandad's study; Max clutched the disk tightly between his fingers. A sharp pain tugged at his insides and for a moment he felt a surge of panic. What if he didn't get home? What if he went somewhere else?

Then suddenly he felt the sharp jolt from deep inside his stomach, his feet abruptly left the floor and he was swirling up into ice-cold nothingness.

Max felt a blast of freezing wind that whipped past his face and hair, stinging his skin like needles. He caught a fleeting glimpse of bright, white, swirling lights as he spiralled upwards, before he clamped his eyes tight shut. Moments later, his feet slammed to the ground, his legs once again buckled from under him and he found himself lying flat on his face.

Max gingerly opened his eyes and tried to focus. It was dark and for a moment, he couldn't see anything. Then, as he slowly lifted himself up onto his elbows, he saw it; Max didn't think that he had ever been so happy to see their purple patterned carpet in all his life. He pushed himself up into a sitting position, his body relaxing with relief and happiness. He was sitting on the study carpet.

He was back.

Max blew out a long breath, his heart rate slowly returning to normal. He looked around as his eyes adjusted to the dim light; he could see the yellow glow of the streetlamp outside the window, the folded maps piled neatly on top of the desk, the bookcase...

Everything was just as he had left it.

Whatever it was that had just happened — wherever it was that he had been — he was home again.

For a moment Max sat very still, feeling the tension in his body release, as though every muscle were slowly unravelling and relaxing.

Then without warning, a tremendous crash broke the tranquil silence of the house and Max tensed once more. Breathing in sharply, he drew his knees in towards his chest. He suddenly became aware of the muffled sound of voices somewhere in the house. Seconds later, there was a gigantic thud and a terrible high-pitched shriek that pierced the silence of the night.

Max's stomach lurched with fear. Scrambling to his feet, he lunged towards the door.

There was a thunderous crash directly outside the room, the door shook, rattling on its hinges.

'Stop!' a man's voice bellowed.

Max froze mid step.

There was the sound of splintering glass, followed by a scream and then heavy receding footsteps along the landing.

'Grandad!' he yelped, lunging for the door handle. It was locked.

Spinning around, Max dived back towards the desk, scattering the maps in his efforts to retrieve the key. He found it hidden beneath the ornate wooden box and snatching it up, stumbled back towards the door, barely registering the eerie silence that had suddenly descended on the landing.

Fumbling with the key, Max tried desperately to unlock the door. As he did, there was a gentle but precise knock from the other side of the door.

Max froze, momentarily taken aback by the normality of the sound.

'Grandad?'

There was a pause.

'No,' a woman's voice replied gently, 'but I'm a friend.'

'Where's my Grandad? Who are you?'

He heard her take a breath and in the seconds pause between the end of that breath and the start of her speaking, Max got a very bad feeling.

'I'm Imeda,' the voice said softly, 'Max, please will you open the door?'

Max hesitated then fingers trembling he clumsily placed the key in the lock and slowly unlocked the door; he noticed that his fingers didn't seem to be working properly.

A distinguished lady with piercing blue eyes, blond hair, and a kind but strained smile was standing on the landing. Jagged pieces of glass lay strewn across the carpet, along with the mangled remains of the little table. A cool breeze was drifting along the landing, flapping at the landing curtain and casting fluttering shadows across the wall. Max realised dimly that the window must be shattered.

'Who are you? Why are you here?'

'We're–' she hesitated and gave him a strained smile, 'It's complicated Max...'

'Where's my Grandad?' he demanded, fear welling up inside him.

'Your–' She glanced past him, then down at her hands.

A chill swept through Max. Her eyes wouldn't meet his.

'W-What's happened?' his voice quavered.

He watched her struggle to find the words and a terrible wave of dread rushed through him. She wouldn't look him in the eye.

She couldn't.

'There's been an accident Max. Your grandad's been hurt,' she hesitantly reached out to touch his shoulder, an anxious frown flickered across her face.

'What?! Where is he?'

'He's–' her voice faltered again.

And then Max knew; knew that the unthinkable had happened. For a moment he felt as though his heart seemed to stop. Horror rose inside him. Pushing past her, he ran towards his grandad's bedroom, his mind filling with dreadful certainty.

'No Max!' she followed him, grabbing his arm.

But it was too late. He had seen it. His grandad was lying face up in bed, his eyes were open, glazed, staring sightlessly up at the ceiling.

SAM KINI

Chapter 5
The Other Crowd

After that, Max didn't really remember much. After that, nothing much mattered.

Two other people arrived wearing grey hooded cloaks, a man and a woman. The man had a gruff, vaguely familiar voice and was introduced as Krake; the woman was young and athletic, with short blond hair and was introduced as Otty. They appeared to have been outside and the man was sweating hard. He had a small bleeding gash on the side of his head and looked dishevelled, as though he had been in a fight. They stood in a tense, nervous huddle, casting Max awkward glances; their voices sounded muffled somehow, as though they were underwater.

He dully remembered the man disappearing back outside and the women asking him lots of questions as they gently ushered and manoeuvred him around the house. Was anything missing? Did he know where his grandad's things were? They were taking him to safety, they told him.

But he didn't really care. He felt distant somehow, numb, as though he had suddenly stepped into a giant cushion, and everything was being viewed through thick swaths of padding.

They carefully eased him around the house,

gathering things and looking awkward and unhappy. They seemed alarmed, when Max confirmed that there was a photograph missing from the mantelpiece, of him and his grandad taken the previous summer. He didn't know why and didn't care to ask. After that, they seemed to speed up their preparations significantly and there were lots of urgent, muted mutterings and worried, expressions exchanged. Max didn't bother to ask about that either.

He wondered vaguely where they were taking him and whether it was wise to let strangers take him anywhere, but he was finding it difficult to decide what to say.

'Why are you here?' he heard his voice ask finally in a whisper.

'We'll explain everything Max, I promise,' said Imeda, 'but we need to get away from here first.'

'But what if I don't want to leave... what about my grandad?' His voice broke off.

'We'll come back for him Max, I promise,' she reached out and touched his arm gently; her blue eyes were filled with sadness.

The two women quickly went through each of the rooms, gathering a strange assortment of things together: photographs, the strange disk, the maps and all of the books from the office. In fact, Max realised dully, most of the things were from the office, which they proceeded to pack into a couple of his grandad's bags, before slowly herding Max down the landing and towards the stairs.

Glancing back, Max looked quickly into his grandad's bedroom, noticing with a stab of pain that someone had covered his Grandad's face with the sheet. There was something very final about seeing him lie there like that. Max swallowed hard, his eyes and throat burning.

He numbly descended the stairs, noticing vaguely that the man named Krake had returned, then they stood in a sombre circle in the middle of the sitting room floor and Max watched as Krake held a second disk, identical to his grandad's, and slowly began to twist and position the dials. Imeda gently touched his shoulder and moments later he felt the same strange jerk from somewhere deep within his stomach and his feet once again left the ground.

The journey this time felt more controlled somehow and he was vaguely aware of the feel of Imeda's hand on his shoulder, as they spiralled upwards through the howling wind and raw, freezing air. Max's eyes burned and he felt the salty sting of tears; he shut them quickly as he realised suddenly that he was crying.

They landed in a neat circle, a few minutes later. Blinking furiously, Max bit his lip and glanced around. He could see that they were standing in a large, deserted stone courtyard, surrounded by a high stone wall. Two huge, stepped pyramid shaped buildings stood at one end of the courtyard. Imeda slowly steered Max across the courtyard and into the closer of the two pyramid buildings. He followed her silently. He didn't know where Krake and Otty had gone and didn't look back to check.

He was led through a large wooden doorway and into a beautiful entrance hall, a magnificent marble stairway swept up out of the hallway to unseen floors above. She led him silently up the stairs, and along a second-floor corridor. The staircase appeared to rise indefinitely, disappearing into the shadowy depths of the roof. He followed her quick pace and the gentle 'click click' of her feet along the corridor numbly and unquestioningly.

Eventually they reached a large wooden door, which she opened before ushering him inside. It opened out into a large room that looked something like a cross between a rather plush office and a lounge. A padded brown leather sofa stood on the wall to his left and an enormous heavy wooden desk and plush winged high back chair farther along to his right. Elegant drawings and sketches hung on the dark panelled walls. The overall effect was one of subtle grandeur.

'Please can you wait here, Max,' she stated in a gentle voice, 'We'll be back in just a moment.'

Max wandered over to the sofa and sat down heavily. He felt exhausted, too weary to be afraid anymore. He stared blankly around the room, vaguely registering that he was still wearing his muddy ripped pyjama bottoms, a jumper and some trainers that they had suggested he put on, when they had packed the things at home.

Home.

Max swallowed hard.

He was distracted by the sound of quickly approaching footsteps and muted voices out in the corridor, and then a moment later, the door swung open and a man swept into the room, followed closely by Imeda. The man was probably about the same age as Max's grandad with short, thick, snowy, hair and intelligent, bright, blue eyes. He had the air of a wise distinguished gentleman who was used to carrying the authority of the room.

'Max,' he said gently, his eyes full of sadness. 'I'm Cade, I'm a great friend of your grandad's.'

'He's dead,' Max whispered numbly. The words felt hard as they fell into the silence of the room.

There was a pause.

The man sighed deeply, and then he pulled a chair out from in front of the desk, positioning it next to Max on the sofa. 'I know, Max, and I'm sorry. I'm so, so sorry.'

Max said nothing. He continued to stare blankly ahead. He wasn't sure what he was supposed to say to all of these people that had suddenly appeared on the day his grandad had died and claimed to know his grandad so well, even though he had never met any of them before.

Seeming to realise this, Cade continued gently, 'I realise that there is a lot that we should explain to you Max, a lot that you should know, but now is not the time. You've had a terrible–' His voice wavered and he paused, seeming to struggle with his own emotions for a moment, '...shock this evening.'

Cade glanced towards Imeda who was hovering over by the door, a look of deep concern etched across her face.

'It is late in your time. You must be exhausted Max. I've asked Imeda to look after you for this evening. She will arrange a bath, some food and a warm bed for you and then tomorrow, I promise, I will explain things.' He glanced towards Imeda and she stepped forward immediately. Then he pushed back his chair and stood. 'I'm so sorry for your loss, Max.'

After that, Max remembered following Imeda down a blur of corridors and up various flights of stairs, until they finally reached a heavy, dark oak door. She opened the door, ushering Max gently inside and Max found himself standing in a bedroom. A large plush bed stood against the wall to his right, the floor was scattered with rugs and lamps stood in the corners of the room, casting a soft, warm glow. A small bathroom opened off to the left and she quickly ran him a bath and then disappeared whilst he bathed, saying that she was going to fetch him some soup. When he got out of the bath ten minutes later, feeling steamy and light headed, there was a blue top neatly folded on the bed and a bowl of steaming soup and some buttered crusty bread waiting for him.

Max pulled the shirt over his head, without properly undoing the buttons and sat down, eyeing the soup sceptically. He was unsure whether he could stomach it. He was still gazing numbly at the bowl and trying to decide when there was a light knock on the door and Imeda returned. Glancing down, Max noticed with some surprise, that the soup looked cold.

How long had he been sitting here? he wondered. Why is it so difficult to think?

'It was all I could get,' she said pointing at the blue top he was wearing, 'there's no one around now. We'll sort things out properly in the morning.' She hesitated and looked embarrassed, as though realising that she was talking about irrelevances considering everything that had happened. 'I'm sorry Max,' she said awkwardly. 'Is there anything else I can get for you?'

He shook his head. 'No. Thanks,' he whispered hoarsely. 'Do I sleep here then?'

'Yes, I'm staying just down the hall tonight. If you need anything...' her voice trailed away.

'Thanks.'

She left him then, softly closing the door behind her.

Max stared around the room blankly, too exhausted to think. Then he wearily clambered into bed and curled up on his side. Moments later, he fell into a deep and dreamless sleep.

Max slept for what felt like a very long time and awoke suddenly, having absolutely no idea where he was. Then the evening's events came crashing back into his mind, flooding his consciousness and a heavy, aching sadness settled into the pit of his stomach.

He slowly sat up in bed and looked around, realising that he had absolutely no idea what time it was. To his surprise, he realised that the only light in the room appeared to be coming from the lamps which he had forgotten to switch off the night before; the room appeared to have no windows. Deciding to investigate further, Max eased himself out of bed and began to wander around the room.

He quickly found what appeared to be a clock on a small wooden table over in the corner. However, it was like no other clock that Max had ever seen before. The clock was carved from heavy grey marble, with five hands that slowly moved around the clock face, pointing towards a complex series of strange numerals and coloured symbols that ran around the edge. A second smaller ring revolved around the inside of the clock face, upon which were a series of curious swirling symbols and a third dial rotated around the outside edge of the clock, covered in what appeared to be a number of small, coloured spheres. On closer inspection, Max realised that the strange, coloured spheres actually appeared to look like tiny intricately painted planets each of which had a tiny word written beneath.

He was busily peering at a tiny planet with the words Shadowlands inscribed beneath it, when there was a gentle knock at the door.

'Hello?' Max called hesitantly.

'It's Imeda; I just wanted to see if you were awake Max. Can I come in?'

He was half way across the room when the door slowly pushed open and Imeda stood in the doorway.

'Good morning Max.'

'Morning,' he replied.

'How did you sleep?' she asked gently. She smiled, but Max noticed that the smile didn't quite reach her eyes; she was studying him carefully, her blue eyes filled with concern.

Max realised suddenly, that he hadn't properly looked at her the previous evening and that she was actually quite a lot younger than he had realised. There was a strong and capable air about her and he could imagine that at times she could be quite formidable. Today however, her blond hair was tugged back into a loose knot, her face was lined with worry and she was wearing a crumpled pale blue tunic and grey trousers that Max vaguely recalled she had been wearing the previous evening.

'I-I slept okay, thank you.'

'I've brought you a change of clothes. If you want to have a wash and change, I'll get you some breakfast and then we'll go and meet Cade.'

'Okay,' he said taking the clothes from her.

'Can I get you anything else Max?'

'No. I'm okay,' he said, not altogether sure that he was.

'Fine...' She glanced around awkwardly, as though she didn't know quite what else to say, before finally adding, 'I'll be back in a few minutes then.'

Max watched the door close softly behind her, then wandered over to the bathroom. He washed quickly and dressed into the blue t-shirt and baggy grey trousers she had brought him. He wondered vaguely how they'd known his size, but decided he didn't care. He then perched on the edge of the bed, waiting for her to return.

A blur of questions churned through Max's mind. They had said that they would explain everything to him this morning. But what could they say – what explanation could they possibly give that could explain all of this? He didn't know who these people were. He didn't know where he was, he didn't understand... anything.

His thoughts drifted to his grandad and Max felt a cold emptiness settle inside him again. A lingering doubt resurfaced in his mind. Could it be that these people were somehow involved with what had happened to his grandad? Something about this seemed unlikely and, he reminded himself, he had definitely heard Imeda talking to his grandad the previous evening. But then again, he wasn't sure. He wasn't sure about anything anymore.

He was still deep in thought when Imeda returned with some warm bread and a hot steaming mug of scented tea. He ate the food quickly and drank the tea gratefully, eager to finally get some answers and realising to his surprise that he was actually now quite hungry. Imeda moved around the room, making the bed and gathering his discarded clothing from the previous evening.

'Where are we? What is this place?' he asked between mouthfuls.

'I think that it's probably best if Cade answers that, Max.' she said turning down one of the sheets on the bed.

'But what was that disk thing?'

'Cade will explain that too Max.' She stopped what she was doing and looked at him intently. 'I promise that Cade will explain everything.' Then eyeing his empty plate, she added, 'Can I get you anything else?'

'No I'm fine thanks,' Max swallowed down the last mouthful, 'Can we go now?'

She placed his folded clothes neatly on the bed, and then smiled gently, 'Okay,' she said simply.

He followed her out of the room and along a maze of hallways and stairways. He noticed now that bright sunlight was streaming from the uppermost reaches of the building and that in the daylight, it was obvious that they were descending through staircases and hallways in a giant pyramid shaped building. The building appeared to be comprised of tiers and each tier had a staircase that wound around leading up to the next level with small hallways and rooms leading off in various directions. The higher you got in the pyramid, the fewer rooms there appeared to be, as the space available on that floor diminished. A huge, cavernous drop stretched down the centre of the pyramid between the floors. Long white cylindrical lights hung down the centre space at regular intervals and heights. The walls were burnished stone, the floor pale marble and a huge polished wooden banister wound around the stairways and floors and disappeared towards the light. A number of people were milling around the various floors that morning, going about their business. Max noticed that when they passed Imeda, they almost always appeared to recognise her and usually smiled or nodded in greeting.

They finally reached the same floor that they had been on the previous evening and Max followed Imeda as she strode purposefully down the corridor in the direction of the same large, polished wooden door that stood imposingly at the far end of the hallway. She came to a halt outside the door and gave it a firm knock.

A deep male voice immediately rang out from the inside. 'Come in!'

Max's stomach gave a funny nervous jolt.

SAM KINI

Chapter 6
The Unexpected News

Cade was sat behind his desk as they entered. 'Max,' he said warmly, standing and moving across the room towards them, 'Why don't we sit over here.' He led Max over to the sofa.

Max nervously perched on the edge of the seat and clasped his hands in his lap; he noticed that his palms felt sweaty.

Imeda quietly retreated from the room, the door clicking softly shut behind her. Silence fell between them for a moment.

Cade coughed quietly and drew up a chair.

Max glanced awkwardly towards him. Earlier his mind had been full of questions, now he couldn't think of anything to say.

'How are you?' Cade asked gently.

'I'm okay,' Max said quietly.

'No, you're not,' he said kindly, 'and I'm not either really. Your grandad Quinn was a great friend of mine, my closest friend actually.'

Max hesitated, 'But how? How can you be his closest friend? I don't know you; I've never even met you...' his voice trailed away awkwardly as he realised that perhaps he should be being a bit more cautious, but the numbness that had descended on him on the previous evening seemed to be blunting his fear.

Cade smiled at Max, but his eyes were full of sadness. 'I know Max, I'm sorry, there is a lot to explain,' he hesitated, looking as though he was not really sure where to start. 'If you can forgive me, this is going to take me some time to explain and what I am about to say, may come as something of a shock to you.'

Max looked steadily into Cade's bright blue eyes and felt his pulse begin to quicken.

'I think—' Cade said slowly, his bright blue eyes never leaving Max's face, '—that I should probably start at the beginning.'

Max caught his breath. He wondered what could possibly come next.

'This... is... Lucem, Max,' Cade stated these words very carefully and deliberately as if each word carried significant meaning. 'That is to say, that it is not Earth. Not your Earth, anyway.' He paused and gazed at Max intently, waiting for the impact of these words to register, as if scared of the impact of each word he uttered. 'Max, I really don't know how to say this to you in any other way; but this is a different universe. You... are... in... a... different universe.'

There was a long pregnant pause.

Max stared at Cade in shocked disbelief.

'I don't understand.' he finally croaked, 'How? How is this not Earth? Are you joking?'

'No.' Cade shook his head, his eyes no longer twinkled. Instead, they had become intensely serious. 'I promise you Max, that I will be nothing but truthful with you, no matter how farfetched this may sound.'

'But how? How can this be true?'

'I know how this sounds Max, I realise that this may seem a bit strange, but it is true.'

Max thought that saying it sounded 'a bit strange' was something of an understatement. He felt stunned; his mind a blur of questions.

'I don't understand. Are we on a different planet or something?'

'No. All of the planets around your Earth, in your world, exist just as you know them to be. This world – this universe – is sort of parallel to yours.'

'What do you mean parallel?'

'It's very hard to explain Max, but there are dimensions that exist. There are dimensions that you can't see with the naked eye, but that exist all around us. Other worlds exist within these dimensions, Max. Lucem is one of them and so is Earth.'

'Worlds?' Max was bewildered. 'You mean

there's more?'

'Yes, an unlimited number. We don't know how many in fact. We've charted and explored many, but no one really knows.'

'I don't understand; why doesn't anyone know this?'

'Well you do, I believe. At least your scientists on Earth can prove mathematically that these dimensions exist, Max, but they just don't understand it fully yet and they don't know how to get there. They haven't worked that part out yet. It's still just a theory for them, at the moment; they call it String Theory[2] on Earth.'

Max thought about this for a moment, attempting to digest all that had been said. How could this be true? he wondered. How could there be worlds that existed parallel, but invisible to each other? It just didn't make sense.

'But this can't be right, it can't be possible,' he said definitively, shaking his head.

'Why can't it be right, Max? Just because something cannot be seen, does not mean that it is not there. Just because something isn't understood,

---

[2] Did you know that String Theory is a real concept or theory in Quantum Physics? Essentially it is believed that String Theory could fully describe our universe making it a theory of everything. Through String Theory, scientists have identified that certain aspects of the theory only make sense if there are more dimensions that exist than the three dimensions we recognise today in our everyday life. It is in these other dimensions that other worlds or universes could exist.

does not mean that it is not true.'

'But...' Max's voice faltered, 'I can't – I don't understand this. How?'

'Max, there are many ideas in history that people have held onto and adamantly believed, that have later turned out to be entirely wrong. Why do you think that everyone has all of the right answers now? For a long time, some people on Earth thought that the world was flat,' he chuckled, the intensity leaving his face for the first time. 'As we evolve, we learn and our understanding of things changes.'

'It just seems so...' Max's voice trailed away. He didn't know what else to say.

'Unlikely? I know,' Cade said simply and smiled. 'But why can't it be right? Have you never thought that something else might exist? Something beyond what is obvious and what can be seen?'

Max's mind churned with questions, the idea that there might be, that in fact there were, mysterious hidden worlds beyond our human senses, left him dumb struck. Whatever explanation he thought he'd hear that morning, he definitely hadn't been expecting this.

'And how did you work out that it existed? How did you work out these worlds?' he said.

'Well we found out about them around five thousand years ago and that's when we started to explore them. Max, we came from Earth once, that was our home. We were... well, we are... humans. We descended from an ancient great seafaring nation[3], who lived on Earth thousands of years ago. We explored the farthest corners of the Earth and then we discovered how to move between the dimensions, to other worlds and we carried on exploring there. We left Earth and traces of our existence was all but gone. We were forgotten and as time passed, all that was left of us on Earth were faint memories and some ancient lost relics of our existence. As time passed, we could not go back. Earth had moved on and we had no choice but to stay away. We travelled back of course. We still do.'

Max thought of the strange stone disk that had bizarrely transported him from the study to the woods on the previous night and the girl with the odd, overexcited orange pet and then the second identical disk that Krake had used that had brought them here.

'Oh, right, so that disk thing – is what you use to travel between worlds? And I accidentally transp– ' he stopped abruptly, realising that maybe they hadn't known about that part and that perhaps it wasn't wise to have said anything.

'Don't worry Max; yes, we know you used the

---

[3] Did you know that there is evidence throughout the world of many great ancient civilisations that were very advanced a very long time ago? There are many mysteries and theories around why these advanced ancient civilisations died out and eventually disappeared leaving only ancient ruins and relics behind.

Key. It's called a Uroboros[4] Key by the way. Must have given you quite a shock,' his face broke into a smile. 'You landed in the back garden of one of our Elders, lucky for us and for you.'

'What?! So I came here then... to Lucem?'

'Yes, you gave us quite a fright to be honest. We were looking for you...'

'Sorry,' mumbled Max. Then a thought occurred to him, 'So, why did my grandad have one of these key things then, if people on Earth haven't yet discovered how to get to these worlds?'

Cade sighed and looked at Max intently, appearing to gather his thoughts. 'Well that's where the next part of what I need to tell you comes in. You see, Max, you and your grandad aren't really from Earth. You were originally from here. You were – you are – from Lucem.'

'What do you mean?' said Max. But even as he said it, he knew it to be true. He remembered the maps he had found in the study and then how his grandad had always seemed slightly out of place, as though he didn't really understand things. He remembered with a grimace the time when his grandad had attended his School Parents evening and on hearing a good school report about Max, had jumped up and invited the rather startled

---

[4] Did you know that the Uroboros or Ouroboros is an ancient symbol depicting a serpent or dragon eating its own tail? The symbol is thought to originate in ancient Egypt but has also featured in Greek mythology, India and writings about alchemy and the Renaissance.

Headmaster for dinner. Then when Max, mortified, had attempted to discuss it with him later, he'd dismissed it and said that he thought that was what people did. Max shuddered at the memory even now; he'd been taunted by Bigsy for weeks after that.

Max glanced back up, to find that Cade was watching him intently. The bright blue eyes were studying him, taking in every detail, and every reaction to what he was saying, as if trying to work out how best to deliver all of this.

'Do you remember anything about your life when you were younger, Max?' Cade hesitated, 'Before about nine years ago?'

Max thought hard. He'd been five years old when they had moved to Wiltshire. He could remember bits or, at least, he thought he could. Their house, his mum and dad, the fire, him and his grandad moving to Wiltshire, it had all sort of blurred and muddled in his mind. He didn't really know, now that he really thought about it, what things he actually remembered and what bits he'd been told by his grandad.

'Max,' Cade said gently, 'All of those memories that you have from when you were a young child, before you moved to Wiltshire with your grandad, they are all memories of here. You lived here in Lucem...'

'But what about my mum and dad, the fire, moving to Normington for a fresh start?'

'All true Max, but it was here. All of that happened here. After the deaths of your grandmother and then your parents, your grandad was devastated.' He paused as if there was more, 'It was a terrible time Max. Your grandad decided to get away. He felt that it would be best for you both, if you could have a fresh start somewhere, just the two of you, away from the memories and the pain of everything that you had lost.'

Max swallowed but said nothing. So, his grandad had left Cassini because of the deaths of everyone that he'd loved. Everyone except Max, and now he was dead too. Suddenly, Max felt very alone. The sadness that had momentarily been forgotten suddenly descended upon him again. Why had they moved there, moved away from everything that they knew? It wasn't like they'd had a great life or anything. They hadn't been particularly happy in Normington.

'I don't understand this,' he said, 'I don't understand why my grandad moved to another world. I mean, it's not like moving to another town or city or even another country, is it?'

Cade shifted uncomfortably and twisted his ring around his finger. Max noticed with some surprise, that the ring was identical to his grandads.

'What you have to understand Max, is that there was quite a lot of pressure on your grandad Quinn here. There are four regions in Lucem, like your countries I suppose. This place, this region where we are now, is the capital and is called Cassini. I'm–' he hesitated, 'I'm the leader of the Elders here in Lucem Max, so I govern Lucem. But your Grandad, he used to be the leader before me. When all of this happened, it was too much pressure and it was hard for him to get away from it all; he needed to break away completely.'

Max sat silently absorbing this. The man that he had known, his grandad, just didn't seem like the kind of person who could lead lots of people. It was hard to imagine, picturing him sitting in this office, giving orders to people like Imeda and Krake.

'So, he was really a leader then?' Max asked hesitantly.

'Yes for a long time,' Cade paused. Then as though reading Max's thoughts, he added, 'But after so much grief, so much loss; it's hard. A thing like that can break a man. Your Grandad was a very good man.'

Max fell silent. His thoughts drifted back to the previous evenings events. With a jolt, he realised that they hadn't actually discussed what had happened to his grandad.

'So who killed... him?' he asked.

Cade sighed, 'At this point in time, we are still trying to understand what has happened. But it would seem that your grandad was killed by some fierce creatures. The creatures are called

Mothmen[5], Max.'

'What are Mothmen?'

'They are nasty creatures, evil of the worst kind. They come from another world called the Forbidden Lands and they–' he stopped suddenly, as though he had said too much. Sadness flickered behind the blue gaze.

Max dully recalled the strange sounds that he had heard in his house the previous night: the crashes on the landing, the terrible high-pitched shriek. Haunting images of his grandad, lying rigidly in his bed, his blank eyes staring sightlessly at the ceiling, whirled at the edge of Max's mind. He swallowed. Hard.

'But why?' his voice faltered.

Cade gazed steadily at Max; his blue eyes looked deeply troubled and sad. He sighed, 'We don't really know why. What is extremely alarming about this, is that until recently the Mothmen did not even know of the existence of other worlds. It would seem that these nasty creatures not only now know, but they have found a way of being able to travel between the dimensions and universes as well. It's very, very worrying.'

Max said nothing. A heaviness had settled inside him. He tried to push the haunting images

---

[5] Did you know that in the US in West Virginia folklore, the Mothman is a legendary creature that was reportedly seen in the Point Pleasant area from November 12, 1966, to December 15, 1967.

from his mind.

Then a thought occurred to him, 'But how did Imeda and Krake know? How were they already there when I got back last night?'

'We were alerted because you landed in the garden of one of our Elders. You met his daughter, I believe. She realised that there was something wrong and alerted her parents. You see, Uroboros Keys are not that common, Max, and young boys using them in their pyjamas even less so.' Cade paused, his face breaking into a half smile.

Max remembered the look of recognition on the girl's face, when she had seen the key in his hand.

'We realised that something unplanned had happened,' Cade continued, 'As I said, your appearance was something of a give-away. We obviously knew that your grandad had a Uroboros Key and that he had used it to travel to that location near Templar's previously, so we immediately dispatched Imeda and Krake to check on you and your grandad. Unfortunately, there was already somebody in the house when they arrived and it was too late... The rest, you know, of course,' he finished quietly.

Max swallowed but said nothing.

'I think that is enough for today Max. I have some things that I must attend to now, and you I think, have had more than enough to absorb for one day,' the piercing blue eyes studied Max intently. 'I promise that I will explain more to you tomorrow.' He glanced briefly at a clock on the wall.

Max noticed vaguely that it had the same strange numerals, swirling symbols and planet shapes as the clock that he had seen earlier. Then with a little jolt, he suddenly realised that he now understood what the planet shapes meant.

Cade paused then added, 'It will be okay Max; I promise that we'll take care of you.' A shadow passed across Cade's face and he looked for a moment deeply sad. 'I've arranged for someone to take care of you for the moment. You're going to stay with one of our Elders, Templar and his family, he has a daughter the same age as you – oh, but you've met her of course,' he smiled gently, 'Imeda will be back shortly and will arrange everything.'

And he left the room, leaving Max alone on the sofa, deep in his thoughts.

SAM KINI

Chapter 7
The Elders

Max sat alone, in Cade's office, lost in his thoughts and attempting to absorb all that he had heard. He had known that there was something that his grandad was keeping from him; he had always known that there was some big secret. But this? He had never, ever in his wildest dreams expected this.

He supposed now that he thought about it and remembered his grandad and the way that he had been, that in some strange, rather bizarre way, it did all make sense. But then, there was another part of him that still wasn't entirely convinced that this wasn't just some giant hoax. Could he really be sitting in another world that existed somewhere hidden alongside his own?

Max sat silently turning this thought over in his mind. He thought about the maps that he'd found in his grandad's study. So, they had been worlds then, maps of the many mysterious worlds that existed. He frowned, trying to remember the names that he'd read; Lucem had definitely been there, The Shadowlands, The Forbidden Lands, Earth.

It was strange to think that somewhere in Normington right now, somewhere parallel to this; his classmates would be going to school. Would anyone miss him? He doubted it.

He would miss detention that night, he realised. He wondered if he would get into trouble. But then he realised that he might never go back, he might never have to face Bigsy and his stupid friends again. He felt momentarily elated at this thought, but then suddenly he remembered all of the other things that would never happen again and at this a deep aching sadness threatened to engulf Max once more. Grief rose in his chest. He swallowed hard and tried to push the thoughts from his mind.

Attempting to avert his own thoughts, he tried to focus on the other things that Cade had said. So, his mum and dad, his grandad they'd all come from here and he had too. This was his real home and his grandad had been the leader of it all. He tried to absorb all of these new facts about himself. It felt strange, almost as though he had to revise his own understanding of himself, rewrite his own history. Almost as though he didn't know himself at all.

He was still turning this over in his mind when there was a light knock on the door and Imeda entered.

'Hello Max,' she said, distracting him from his thoughts.

'Hi,'

'I guess that Cade has explained everything to you now?'

'Yes,'

'It must have been a lot to take in?' she smiled kindly.

'Yes, a lot.' Max nodded.

'And you know that you are going to stay with one of our Elders, Templar and his family, for a while?'

Max nodded stiffly, 'Did I frighten her, the girl, appearing in the middle of her garden like that?' he asked awkwardly. He suddenly felt quite apprehensive about going back.

'Well, I expect it was a bit of a shock, but nothing to worry about Max,' she smiled at him, then added, 'Don't worry. They're a lovely family.'

'Imeda,' he said, 'Can I ask you something?'

'Yes, of course.'

'You were at my house, a couple of nights ago, weren't you?'

She stared at him, a look of surprise registered on her face, 'But how did you know?'

'I woke and heard you. I listened for a bit,' he flushed slightly, then added, 'I couldn't help it; I thought we were being burgled.'

'I'm sorry,' she said.

'Did you come often, to see my grandad?'

She hesitated. Her blue eyes narrowed

slightly and she regarded him for a moment as if uncertain about how much she should say. 'Yes, usually every two months or so, Max, we had to occasionally bring you money and things. Your grandad had never lived or worked on Earth, so you had nothing to live off effectively. And we gave your grandad updates on what was going on here.'

For some reason the confirmation that his grandad had such regular secret contact with this world and his previous life, but had kept Max completely shut out of it all, made Max feel a little angry.

'And where did you get the money from?'

'There are ways Max, the Wokulo are a race of smugglers that travel amongst the worlds and trade in most things. We just kept exchanging your money from here, into money that you could use there.'

'Oh, right,' Max didn't really know what to say to this.

'We should go,' she said turning to head back towards the door, 'They're expecting us in time for lunch.'

Max rose from the sofa and followed Imeda towards the door.

'Can I ask you another question please, Imeda?'

'Mmm?' she said; her back to him.

'Last night, how did you know to come and how did you know that I was in the study?'

She turned around to face him, her back to the closed door. Her eyes studied him carefully.

'Well, we got this emergency message from Cade and Templar that someone – and they thought that it was possibly you – had been seen in Templar's garden. We were worried for your safety; we didn't know how you'd found out, whether your Grandad knew, whether you'd managed to get back there safely. It was decided that we – Krake, Otty and I – should immediately go to the house to check that everything was okay. Of course it wasn't...' she finished quietly.

'What was there, when you arrived?'

'Has Cade not told you, Max?'

'Yes, but... I suppose I just wanted to ask you about it.'

She smiled kindly, but her eyes were full of sadness, 'Well, when we arrived, Valac and one of the other Mothmen were there and your grandad... he was already... well... they'd already got to him Max. We fought them, but they escaped by flying out of the landing window. Krake tried to catch them, but he couldn't. I'm so sorry Max. There was nothing we could do. It was already too late.' She sighed and looked intently at Max, sadness flickered in her eyes, 'I heard a crash as you landed back in the study and when Krake and Otty had gone outside to chase the Mothmen, I came to get you.'

'And what are these Mothmen exactly?' Max asked, trying to ignore the images of his grandad that came flooding into his mind.

'Mothmen are terrible creatures Max, they come from the Forbidden Lands. Valac is one of the leaders of the Mothmen; he is also one of the fiercest...' Her voice trailed away awkwardly.

'Cade said that the Mothmen never knew that parallel worlds existed before.'

She nodded but Max saw a tiny flicker of surprise register in her eyes, 'What did Cade say?'

Max hesitated, 'Erm... just that really.'

She nodded, 'Until very recently, Mothmen had never been seen before outside of the Forbidden Lands. It's a terrible worry.'

Max nodded, but he was left with the sense that there was far more that she wasn't telling him.

She reached out and touched his arm gently, 'I'm sorry. We should really go.'

'Okay,' Max said hesitantly, 'But please can I just ask you one last thing though?' A slightly disconcerting thought had just occurred to him. 'How did I get back? Cade said that the Key, the Urobo – whatever it's called – key thing, takes you to different worlds. How did I happen to make it to here and then back home again?'

'Uroboros Key,' she corrected him, smiling. 'Well I guess that the last time your grandad used the key, he must have used it to travel from your home to here, perhaps to visit Templar, so it was already configured for Lucem. In terms of getting home, well I guess you didn't change the configuration did you... you used the Return?'

Max shrugged blankly.

'All Keys are configured for the same list of set, pre-agreed locations.' She continued, 'It has to work this way, otherwise people could just turn up everywhere and anywhere, uninvited. With one exception, some of the Keys have a return home feature that allow you to travel back home. Your grandad's Key must have been configured to allow him to travel to and from the study if he ever needed to in secret. To be honest though, Max, you were extremely lucky, you could have ended up anywhere and we might never have found you...'

Max followed Imeda out of the office, silently digesting this unsettling thought. He found the idea that he could have so easily transported himself into another world entirely, to a world like The Forbidden Lands, deeply unsettling.

He followed her down through the labyrinth of corridors and stairways through the vast light hallway and out into the bright sunshine of the courtyard. The courtyard was now alive with the hum and buzz of activity as people bustled around attending to business. A large stone archway led out of the courtyard at one end of the large courtyard and a number of smaller archways led off in different directions. An ornate fountain of marble circles and spheres bubbled and sparkled at the centre of the courtyard, and a blue and white flag bearing a circular symbol flapped proudly at the far side. Max noticed that the symbol was the same symbol as the one on his grandad's and Cade's rings.

'Who are all of these people?' Max asked Imeda, as she strode purposefully in the direction of a narrow arched entranceway on the far side of the courtyard and he followed hurriedly in her wake.

'Some of them are local business people, they might be here on business or for meetings, but a lot of them work here, for the government, for the community.'

'OK. And the Elders lead these people or something?'

'Yes there are six of us.'

'Oh! So you're one too.' Max felt himself flush slightly. He felt a little embarrassed that he hadn't realised this before now.

'Yes,' she said smiling 'I'm one too. But just for Cassini, there are four regions here in Lucem.'

'Oh, right,' said Max. He felt that he might burst from all of the questions that he needed to ask.

They had reached the archway and stepped out of the courtyard onto a wide flagstone walkway that lead off to the left and right. A number of stone buildings interspersed with trees were dotted about on either side of the walkway. They were mostly three or four storey buildings with sharply gabled roofs. In the distance, Max could just make out a ragged range of very high mountains, the highest of which appeared to have snow on its summit. A dense dark green forest stretched away into the distance, reaching up the side of the mountains before slowly petering out.

Imeda turned left and headed up the street at a brisk pace.

'And Cade – he is the leader and my grandad was too?'

'He is the Lead Elder, and yes your grandad was before him, before you left.'

'And what does Lead Elder mean exactly?'

'I guess it means that we all have an input, but that the final decision comes down to him in the end.'

Max thought about this for a moment. He still found it very hard to imagine his grandad, the man that he had known, having that much power and influence.

He was distracted from his thoughts by some

rustling in the shrubs to their left. Then unexpectedly a small brown creature burst forth from the shrubbery, took a quick sideways glance at Imeda and Max, before bouncing happily across the walkway and into the bushes at the far side. It was a tiny kangaroo-like creature that stood no more than a foot high, had large brown eyes, tiny round ears and appeared to be able to bounce at least two or three times its own height.

'What was that?!'

'That?' said Imeda looking entirely unconcerned and continuing off down the street, 'was a Nomo.'

'What's a Nomo?'

'It's just a wild creature that lives around here; they're a bit of a nuisance to be honest.'

Max followed Imeda in silence for a moment, his mind still buzzing with questions.

They had reached the end of the street now and the walkway met a second road that lead off to their left and right. Imeda paused to look in both directions, before turning right and setting off again at a brisk pace.

With a start, Max noticed that there were some extremely odd-looking creatures mixed in amongst the crowd and any final lingering doubts that this was perhaps some giant hoax immediately dissolved from his mind.

He spotted three small, cloaked creatures deep in discussion. They were about three feet tall and all wore full length, hooded grey cloaks that covered their bodies entirely. Their faces were almost completely concealed beneath the shadow of their hoods. Max could just make out the suggestion of large heads, brown rather abundant beards that protruded and stretched down the front of their cloaks and the faint luminous blue glow of their eyes.

They appeared to be talking in some strange language, but they stopped their discussion as Max and Imeda passed and all three turned to watch them from the shadowy depths of their hoods. There was something faintly intimidating about them and Max decided to wait until they had passed further down the street before asking Imeda what they were.

However, as they passed a little further along the street, he was immediately distracted from his question. Set back from the main walkway, in a little square there appeared to be a series of large standing stones placed in an orderly circle. A number of people and strange creatures were milling around and forming a rather disorderly queue. Amongst them Max could see a huge lizard like creature that stood over six feet tall on its hind legs, with green scaly skin and slanted pale yellow eyes. It wore a grey cloak and trousers from which its long, muscular tail protruded. Next to this, stood a huge hairy creature that must have been about seven feet tall and was covered from head to foot in thick brownish, black fur. It had dark brown eyes and a face that looked almost half ape and half bear. It reminded Max vaguely of a Yeti or Bigfoot[6] that he'd seen in photographs of sightings, on TV or in the newspapers, back at home.

He was busily staring at these creatures, when suddenly a series of bright white lights appeared in the centre of the stone circle[7] and began agitating and weaving, bobbing and swirling as they circled and span around. Moments later, a number of strange creatures appeared in the centre of the circle with what appeared to be crates of vegetables and sacks of grain, which they immediately began to drag beyond the periphery of the stones.

They were about three feet tall, had long bony legs, arms and fingers, pot bellies and moved with a slightly awkward gait. There were six of them in total, all of which had large wrinkly foreheads and big brown eyes. Oversized ears stuck out and protruded from amongst tufty hair, on top of which they were all wearing rather elaborate knitted hats

---

[6] Did you know that in the folklore of many countries there are strange tales of huge half-bear, half-man or ape-like creatures? The creatures have names like 'Yeti' or 'Abominable Snowman' in the Himalayan region of Nepal, Bhutan and Tibet and in American folklore, a similar described creature is called 'Bigfoot.' There have been many claimed sightings over the years

[7] Did you know that stone circles have been found all over the world? Stone circles are a monument of stones erected in a circle, most of which were built during the Neolithic and Bronze Age era's. Their purpose and meaning is widely debated and still not fully understood.

in variety of colours and designs. Some of the hats had huge oversized multi-coloured pompoms whilst the tips of others stretched down and almost reached the ground. They wore grey or dark nondescript clothing and had bare sandaled feet, almost as if they intended the hats to make the biggest statement possible, which undoubtedly it did.

Max watched mesmerised, as one of the creatures wearing a particularly flamboyant hat got the tip of his hat caught beneath a heavy looking crate of vegetables and then struggling, had to call for help to successfully extract himself and his hat. Once free from the crate, he then commenced patting it down and delicately dusting it off, before replacing the hat upon his head with a little flourish. One thing was clear to Max, these creatures were very proud of their hats.

The strange creatures quickly finished dragging all of the crates and sacks beyond the edge of the stone circle and then set about organising everything into neat piles. The queue that included the lizard and bear-like Yeti creature – that had until now stood observed the six odd creatures with extravagant headwear – then piled forward in a small, congested huddle and entered the circular perimeter. Moments later, they vanished.

Max halted in the middle of the walkway, dumb struck.

'What is that? What's going on over there?' he

called to Imeda, as she strode on ahead of him.

'Hurry up,' she said briskly, then as he caught up with her, she added, 'It's a bridge. We use them for travelling between the Five Kingdoms. There is a scheduled timetable for bridge departures to each of the Five Kingdoms regularly throughout the day.'

'Oh,' said Max thoughtfully, 'But what are the Five Kingdoms?'

Imeda paused, 'That is a long conversation Max, but essentially there are five separate kingdoms and a number of people and beings that live in those worlds that are aware that parallel universes exist. We have a treaty and agreement between these Five Kingdoms about open travel and free movement and trade.'

'OK,' said Max, feeling rather confused. 'And what are these Five Kingdoms?'

'They're called Hyperborea, The Shadowlands, Arcadia, Naburu and Lucem, of course. People travel freely amongst these worlds but outside of that... it's limited and you have to use an Uroboros Key or something similar. But it isn't really encouraged; we have lots of rules about inter-world travel.'

'Oh, right,' said Max again, his mind awash with questions.

He was still reeling from this new piece of information when he noticed that heading towards him was another of the flamboyantly hatted creatures.

This one was wearing an elaborate orange, purple and red intricately designed hat with three huge pink pompoms that hung pendulously down the right side of his head and balanced at a jaunty angle. Max noticed with some surprise that he was actually knitting a second hat as he walked along. Four crochet hooks moved swiftly between his long nimble fingers as the hat slowly weaved into existence, whilst the creature scarcely so much as looked down.

'What... are... they?' Max asked, in wide-eyed wonder.

'They're Ebu Gogo[8]. They knit,' Imeda said quite simply, as if it was the most ordinary thing in the world for strange gangly creatures to wear flamboyantly designed hats that they knitted as they walked down the street. 'The house is just down here,' she added.

Turning right she marched off down a narrow, secluded pathway in the direction of a large three-storey house, partially obscured behind heavy wooden gates.

Max stopped abruptly on the path and peered cautiously at the house. His stomach gave a funny,

---

[8] Did you know that in 2004 on the Island of Flores in Indonesia the remains were found of a small human like creature? The skeleton matched with mythology from the island of a small hobbit sized people that had once inhabited the Island.

nervous jolt. He had been so busy observing everything, that he had completely forgotten where they were going.

Imeda had stopped a few feet in front of him and was unlatching the gates. She turned and glanced quickly over her shoulder.

'Come on.'

Feeling oddly as though his legs had just turned to lead, Max reluctantly followed her through the gate and up the stone path in the direction of the front door.

The house was larger than he remembered and surrounded by trees and shrubs which swept around both sides of the building and towards what Max presumed, must be the back garden – the garden that he had accidentally visited the day before, when he'd hidden in their bushes and then jumped out at their daughter in his pyjamas. Max swallowed and glanced nervously towards the door.

Then out of the corner of his vision, Max caught a furtive movement over near the corner of the house. Startled, he looked back. Suddenly from around the corner of the house, appeared a greenish, grey scaly-skinned creature which moved swiftly towards them and let out a deep rumbling growl. It snorted gently and a menacing wisp of grey smoke slowly emitted from its two slanted nostrils.

ANCIENT SECRETS

Although Max had never seen one before, it looked, he thought, remarkably like a very small dragon.

SAM KINI

Chapter 8
The Unusual Invitation

Imeda lurched to a halt on the path.

The dragon, which was about five feet long from its nose to the tip of its tail, eased its way across the path, its claws scraping gently across the gravel and then stood blocking their way.

'Elea?' Imeda called loudly and Max was disconcerted to hear more than a touch of urgency to her voice.

The dragon's eyes narrowed, and it snarled, snapping its teeth as it let out a second deep guttural growl which ended as it belched and more smoke shot from its nostrils.

'Elea!' Imeda shouted.

A moment later, a dark-haired attractive woman wearing an apron and kind expression appeared at the front door.

'Imeda!' she exclaimed, smiling widely and stepping towards them, 'Come on Gog, out of the way, these are our guests.'

The dragon reluctantly moved to one side and then slowly ambled away, throwing them a suspicious glance over its shoulder. It looked, Max felt, distinctly disappointed.

'It's a watcher. Just security measures,' Imeda said lightly, 'Lots of people have them; I guess they're like your guard dogs.'

Max nodded his head dubiously. He felt that a dragon no matter how small it looked, was infinitely more menacing than any guard dog he had ever seen on Earth.

'And you must be Max!' Elea said brightly, 'I'm Elea. Welcome to our home. Please do come inside.'

Max stepped into an impressive, pale marble hallway, and then quickly followed them through the house and towards the smell of food. Moments later, he found himself standing in a bright homely kitchen. A table adorned with a large bunch of purple and grey spiky flowers was off to the right and a large stove stood against the farthest wall. A series of pans were bubbling and spitting on what Max took to be a stove, filling the room with mouth-watering smells. Two large windows looked out onto the garden beyond and Max vaguely recognised the garden that he had been exploring two days earlier. In the centre of the kitchen was a large unit upon which sat a chopping board and various cooking implements. Sitting on a stool, leaning against this unit and idly flicking through a book, was Anna.

She looked up as they walked in and gave Max a confident smile.

She looked much as Max had remembered, about the same age as him, with tanned gangly limbs, shiny blond, brown hair that was cut into chin length bob and big dark brown eyes.

'Max, this is Anna. I know you two briefly met the other day,' Elea smiled at him kindly. Her eyes were warm and reassuring and he saw now how very much alike she and Anna looked, except that she had darker shoulder length hair and deep brown eyes.

'Hi,' said Anna casually.

'Hi,' Max replied awkwardly. He put his hands in his pockets and hovered in the doorway, wondering what to do.

'We're very glad to have you here, Max.' said Elea, glancing pointedly towards Anna.

'Thanks,' said Max. He didn't know what else to say.

'Well, lunch is ready so we can sit down straight away.'

She herded everyone through to the dining room and proceeded to serve stew and warm freshly baked bread. A slight awkwardness fell between Max and Anna as they ate, as neither of them seemed to know quite what to say to one another. Max concentrated on his food, realising that he was actually quite ravenous and instead listened to Imeda and Elea talk. It was mostly just conversation about the Five Kingdoms, and a lot of people who seemed to work at the Ancient Council with Imeda and Templar. Max ate his lunch and let the conversation wash over him; happy to have a moment to collect his thoughts after everything he had learnt.

'Whilst you are here, Max, you must treat this as your home,' Elea said just as Max was finishing his food. She glanced towards Max and Anna's empty plates then added, 'Anna, why don't you take Max upstairs and show him his room.'

'Okay,' said Anna sliding out from her chair, 'Come on.'

Max followed Anna out of the dining room, back into the hallway and up two flights of stairs.

Two doors led off the narrow landing; the first was closed and had a small plaque on it that read 'Anna's room.' The second door stood ajar. As Anna pushed open the door and Max followed her in, he found himself standing in a large room that was decorated in blue and white. Sunlight was streaming through a large window which looked out onto the back garden. Thick blue floor length curtains framed the window and a large cream rug covered most of the polished wood floor. A small bathroom opened off to one side and a large wooden bed stood in the centre of the room. Neatly folded and placed on top of this were some trousers, a smart shirt, shorts, T-shirts, two jumpers, socks, underwear and some pyjamas. A grey rucksack had been placed at the foot of the bed along with the two bags of his grandad's things.

'Mum didn't know what size shoes to get you, so she didn't get those yet, but she guessed the clothes' size. She thought they should fit.'

'Oh, right,' said Max. He didn't really know what to say; he felt slightly overwhelmed.

'There's some things there, that Otty brought over, that apparently came from your house.'

'Oh, right,' said Max again, 'They weren't really mine, they were my Grandad's...'

'Oh,' said Anna. An awkward silence hung between them for a moment, 'I'm sorry about that — about your grandad.'

'It's OK,' said Max quietly. 'I'm — erm — sorry I jumped out of the shrubs like that and scared you yesterday.' He glanced awkwardly towards the window.

'Oh you didn't scare me, not really,' she said plonking herself down on the bed, 'I was just a bit shocked that's all. Then I saw the Key and I thought that something must be up.'

'Why? How did you know?' he asked, perching on a chair over by the window.

'Well, most people don't have Uroboros Keys, you see. They travel around the Five Kingdoms using the Bridges. I knew something wasn't right when you arrived with it in your hand, looking all shocked and everything, and we've been told at school to look out for anything strange.'

'What do you mean anything strange?'

'Well, you know, boys landing in your back garden in striped pyjamas – that kind of thing.' she grinned.

Max forced an embarrassed laugh.

'No, they just ask us to look out for anything unusual. They don't say much really. But... I have heard them talking...' she leaned forwards slightly and lowered her voice, her eyes gleaming conspiratorially, 'Well, I've known something has been going on for weeks. Everyone has been getting really twitchy, so I've listened in to my parents talking a few times. There's these creatures that have suddenly been sighted outside of the Forbidden Lands. They've never travelled between worlds before, and it's got everyone really nervous–'

'What, the Mothmen?'

'How do you know about Mothmen?' Anna's eyes widened in surprise.

'Well, they were at my house. They were the ones...'

'Oh, right, sorry,' said Anna quickly.

'What do you know about them?' asked Max carefully. He glanced down at his hands, not actually sure that he wanted to hear the answer.

'Not much; I've never seen one. But they say

they're terrible, sort of half-human and half-moth or bird, they're supposed to be huge and really strong and vicious...' her voice trailed away awkwardly, and her cheeks flushed.

'Oh, right,' said Max. His heart sank.

'And you really have no idea why the Mothmen would want to hurt your grandad?' Anna asked cautiously.

Max shook his head, a hard lump had begun to form in his throat, 'No I asked Cade, but he didn't know, he said they were trying to find out.'

Silence fell between them for a moment.

'Oh,' said Anna, 'And when I've been listening in they've also been talking about someone called Xegan. They seem really worried about him. But I haven't managed to find out much about him yet.'

Max felt a sudden spark of recognition. 'I think I've heard something about Xegan,' he said hesitantly, 'I overheard Imeda and Krake talking about him to my grandad two nights ago.'

'Really? What did they say?'

'Well, I'm not exactly sure now, but I think they were talking about him breaking something and being the first person in a very long time.' Max shrugged. 'Do you have any idea what that means?'

Anna frowned thoughtfully, 'No, I don't, but I

do know that he's someone from Cassini, who went missing a long time ago and seems to have suddenly reappeared again. But that's all I've managed to find out so far.' She hesitated, 'Do you mind me asking – what was it like there on Earth?' Her eyes were bright with excitement.

'It was OK, a bit boring compared to here to be honest,' said Max, thinking of the strange assortment of creatures he'd seen that morning.

'I've hardly been out of Lucem,' Anna said wistfully.

'Well, I didn't even know anything outside of Earth existed until this morning. Beat that!' Max said with a wry smile.

'Really? What? Even though your grandad used to be the Leader of the Elders and everything – you didn't have any idea?'

Max gazed out of the window for a moment, a tiny knot of anger was growing inside him. He'd been asking himself the same question and feeling a little angrier each time he'd thought about it, ever since the conversation with Cade that morning. There were so many secrets. Why hadn't his grandad shared any of this with him?

'No,' he said darkly, 'I didn't know a thing. I mean I guessed there was something going on, but he didn't tell me a thing.'

Anna studied Max for a moment and then

said, 'I wish that I'd seen Earth. Do you want to come outside? You can meet Lokie.'

'Is that the orange thing?' said Max, remembering the strange orange pet that he had seen in the garden with Anna.

'That thing,' she grinned, '...is Lokie. It's – well – I think it's a Pamba. My uncle Bron gave it to me. He's got this great shop. I'll take you. He deals with the Wokulo and they get him all of this great stuff from loads of different worlds from outside of the Five Kingdoms; I think that's where Lokie came from, I've certainly never seen one before.'

'What are the Wokulo?' asked Max, following her downstairs.

'Oh they're this race of traders and smugglers. They live mainly within the Five Kingdoms, but they travel all over, to loads of different universes and they trade and sell all kinds of things.'

Max tried to remember where in the mass of information he had been bombarded with during the last twenty-four hours, he had been told about Wokulo and then remembered Imeda's comment about the money being exchanged. So, he thought, they must smuggle money and things from Earth too.

'What do they look like?' said Max, thinking of the strange variety of creatures he had seen on the walk from the pyramids to the house.

'Oh they're a bit creepy,' she said, 'short, hairy and hooded with these eerie pale blue eyes.'

So that was the Wokulo, Max thought, thinking of the three strange bearded and cloaked individuals that had watched them walk down the street earlier.

They wandered outside into the sunshine of the garden and headed over towards a sunny, secluded stretch of grass surrounded by shrubs.

'Oh – while I remember – we're not supposed to tell anyone who you are at the moment. You're my pretend cousin who is staying with us as your parents have gone away. I haven't really got a cousin, but I guess I have now,' said Anna enthusiastically. It was clear that she was thoroughly enjoying this.

'Oh,' said Max pondering, 'I wonder why they're pretending that we're cousins.'

'I don't know, I guess it's something to do with what's just happened with your grandad and all this other stuff that's going on. I told you, they're being twitchy and secretive about everything at the moment.' Anna wandered over to a small pile of orange fluff curled up in a blanket, 'Here's Lokie!'

Lokie was fast asleep and snoring gently. His rust coloured fur shone in the afternoon sunshine and one of his oversized green ears twitched.

'He sleeps a lot,' she said, then added loudly,

'Lokie! This is Max!'

Lokie opened one huge droopy brown eye with what appeared to be a supreme effort of will, before he rolled over turning his back on them both and started snoring again gently.

'Oh well,' said Anna, plonking herself down in the sunshine and leaning back on her elbows.

'How did he know where I was hiding? When I was over there in that bush?' said Max looking across the garden. It seemed surprising to Max now that Lokie had ever managed to find him in his hiding place.

'Oh, when he's awake, he's quite alert,' she looked over at him in the blanket and raised an eyebrow. 'I know you wouldn't believe it, to see him now. He just seems to conserve energy a lot!' She grinned at Max.

'No kidding,' laughed Max, 'And that was where I landed, I suppose?' He nodded over towards the woodland that stretched beyond the garden.

'Yes. How did you know to configure the Key for here?'

Max shrugged, 'I didn't. Imeda reckons that this was probably the last place my grandad must have travelled to, so the Key was already configured for here. I just sort of accidentally moved one of the rings and then moved it back again to its original position.'

Anna frowned. 'I wonder if your grandad came to visit my dad then?' She paused, 'And how did you get back? After I ran in to tell my mum and dad, they came looking for you, but they couldn't find you.'

Max realised suddenly that it must have been her parents that he had heard when he was crouched in the shrub.

'Well, at first I didn't think I could get back. I just moved the dial and moved it back again, but nothing happened the second time.'

Anna nodded. 'Well the configuration was set for here, so nothing would happen. You would have had to change the dials to a different location or world to get it to go anywhere. You see, the outside dial is the World ring, and the middle dial is the Region ring. You change that for the region or country that you want to travel to within the world you've selected and the inside ring is the Location ring and represents the actual place or area that you specifically want to travel to within the region and world you've selected. There are hundreds of different configurations and locations.'

'Oh, right,' said Max. Even though it all still seemed incredibly strange, it was starting to make a lot more sense. 'Well, I eventually found this little switch on the back, Imeda said that it was a return switch or something...'

'Only the expensive ones have the return

home feature. Most just have configuration options for the standard list of locations.'

'But why?' said Max, 'Why can't people just use them to travel anywhere?'

'It isn't allowed. Can you imagine if people could configure the keys for anywhere? People could land in your house uninvited, it would be annoying, not to mention dangerous! The only exception to the standard list of locations is that the better Keys allow you to return directly back to your own home. It's so that people can discretely travel to and from home without having to travel to the closest landing site. Sometimes the closest landing spot is nowhere near your house – kind of annoying really. Anyway, your grandad's Key must have had this feature because of his job. Lucky you found it really or you could have ended up anywhere.'

'I know, really lucky,' said Max, suddenly feeling the full enormity of how unbelievably fortunate he had been.

'I've never used a Uroboros key. What was it like – you know – *really* using one?' Anna's eyes sparkled with excitement.

Max thought about this for a moment. 'It was strange and kind of painful,' he said, thinking of the slamming into the ground part of the experience, 'Did you see that flattened grass up there?'

'Yes but that's kind of usual.'

'Really? What the whole landing on your face thing?'

'Oh I don't know about the landing on your face part,' she laughed, 'but the grass being flattened is part of the energy as the bridge opens up or something. I don't exactly understand it; I've only ever travelled by the centrally controlled bridges, but I've seen the grass flattened in circles like that loads of times. Whenever a bridge seems to open up, it always leaves a mark like that, it's just that if you land on hard surfaces like stone or whatever, it doesn't really show.'

'Oh, right. Well, I'm glad I didn't land on stone – I'd have probably knocked myself out!'

An easy silence fell between them for a moment.

Then Anna grinned at Max, 'You really don't know anything, do you?' she smiled, her eyes twinkling, 'This is going to be fun.'

'No,' Max said simply and smiled, 'I really don't.'

Max closed his eyes and tilted his face towards the sun, basking in the warmth of the afternoon sunshine. The heavy sadness that had been pressing down on him since yesterday and the dozens of questions that had been whirling around in his mind gently receded and as they stretched out on the grass, Max felt himself start to relax.

It was dinnertime and Max was enjoying his second portion of desert: a delicious fruit pie and custard, filled with some kind of strange purple sweet berries that Max didn't recognise, when Anna's father Templar arrived home from work.

He was a tall lean man with dark silver-flecked hair and serious dark brown eyes.

'You must be Max,' he said in a deep melodic voice as he hovered in the doorway and took off his jacket, 'I'm very pleased to meet you.'

'Pleased to meet you too,' said Max.

'Are you settling in OK?'

'Yes, thank you.'

Elea who had disappeared from the room, suddenly reappeared with a plate filled with fish, vegetables and potatoes and a bow of freshly cut bread, 'There you go dear,' she said, as she set the plates down on the table, then glancing towards Max and Anna she added, 'Would you two like anything else to eat?'

'No thanks, mum,' said Anna.

'No thanks,' said Max.

'I spoke to Cade earlier, Max,' said Templar as he drew a chair out from the table and sat down. 'He was wondering if you could come into work with me tomorrow. The Ancient Council have called a meeting that he needs to attend and he would like you to meet them.'

Anna met Max's eyes across the table and she frowned slightly. He could tell that she was more than a little surprised by this.

'OK,' said Max hesitantly.

'You won't need to come in until about 10am,' he said, 'So I'll go in to work and then come back for you. There's no point in you coming in sooner than you're needed and I expect that you'll need a good night's sleep again tonight.' He smiled at Max and began to butter some bread.

'Why do the Ancient Council want to meet Max?' Anna's eyebrows rose inquiringly.

Templar glanced at Anna and began to pile vegetables and fish on his plate. 'Well, I expect it's something to with his grandad once being the Leader of the Elders here in Lucem, Anna. He is a member of our community who has been living outside of our community for a number of years now. It's natural that they should want to meet him.'

'So, are the other leaders of Lucem going to be there?' asked Anna, her brown eyes narrowing suspiciously.

'Erm, no I don't think so. This is just a meeting between them and Cade and they'd like to meet Max.'

'Who is the Ancient Council?' Max asked

bewildered, feeling as though he was missing the point entirely.

'It's the leaders from the Five Kingdoms,' Templar said gently. 'Each leader sits on the Ancient Council and ensures that his or her community or world, abides by the rules of the Covenant.'

With a start, Max realised that he'd heard of the Covenant before. It was the Covenant that Imeda and Krake had discussed with his Grandad two nights ago; this was what the person called Xegan was supposed to have broken. Max glanced quickly towards Anna, wanting to catch her eye, but she was still watching her father, her brows furrowed into a deep frown.

'What's the Covenant?' he asked hesitantly.

Templar swallowed his mouthful of food, 'Well, there are certain rules, Max, that all the leaders have agreed to. These rules are designed to help maintain and manage the secrecy over the fact that parallel universes exist.'

'But why is it kept so secret?' asked Max.

Templar smiled at Max, 'Well, a long time ago, an agreement was made between the rulers of the Five Kingdoms that each world should be allowed to evolve naturally and individually and to find out for themselves – or not.'

'But why?' said Max. His mind had suddenly begun to buzz with questions again.

'Well, what you have to understand Max is that not all civilisations are ready to hear this kind of information. Some would immediately want to conquer all of the worlds and rule them. Others have developed into strange, frightening places and it would simply be unwise to let their inhabitants' know.'

Max thought again about the Mothmen and nodded slowly.

'The Ancient Council has always taken the view that if universes and civilisations do not know, then maybe they are not ready or were never meant to know,' Templar added, before taking another mouthful of his dinner.

Max turned this information over in his mind. He thought back to the conversation he'd overheard between Imeda, Krake and his grandad; he still wasn't certain that he really understood what breaking the Covenant meant but something told him that perhaps he shouldn't ask the question outright. 'So, what does the Covenant say exactly?' he asked hesitantly.

'Well,' Templar paused, his knife and fork hovering over his plate, 'It's essentially a list of rules and guidelines about how we should travel between universes and interact with worlds outside the Five Kingdoms to protect the local populations and to protect ourselves.'

Max slowly nodded. He still didn't think he really understood, but he wasn't sure what he should ask next. He paused, 'So the Covenant doesn't ban travel between worlds outside the Five Kingdoms then?' he asked carefully. He glanced towards Anna; she met his gaze and gave him a puzzled frown.

'No it doesn't ban travel outside the Five Kingdoms. We can and do travel to other worlds, but it does control it, to ensure the minimum impact to the local populations. Free movement and trade are encouraged within the Five Kingdoms, but outside of that, the Covenant lays out certain restrictions and controls over how people should visit these worlds and it is each Ancient Council member's responsibility to make sure that their people abide by this.'

Max thought about this for a moment, it seemed odd to him that with such strict controls over movement outside the Five Kingdoms, that Max and his grandad had been living on Earth for the last eight years.

Anna caught Max's eye across the table. She looked directly at him, her dark brown eyes drilling into his and he immediately caught her meaning. Returning his attention to his plate, he quickly finished the last mouthful of his desert. Then they immediately excused themselves from the table and disappeared upstairs.

'Well, that's a bit weird.' whispered Anna, the moment they reached the small landing outside their bedroom doors.

'Do you think it could just be because we've been living outside the Five Kingdoms for the last nine years and maybe they made some special exception or something?' Max said, as he followed Anna into his room.

'Probably, but I've never heard of it happening before. To call a meeting just with Cade and to want to meet you without all of the other Lucem leaders, just seems a bit strange to me. This is a big deal Max; I don't think my dad has even been to an Ancient Council meeting.'

Max stared at Anna in alarm.

'I'm sure it'll be fine though,' she added quickly.

'Mmmm,' Max muttered, thoroughly unconvinced. 'Listen, I've remembered something,' he said, 'the Covenant is what Imeda and Krake were talking to my Grandad about that night. It was the Covenant that they said Xegan had broken. I didn't remember before because I'd never heard of it before, but that's definitely what it was. They said that they thought that Xegan had broken the Covenant.'

Anna's eyes were wide, 'Well, that explains everything!'

Max sat down on the chair by the window. He felt as though his head was swimming with all of this new information. 'What exactly does it explain?'

'Max, if Imeda and Krake said that Xegan's broken the Covenant, it means that they think Xegan has told something or someone outside of the Five Kingdoms. It means,' she said with a meaningful look, 'that they believe that Xegan is the reason why the Mothmen have suddenly appeared.'

Max turned this news over in his mind.

'It's obvious, really,' Anna muttered to herself. 'I should have realised before, what with them both suddenly appearing at the same time.'

Max watched Anna pace around the bedroom, 'Anna,' he said slowly, 'Why do you think that Imeda and Krake would come to tell my grandad about Xegan breaking the Covenant? Isn't it a bit odd? Why would he care?'

Anna paused midway across the room and frowned, 'Well, it is a really big deal, you heard what my dad said: I don't think it's happened for a really long time and your grandad was once the Leader of the Elders. I suppose if he was being kept updated on things from time to time, then this would definitely be the sort of the thing they would tell him.'

Max nodded, an even bigger question forming in his mind.

'Anna,' he said again, 'If Xegan is the reason why the Mothmen have just appeared, do you think that he's the reason that Valac and the other Mothmen came after my grandad?'

Anna was silent for a moment, 'Probably,' she said slowly. 'It would make more sense really. We know that Xegan was from here originally. Your grandad was probably the leader when Xegan lived here.'

'But why? Why would Xegan send the Mothmen after my grandad?'

Anna shook her head solemnly, 'I have absolutely no idea.'

Max felt the tiny knot of anger tighten in his stomach. Yet another mystery about his grandad. Yet another secret.

'I wonder if this is linked to why the Ancient Council want to see you tomorrow,' Anna said thoughtfully.

Tomorrow. Max gave a start. For a moment, he had forgotten all about it.

'What is the Ancient Council like?' he asked, picturing a group of grey haired, wizen and wrinkly individuals and suddenly feeling quite nervous.

'Well, I've only ever met Cade,' she said, 'but I know who they are; my dad has mentioned them. There's Chandra – she's the leader of the Hidden People.'

'What do you mean Hidden People?' said Max.

'Well exactly that. They can make themselves

invisible.'

'What, for real?'

'Yes, for real. Most of the other communities — if they've lived and moved around in the worlds for a long, long time — have some kind of ability or skill that enables them to be able to move around and not get spotted so easily.'

'Oh, right,' said Max, bewildered.

'So there's Chandra,' she continued, 'from the Hidden People and they're one of the oldest civilisations, they move around a lot. Then there's Maya, she's the leader of the Nix, they're a race of Shapeshifters and they live in Hyperborea. They can disguise themselves by changing into animals and other creatures. Then there's Manu, he's the leader of the Shadow People, and they have shadows that can move around without them.'

'What?!' said Max a little too loudly, 'you're joking.'

'Shhh,' she said, 'They'll hear us. Yes, their shadows move around independently, well if they want them to anyway. They live in The Shadowlands... obviously. Then there's the Yeti's — they're not so good at hiding to be honest. They also live in the Shadowlands, mostly.'

So they were Yeti's, Max thought. He wondered if they were the same creatures that had been spotted on Earth.

'Then there's the Buru,' Anna continued in a whisper, 'They're like these huge lizard things – they give me the creeps, to be honest. The leader is called Rague and they come from Naburu.'

Max thought of the large lizard-like creature he had seen earlier queuing up at the bridge.

'Whom have I missed?' she said absently, 'Oh and Pangu, he represents the Ancient ones. Along with the Hidden People, they're one of the oldest civilisations. They don't move around much now, but apparently, they used to explore loads of worlds.'

Max stared at her, his mind boggled. 'What about those funny Ebu things who do all of the knitting and the Wokulo?'

'Well the Ebu Gogo only live in The Shadowlands and Lucem. They are happy to be governed by either the Shadow People or us, so they don't sit on the Ancient Council. Apparently, they used to live on Earth too, thousands of years ago, but they couldn't live in harmony with the people. I learnt about that in my History and Civilisations of the Worlds class at school.' She paused, then continued in a whisper, 'And the Wokulo, they haven't really signed the Covenant and aren't members of the Ancient Council, so they aren't really governed by the rules of the treaty, that's how they get away with so much. But they do have to make sure that they aren't seen, when they are in the worlds that they travel to. My dad says that they get away with too much really, but that people turn a blind eye because they like buying the things that they smuggle and trade from the different worlds. I don't think he likes my uncle Bron's shop much either.' She added thoughtfully.

Max sat in a stunned silence for a moment. He could see now why Anna was wondering why these people would possibly want to meet him. They were the leaders of civilisations and worlds. It did seem strange and very intimidating.

Anna shrugged, 'Anyway, it'll all make more sense tomorrow, after you've been to see them,' her dark brown eyes twinkled with excitement.

After that, Anna disappeared off to her room and Max wearily clambered into bed. He wished that he shared some of Anna's enthusiasm about tomorrow's meeting with the Ancient Council. He couldn't imagine what they could possibly want to ask him and even less what he could possibly think to say.

SAM KINI

Chapter 9
The Overheard Conversation

Max slept heavily and dreamlessly and woke the next morning with Elea knocking on the door.

'Wake up, Max,' she called through the closed door. 'It's 08:30, breakfast time!'

Max opened his bleary eyes. He could see sunlight streaming through the gaps in the curtains. He rolled over and looked at the clock by the bed. Sure enough, it was 08:30.

Then with a jolt, he realised that he should be meeting the Ancient Council in an hour and a half and he jumped out of bed. Dashing to the bathroom, he washed and then quickly dressed into a pair of soft grey trousers and a white T-shirt that had been sitting in the pile of clothes left by Elea on the bed. Anna had been right; she had judged the size well and they were a good fit.

'They look nice,' said Elea as he bounded into the kitchen moments later.

She was busily cooking at the stove and the smell of fresh bread filled the room.

'Thanks,' said Max. 'I mean, thanks for getting the clothes and everything.'

'Oh it's no problem at all,' she said, 'You're

very welcome. If you can manage with those trainers for now, I'll get you some more shoes sorted out as soon as I get chance. Now, would you like some eggs?'

There was no sign of Anna yet, so Max plonked himself down on one of the stools at the kitchen unit watching Elea as she swept around the kitchen preparing the eggs, fresh coffee and fruit juice and buttering thick wedges of fresh bread.

'Where's Anna?' he asked, as Elea poured him a large glass of purple fruit juice and proceeded to pile bread and scrambled eggs onto his plate.

'Oh, she'll be down shortly,' she smiled at Max, 'Templar will be here in about half an hour too,' she added, 'So you'll be there in good time for the meeting at 10am.'

Max swallowed the mouthful of egg he was eating with a gulp and glanced at the clock on the wall. It was 9am.

'Oh, right,' he said suddenly feeling as though some small animal was doing backward flips in his stomach. He wished Anna would come down. He needed the distraction of her conversation.

Seeming to realise his nervousness, Elea looked at him and smiled kindly, 'Try not to worry, Max. It will be fine. Don't forget, Cade will be there too.'

Max gave Elea a tight smile and continued

focusing on his eggs.

Moments later Anna bounced into the room.

'Morning!' she said loudly as if announcing her arrival, 'That stupid watcher kept me awake half the night growling outside my bedroom window.'

'Oh, he'll settle down,' said Elea, 'It's only because Gog hasn't got used to things here yet.'

'Oh, so he's new?' asked Max.

'Yes we just got him last week,' Anna gave Max a meaningful glance. 'Dad's work provided him. Mum, why did you say we've got to have him?'

'Anna, I told you already, all of the Elders are being provided with them. It's just a new policy, nothing to worry about.'

'Oh, right. I forgot,' said Anna lightly, 'Mum, please can I have some plum juice?'

When Elea had moved away to pick up the purple juice up off the side, Anna leaned into Max and said in whisper, 'I bet this is all linked to this business with Xegan and the Mothmen.'

Max nodded.

Anna leaned back again and began piling eggs onto her plate as Elea approached the table. 'Thanks Mum, I'm starving.'

Then as Elea swept out of the room for a moment, Anna leaned back towards Max for a second time and whispered, 'How are you feeling about this morning? You know, about the thing with the Ancient Council?'

'Umm. OK,' said Max, feeling anything but OK. He glanced at the clock again. It was 09:15. 'What do you think they are going to want to ask me?' he asked Anna in a tight voice. The small creature in his stomach had just resumed doing its backward flips.

'I don't know,' she whispered, 'I've been thinking about it last night and I just can't imagine.' She paused and then added, 'I wish I was coming with you, instead of going to stupid school.'

Max gave her a weak grin. 'To be honest, I wish you were going instead of me!'

A noise out in the hall halted their conversation and moments later Templar entered the room.

'Morning both of you', he said smiling, 'Nearly ready, Max?'

'Nearly,' said Max reluctantly chewing the last mouthful of his breakfast and sincerely wishing he still had a plateful of food.

They left the house shortly afterwards and headed out of the garden and back up the private pathway that led out onto the main road. Max was relieved to find that Gog did not make a reappearance that morning, as they walked down the path away from the house, which led Max to believe that it was either due to Templar's presence or that he was tired from last night's growling activities outside Anna's bedroom window.

The walkways and streets were quieter that morning and the journey seemed to take half the time that it had taken on the previous day with Imeda. All too quickly they were entering the Pyramid courtyard.

'Don't worry,' said Templar, 'It'll be fine.'

Max knew that Templar was only being kind, but the more people kept saying that he'd be fine, the more he began to seriously question and doubt whether he actually would be. He couldn't imagine for a second what they could possibly want to ask him and he couldn't think of a single thing that he could say that such a powerful group of people would be remotely interested in. What if he went into the room, he thought, and they asked him something that he couldn't answer or if he completely froze up and couldn't speak and just stood there like a mute like he had in his Geography class. He might make such a fool of himself that they might decide that they didn't want him here and send him straight back to Normington on his own.

Templar led him through the courtyard and towards the entrance of the second stepped pyramid. Both pyramids led up in precise huge sandy coloured blocks to flattened points which reached high into the sky and Max could see large window like gaps right at the top, which the sun was shining through and which must have been the source of the light flooding into the central chamber of the hall. Max noticed that there was actually a circular glass walkway that was suspended about halfway up the side of both pyramids connecting the two. He could just make out a few people walking through the clear tubular walkway, as Max and Templar briskly walked across the remaining stone flags and disappeared into the cool entranceway of the second pyramid.

The hallway of this pyramid was equally as impressive as the first, with the same tiered floors, long white lights and majestic staircases that stretched up and disappeared towards the source of the sunlight deep in the recesses of the top of the pyramid.

Templar quickly led him up the stairs to the third floor and down a long corridor.

'Please can you wait here, Max?' Templar said, as he led Max over to a handful of chairs, set to one side of the corridor. 'I just need to pop into my office. I'll be back in a minute.'

Max perched on the edge of the seat and looked around with his hands clasped nervously in his lap. He was sitting facing a series of doors which Max assumed must lead to offices, as there were small grey plates attached to each of the doors, each of which was engraved with a name. The door to one was ajar and Max was surprised to hear Cade's voice emanating from the inside.

'We made the only decision we could,' Cade said in a firm voice.

'I don't agree,' came the sound of a second voice, 'He shouldn't be here.'

'What choice did we have, Malik? We couldn't leave him there, it wasn't safe.'

'Quinn made his choices. You know how I feel. Until we know what's going on, the decision to take him was rash. He should be back there, not here.'

'MAX!' A third voice rang out from the corridor; Max turned and saw the man called Krake that had come to collect him with Imeda, striding along the corridor towards him.

The voices inside the room stopped abruptly.

'How are you, Max?' Krake asked smiling broadly.

'I'm OK,' said Max, hesitantly glancing back towards the door. A quieter discussion had resumed inside and Max could no longer hear what was being said.

'We never got properly introduced. I'm Krake; I'm Cade's son.' Krake sat down on the chair beside Max and looked at him thoughtfully.

Max turned his attention to look at Krake fully for the first time; he was heavyset with dark brooding eyes and thick dark hair. He didn't look at all like his father.

'I've been wanting to catch you, Max, to talk to you, to see how you are. I'm so sorry about everything.' He smiled at Max, 'I knew your grandad well and your mother and father.'

Max looked at Krake with surprise, realising that many people had mentioned his grandad since he had arrived but that no one had really mentioned his mother and father.

'Did you know them well?'

'Your father yes, since we were children. I got to know your mother later, when she met your father,' he hesitated and studied Max for a moment. They were good people, Max.'

'What were they like?'

'Your mother was lovely, she had blue eyes like yours and was very kind and generous.'

Max felt a gentle thrill of delight and a warmth that slowly expanded inside his chest. It was nice to hear Krake talk about his parents. He'd never met anyone before, except his grandad, that had even known his parents and his grandad hadn't always been willing to discuss them. Max had always felt that the topic upset his grandad, so sometimes even when he'd had questions about his mum and dad, he'd avoided raising them.

'Oh and she was funny,' Krake continued

smiling, 'really funny.'

'And what about my dad?' he asked.

'He looked a lot like you: dark hair, blue eyes. You're tall for your age and he was too. He was a big man.'

Suddenly there was the sound of approaching footsteps on the corridor. Max reluctantly looked away from Krake and saw Templar approaching them along the corridor.

'Hello Krake!' he said warmly. 'Are you ready Max? It's time for us to go.'

'Hello Templar,' said Krake. Then looking back at Max he added, 'I'll see you again sometime.'

Max gave Krake an attempt at a half smile and then got up to follow Templar back down the corridor. He wished that he could stay and talk to Krake for longer – he wanted to hear more about his parents.

They wandered back down the stairs, through the great hall and out of the pyramid into the sunshine of the courtyard. Although it was still quite early in the morning, the temperature had risen, so it was already quite warm and there was a light balmy breeze. They made their way across the courtyard, through the entrance and into the cool hallway of the other pyramid.

'I didn't check you in before,' said Templar, 'I just need to let reception know that you're here,' and turning he disappeared off in the direction of a marble carved desk which sat to one side of the entrance hall.

Max looked around the busy hallway. He noticed that this morning there were lots of different and rather unusual looking people and creatures wandering around. He noticed three Yeti's deep in a discussion to the left of the main doorway and a Buru lizard that carried himself with some authority and was dressed in a sleek blue cloak, swept up the stairs and disappeared into the upper levels.

Moments later Templar returned and Max followed him as he strode purposefully across the marble floor and then up through the labyrinth of stairways. Up and up they went, Max feeling increasingly nervous with every floor they climbed. Finally, after about fifteen floors, they turned off and headed down a short marble floored corridor at the end of which and dwarfing everything around it, stood a huge thick oak door.

'You'll wait here, Max. The meeting has just started. They'll call for you when they're ready for you,' Templar said. 'When you come out, please can you wait here for me? I'll come back to collect you.'

Max felt his stomach tighten into a knot.

As if noticing this, Templar added, 'Try not to worry, Max. They're all good people and they will treat you fairly.' Then with a kind, sincere smile, he turned and left Max standing alone in the corridor.

Max hovered by the door and wondered about the conversation he had just overheard between Cade and the man named, 'Malik'.

Within moments, however, there was the sound of the door being opened from the inside and a young dark-haired woman wearing a severe bun, a crisp white blouse and a solemn expression appeared in the doorway. Max's stomach lurched.

SAM KINI

Chapter 10
The Ancient Council

'You can come in now,' she said briskly. 'They're ready for you.' Turning sharply on her heel, she retreated into the room.

Max's stomach immediately resumed its backward flips. He swallowed hard, and then hesitantly followed her through the door, around a corner and into a large room.

Before him was a large U-shaped table, around which were sat the strangest assortment of people that Max had ever seen in his life. Seven people sat around the table and Cade was amongst them. He looked up as Max entered the room and gave Max a reassuring smile, but his eyes frowned slightly and he looked, if Max wasn't mistaken, a little embarrassed. Max guessed that they had heard Krake earlier and that he probably knew that Max had overheard them talking.

Next to Cade sat an old man. He was dark skinned, with a short white beard and hair; he had dark wise eyes and a wide generous smile. To his right, sat a huge Yeti. Max wasn't sure whether he just seemed larger, close to, or whether he was in fact much bigger than any of the other Yeti's, that Max had seen so far, but he sat head and shoulders above anyone else at the table, dwarfing the people seated around him.

To the right of the Yeti and in the centre of the table sat an elegant, distinguished lady with short cropped, pearly white hair and silvery grey eyes that twinkled. Her skin was pale and she had an almost luminous quality. Next to her sat possibly the most beautiful woman that Max had ever seen. She had long dark, thick, shiny hair, deep blue eyes and full, rose-coloured lips. Her cheekbones were high, her neck long and elegant and she had an almost swan like quality. She studied Max with her intense blue appraising eyes and Max immediately felt embarrassed.

To the right of this lady was what Max assumed must be the leader of the Buru. Close to, he was even more fearsome and creepy than Max had imagined. He was clearly the Buru individual that Max had seen on the staircase earlier and was wearing the same dark blue cloak. He had grey, green scales, flat slit like nostrils and his yellow slanted eyes scrutinized Max carefully, as if calculating and taking in every detail. An orange forked tongue slithered out of his mouth and disappeared so fast that Max wondered if he'd imagined it. Long hard scaly fingers with grey claws that tapered to a needle-sharp point, gently rested on the table in front of him.

Next to the Buru leader, sat possibly the most peculiar creature that Max had seen since his arrival in Lucem; leaning over the end of the table opposite to Cade was a strange goat like creature, who appeared to be half goat and half man. He was seven feet tall – or more – by Max's estimation. The strength of his body visible beneath the long grey cloak that he was wearing and his long muscular furry legs were wrapped under the table and ended in goat-like hooves in place of feet. He had huge curled grey horns that grew out of his wispy hair and swept back over his shoulders. His face was clearly that of a man's but had an animal like quality with a flattened nose and a thick white beard with flecks of brown through it. His slanted large dark eyes held a deep wise intelligence that contemplated Max carefully and it appeared to his relief, with some warmth. The brisk lady who had brought Max into the room was sitting in the corner with a pad and paper; she appeared to be taking notes.

Max glanced awkwardly around the table at the seven incredibly strange faces that were watching him intently. He felt like he'd walked into a scene from Star Wars. He wondered where he should stand; there were no empty seats and in any case, nobody told him to sit down. He wasn't sure what to do with his hands either, so he shoved them into his pockets and then took a reluctant step towards the table. He had never felt so under scrutiny in his life.

The older woman with short white hair and silvery grey eyes sitting in the centre of the group addressed Max first.

'Thank you for coming to meet us, Max. This is the Ancient Council.' She raised her hands and gestured towards the group sitting around the table,

'We have Cade, who represents Lucem and who of course you know, Manu the leader of the Shadow People,' her right hand panned around, 'Mirka the leader of the Yeti's, I am Chandra the leader of the Hidden People. This is,' she gestured towards the beautiful dark-haired lady to her left, 'This is Maya, the leader of the Nix. She represents all of Hyperborea. This is Rague, the leader of the Buru and finally, Pangu who represents the Ancient Ones in Arcadia,' she said as she finally gestured towards the strange goat-like creature.

Mirka the Yeti nodded at Max and Manu the leader of the Shadow people and Maya the beautiful dark-haired woman, both smiled and said hello.

Chandra paused and then said, 'Please accept our apologies that you have had to come here today, Max, particularly under the circumstances. I'm sure that everyone here would join me in expressing our condolences to you; your grandad was a great man and his death is a loss to us all.'

Max nodded stiffly. He was aware that a few people were nodding around the table and murmuring in agreement.

'I expect you're wondering why you're here, Max,' she said fixing Max with her silvery gaze.

Max didn't say anything. He wasn't sure he could. His mouth had suddenly gone very dry.

'The reason why we wanted to meet you, Max, was because granting permission for someone to live permanently outside of the Five Kingdoms is a highly unusual step and was done largely as a favour to your grandad Quinn. Strictly speaking the rules of our covenant wouldn't usually allow it and it obviously didn't end as we had expected.' She finished awkwardly; her silvery eyes studied him closely.

Max was vaguely aware of Cade shifting uncomfortably in his seat to Max's left.

Chandra paused, before continuing delicately, 'Given the severity of everything that has just happened, it is imperative that we quickly come to an understanding over the sequence of events. We called Cade here today so that we could review everything that has happened and we wanted to meet you to understand from yourself how you felt. Clearly, we can cover most of this with Cade. Particularly,' she hesitated, 'the events of the last couple of days. But I really just wanted to understand from you, Max, first hand, how you felt about your time on Earth and whether you felt that the correct decision had been made to allow you to both live there.'

Max glanced around the room, bewildered. He was beginning to feel very confused. He hadn't known about any of this until two days ago, he had lost count of the number of secrets that his grandad had kept from him, most of which he didn't really understand why and so far he hadn't had a choice in any of this. He hadn't made the choice to be on Earth in the first place, he hadn't made the choice to leave and now he'd overheard them discussing whether to send him back. His nerves gone, he realised that he actually felt quite angry.

'To be honest with you, I didn't exactly have a choice, did I?' he said darkly, 'And I didn't know about any of this until two days ago. If you want to know whether I liked being kept in the dark for the last eight years and not really knowing who I am, then, no, I didn't. I knew something was up and that something wasn't right and I kept asking and he wouldn't tell me and now he's dead and I suddenly get told all of this!' Max bit his lip and stared down at the floor, he knew that he had said too much.

There was a taut silence in the room.

Max stared at his trainers. He could feel the blood pounding in his ears.

'Thank you Max,' Chandra said carefully, 'I'm sorry, it's just important that we get the full picture.' She paused then continued, 'We're very sorry for your loss, Max, and all that you've been through.'

Max felt his face reddening. He said nothing and continued to stare at the floor.

'I think that is enough for now, unless anyone else has any questions?'

The silence lengthened; a couple of people shifted uncomfortably in their chairs. Someone coughed.

'Okay then, Max, thank you for your time. You may leave.'

Max turned and left the room, pulling the door to a close behind him. He paused on the other side of the door, breathing hard, his hand resting on the handle. He could feel the blood still pumping in his ears and his heart pounding in his chest. He took a very deep breath and tried to calm himself down.

He'd let his temper get the better of him. They were bound to send him back now, he thought. He wondered dully, how soon it would be before Templar returned to take him home. He needed to get out of here and to escape back into the sunshine.

It took Max a moment to realise that he could still hear the muffled sound of voices from inside the room. He glanced around, realising that the door was still ajar. The low murmur of a man's voice was emanating softly from the gap.

Max hesitated, if he shut the door now, they might hear and then they'd know that it hadn't been closed. A second voice began to speak, it sounded like Chandra. After another moment's hesitation, Max leaned in towards the gap, held his breath and listened.

'Do you think that he knows, Cade?' It was Chandra that was speaking.

'I'm sorry, knows what?' said Cade, he sounded annoyed.

'His eyes changed colour, Cade. You know what that means.'

There was a pause, as no one spoke in the room.

'Are you sure, Chandra? I didn't see that.' It was a different, deep, male voice.

'Absolutely positive,' she said her voice serious. 'The response to what I said was quite immediate – his eyes went a silvery grey.'

'Did you say that purposely to get a reaction, Chandra?' came the sound of another woman's raised voice. Max assumed that it must be Maya.

'That's why you dragged him here Chandra, under this silly pretence?' interjected Cade. His voice was loud, incredulous.

'We needed to know,' she said simply, 'I'm sorry, Cade, I didn't want to cause him any more pain but given the circumstances, we had to know and there was no other way. I had to make him uncomfortable, to create a reaction. You know it's usually the first sign of any kind of ability with

Aether[9].'

'I know, but really, hasn't he already been through enough?' It was Cade speaking again, 'Couldn't we have waited?'

There was another pregnant pause.

'I guess it's no surprise; we know that it has always been in his family.' It was Maya that was speaking.

'You'll have to watch him Cade,' said Chandra, 'See how it develops with him over time.'

'Yes, but right now what he needs is our protection and support,' Cade sounded agitated. 'He's had enough revelations over the last few days!'

'Speaking of which, Cade,' it was Maya again, 'I don't understand how Xegan managed to find them? I thought that it was only the Elders that knew their location.'

'It was only the Elders; the information had always been managed very tightly. We don't know how Xegan managed to find them,' said Cade. 'Understanding that, is our main concern at the

---

[9] Did you know that Aether (also spelled æther or ether and also called quintessence), was discussed throughout Ancient and Medieval science and was for a long time widely believed to be the material that fills the region of the universe above the terrestrial sphere? In Greek mythology the word αἰθήρ (*aithēr*) was thought to be the pure essence that the gods breathed. Plato and Aristotle spoke of aether as being the fifth element.

moment.'

'Have you given any consideration to the idea that the Elders have been compromised Cade? That someone in your trusted circle has betrayed you?' It was Maya again.

'Never,' said Cade emphatically. 'I would personally vouch for every one of my Elders. I trust them all implicitly.'

'Well, something has happened Cade, because Xegan found them.' Maya's voice was firm.

'Are we absolutely certain of all our facts on this?' said a low rasping, almost gravelly voice, 'Are we sure that all of this is definitely connected to Xegan and that Valac and some of the Mothmen are working for him? Are we even sure that he's broken the Covenant?'

'Absolutely, he's been seen and suspected for years, of course, and we've all heard the rumours, but now we're certain.'

'It's strange, he's been elusive for so long and now suddenly all of this,' said a deep male voice Max didn't recognise.

'I agree,' said Cade, 'we've tried to keep track of him over the years, but it's always proved impossible and now–'

There was the sound of approaching footsteps on the marble floor. Max quickly stepped away from the doorway and stood leaning casually against the wall.

Moments later, Templar walked around the corner. He stopped abruptly when he saw Max leaning against the wall, a startled expression passed over his face.

Max glanced quickly down at the floor, worried that Templar had perhaps seen his eyes.

'Are you okay?' Templar asked, as they passed down through the hallways and descended the stairs. He gave Max a fleeting sideways glance and frowned.

'Fine,' said Max, quietly. He was trying to keep his head down until he knew he had calmed down and his eyes would be normal again.

Max followed Templar home, silently preoccupied in his thoughts. His mind was swimming with questions. Templar seemed to realise this, as he didn't push the conversation any further. Max desperately wanted to discuss everything with Anna, but he knew that he'd have to wait until she returned home from school.

Lunch passed quickly and afterwards he wandered outside to join Lokie who was dozing again in his blanket in the garden. Positioning himself under the shade of a nearby tree, Max sat down and tried to relax.

Only two days had passed since he'd climbed out of his bed in Normington and crept along the landing to his grandad's study. *Two days.* In just two days, everything in his life had suddenly and inextricably changed and with every moment that passed it seemed that more secrets were revealed; more questions raised. Max was beginning to feel as though everything that he had ever known about himself was a lie and he wondered if he even knew his grandad at all.

Every time, he thought about his grandad, a tiny knot of angry resentment would begin to build inside and the same question would begin to revolve round and round in his mind. Why? Why hadn't his grandad told him anything?

Worse than that even, he wasn't at all certain, that his grandad would have ever told him any of it. He couldn't imagine a point where his grandad would ever have been able to untangle and explain all of this to him. The realisation of this, made him even angrier. This was his history, his life and it had all been kept from him.

It was just after 15:15, when Anna came charging into the garden to find Max. She was wearing the same blue short-sleeved dress that she had worn the day that Max had unexpectedly arrived in the garden and Max realised that it must be her school uniform. She plonked herself down on the grass beside him and looked at him expectantly.

'Well?' she said eagerly.

Max gave her a weary smile, then he started at the beginning. He told her about their arrival at the pyramids and the conversation he'd overheard between Cade and Malik. How Malik had said that he shouldn't be here and how they had stopped talking when they had heard Krake say Max's name. Then he told her about what had happened at the Ancient Council meeting, how Chandra had purposely tried to get a reaction from him and how afterwards he had overheard them talking about Aether and his eyes changing colour and how Maya had seemed very concerned about how Xegan had managed to find them on Earth. Anna sat listening avidly to Max throughout, her brown eyes wide with surprise.

'Wow!' she said when he had finally finished, 'I did *not* expect that!'

'I know,' said Max, relieved to have finally shared it all with her.

'Did you know about your eyes changing colour?'

'Yes, so did my grandad's, but it's just been one of those things; it's always happened to me. I mean I knew it was a bit odd and everything and that it didn't happen to the other kids at school... but I didn't think that it was anything more than that. I didn't know what it meant. My grandad never explained it. Have you heard of it before?'

'Yes, a couple of times, I think,' she said looking at him thoughtfully, 'It's not that common though. I knew it was linked to having some ability with Aether, that's why the Hidden People have silvery eyes I guess. But most humans don't have much ability with it. Do you remember how I told you about all of those abilities that the different civilisations and groups had? Like the fact that the Shadow People can make their Shadows move without them, and how the Hidden People can make themselves invisible and how the Nix can shape shift into other creatures? Well, that's all because they work with Aether. It's like this energy that surrounds us in the universe and all of the older more ancient civilisations have found some ability or way of working with it.'

'I don't understand.' said Max, 'What kind of energy?'

'Well,' she said, 'Every world is comprised of the same five elements. These five elements have to exist in the universes for life to exist. The elements are Earth, Wind, Fire, Water and Aether. Life cannot exist anywhere without all five elements.'

'Oh, yes,' said Max frowning, 'I've heard of four elements, about Earth, Wind, Water and Fire, but I've never heard of five before.'

'Well it's this energy, that sort of binds and connects everything and it connects the universes. When it's channelled correctly, it allows you to cross between the universes and dimensions, so that you can travel between worlds. That's what the

Uroboros Keys and gateways do and like I said, it can give you abilities to be able to do things, if you know how to work with it properly.'

'You seem to know a lot about it.'

Anna shrugged, 'We learn about it at school. I actually find that class quite interesting.' She grinned.

'And I've got this power?' said Max feeling a little bewildered. 'So one day I might be able to make myself invisible or change into a chicken or something?'

'It sounds like they think you might have the power to do that, but I think it's supposed to take a very long time and years of study for humans like you and me to be able to do those sorts of things.' She grinned at Max, 'Wouldn't it be great though... I wish my eyes went silver, can you tell when it happens?'

'Sometimes,' he said thoughtfully. 'But it's more that I can tell when I feel angry or frustrated or my emotions are really strong and then I sort of know it might have happened, as it seems to always be linked to that.'

'Right,' she said thoughtfully. 'Maybe that's because that's when your emotions are most powerful?'

'Maybe.' Max turned this news over in his mind. He was finding it hard to become enthusiastic about this new revelation, even if it did seem decidedly more fun, than most of the other things that had learned about himself in the last few days. It was still another thing that he didn't know about himself. Another secret that had been kept from him. How can I possibly know so little about myself? he wondered. He sighed wearily and looked at Anna. 'How much more am I going to find out Anna? How many more things don't I know?'

Anna's bright blue eyes were for once solemn; she shook her head, 'I really have no idea, Max. Maybe this is all there is to find out,' she said hopefully, her expression sincere. 'But maybe it's not... You know, Max, there could be lots more we don't know.'

They sat contemplating this for a moment and then Anna said, 'So we were right then, Xegan's definitely broken the Covenant.'

Max nodded, 'Yes, definitely. Cade said that they've heard rumours and suspected he'd broken the Covenant for years, but now they know for sure. Valac and some of the other Mothmen are working for Xegan. He's the reason my grandad's dead. Why didn't Cade tell me, Anna, when I asked him about my grandad? Why did he miss that part out?'

Anna shook her head, 'I don't know,' she frowned thoughtfully. 'It's strange, isn't it?'

'And how did Xegan find us?' Max continued. 'Cade said that he trusted everyone in the Elders, but he also said that it was only the Elders that knew where we were on Earth. None of this makes any sense.'

'I know,' Anna frowned. 'Did they say anything else – anything else at all – about what they thought Xegan was up to?'

'No. I think that they might have been about to, but then your dad turned up.'

She rolled her eyes. 'Trust my dad. Well, I heard something else today, after you left this morning. One of mum's friends popped in briefly and I heard them talking and saying that one of the Hidden People who lives in Lucem has suddenly vanished.' She hesitated and grinned, 'I don't mean invisible – I mean really vanished, like they've been kidnapped or something. When I asked mum about it, she played it down, but she sounded really worried when I heard them talking.'

'Do you think its Xegan again?'

'I guess it's probably connected; nothing like this has happened before. It seems a bit coincidental, doesn't it, with everything else that's going on. Who else could it be?'

Max turned this news over in his mind.

'And what about the other things?' said Anna, 'What do you make of that whole thing with Malik and Cade?'

'I don't know, but I definitely got the feeling

that Malik didn't want me here. He seemed to think I should have stayed in Normington.'

Anna frowned thoughtfully, then shook her head, 'I don't know. It's strange isn't it. I mean, what would you do if you were there on your own?

Max shook his head, 'I really don't know. There was only ever just me and my Grandad, we don't have anybody else...' He lapsed into silence again.

'By the way, no school tomorrow,' Anna said chirpily. 'And mum says that we can go to my Uncle's shop to have a look around, but she has to take us and we still have to pretend that you're my cousin. It's OK,' she added, 'It's not as weird as it sounds. Uncle Bron doesn't get on that well with my dad. He's my mum's brother, so he's never met half of my relatives on my dad's side of the family and the shop is great, you'll love it!'

Much later, Max fell into bed exhausted and drained. They had eaten and then spent the evening with Elea; Templar had once again been working late. Max had excused himself and come to bed early, under the pretence that he was still tired from having been awake all night, the night he'd arrived. But the truth was he needed time to think and he wasn't ready to share with Anna, the tiny seed of horror that had been growing inside him, since they had talked that afternoon.

He had remembered what Cade had said at the Ancient Council Meeting, about their location in Normington being secret. Cade has specifically said that only a few people had known their location and that they had no idea how Xegan had found Max and his grandad on Earth. So, how had Xegan found them and why had Valac arrived at that particular time, on that particular night? They had arrived at *exactly* the same time that he had been in Lucem. Max had crept into the study and accidentally used the Uroboros Key; by the time he had arrived back, Valac had already been there. No matter how hard he tried, he couldn't help feeling that it was too coincidental.

A cold dread settled inside him. The idea was so horrible – so horrific – that he could hardly bring himself to think it. He'd used the Uroboros Key and then Valac had arrived. What if *he* had somehow alerted Xegan to their whereabouts in Normington? What if he had actually caused his own grandad's death?

Sometime later, he heard the sound of Anna coming up to bed. She hovered on the landing outside their rooms; then after a moment he heard her footsteps move away and her bedroom door quietly click shut. Max rolled over and curled up on his side, feeling wretched. He didn't think he had ever felt so sad and alone. Much, much later, he finally dozed off and fell into a restless sleep.

SAM KINI

Chapter 11
The Weird and Wonderful Shop

Max woke the next morning, to see bright light flooding through the edges of the curtains. He had finally dropped off to sleep at close to 2am, but even then he'd been restless, his head filled with half awake, half dream like thoughts and worries that kept churning round and round in his mind. He had then eventually fallen into a deeper sleep, after he could already see the faint pale blue light of dawn creeping through the gaps in the curtains.

Max lay in bed not moving, wallowing in the warmth and comfort of his bed and the softness of his blankets. His limbs felt heavy and tired. He was still lying in the same position when Anna came bouncing into the room, some ten minutes later.

'Morning!' she chirped, plonking herself on the end of his bed. 'Did you sleep well?'

Max eyed her cheery expression and brightly coloured striped pyjamas through bleary eyes and wondered whether he could possibly find the enthusiasm to match it.

'Not really,' he said truthfully, then upon seeing her frown and not wanting to expand any further right now, he quickly added, 'I think Gog was growling outside again.'

'Oh, he's so stupid!' she grinned, 'Come on – let's go and get some breakfast and then we can go to Uncle Bron's shop. He has all of these amazing things from faraway lands that the Wokulo bring in for him. I can't wait for you to see it.' She paused and frowned, observing Max's distinct lack of enthusiasm, 'Are you sure you're all right?'

'Yes,' Max lied.

Anna raised her eyebrows, clearly unconvinced.

Max hesitated. What he wanted to say was, 'I think I might have done this terrible thing; I think I might have somehow alerted Xegan and Valac to our location in Normington; I think I might be the reason why they found us and why my own grandad is dead. He knew he should ask her about it, knew that she might be able to help. But he was too scared to hear the answer. He felt too ashamed. So in the end he just said, 'I'm all right, just sleepy.'

'Well come on dopey – it's good, honestly. I'm going to get dressed. I'll see you downstairs in five minutes.' Then she dived off the bed and bounced out of the room; the bedroom door swinging shut behind her.

Max hesitated, lingering in the soft, comforting warmth of his blankets for a moment, then slowly, reluctantly, he dragged himself out of bed and wandered heavily into the bathroom.

It wasn't Anna's fault, he thought grumpily.

She was only trying to cheer him up and they were being so kind to him. He needed to get it together, he told himself firmly.

He gloomily inspected his appearance in the bathroom mirror. His face was creased and he had bluish shadows smudged under each eye. Then he splashed some cold water on his face and quickly got dressed.

He joined them downstairs in the kitchen, a few minutes later. Elea was humming to herself as she prepared breakfast and Anna was sitting at the table already digging into a pile of scrambled eggs. Lokie was perched on the table next to Anna, nibbling a piece of bread.

Sunlight shone brightly through the kitchen windows, flooding the room with a warm golden glow.

Anna looked up and grinned at Max, 'More awake now?'

'Yes, definitely,' he said.

'Morning, Max,' said Elea brightly, 'Would you like some breakfast?'

'Umm, yes please,' said Max then looking at Anna he added, 'Why are you off school today then?'

'Well we have two days off each week but they're split up, three days in school then one day off, two days in school and then another day off, like that. School is sooo booooring!' she sighed.

Elea frowned at Anna and began piling eggs and bread onto Max's plate, 'Anna, haven't I told you about Lokie sitting on top of the table?'

'I know Mum but he's so small, he can't see anything if he sits on a chair!'

Elea frowned again but said nothing and walked back over to the stove.

'What does he eat?' said Max, realising that he hadn't actually seen Lokie do anything but sleep since he'd arrived.

'Well it's kind of strange, he hardly eats anything at all some days and then other days he doesn't stop eating and he eats everything in sight,' she peered at Lokie thoughtfully.

Lokie slowly reached a paw like hand out and gently tugged a piece of bread off Anna's plate.

'I think that today is one of those days. That is his third!' said Anna raising an eyebrow.

Max eyed Lokie munching his third piece of toast. Being less than a foot high, the piece of toast was almost as big as his head. Lokie looked back at them with big brown eyes and gently hiccupped.

'It's hard to see where he puts it,' said Anna frowning, 'He is so cute though, isn't he?'

Lokie hiccupped again and then burped quite loudly.

'Or maybe not!' she grinned.

There was a knock at the front door and Elea disappeared. Voices filtered through the open kitchen doorway and moments later, she reappeared with what appeared to be an Ebu Gogo woman.

The Ebu Gogo was dragging a large box of food rather awkwardly into the kitchen and they appeared to be discussing the contents of the box.

'Oh well, never mind Quonk,' Elea said reaching for her purse on the kitchen unit, 'I'll pay you now, but do you think that you could drop some more off for me later in the week? Maybe after you get the next delivery from Hyperborea?'

'No problem,' said the Ebu Gogo lady in a surprisingly squeaky voice.

Max watched mesmerised. Apart from the Ebu Gogo man that had passed him in the street knitting and that had been brief; he had only ever seen them from a distance. Close to, they were just as strange, with tanned skin, angular bony limbs, large, oversized foreheads, ears that stuck out, potbellies and big brown, doleful eyes. On her body, she wore a neat little grey dress from which her bony knees and large sandaled feet protruded and on top of her head, she wore a huge extravagantly knitted hat[10]. It had a wide front that frilled and framed her head in orange and purple, and which tapered down her back, incorporating almost every colour of the rainbow, until it stopped just short of the floor and ended rather flamboyantly with six large, gold pompoms. The weight of the pompoms was obviously considerable, as she kept tugging it forward to stop the hat from slipping back off her head.

Noticing Max's enthralled gaze, Elea said, 'Oh, this is my nephew, Anna's cousin. He's called–' She hesitated, and gestured towards Max, '...Frederick and Frederick, this is Quonk; she is an Ebu Gogo. She delivers all of our food and is a friend to our family.'

Anna snorted into her orange juice.

'Hi, Quonk' said Max.

'Pleased to meet you, Frederick,' squeaked Quonk, removing her hat with a little flourish to reveal soft tufts of sandy coloured hair.

Elea and Quonk resumed their conversation and Max returned to his breakfast. Anna caught his eye and grinned.

---

[10] Did you know that on the Island of Taquile on Lake Ttiticaca in Peru the local men knit and crochet hats as part of their tradition? They knit the hits in elaborate colours and designs and wear the pompoms in different positions to signal whether they are busy or can be interrupted as they go about their daily business

'Great name, Mum,' said Anna, chuckling again after Quonk had left.

'Oh shush!' she said, her cheeks flushed. 'I had to think fast, I hadn't thought about what we were going to call Max before that moment and I'm not used to lying.'

'I know but – Frederick, Mum!'

Max laughed.

'Quonk's husband likes to knit... a lot!' said Anna. 'I mean they all knit the Ebu Gogo, but Quonk's husband he really knits, he enters all of these hat competitions and things. She's always turning up in these unbelievable concoctions. I'm not sure she likes some of them that much to be honest, they look pretty uncomfortable.' she added thoughtfully, biting into her piece of toast.

'But *why* do they knit so much?'

Anna munched her toast for a moment, then shrugged, 'I don't know. They just do. It's like their tradition or something. The patterns on the hats mean all sorts of things, like their family name, where they come from and the way they wear their hats mean something too, I think...'

'What do you mean, the way they wear their hats?'

Well you know, if they wear the pompom on one side it means that they are in a rush and too busy to talk today and if they wear it the other way it means something else.'

'Wow that's weird!' said Max, marvelling again, at how different everything was to anything that he knew. He was starting to feel that nothing would surprise him.

They set off for Bron's shop just after breakfast. The morning had started bright and clear and as they wandered down the garden path in the direction of the gate, despite everything, Max felt his spirits lift.

Gog ambled around the side of the house and stood near the gate observing them suspiciously through narrowed eyes, a menacing wisp of grey smoke slowly seeping from his nostrils. Max could have sworn that Gog was watching him with a mean glint in his eyes and as he followed Elea and Anna out through the garden gate, Gog gave him a threatening growl and irritably snapped in the direction of Max's heals.

'Are you absolutely sure he knows I'm a friend of the family?' Max laughed, as he joined her on the path.

Anna grinned and rolled her eyes, 'I know, he's a menace isn't he!'

They set off up the street, Lokie, who had come with them, was perched in the back of Anna's rucksack, his head peeping out of the top. His oversized ears stuck vertically in the air and he gazed around with wide curious eyes. Upon reaching the main street, they turned left in the direction of the pyramid buildings. The walkways and streets were busy that morning and Max watched with fascination as the strange assortment of people and creatures went about their daily business.

'Don't you have any cars or bikes or... anything here?' Max asked, looking around and realising with a sudden jolt that he hadn't actually seen anything remotely like that, since he'd arrived.

'Oh, do you mean those things that you drive around in, on Earth? Yeah I know what you mean; I've seen them in a book at school. No we don't, we don't really need them as we have Bridges. We've got a few trams and boats, but most of the time people just travel around using the Bridges.'

Max nodded. Glancing up, he noticed that they were approaching the stone circle that Max had seen on his previous journey with Imeda. Just as before, a disorderly queue was slowly forming to one side of the standing stones and Max could see a string of bright, white lights that were bobbing and swirling within the stone area.

Max watched as the lights slowly dissipated and a group of people suddenly appeared before him within the circle; a young blond haired woman with silvery eyes, an Ebu Gogo and two Buru lizards quickly came into focus and clarity. The Buru both looked around sharply, before immediately resuming a heated conversation with each other, then they stalked off in the direction of the main street.

Elea turned and began heading towards the circle and for an excited moment, Max thought that they might be getting a bridge to somewhere, but she swept past it in the direction of the other side of the square.

'See – look,' said Anna gesturing towards a board to their right which had lots of place names and times scribbled across it, 'That bridge was just in from Naburu, the next bridge leaves in five minutes for Pavel which is another region in Lucem and the next one after that leaves for The Shadowlands. They're coming and going all the time.'

'Oh, right,' said Max somewhat amazed by it all. It felt good to be walking along the streets with Anna explaining things to him.

They headed towards the far side of the square and wandered down a road between a series of stone three storey buildings, a second large square suddenly opened out in front of them to reveal the hubbub and clamour of a busy market. However, it was the strangest market that Max had ever seen. Max noticed that most of the traders were either Ebu Gogo's or Wokulo and due to their diminutive size and the relatively large size of many of their customers, some of which were seven or eight-foot high Yeti's, they were all perched on small platforms behind their huge stalls which they clambered onto by using little ladders. The Ebu Gogo's tended to be trading in food and had stalls overflowing with fresh vegetables, fruit and fish. The Wokulo were selling all manner of wares and strange things.

Max passed a Wokulo stall that was selling a variety of strange creatures and insects in ornate cages. The foremost cage contained a giant hairy spider that looked something like a tarantula except that it was over two feet in size. Fine black spiky hairs covered its chunky body and eight arched legs. The spider turned, as they walked past, clacking its fangs gently and watching them with eight dark, unblinking eyes. Lokie who had until this moment been happily observing the clamour of activity in the marketplace, suddenly dived, droopy eared into the bottom of Anna's rucksack, quivering.

'I hate insects,' said Max shuddering, 'Did you see that? It was as big as a cat!'

Anna grinned and shrugged, 'This is nothing; wait until you see my uncle Bron's shop.'

'What?' said Max in alarm, 'He doesn't sell even bigger spiders and creepy crawlies, does he?'

'No!' said Anna laughing, 'I just meant that the stuff he sells is better than this.'

They wandered out of the marketplace and down a wide street flanked by tall stone buildings on either side; Max slowly became aware of the rushing sound of water and moments later, they found themselves standing on the embankment of a large fast-paced river. The river led down from the ragged range of mountains that jutted starkly into the bright blue sky dominating their view to the right and swept past them in the direction of five immense water wheels that turned and churned through the water creating white frothy foam a little way down the river to their left.

A large stone bridge with ornately carved pillars at both ends, stretched across the expanse of water in front of them and to their left further down river was a second bridge, upon which a blue tram covered in a strange intricate swirling pattern with three carriages could just be seen slowly trundling its way to the other side.

'The big docks are down by the sea,' said Anna, waving her hand in the direction of the water rushing away from them to their left.

They crossed the bridge and upon reaching the other side of the river, turned almost immediately down a narrow side street. An imposing stone building stood in front of them with a huge heavy oak door. However, instead of going through this door, they turned sharply down a second side street to the left of the building and descended some stone flagged steps that led to a blue heavy, wooden door and presumably into the basement of the building.

A faded blue sign that read Bron's Goods in gold letters creaked and swung at the top of the steps. Elea quickly led the way down the stairway and through the door. A tinkling bell rang somewhere in the dim interior of the shop.

'Uncle Bron!' yelled Anna.

A tall dark-haired man quickly strode towards them. He had a mop of dark, silver speckled hair, dark brooding, shrewd eyes and thin lips that looked at once pensive and serious and then suddenly broke into a wide welcoming smile that crinkled his eyes.

'Anna, my favourite niece!' he boomed.

'Well, that's not hard Uncle; I'm your only niece!' Anna said grinning.

'True, true, and who's this?

'This is Anna's cousin, Frederick, from Templar's side of the family, Bron,' said Elea.

'Oh, from the posh side of the family!' said Bron laughing, 'Well you're very welcome here Frederick.'

'Thanks,' said Max awkwardly.

They left Elea and Bron talking and began to wander around the shop. It seemed that everywhere Max looked, there were weird and wonderful objects and strange unidentifiable things crammed, hidden and balanced on top of one another. Animal skins, pictures and intricately drawn maps depicting faraway lands and ancient charted worlds, hung from the walls and the whole room was lit in a soft subdued light, which bounced off some of the strange objects in the room casting eerie shadows across the walls. Small, neat labels were balanced near many of the items detailing what the objects were and where they came from.

'Does all of this come from the Wokulo?' said Max, eyeing a label that read, 'Woolly Mammoth skin – Location unknown' that was balanced on top of a large folded, dark, hairy skin and next to this, another label that read 'Dragon hide – Dragonia' which was balanced on top of a section of grey hard, scaly leather.

'Most of it,' said Anna. 'Although there are some things that come from Naburu, I think.'

'So what, they travel to all of these places and just take all of these things?'

'I don't know – I suppose so.'

He moved over to another table which was crammed with objects teetering precariously. A large jar sat in the centre of the table within which were a number of small white balls of fluff that whizzed around the jar at great speed, bouncing off the sides. The jar was labelled 'Unknown Item – Cloudlands.' Next to this was a huge blue crystal that glowed luminously at its centre before fading out towards its translucent edge, that read 'Blue Glowing Crystal – Arctica', and next to this was a large jar filled with twinkling sand coloured dust that read 'Crystal Dust – Barren Lands.' There were small carved statues, elaborate candlesticks, beads, strange masks and a strangely eerie but beautiful skull carved from purple crystal that read 'Crystal Skull – Forbidden Lands. A strange pearly white luminous horn leaned against a table to his left; the label that hung neatly from its point read 'Unicorn Horn – The Ancient Lands.'

There were gold coins, an old, battered medallion with a skull and cross bones etched into each side, a strange, elongated skull, gems and jewels and an iPod. Except that the label didn't read iPod, it read 'Fortune telling device – Earthe.'

'Ooooh, this is great,' said Anna, when she realised what he was looking at. 'Look, you do this,' and she picked up the iPod, which had no earphones, and began running her finger around the circular dial.

'Erm Anna...' said Max hesitantly, wondering how he should break this to her.

'Oh, I know it's not real,' said Anna, 'It's just a silly gadget, but its good fun. I just usually ask it a question and then do this, see?' She ran her finger around the dial and then held it out to show Max the words, 'I Will Survive – Glorya Gayner.' 'I don't know what the Glor-ya Gay-ner part is,' she frowned, then added, 'Oh well. Maybe not today. You try.'

Seeing no reason to spoil her fun, Max shrugged and took the iPod off Anna.

'Okay,' he said and ran his finger around the dial. It read, 'Run For Your Life – Beatles.'

'Umm,' said Anna peering at the iPod in Max's hand thoughtfully and sounding a bit deflated, 'I wonder why its saying that beetles should run for their life... how strange! Oh well!' she shrugged and moved off in the direction of another table.

Max smiled to himself and wondered whether Anna's uncle knew that the Wokulo were selling him things that they were making up uses for, as they obviously had absolutely no idea what they really were.

'Look at this Ma–... Frederick,' said Anna remembering to keep up the pretence and quickly correcting herself. She was standing in front of another table upon which were displayed a number of gadgets.

Max watched, fascinated as a number of small, strange insect-like robots, squabbled and scrambled over the surface of the table. Two of the beetle-like robots watched Max with metal beady eyes, as they bounced up and down on the edge of a book, whilst two others appeared to be having a fight. One had grabbed hold of the other's antennae and they were tumbling and rolling around the table top. A small rather battered label, that looked distinctly as though it had seen better days, was positioned nearby and read 'Trackers – Naburu.'

Max touched one of them lightly on the top of its head and watched as it scuttled away in alarm, to hide behind a box of shiny metal discs and a label that read 'Poca Smoke screens – Naburu.'

At the edge of the table, something else caught Max's eye. It was a small dagger with an intricately crafted handle, carved with a series of strange symbols and set with gleaming emeralds. Max gazed at it for a moment, before reaching out to gingerly touch the blade. It felt hard, cold and unforgiving against his fingertips.

'Oh and look at this too,' said Anna, 'More things from Earth!'

Max's gaze lingered on the strange dagger for a moment. Then he wandered over to join Anna. She was peering at a huge stone tablet that was leaning against the wall. Etched into the tablet was a series of intricately carved symbols. To Max's utter amazement, he realised that the symbols looked remarkably like the Egyptian hieroglyphs that he had seen on a trip to the museum with school.

Next to this, hanging on the wall, was a painting that looked strangely familiar to Max. It was a rather angular painting of a lady with dark hair, painted in bold blocks of colour and a thick black outline. Max looked to the bottom corner and saw with some shock, that it read in scribbled writing, Picasso. Even he had heard of Picasso the painter.

'Anna!' he said slightly astounded, 'Some of these things are worth an awful lot of money. This is a really famous painter, you know!'

'Ummm, but not here,' she muttered distractedly, and wandered off in the direction of the next table.

They spent a little longer wandering around the shop investigating before Elea finally called them over.

'Time to go. I want us to get back in time for lunch.'

'Already?' said Anna, in a pained voice.

'Yes,' Elea said firmly, 'And please can you wait for me outside? I just need to discuss a couple of things with your uncle Bron.'

'Okay,' said Anna, then added in whisper, 'I'll join you in a minute Max. Uncle Bron, I'm just going to collect that book I forgot for school,' and she disappeared towards the back of the shop.

Max looked around and then hesitantly made his way across to the thick oak door standing to his left. He pulled the door open and stepped outside. The door quietly clicked shut behind him.

Too late, he realised that instead of standing, as he had expected, at what should have been the base of the stone steps leading up to the main street, he was standing in a small yard that was sunk down below street level and with no obvious exit. He had somehow taken the wrong door.

Max turned, feeling foolish, and twisted the door handle. The handle didn't budge; to his utter dismay, Max realised that the door had locked behind him. A ten-foot-high wall bordered the yard, on top of which ran a high spiked railing, located at street level above him. Despite it being a bright sunny day, no sunlight shone into the grey, gloomy yard. A series of large storage boxes, bins and crates stood to one side.

He was going to have to bang on the door he realised, in order to attract their attention and turning he was just about to do this, when he became aware of a deep rumbling snarl from somewhere behind him.

Max's heart sank. Turning, he looked cautiously across the yard.

With a soft scraping sound, as its claws dragged gently across the hard stone floor, an enormous Watcher stepped out from behind the bins.

Fear flooded Max's body.

SAM KINI

Chapter 12
The Covenant

The Watcher was bigger than Gog, reaching almost seven feet in length. Its skin was a darker, bluish grey and a long menacing ridge of scales ran from its head to its tail, ending in a razor-sharp point.

It blinked at Max, its yellow, slanted eyes seemed momentarily surprised to see him standing in the yard, then they narrowed, it snorted and grey smoke shot from its nostrils.

Max stepped back, pressing himself against the door and cursing his stupidity. He wondered what he should do, he knew that he needed to quickly attract their attention, but he was scared to turn his back on the Watcher in case it took this as an opportunity to strike.

The Watcher blinked, it's tail twitched, then it took a step towards Max, its claws scraping softly on the hard stone flags. A thin tendril of smoke seeped menacingly from its slanted nostrils.

Max leant back hard against the door, his eyes never leaving the Watcher. He began urgently knocking on the door with the knuckles of both hands. But to his dismay he realised that the door was so heavy and the wood so thick, that the knocking didn't even sound loud on this side of the door.

'Help!' he shouted, hoping that someone from street level would hear. His voice quavered, sounding surprisingly shrill.

The Watcher took another step towards Max, snapping its teeth as it let out a second, deep guttural growl which ended as it belched and more smoke shot from its nostrils.

Max felt the sweat start out on his forehead.

'Help!' he yelled, urgently banging again on the door again, 'Help me!'

The Watcher took another step towards Max. Then it lunged.

Max dived out of the way, just as a shot of fire and smoke erupted from the Watcher's mouth and scorched the door behind him.

'Helppppppp!' Max yelped as he dived across the yard for the safety of some other boxes at the far side, which looked, close to, disappointingly flimsy.

'Helppppppp!' he shouted again, just as a second bout of fire erupted across the yard and the Watcher roared.

'Max?' a scared voice rang out from somewhere above him.

Glancing up Max could see Anna leaning over the railings, a look of horror etched across her face.

A low roar jolted Max back to his senses. The

boxes he was hidden behind were smouldering gently and he dived across the yard again, praying that he would reach the relative safety of some heavy-duty bins in time.

'Graul, stop that!' yelled Anna, her dark eyes wide with panic, 'Uncle Bron! Hang on Max!'

Max hurled himself behind the bins just as a wave of searing heat shot past him. He crouched behind the bins praying that they would come quickly and that the bins wouldn't melt before they arrived. The faint smell of singed hair lingered in the air.

Another roar rang out across the yard. Max didn't dare move. He anxiously crouched behind the bin, his heart thumping hard in his chest. He ran his hands across his face and into his hair, a mixture of sweat and tiny bits of burnt hairs, which Max presumed to be his eyebrows, streaked his palm. There was another blast of hot air and a strong smell of melting plastic that meant Max guessed, that the front of bin had just had another roasting. Then suddenly the sound of a door banging open on the far side of the yard.

'Graul! Stop now!' bellowed Bron.

The silence stretched out for a moment. Max stayed crouched behind the bin, not wanting to take his chances on the obedience of the Watcher.

'It's okay. You can come out now, Frederick,' called Bron.

Shaken and his face burning with embarrassment, Max cautiously peeped out from behind the bin. The yard looked blackened, faint wisps of smoke were rising from the flagged floor and the charred remains of the boxes were gently smouldering in the corner. Graul was standing off to one side looking thoroughly disgruntled, a long tendril of smoke was seeping from his nostrils and his yellow slanted eyes narrowed grumpily on Max as he slowly stepped out from behind the bins.

Unsure whether he should feel more embarrassed or relieved, Max slowly picked his way across the blackened yard towards them.

They left the shop shortly afterwards. Luckily, in the commotion, Anna's uncle Bron did not seem to have noticed that Anna had been calling him Max instead of Frederick throughout the incident, and the need for any explanation was avoided.

Elea was mortified by the whole thing and kept repeatedly saying, 'But are you sure that you're all right Max?'

Max just felt embarrassed; he had singed his hair and was definitely short of half his eyebrows.

Once over the initial fright of the situation, Anna was finding it all rather amusing and kept giving Max sideways glances and then bursting into fits of giggles.

'Seriously, how did you manage to get the wrong door Max?' she snorted as they headed home, 'I mean it's not like it even looks the same – the shop door was blue for a start.'

'I realise that now!' Max laughed, brushing his hands through his singed hair.

'Ooooh,' she cooed, 'Look even your eye lashes are curly!'

'Oh, shut up,' said Max laughing with relief as much as anything else.

The journey home was uneventful and as they arrived back at the house, Max was grateful to see that Gog did not make an appearance. They ate a hearty lunch and then quickly made their way outside into the sunshine.

Max followed Anna as she wandered over to a shady patch of grass in the garden and flopped down next to her. Lokie, after the morning's excitement, was once again curled up in his blanket, snoozing in the afternoon sun.

'So, anyway,' said Anna stretching out on the grass, 'I listened in on mum's conversation to uncle Bron.'

'Oh! So, you didn't really need to collect a book then?'

'Of course not,' Anna shrugged. 'It was just an excuse; I figured that if she wanted us out of the way, then it was probably worth listening to.'

Max grinned. 'Go on.'

'Well, it was interesting,' she said, her eyes gleaming. 'They were talking about some of the strange goings on. My mum was telling uncle Bron about the Hidden Person going missing and he was saying that that's not the half of it, that he's heard all kinds of rumours. Two of the Wokulo that he trades with a lot, Lempo and Domovoi, have been telling him that they've been picking up some really weird reports as they've been travelling between the different worlds. There have been quite a few sightings of Xegan with Valac now and there are rumours in the Forbidden Lands that Xegan is after something. That he's frantically searching for something that's crucial for his plans...' She paused for a moment, her eyes suddenly serious and then said, 'What do you make of that, Max? Do you think it could be linked to what happened to your grandad?'

With a pang, Max thought about his grandad and a cold wave of dread crept over him once more. Could he really have accidentally revealed where they lived by using the Key?

'Listen, are you sure that you're OK?' Anna said frowning.

'I'm fine,' he said quickly. 'What do you think this means?'

Anna threw him a disbelieving look but didn't push him any further. 'Well, it makes me wonder whether Xegan thought that your grandad had the thing that he's searching for and that's why he sent Valac to your house. Do you think that's possible?'

Max frowned, 'I guess so, but I've got absolutely no idea what it could be.' He thought about the ordinary, everyday and sometimes slightly shabby belongings that he and his grandad had owned on Earth. It was hard somehow, to believe that his grandad Quinn had kept something in their little house in Normington that Xegan would want so badly and that was crucial to his plans. But then, thought Max reflectively, it was just as hard to believe that his grandad had been the Leader of the Elders and that he had kept all of these things secret from him for so long.

As if reading his thoughts, Anna said, 'Your grandad could easily have had something from the time when he was the Leader of the Elders,' she paused, frowning for a moment. 'The problem is, I'm not sure how we can find out now. How would we even know whether Xegan and Valac got what they were after when they came to your house that night? Would you have noticed that night whether anything had been taken?'

Max thought back to the horror and confusion of the evening, when he had left Earth for Lucem, 'No, not really,' he said truthfully.

Anna frowned thoughtfully. 'But then, I suppose, if Xegan is *still* searching for this thing that he wants, then maybe your Grandad didn't have what he was looking for after all, maybe they just thought that he did.'

'Maybe,' Max nodded slowly, 'Anna, you said that this thing Xegan wants is crucial to his plans – what do you think that means?'

'I don't know, but from what we know about Xegan so far, it can't be good, can it?' she shuddered.

They lapsed into silence for a moment.

'By the way,' said Anna, 'I noticed that your eyes didn't go silver today, which is just as well, as it would have been interesting to try and explain that to my uncle Bron, on top of everything with Graul and me nearly letting it slip about your name!'

'I hadn't thought about that,' Max said, pondering this for a moment. 'Maybe it just happens when I'm angry. To be honest, I wasn't angry today, I was just scared to death, I thought I was about to be barbecued!'

'I think your eyebrows have been!' Anna laughed.

They spent the rest of the afternoon in the garden chatting and then later ate dinner with Elea; Templar was working late again and did not join them. However, when Max arrived downstairs for breakfast the next morning, Templar was sitting at the breakfast table with Anna, looking tired and strained.

'Morning, Max,' he said looking up from his paper as Max entered the kitchen.

'Morning,' said Max.

'Cade wondered whether you would come into work with me this morning Max, he thought that maybe after yesterday, it was time you two should have another chat.'

'Okay,' Max said hesitantly. He wondered what Cade had told Templar about what happened.

'Great,' said Templar. 'We'll leave straight after breakfast then, if that's OK?'

Max glanced over at Anna and caught her eye; she raised her eyebrows and gave him a knowing look. He knew what she was thinking. Would Cade mention what had happened at the Ancient Council meeting and the conversation Max had overheard with Chandra about Max's abilities with Aether?

At that moment, there was a knock at the back door and Quonk arrived to deliver the missing potatoes from the previous day's delivery.

'Good morning, Quonk,' called Templar as she followed Elea into the kitchen, wearing an even more spectacular hat of purple and orange zigzags that frilled extravagantly around her face and then billowed down in giant knitted ruffles to a point, upon which a giant maroon pompom quivered. It looked Max felt, rather like someone had been sick on Quonk's head.

'Good Morning!' Quonk squeaked. 'Morning Anna, Morning Frederick!'

'Morning!' said Max and Anna together.

Templar frowned slightly and glanced at Elea questioningly; it was clear that Elea had not yet told him about the name she had selected for Max's new secret identity.

'Great new hat!' said Anna, eyeing Quonk's head.

Quonk looked at Anna, a rather resigned expression on her face, 'Thanks,' she squeaked, 'My husband finished knitting it last night.'

As soon as they had finished their breakfast Max left the table and went upstairs to gather his things together, ready for the trip in with Templar. Anna caught up with Max on the landing outside their rooms.

'So, what do you think then?' she whispered immediately, 'I bet this is something to do with what happened at the Ancient Council meeting. I bet he'll tell you about your eyes.'

'I don't know,' Max said thoughtfully, 'I really hope he does mention the Aether thing and my eyes so I can ask him some questions about it. But I suppose it could be something completely different. He did say that we'd talk again after that first meeting and he hasn't even told me about Xegan yet.'

They left soon afterwards. The journey to the pyramids now felt quite familiar to Max. Glancing upwards, Max noticed with some shock that he could see a cluster of five pale grey moons or planets faraway in the distant sky and was reminded once again how little he knew about the worlds he now found himself in. He passed the Bridge Gateway and there were the usual strange assortment of creatures and people queuing and jostling for the next bridge and there appeared to have been a recent arrival of six Wokulo that were speedily dragging and bumping a large number of crates and boxes out of the stone circle. Max wondered if there was a delivery somewhere in the pile that was destined for Bron's shop.

A little further along, Max suddenly became aware of some rustling in the shrubs close by and a small group of Nomo's, comprised of three adults and two young, unexpectedly burst forth from the bushes. The tiny kangaroo-like creatures paused momentarily to contemplate Templar and Max, with their huge brown inquisitive eyes, before they bounced off in the direction of a wall and some shrubs on the other side of the path, the two baby Nomo's in tow. The smallest and last of the Nomo's appeared to hesitate for a moment at the sight of the wall which was at least twice its own height, then after bouncing on the spot for a moment and appearing to gain some confidence, it jumped neatly over the wall and disappeared into the shrubbery to join the others.

'How have you been finding things, Max?' asked Templar, interrupting Max from his thoughts. They were approaching the archway to the pyramid courtyard.

'I'm fine, thanks. Everything's great,' said Max, before adding, 'Thanks for letting me stay.'

'Good, I'm glad,' Templar said as they entered the courtyard and set off in the direction of the pyramids. The courtyard was bustling with activity this morning with people arriving ready to start work. Max couldn't believe that this many people could work here at the pyramids.

'Do all of these people work here?' he asked. There seemed to be at least ten times more people today than he had seen on any of his previous visits.

'Yes, but there's a lot to do, a lot of administration staff needed and some of these people are Ancient Council workers; not just people who are employed by the Elders. There's a lot underground too. The pyramids actually go down as far as they go up Max.'

'What, so they go right down into the ground? There's more offices and stuff down there under our feet?'

'Oh yes,' said Templar laughing.

So are the Ancient Council based here then?'

'Not just here, they have offices all over the

Five Kingdoms, but there are quite a lot of Ancient Council workers based here. There are representatives from each of the civilisations that work at the Ancient Council, so everyone's views get represented.'

They strode across the yard and entered the first pyramid building where Cade's office was located. As on their previous visit, Templar left him momentarily to check him in at the front desk.

Max thought back to the last time he had visited Cade's office, the day that Cade had told Max the shocking news about all of this and explained how parallel worlds exist and that he and his grandad weren't really from Earth but were from here — a different world entirely.

How much he had learnt since then, he thought. It felt like a lifetime ago rather than the few days it actually was. He still couldn't really take it all in.

Moments later, it was with a combination of fear, eagerness and apprehension that Max once again knocked on Cade's office door.

'Good morning Max!' said Cade, his bright blue eyes twinkling as usual.

'Good morning,' said Max as he followed Cade over to the sofa in his office.

'How are you?' Cade smiled, but his eyes looked at Max searchingly, taking in every detail.

'I'm OK.'

'I thought that it was time that we should have another chat. I went through a lot of information the other day. It must have been a lot to take in and there was the Ancient Council meeting as well, of course,' he hesitated. 'I wasn't expecting you to have to attend that meeting, Max, I'm sorry. I hadn't really had chance to explain anything to you about the Ancient Council before you met them all.'

Max nodded but said nothing.

Cade pulled up a chair and sat down next to Max, 'I should probably start with explaining a bit about the Ancient Council and what it's all about.'

'OK,' said Max, thinking that it was probably better to just listen to what Cade had to say rather than telling him that he already knew some of it.

'All of those people that you met were members of the Ancient Council.' He paused and looked at Max intently, 'I know this sounds complicated Max, but there are, as I guess you have now realised, Five Kingdoms or Worlds that co-operate and support one another. The civilisations that live in these five worlds have all been aware, for some considerable time now, about the true nature of our reality; about the fact that parallel universes exist.'

Max watched Cade waiting for him to continue.

'For a long time everyone just got along, and pretty much did as they pleased. There was freedom of movement and free rein to explore anywhere, even uncharted worlds. But it didn't work Max; people would go wandering off and would never come back. We lost people...' Cade hesitated and sighed.

'But where did they go? How were they lost?'

'Well, they probably landed in some barren or strange, remote world and couldn't for whatever reason make it back. Sometimes people would be captured by the monsters or natives of the world that they visited. We, the humans, were particularly hard hit, as we didn't have any real way of being able to hide ourselves when we landed in the worlds very easily. Unlike, say the Nix who could immediately shape shift into the form of one of the animals that naturally lived in that world, the Hidden people who could arrive invisibly or the Shadow people who could just send their shadows to the place and assess how friendly or dangerous the place was first.'

Max shifted in his seat watching Cade avidly now, somehow even though it all still seemed incredibly strange, it was starting to make a lot more sense.

'You see, it isn't possible to open a window to a universe and peep through before you go. If you want to see what's there, you have to go and so travelling to new uncharted worlds or even to be honest some worlds which we have already explored, like The Forbidden Lands, Dragonia or Arctica, are absolutely fraught with danger. You could land and be ambushed, anything could happen.'

Max suddenly remembered the maps that he had looked at in his grandad's study. He had seen a map of the Forbidden Lands then. Max remembered the dark uncharted area that had stretched across the southern part of the map, where the drawing and landscapes had suddenly petered out and a single word had been written: Danger. He shuddered and wondered how many people had been lost, ambushed or killed in the Forbidden Lands by creatures like the Mothmen, whilst trying to complete that map.

'But it wasn't just that,' Cade continued, 'It wasn't just our safety. There was sometimes no real thought or consideration for the impact it might cause to the inhabitants of the world that was visited. You can imagine how myths are made, Max, when the inhabitants or natives of a world are happily getting on with their lives and suddenly a strange person or creature, unlike anything they have ever seen before, pops up out of nowhere.' He chuckled, his face breaking into a proper smile for the first time that morning. 'It happened a lot in the early days. The Yeti's were especially bad for a time, always accidentally popping up in places and not being able to get back. That was when we realised that we needed some control; both for our own sake and to protect the worlds that we travelled to, and so the Covenant was created.'

'Oh, right,' said Max. Suddenly everything made a lot more sense, it was like piecing together a giant jigsaw.

'So the Covenant protects all of that.' Cade continued, 'It is a treaty that most of the groups that you've seen since you have arrived here and the leaders you met the other day, have agreed to and it essentially says that each world should be allowed to evolve and to find out the truth about parallel worlds existing for themselves.'

Max frowned, 'But what about the Wokulo and the fact that my grandad and I lived on Earth for nine years? That doesn't exactly fit into the Covenant, does it?'

'The Wokulo have always refused to sign the Covenant, Max. Their way of life, whilst not desirable to everyone, is one that they have chosen for millions of years. However, broadly speaking, they do follow the Covenant. They are masters at hiding and so rarely get seen by the local inhabitants when they shouldn't and they have *never* broken the Covenant and told another civilisation.'

'But they travel all over the place and steal stuff, don't they?' said Max abruptly. He knew it had come out a bit more aggressively than he had planned, but it was true.

'I'm not supporting or condoning what they

do, Max. I would be much happier if they signed the Covenant and settled in the Five Kingdoms fully.' Cade sighed, 'But you have to understand, we walk a fine line with races like the Wokulo and the Hidden People who are ancient civilisations and who have always followed a particular way of life. Neither of them has a fixed world that they appear to have come from, like we came from Earth. They have migrated and moved around worlds since the beginning of time. It is hard to – millions of years down the road – say that a lifestyle that they have adopted for forever is now no longer acceptable. What right do we have to do that?'

'What, so they just moved around all of the time, living in different worlds?'

'Yes. The Hidden People and Wokulo have moved between worlds for as long as anyone can remember. The Hidden People have largely settled now in Lucem, the Shadowlands and Hyperborea, but there are still a handful that roam around in different worlds. There are many different and strange creatures, Max, as I'm sure you've now seen.' He smiled again, his blue eyes twinkling. 'And we just have to try to live in tolerance of one another.'

'And what about my grandad and me then? Why were we allowed to live outside the Five Kingdoms?'

'Well,' said Cade, for a moment his blue eyes looked deeply troubled and sad, 'As Chandra said, it was due to special circumstances. We made an exception, as your grandad Quinn really needed a break, to get away. Any exceptions have to be agreed by the leaders of the Five Kingdoms, the Ancient Council. Your grandad was the leader of the Elders here in Lucem for a long time Max; I guess he was owed a few favours.'

Max thought back to his life in Normington; he was unsure whether he would consider the past nine years a favour.

'But Max you need to remember that although you lived there, the Covenant wasn't broken. No one knew who you really were. It wasn't as though you had been given permission to go and live in the Cloudlands or anything, as a race we came from Earth originally. You were able to live there as humans, there was no risk to you or to the people on Earth. No one was told; all of this was kept a total secret.'

Even from me, thought Max darkly, feeling the familiar anger and resentment well up inside him again.

'So does anyone ever break the Covenant, then?' he asked, glancing awkwardly towards Cade.

Cade paused, his eyes narrowed, 'Yeesss,' he said cautiously, 'we believe, in fact we are fairly certain, that someone from within our society has broken the Covenant.'

'You mean Xegan?' Max said without thinking,

then quickly added, 'I heard Imeda and Krake talking about him that night to my grandad.'

Cade paused and blinked, a tiny flicker of surprise registered in his blue gaze. Then when he did speak, it was in a carefully neutral voice with all of the reactions excluded from it. 'Yes, Xegan,' he said flatly.

Max felt a spark of annoyance. Why was it always so hard to get to the truth?

'Why didn't you tell me?' he asked. 'When I asked you what had happened to my grandad, why did you just say it was the Mothmen?'

Cade paused, 'Well it was the Mothmen, Max.'

'But they were working for Xegan, weren't they?' Max said abruptly.

Cade gave a stiff nod. 'We believe so. But Max, you have to understand that we are still trying to understand what is going on here. We don't have all of the facts yet.'

But that wasn't right, Max thought. They had known. At the Ancient Council meeting, they had all seemed to know that Xegan was involved and that he was behind Valac's attack.

'So, who is he?' Max asked bluntly.

Cade hesitated, 'He's a person from our society here in Lucem who disappeared many years ago now. Unfortunately, he seems to have suddenly reappeared and, well, we're fairly confident now that he's brought some of the Mothmen with him.'

Max nodded stiffly, 'Why? What does he want?'

Cade paused and looked at Max intently, 'Well we don't know, we can only guess. He was always… ambitious… he had very different ideas. He didn't agree with the way your grandad ran the Elders – or me, for that matter.' Cade paused again, before continuing carefully, 'The knowledge of parallel worlds has always brought out the worst in those motivated by greed and power, Max. That's why this knowledge is guarded so carefully. The Ancient Council believes that worlds should be allowed to evolve naturally. It promotes tolerance, understanding and acceptance between different worlds, societies and cultures. In the history of civilisations, imposing one world or society's view on another has always inevitably caused problems. Not everyone agrees with this. Some people have very different ideas about how we should handle the truth. They see other societies and worlds and they see more opportunities for power, opportunities to dominate and rule worlds.'

'And Xegan believes this?'

'He used to yes. He thought that the Ancient Council's approach was weak.'

'And that's why he left?'

Cade hesitated, 'That was definitely part of it,

yes.'

'So, where did he go?'

'He's been missing for years; we didn't know where he was. Time passed and everything went very quiet – until recently. It would now seem that Xegan has just been biding his time.'

'Biding his time for what?'

'That's the problem Max; we're not exactly sure. What we are now certain of, is that he has been travelling between worlds, travelling to places that previously may not have known about the fact that parallel worlds exist and telling some of them. Breaking the Covenant. Gathering support. Xegan doesn't care about the Covenant and the fact that we try to live in harmony with one another, he cares only about gaining more power. Trust me Max; there are some creatures, like the Mothmen, where it would be better if they never knew about anything outside of The Forbidden Lands. Unfortunately, thanks to Xegan, they do now know and we really have no idea who or what else he has told.'

'What is he trying to do though?' asked Max.

Cade sighed. 'Gain power? Rule worlds? One can only guess at this stage, Max.'

'And do you have any idea yet why he wanted to harm my grandad?'

Several emotions fought on Cades face for a moment, 'No,' he said slowly, 'Not really. Not yet.'

Max sat silently absorbing this. There was something about Cade's manner, how awkward and uncomfortable he seemed that left Max convinced that he still wasn't being entirely truthful with him. More mysteries, he thought dully. More secrets. He was becoming sick of it.

'That was quite an outburst at the Ancient Council meeting the other day,' Cade said quietly, his blue eyes studying Max intently. 'I do understand how this must be hard for you Max. I know this is a lot to take in.'

Something snapped inside Max. The pressure and uncertainty of the last few days was too much to take. 'Do you?' he flared, 'Do you really understand what this is like?' He stopped abruptly and looked at his hands clasped in his lap; he didn't know whether he trusted himself to speak.

Cade said nothing. He simply sat watching Max inspect his hands and waited for him to speak.

'What did you expect?' Max said finally, 'I've lived on Earth all my life – well, all of the bits I can remember anyway – and then I suddenly find out all of this, all of these secrets, all of these lies. I don't even know who my grandad was now, I think back to all of these things that he said and I don't know whether they're true or whether they're made up too. I don't feel like I know who my parents were. I don't feel like I know who I am anymore–' his voice faltered and he stopped abruptly.

'I'm sure that everything he told you would

have been as close to the truth as he could make it. He wouldn't have wanted to lie to you anymore than he had to. You may not see this now, but your grandad was a good man and he was just trying to protect you. He loved you more than anything.'

Max folded his arms across his chest, he realised his eyes would probably have changed colour, but didn't care. It was easy for everyone to say kind, reassuring things, when they weren't the ones that had suddenly found out that everything they knew about themselves was a lie.

Cade seemed to realise that he wasn't going to convince Max of his grandad's good intentions, because he abruptly changed the subject and said, 'Your father travelled to many worlds, Max. We used to have an exploration programme that ran called WEAM – the World Exploration And Monitoring programme. Your father served in WEAM for many years and was extremely successful in the programme, finding and charting many lands.'

Max was silent for a moment. 'Really?' he said reluctantly, 'So he travelled and went to loads of worlds then?'

'Yes, he worked for the Elders when he finished studying and he was in WEAM for many years before he met your mother and they had you. He was a brave man, Max.'

'So where did he go? What did he do?' said Max feeling his anger subside a little.

'Well, he travelled and explored new worlds, charted lands and monitored the inhabitants, so that our understanding of the extent of the worlds out there grew.'

'But where did he go exactly?'

'To be honest, the best person to talk to about this is my son, Krake. They served together.' Cade smiled kindly, 'Do you have any other questions about anything else, anything we haven't yet discussed?'

'I'd like to know about Aether,' Max said immediately.

'OK,' Cade paused. 'Well there are Five Elements that must be present in worlds for life to exist – Earth, Air, Water, Fire and Aether. Aether is the fifth element and it is a universal power or energy, which is inherent in everything. All life, in fact everything in the universe, in every universe, is interconnected and participates in this same energy – Aether.'

'But this Aether, this energy, what does it do? How do you even know that it's there?'

'We do not understand it fully. We do not even know completely what it can do, but we do know that it's there. It's the dark matter, the invisible energy that exists between things. As I said to you before, Max, as with the parallel worlds, just because it cannot be seen does not mean it is not there. What you cannot see in life, frequently supports what *you can* see.'

'Do humans have power with it?' Max asked hesitantly, 'You know like The Nix, the Hidden People and Shadow People?'

Cade paused and looked at Max intently. Max felt as though the bright piercing blue eyes might almost be able to read his thoughts and he quickly dropped his gaze and stared awkwardly into his lap.

'Rarely,' Cade said after a moment. 'It is highly unusual for humans to have any kind of ability with Aether. Now we've been talking for a long time again, so we should probably wrap up. Is there anything else you wanted to ask?'

Max sat processing this for a moment, realising that Cade clearly wasn't going to tell him. So, he thought, it was just another secret to be left in the dark about, another secret about him.

'No,' he said in a resigned tone.

'OK,' said Cade, 'Well, there is just one final thing that I needed to mention to you. It's about your grandad.'

Max hesitated. Maybe he was wrong, maybe Cade was going to tell him after all.

'It's about his funeral, Max,' Cade continued carefully. 'We went back to the house and we brought your grandad back. We thought that in keeping with our traditions, we would bury your grandad the day after tomorrow.' He hesitated, 'We thought we'd do a traditional funeral. We think it's what your grandad would have wanted.'

'OK,' said Max simply. He wasn't sure how he felt, nor how he should react to this. With everything that had happened over the last few days, he hadn't really given any thought to his grandad's funeral at all. Despite his anger towards his grandad, the realisation of this made him feel a little guilty.

'There's something else,' Cade sighed, his blue eyes looked deeply troubled and sad, 'When we – when we went back to the house it had been, well, it's been robbed Max and the house is a bit of a mess. We were hoping to collect some more of your belongings, but we haven't really been able to salvage anything... and on top of everything else... I'm so sorry, Max.'

'OK,' said Max, again uncertain of what he should say.

'Let's leave it there then, Max,' said Cade.

Max sat glumly in the chair his hands clasped in his lap. The meeting was clearly drawing to a close, but Cade hadn't told him anything about his eyes and possible ability with Aether and he wasn't entirely certain that he'd really told him everything to do with Xegan. He also didn't think that he could possibly bring himself to ask about the other worry that was churning away at the back of his mind. Had he accidentally caused the death of his grandad by using the Uroboros Key when he shouldn't have?

Cade obviously taking Max's silence to mean something else entirely, smiled kindly and said, 'Don't worry about the funeral, Max; we'll take care of everything.'

'OK thanks,' said Max despondently. He had never felt so confused in his life.

Chapter 13
The Burden of Guilt

Max followed Templar back to the house in silence, gloomily aware that his moodiness probably wasn't the most polite way to repay their kindness, but he felt utterly confused and besides, he couldn't think of anything to say.

The more Max considered it, the more Max felt devastated at the thought that he might have somehow alerted Xegan to their whereabouts in Normington and inadvertently caused his own grandad's death. But then he thought, struggling to his own defence, maybe if his grandad had been a little more honest with him in the first place then he wouldn't have had to take matters into his own hands and go rummaging through his study. When he thought back to his grandad, his memories and the things he'd been told, he didn't know what was true anymore and a deep resentment and anger would well up inside him. But then he'd remember his grandad doing something or saying something at their house in Normington and them laughing together and a deep aching sadness would descend upon him again. His mind was a blur of troubled thoughts and muddled hurt emotions and the confusion of feelings he was experiencing was finding its expression in anger. It probably wasn't the best way to handle things, but he didn't know how else to act. He just felt so confused about everything.

He noticed vaguely as they were walking back up the path towards the house, that Templar was speaking to him.

'I hear you had a run in with Bron's Watcher yesterday, Max,' he said smiling, 'Are you OK?'

'I'm fine, thanks,' muttered Max distractedly. He was struggling to drag himself from sad thoughts.

'You'll get used to them,' said Templar, 'Watchers aren't too bad once you know how to deal with them. It's really all in the confidence and tone of voice.'

Max followed Templar up the garden path towards the front door and eyed Gog, who was prowling around at the side of the house and snapping grumpily at everything around him, doubtfully. He couldn't imagine how a confident tone of voice would do very much to help him with Gog.

They wandered into the house and into the bright warmth of the kitchen where Elea was humming as she prepared lunch.

'Hi, you two,' she said smiling warmly. Then, upon eyeing Max she added, 'Tough morning?' And then pulling him towards her open arms, she gave him a hug.

'I'm OK,' said Max a little awkwardly as she

pulled away.

The hug had been warm, soft and comforting and smelt faintly of soap, clean linen and fresh flowers. Max sighed. His grandad hadn't been much of a hugger and he didn't remember ever being hugged by anyone else. Sitting in the kitchen with Templar and Elea, Max momentarily felt as though he'd had a fleeting glimpse into a life he could have had, the life he would have known, had his parents not died in the fire and had his grandad not decided to leave Lucem and move them both to Earth. He remembered so little about his mother and father, just fragments of information that he'd been told and distant faint glimpses of memories that he wasn't even sure were real.

'Have you time to stay for lunch with us, Templar?' Elea asked, 'I've made your favourite stew.'

'That's great,' said Templar hungrily, 'But I'll have to be quick as I need to get back, I've got a lot on this afternoon and I have to get back early for us to go out this evening to Krake's ceremony, remember?'

Elea sighed. 'Yes I remember,' she glanced at Max and a frown flickered across her face.

Max glanced towards Templar, but he appeared not to have noticed and was immersed reading a newspaper called The Lucem Times.

They ate lunch together sat around the

kitchen table and afterwards Max headed upstairs to change into some shorts. He'd gone to the meeting dressed smartly and he was dying to cast off anything that reminded him of his old school uniform and to get into something cooler and more comfortable. Moments later as he descended the stairs again, he could hear Elea and Templar having a discussion in the hallway below.

'Are you sure we should go tonight, Templar?' Elea was saying, 'With the way things are at the moment, I just don't feel good about leaving Max and Anna on their own.'

'It's only for an hour, Elea,' said Templar softly, 'We'll only be a few doors away at Krakes. We can just pop in and then we'll come home again and don't forget, that's why we've got Gog.'

'I guess,' said Elea hesitantly, although she sounded Max felt, thoroughly unconvinced.

'I think that it's really important to Krake that we attend, Elea. You know how long he's been waiting to become an Elder, if we just pop in for an hour.'

'I know it's just that with all of the odd things going on at the moment...'

'No one outside of The Elders even knows Max is here and besides Cade thinks that Max isn't actually in any real danger, no more than the rest of us anyway. All of this secrecy over Max is just precautionary.'

Max loitered on the stairs for a moment straining to hear, but they seemed to have moved off into another room and he heard nothing further. He set off quickly down the stairs and went outside to find Lokie; he didn't think that he'd ever listened in to so many people's private conversations in his life.

Lokie was for once not asleep in his blanket in the sunshine. Instead, Max found him ambling around the garden chasing flies and butterflies; and appearing to demonstrate some of the alertness and energy that Anna had tried to convince him of the day before. Max found a patch of grass in the shade of a nearby tree and plonking himself down, stretched out to watch Lokie.

Lokie was balancing on top of a series of plant pot shaped containers and appeared to be attempting to stretch up and grasp what looked like a giant bright green slug that was happily making its way up the wall just out of his reach. Just as he attempted to take a swipe at the slug, he overbalanced and wobbled over, he fell with a crash, scattering the plant pots everywhere. Jumping up he looked over at Max with an embarrassed, perplexed expression, a plant pot teetering precariously on one of his oversized, green ears.

Max was still sitting stretched out on the grass, laughing at Lokie moments later when Krake suddenly appeared from around the corner of the house and headed over towards Max.

'Hello Max,' he said beaming, his dark brooding eyes creasing at the edges.

'Hi Krake, what are you doing here?' said Max sitting up. He was somewhat surprised by Krake's appearance in the garden.

'I have a party this evening,' he said, 'So I'm dropping off these things,' he indicated a large black bag that he was carrying that looked as though it was crammed full. 'I've just recently become an Elder,' he said unable to hide his pride, 'and this is a sort of ceremonial party. It's quite low key, what with everything going on at the moment, but it should be good.' He grinned.

'Congratulations!' said Max, uncertain what it was customary to say under the circumstances.

'Thanks,' said Krake, sitting down awkwardly next to Max; his bulky frame looked uncomfortable on the grass.

'I was passing and I just thought that I'd pop in and see how you were doing. My father, Cade said that you two met today.'

'I'm OK,' said Max unconvincingly.

'I understand Max. All this is a lot to take in...'

Max gave a jerky nod. 'Cade said you were in WEAM with my dad?'

'Yes,' said Krake his expression softening. 'We all served together, after we'd finished studying, we were employed by WEAM. We ventured into faraway, unknown worlds together, exploring, charting and mapping. They were good times. Scary, but good.'

'What did you see out there?'

'Oh, things that would make your hair stand on end, Max. You've seen the variety of creatures here, well this is nothing compared to what's really out there...' His voice trailed away.

Max watched Krake's wistful expression for a moment and wondered what he was thinking about. 'So, where did you travel to with my dad?'

'Oh, all over: The Lost Kingdoms, Arctica, Dragonia, Gollinrod, The Frozen Lands. It's such a long time ago now, it's hard to remember them all. But here I've got something for you.'

Krake fished deeply into his jacket pocket and then held his open palm out towards Max. There, nestling in his hand, was what looked like a strange necklace with a strange ball shaped pendant dangling from the chain.

'It's for you,' said Krake, 'Your father and I found it on one of our travels with WEAM. I know it's a necklace and everything, but I thought you might like it. The amulet is supposed to channel Aether in a certain way, so that it's got protective qualities.' he shrugged and held it out towards Max.

'Oh no, it's great,' said Max eagerly taking it,

'Thanks!' He'd never had anything of his father's before, almost everything of his parents had been burned in the fire. Max held the chain between his fingers and regarded it carefully. Upon closer inspection, he could see that the pendant was a small intricately etched cage, encased within which was a pale blue stone which glowed softly at its centre, and rotated and spun freely within the tiny cage as the necklace moved in the palm of his hand. It was strange and weirdly beautiful.

'Well keep it on you,' said Krake, 'I don't know whether the protection it provides really works or not, but with everything that's going on right now, it can't harm, can it?' He grinned.

'No,' said Max, 'Thanks, I'll definitely wear it.' He placed it over his head and tucked it inside his t-shirt, it felt cold and reassuringly solid against his chest, 'Thanks Krake,' he said again smiling.

'Right,' said Krake standing, 'I'll be going then, I've got to drop these things off and then I need to get back to work. Bye, Max.'

'Bye and thanks,' said Max, as he watched Krake lumber disappear across the lawn and around the side of the house.

Max fingered the shape of the amulet through his t-shirt absently, feeling the weighty shape of the amulet and chain.

A bird squawked in a nearby tree distracting him from his thoughts, glancing up he saw a large raven like bird with sleek black feathers that was watching him inquisitively from a nearby tree. The bird seemed to observe him with dark enquiring eyes for a moment and then suddenly it took off, swooping low over the garden and disappearing around the side of the house, in the direction that Krake had just left.

Anna arrived home from school a short while later and immediately came hurtling into the garden to join Max, her face flushed with barely contained excitement.

'So?' she said expectantly, 'Go on – what happened then?'

'Well to be honest, he told me about lots of things that I'm sure you already know about, like the history of the Ancient Council and why the Covenant was formed and stuff, how the Yeti's used to turn up all over the place and get themselves lost. Things like that.'

'And?'

'Well he told me a bit about Aether. But only because I prompted him.'

'And? What about your eyes, did he mention what Chandra said about your eyes?' Anna asked excitedly, her expression vivid.

'No.'

'Well that's a bit rubbish, what did he say exactly?'

'Well he said,' Max paused to remember Cade's exact words, '"It's highly unusual for humans to have any kind of ability with Aether," and that's it!'

Anna frowned, 'Well that's a bit weird; I wonder why he didn't tell you the truth? Why keep it secret from you?'

'Well that's hardly anything new, is it?' Max said flatly.

'And what else did he say then?'

'Well he did tell me a bit about Xegan. But only because I pushed him about that too!'

'Really?' Anna said eagerly, 'What did he say?'

'Well, you were right – he's definitely someone from this society who disappeared years ago, he said that they lost track of him but now they think he's been travelling between worlds and breaking the covenant, gathering support–'

'Gathering support for what?' interrupted Anna, her expression suddenly very serious.

'Well, he said that Xegan was always,' Max hesitated, 'ambitious, I think, and that he never agreed with the way my grandad ran the Elders or Cade. He said that he thought Xegan was motivated by power and he said–' Max paused and frowned, as he again tried to remember the exact words Cade had used, 'that some people have very different ideas about how we should handle the truth, about how things should be run with other worlds. That rather than living in harmony, some people see other societies and worlds and they see more opportunities for power, opportunities to rule worlds.'

Anna's eyebrows raised in alarm, 'And that's what Xegan's trying to do?'

Max paused, 'Well, Cade said they didn't know exactly, but he thought it might be.'

Anna blew out a long breath, 'Wow, that doesn't sound good at all. What else did he say?'

'He said that they still didn't know why Xegan had sent Valac after my Grandad, but–'

'But what?'

'I don't know, it's strange,' Max hesitated, trying to make sense of his thoughts, 'I just got this feeling that there was something else. Something he wasn't saying.' He shrugged.

Anna frowned. 'Well, I heard something else about Xegan today too. Apparently that hidden person who has gone missing is a Key Maker!'

'What's a Key Maker?' Max asked blankly.

'You know how the Hidden People make Uroboros Keys? Well, they have key makers. That's their job.' she hesitated, 'Don't you see? That must be how the Mothmen are getting around. Xegan must be using this person to make Uroboros Keys for them.'

Max's heart sank. 'So, if this person is working for Xegan they'll have a lot of knowledge about Uroboros Keys then?' he asked hesitantly.

Anna shrugged, 'I guess so – why?'

Max fell silent. A sickening feeling settled into the pit of his stomach.

'Look, what's up?' said Anna, 'And don't say nothing!'

Max hesitated, 'How do you think that Xegan found us on Earth, Anna?'

Anna shook her head, 'I don't know. Why?'

'Well,' Max swallowed, 'You don't think... It's not possible to... trace Keys, is it?' he asked hesitantly.

Anna frowned, 'What do you mean?'

Max took a deep breath. 'Anna, don't you think it's a bit coincidental, that on the same night at the same time I accidentally use the Key, Valac arrives?'

Anna looked blank for a moment then her eyes widened, 'Oh! So you think that you–' Anna shook her head firmly, 'No, I don't.'

'But... are you sure? How can you be so sure?'

'Well, they just can't be. Everyone knows that.'

'But are you sure?'

Anna shrugged, 'Look Max, your grandad obviously used the key to travel here sometimes. Don't you think that if Xegan was somehow tracking the key, he'd have found you a long time ago?'

'But Xegan's got this Key Maker working for him now,' Max said cautiously, 'what if they've found a way...'

'Max, they've been using Uroboros Keys for thousands of years. If there was a way of tracing their movement and the configurations they use, they'd have found it before now.'

'Doesn't it seem a bit coincidental though? And if it's not that, then how did Xegan find us?'

Anna shook her head firmly, 'I don't know Max, I can't explain how they found you and your grandad, but I really don't think the key was traced. I just don't think that it's possible.' Anna's face broke into a smile, 'If you were worried about it, why didn't you just ask me?'

Max gave Anna an awkward shrug and smiled, he felt embarrassed. Why hadn't he just asked Anna? It seemed so silly now. After all, what did he really know about this world?

'Anyway, what else did he say?' she asked brightly.

'Well he talked a bit about my dad being in WEAM and how he used to explore lots of different worlds,' said Max. Having his doubts removed had immediately lifted Max's spirits.

'Was he? I didn't realise he was in WEAM. That's really cool.'

'Oh and Krake stopped by and gave me this, he said that my dad and him found it when they were off exploring somewhere,' Max tugged the pendant out of his shirt and held it towards Anna for her to inspect.

'Krake doesn't come round very often, let's see,' she said, 'Ooooh, I wonder where it came from. I bet my Uncle Bron would know.'

'I know,' said Max, inspecting it again, before carefully placing it back under his T-shirt.

There was a soft rustle of leaves overhead. Glancing up, Max saw that the black bird had returned. It was perched on a branch in a nearby tree, watching them with dark inquisitive eyes.

'And what else then? What were the other things?'

'Well there were a couple of things that he said that were quite interesting. He told me a bit more about why the Ancient Council allowed my grandad and I to go and live on Earth. He said that my grandad was owed some favours, that he'd been the leader for a long time and that it was an exception due to the special circumstances – I suppose that's the deaths of my Mum and Dad – and he said that we were allowed to go to Earth to live because strictly speaking the Covenant wasn't being broken as this race was originally from Earth and we could live there without anyone knowing or it affecting anybody; that because it was kept a secret and we could blend in, that's why they let us do it.'

'OK,' said Anna, frowning thoughtfully. 'Makes sense, I suppose. Anything else?'

'Well, that they've brought my grandad back and they're arranging his funeral for the day after tomorrow,' Max said heavily, 'Oh and apparently our house has been robbed.'

'Really?' said Anna her eyes wide, 'That's weird.'

'Yeah, apparently they're going to give him a traditional funeral – whatever that is.'

'No, the bit about the robbery, is there anything there that you're bothered about?'

Max thought about this for a moment, 'No, not really I don't suppose.'

'Hmm,' said Anna thoughtfully.

'So, I suppose I did manage to find out quite a bit about Xegan,' said Max, 'But he didn't tell me about the Aether thing and I'm absolutely positive that there's something he's not telling me. Why won't anyone give me the full story?'

'I know,' agreed Anna, 'But he did confirm one thing whether he realised it or not.'

'What?' said Max.

'Well, we know that Xegan is searching for something, don't we? Don't you think it's pretty coincidental that the house has been turned over when we think Valac was there looking for something a couple of days before? The reason your house was ransacked Max, was because Valac went back. That means Valac and Xegan definitely didn't get what they were looking for the other night when you were there. But they still thought that your grandad had it at your house. That's why they went back.'

Max stared at Anna for a moment. He knew she was right.

'Is there nothing that you can think of that they might have wanted, Max?'

'I don't know; it's not going to be something from Earth is it? If Xegan wants it and knew my grandad had it, it's bound to be something from here and all of that stuff was hidden away in his study and I never saw it. Apart from–' Max stopped abruptly, 'I've just thought of something,' he said, his face had gone white. 'Anna, it could be in those bags upstairs.'

'What! Why, what's in them?'

'Well I don't really remember, it's just a load of my grandads old things; maps and stuff, I haven't even looked through them since I arrived here. I didn't particularly want to be reminded of my grandad every time I walked in the room, so I sort of chucked them in the bottom of the wardrobe.'

Suddenly the sound of Elea's voice was calling them in for dinner.

'This is early!' said Anna, dragging herself reluctantly off the lawn.

'They're going out tonight.'

'Really?' said Anna raising her eyebrows, 'Well, we'll have the perfect opportunity to go through those bags then, won't we?'

SAM KINI

Chapter 14
The Map

'I thought they were never going to go!' said Anna, flopping back onto Max's bed.

Dinner had finished, and they were in Max's bedroom. Moments before, Elea and Templar had left for the party at Krake's house and they had immediately charged upstairs to his room.

'Mum fusses so much sometimes,' Anna rolled her eyes, 'So go on. Where are these bags then?'

'They're here,' said Max dragging them out of the wardrobe and dumping them on the floor at the foot of the bed. 'Right,' he said unzipping them, 'What do you think we're looking for? I mean, do you think it'll be obvious if there is anything in here?'

'I don't know, it's not going to have a 'Xegan' name tag on it, is it? I guess we just have to look for anything unusual.'

'Yeah, I guess,' said Max, uncertainly. He couldn't help feeling, as he slowly tipped the contents of the two bags out onto the bedroom floor, that everything in Lucem seemed unusual to him at present. He wasn't at all convinced that he was going to be able to spot whether one thing was more unusual than the next.

They sat on the bedroom carpet spreading the objects out around themselves in a giant fan. Many of the books that Max had seen on the bookcase in his grandad's study were there: 'Leading the People', 'Great Sea Navigators of the Worlds', 'Lucem Life', 'The Ancient Council – Yearly Review', 'I Win, You Win – Great Negotiating Tactics for Dealing with the Wokulo' and 'The Hidden History of the Hidden People Revealed'.

Max picked them up one by one, flicking through the pages and then setting them to one side. He remembered how he had read many of these titles that night in his grandad's study. It was strange, he thought, how each of the book titles now carried so much more meaning.

'I don't suppose there's anything particularly unusual here, is there?' he said gesturing towards the pile of books.

Anna gave them a cursory glance and then shook her head. 'My dad's got most of them. Apart from maybe that one there,' she said, pointing at 'The Ancient Council – Yearly Review'. 'I suppose Xegan could be mentioned in it or something. But then, on second thoughts, why would he want it? There are probably loads of them been printed. Forget it.'

'Okay,' said Max, dumping the book back down on the pile.

'Ooooh, now this is interesting. I haven't seen one of these before,' said Anna. She had picked up the small dark wooden box with intricate little carvings and tiny clawed feet which Max had found on his grandad's desk.

'Yeah, I found that on the night,' said Max. 'There were two keys in it: one which opened the desk drawers and the other which opened the box that the Uroboros Key was in.'

'Hmmm,' said Anna flipping open the lid. 'Nothing in it now though. Where's the other box?'

Max pointed towards a larger dark wooden box that was set off to one side and lifting it, held it out towards Anna.

'Oh yeah, look it has the Hidden People symbol in the top,' she said, pointing to the ornate metal coiled snake that was inlaid into the lid of the box. She opened the box carefully; the Uroboros Key had been placed neatly back inside on top of the blue cushioning. 'It's like my dad's, but much better. Look, it's got more World symbols on it,' she said, pointing at the innermost dial. 'They're all made by the Hidden People, but the better ones have more places that they're configured for. This is a really good one: it's got symbols for lots of worlds on it. I don't even recognise most of them.'

'Why are they all made by the Hidden People?'

'Well, I suppose it's because the Hidden People are supposed to be the most well-travelled. They've always moved around so much; they're supposed to know the most about the worlds that exist out there.'

'But there's nothing unusual about it?' said Max enquiringly, 'I mean, nothing that Xegan would be hunting for?'

'No, I doubt it,' said Anna, setting the Key down to one side.

There were a few things that Max assumed must have been found by Imeda, Krake and Otty in drawers that Max had not yet reached by the time he had taken his unexpected trip with the Uroboros Key. Max found a fountain pen with the same pattern of two circles etched into one side; that he had seen on his grandad and Cade's rings, a magnifying glass and, wrapped in a small square of dark grey velvet, a ring. Max considered it for a moment, turning it over in his fingers. It was smaller than the ring that his grandad had worn and clearly made for a more delicate female hand. As he twisted it gently between his fingers, inspecting it carefully, he saw that it was made from the same dull grey silver as his grandad's ring. Tiny intricate etchings ran around the surface of the ring and neatly inscribed on the inside edge was a tiny message that read, 'For Indah. With all my love, Quinn.' Max realised with a little jolt that Indah was his grandmother and that the ring had probably been her wedding ring for her marriage to his grandad, many years earlier.

'What about these?' said Anna interrupting

Max from his thoughts, indicating to the little stack of diaries.

Max glanced distractedly towards Anna. 'No, I went through those on the night in the study. There's nothing much in there; just dates when Imeda came to visit. That's about it.'

'Oh, right, okay,' said Anna, giving them a cursory glance and then tossing them to one side.

Max returned his attention to the ring and after studying it for a moment longer, carefully folded it up inside the square of grey velvet. He looked around wondering what to do with the tiny little package to keep it safe. His eyes fell on the intricately carved box with the clawed wooden feet and then lifting the lid, he gently placed the grey velvet parcel on the soft red lining and closed the lid. He wondered for a moment what had happened to his grandad's ring now that they'd brought him back. The thought of his grandad's body being returned brought a hard lump to his throat and he quickly pushed the thought from his mind. Then lifting the lid for a second time, he carefully placed the fountain pen inside the box and looked around.

'These are interesting,' said Anna, opening the first of the old maps and leaning over to closely inspect the circular shapes and drawings on the map that was entitled Hyperborea. Tiny pictures of strange animals and creatures adorned the edges of the map and were drawn on some of the landmasses and seas. A huge octopus with many tentacles and a spiny, fierce, sharp-toothed fish had been carefully drawn lurking in the choppy seas alongside elegant ships with tall masts and white billowing sails.

'Mmm,' said Max opening another, 'But do you think any of these could be it?'

'I don't know,' said Anna, as she carefully inspected each map in turn and then slowly placed them all to one side. 'I'm not sure. I mean, they're really nice and they're much fancier than anything you'd usually see and they're obviously quite old, but apart from these two–' she pointed at the maps of 'The Forbidden Lands' and 'Earthe', 'they're all just maps of the Five Kingdoms. Look, there's "Hyperborea", "The Shadowlands", "Arcadia", "Naburu" and "Lucem". I mean, we've studied these maps in school and they look normal. I can't see anything on them that would be so special or difficult to get hold of.' She frowned deeply.

'Do you think it could be that map of "The Forbidden Lands" then?' said Max.

'I don't know. I suppose it could be. We definitely know Xegan has been there, but the map is only half complete. What about the map of "Earthe"? Does that look OK to you?'

Max took the map from Anna and studied it for a moment. It was just like any map of Earth, more decorative and older, but it had the same landmasses and seas as any other map of Earth. He understood what Anna meant, apart from the obvious beauty and age of the maps, he couldn't imagine that there was anything that Xegan could be so desperate to get his hands on.

'Seems OK to me.' He placed the map of Earthe back down on the floor. Then, seeing the last map, picked it up. It was the double-sided map of Lucem, which covered the area surrounding Lucem and Ridgefield.

'What about this one?' he said, holding it out for Anna to inspect.

'Let me see—' said Anna taking the map from him. Max watched her silently, as her dark brown eyes flicked across the map taking in every detail.

'Now, this one is interesting.'

'Really?'

'Well, look, it's quite old. It doesn't look like that here now. There are many more buildings now for a start,' she held the map out towards Max for him to inspect.

'And look how much of the forest is shown on the map here; most of the maps I've seen don't cover the forest and mountains around Cassini quite so much.'

Anna laid the map carefully on the floor, unravelling each of the folds, so that the whole map was revealed. It was true that many of the buildings that Max had seen since his arrival in Cassini did not appear to have been documented on the map and now that he could see the map fully, Max realised that the city of Cassini was quite a lot larger than he had first thought.

A huge section of forest and a jagged range of mountains dominated the area to the east. The river that they had crossed on the previous day, could be seen as it sliced its way through the giant gorge, mountains and forests, meeting the many smaller, meandering rivers and streams, before it eventually passed through the city and broadened out, stretching towards the sea to the far left and west of the map. Several smaller villages and hamlets were scattered along the rivers many tributaries, away from the main centre of the city and towards the edge of the map.

'So, is this the whole of Cassini then?'

'Oh, no, it's quite a lot bigger than this. This is just central Cassini,' Anna said thoughtfully. She was crouched over the map, peering at one of the villages located to the south of the city. 'I've hardly been anywhere,' she muttered grumpily.

'What about the other areas,' Max began.

'Hmmm.'

'How big are they?'

'Cassini is the biggest. That's why so much Ancient Council activity goes on here. Mimas is second biggest, then I'm not sure between Pavel and Taquile.'

'And that's it then on the whole world? There are just these four places?' The question had been slowly forming in Max's mind for days when he thought back to his Geography classes and the billions of people that Mr. Crawlie had told them lived on Earth.

'Well, no, not really,' she said, 'People do live in other places too; farmers and stuff. But the four main centres are where most of the population on Lucem live. It's just not as populated as your world,' she added. 'I suppose we live in the Five Kingdoms and when there are five worlds to choose from, well I guess it's bound not to be so crowded.' She shrugged. 'We should get on with this. They might be back soon.'

'Well, if you turn it over,' said Max, returning his attention to the map, 'I think there's a map of Mimas on the back.'

'Oh, yes!' said Anna, quickly flicking the map over and beginning to inspect the other side.

The map on this side depicted a vast valley, flanked on both sides by a series of steep, rugged mountain ranges. A wide river expanse twisted and meandered its way through the valley before disappearing off the west section of the map. Farmland dominated much of the valley to the north, stretching towards the steep range of mountains and hills and cutting into the lower sections in tiers. A large city sat in the centre of the map straddling both sides of a narrower section of the river and a huge forest, the Grigori Forest, dominated the area to the south, stretching into the lower reaches of the mountains. They crouched over the map, inspecting it closely. Several trails weaved through the forest, stretching into the lower reaches of the mountains and hills, but they all eventually seemed to peter out, leaving areas of what appeared to be impenetrable dense green forest.

Max was busy studying the trails to see whether any of them penetrated any further into the dense foliage and trees, when he suddenly noticed a tiny building far off to the right of the map, deep within the forest and far beyond the point where the last of the trails and pathways ended. As Max leaned in closer he could see that the tiny building had been hand-drawn in ink, next to which, written in small spiky handwriting, were the words: 'Temple of Fangs' and 'Uroborologs'.

'There are some markings here,' he said, jabbing his finger onto the map and indicating the spot where the temple was drawn. 'Look at that! There's some writing – that's not part of the original map!'

'Really!?' said Anna, leaning forward to take a closer look. 'I didn't notice that before.' She glanced up, her eyes gleaming excitedly, 'This could be it!'

Max, peered thoughtfully at the map, 'What do you think it means?'

Anna leaned forward again and began to

eagerly inspect the writing, 'I'm not sure. It's not exactly easy to see.'

'I know! Have you heard of the "Temple of Fangs" or "Uroborologs" before?'

'No, I haven't...' She frowned thoughtfully.

'I wonder if this could be it; if this could be what Xegan is after?' said Max.

'I don't know, but it could be. It seems to be the only thing that we've found.'

'What do you think we should do with it?'

'We should give it to my dad and he'll take it to Cade tomorrow. I'm sure Cade will know what to do with it.'

'OK, good idea.' Max leaned back and stretched; suddenly aware that they had been studying the map for some time. His back ached from leaning over and his legs cramped. He glanced towards the window, wondering vaguely what the time was. The light was beginning to fade outside and the blue sky had given way to a subdued grey. Max could see the dark outlines of the trees outside jutting starkly against the darkening sky.

'What time do you think it is?' he asked.

'Dunno,' Anna murmured. She was peering at the map.

Max shifted sideways on his knees so that the

clock at the side of his bed came into view. He was surprised to see that the clock read 19:45 – much later than he had expected. Out of the corner of his vision, Max suddenly saw a dark ragged shape flash past the window. He gave a start.

'What was that?' he said sharply, his head jerking back towards the window.

'What was what?' Anna said distractedly; her head still bent low over the map.

Max stared at the window and the view of the garden beyond. There was nothing, just the still fading light and the dark silhouette of the trees. He glanced back towards Anna. She was still crouched low over the map frowning deeply, her lips pursed together as her fingers slowly traced the area around the tiny words that read 'Temple of Fangs' and 'Uroborologs'.

'I thought I–' He hesitated and glanced back at the window again. Everything was still. A black bird chirruped and fluttered past, then turned and swooped back towards the trees. He sighed. With everything that had happened over the past few days, he was getting jumpy. He needed to calm down.

'Oh, nothing,' he muttered, returning his attention to the map. He was beginning to investigate the forest area again when there was a loud bump directly outside the bedroom door.

'What was that?' he said again with a start.

'It's probably just Lokie,' said Anna casually. She glanced up, 'He always bumps against the door when he wants to come in. Lokie?'

Sure enough, a moment later, there was the sound of Lokie's muffled murmuring from the other side of the door.

'You're a bit jumpy, aren't you?' Anna muttered, returning her attention to the map.

Feeling embarrassed, Max stood up stiffly and wandered across the room. He opened the door and Lokie immediately waddled in, his large oversized green ears twitched and his eyes darted around the room, seeming momentarily surprised at the clutter spread out across the floor. Then he ambled over to the edge of the map and sat down with a soft thud, taking in every detail with wide inquisitive brown eyes.

Max closed the bedroom door and followed Lokie back across the room. He was just about to sit down, when suddenly a black winged shape swooped past the open window, closer and clearer this time. It was accompanied by the soft rush and hiss of wings cutting through air.

Seconds later, a hauntingly familiar, high-pitched screech broke the quiet of the house.

Max's stomach lurched with fear.

Anna's head shot up, her dark brown eyes met Max's, wide in alarm. In one swift movement,

Anna leapt to her feet, any excitement over the map immediately forgotten. 'What was that? That noise?' she said in a frantic whisper.

A second high-pitched shriek rang out through the house. Moments later, there was the sound of a tremendous crash from somewhere downstairs.

Anna's eyes met Max's. Their eyes locked in silent horror.

'I think it's Valac,' Max whispered, gulping down a wave of panic. 'I heard noises like this that night at my house.'

Terror swam to the surface of Anna's face. 'What should we do?'

A thunderous crash reverberated throughout the house. Lokie froze, bat ears quivering, and then dived into the bottom of the empty rucksack that was lying near the foot of the bed.

'What should we do? We're trapped!' Anna gave a strangled whisper.

Max tried to think, but his mind had gone white. His eyes darted around the room, a blur of frantic thoughts began to churn through his mind. Then suddenly, his eyes fell on the Uroboros Key. Lunging forwards, Max snatched the Key and the map off the floor.

'Anna, get hold of me – grab my arm!'

There was a deafening bang, followed by the sound of splintering wood that sounded as though it came from the stairs.

'Wait! What about Lokie!' said Anna, diving forwards and quickly snatching the rucksack off the floor. She hurtled back towards Max, grabbing hold of his arm and clutching the bag and Lokie to her chest.

Swallowing down his fear, Max forced himself to focus on the Uroboros Key, then quickly twisted the inner most dial sharply to the left.

There was a tremendous thud on the landing directly outside the bedroom door. The door shook, rattling on its hinges.

'Hurry!' Anna gasped.

Max stared helplessly at the snake, frantically willing it to move. But it didn't; the snake remained still, the pale blue eye was dull.

'Hurry!' she shrieked again.

Panicking, Max twisted the dial sharply to the left again, feeling the second click of the dial, just as the snake as though waking from a deep sleep, began its slow grinding journey around the centre of the Key.

There was another enormous crash and the door burst wide open, splintering on its hinges.

Max caught a brief glimpse of a huge black

figure with spiny folded wings and razor-sharp clawed hands that loomed through the fractured doorway and two fiery, red unblinking eyes that burned intensely with what seemed like fathomless depths of contempt, deep hatred and pure rage. Then he felt the sharp jolt from deep inside his stomach, their feet abruptly left the floor and they swirled up into the ice-cold nothingness, a furious, exasperated howl echoing after them into the void.

Chapter 15
The Escape

Higher, higher and higher they spiralled, swirling through the void. The wind whistled past Max's ears, whipping his face and hair and stinging his skin like needles.

Then suddenly they were slowing down. He could feel that they were spiralling downwards before they abruptly slammed into the ground. Max's legs buckled from underneath him and they landed in a heap on top of one another on the floor.

'Ouch!' yelped Anna, who had unfortunately landed beneath Max.

'Sorry!' said Max, untangling himself from her. He quickly pulled himself into a seated position and looked around. Pearly white beads of light were twinkling and slowly dissipating above them in the darkness.

'Wow, that was more painful than I expected!' Anna said, rolling onto her back, 'Am I concussed? I can see twinkly things.'

'No, that always happens,' said Max, rubbing his head and blinking. 'Anyway, are you OK?'

'Yeah, I think so, but the rucksack's empty. Where's Lokie?'

Max looked around quickly in the darkness. Lokie had bounced and was sitting a few feet away quivering; his huge green ears were folded over and completely concealed his eyes and most of his face, revealing only his mouth, which was turned distinctly downward.

'He's here,' said Max, scooping Lokie up. He blinked, struggling to get his bearings in the gloom. They were outside, sitting on some kind of firm but grassy ground and it appeared to be night-time, as it was extremely dark.

Something rustled softly in the darkness and Max looked around, his eyes slowly adjusting to the murky shadows.

'Phew,' said Anna still lying on her back rubbing her head, 'For a minute back there I thought we weren't going to make it. Did you see that thing? Those red eyes!'

To Max's utter horror, as his eyes slowly adjusted to the darkness of their surroundings, twelve startled eyes came into view.

Max stared at the eyes in stunned silence.

The eyes stared back, unblinking.

They appeared to be in some kind of clearing. There was no moon and a recently extinguished fire gently smouldered somewhere off to their left, the last embers flickering and fading away.

The eyes, Max could now see, belonged to six

little men with bald heads and wide noses, who wore loin cloths and were adorned with tattoos and strange-shaped bones which dangled from their ears, neck, waist, legs and arms.

'Where are we?' said Anna as she slowly sat up, rubbing her head.

Max watched with dismay as the six shocked, wide-eyed stares slowly became narrow, angry and irritated. One of the tribe with red paint smeared across his face slowly stepped forward and pointed his spear directly at Max. The bones dangling from his ears, wrists and ankles rattled and clunked gently in the dim light.

'Anna...' whispered Max.

Anna blinked and looked around, her eyes widening with shock and fear.

Tugging his eyes away from the heated gaze of the six tribesmen, Max glanced down at the Uroboros Key, which was lying next to him on the floor. The red-painted warrior murmured something to the rest of the group and then thrust his spear towards Max for a second time, gaining confidence. The others nodded and murmured in agreement. A second tribesman stepped forward, prodding his spear towards Anna.

'HEY!' Anna said indignantly, as the sharp spike grazed her arm.

The sound of her annoyance seemed to

momentarily faze the group and they looked at her inquisitively.

Realising that their attention was distracted and that delaying action would only give the tribe time to further regain their confidence, Max lunged for the Key and seizing it in his hands, twisted the innermost dial sharply to the right.

'Anna, grab Lokie! Hold tight!' he yelped, grabbing Anna's arm.

The tribe's attention swung swiftly back to Max, bristling and murmuring agitatedly and then in a flurry of rattling bones, six spears were raised, stopping centimetres from Max's head.

Max breathed in sharply, looking up at the long shaft of the red-painted warrior's spear which was almost touching his nose. He could feel Anna gripping his arm tightly. Then suddenly, Max could feel the gentle vibration of the snake, as it began to slowly coil and wind its way around the centre of the key. He felt a sharp jab in his cheek and the familiar jolt deep inside his stomach and their feet once again left the ground and they were spiralling upwards at great speed through the cold, howling wind and frigid, freezing air.

A hand grabbed his arm tightly and he grabbed Anna's wrist again to steady her, keeping his eyes tight shut.

Higher and higher and higher they spiralled and then slowly but surely, they began to slow down and make their descent, before moments later they once again fell to the ground with a dull, heavy thud.

Max lay dazed, watching the bright white lights dissolve around them. Then, wondering where they might have landed this time, he quickly rolled over and sat up with a start.

Looking around, Max saw that lying a few feet away face down and groaning, her arm on top of a thoroughly disgruntled-looking Lokie, was Anna. Lying a few feet further over to the left and sitting up, looking exceedingly startled and unhappy, was one of the tribesmen.

'Oh no!' he groaned, 'We've brought one of them with us!'

'What do you mean we've brought one of them with us?' said Anna in a horrified voice, sitting up sharply. 'What are we gonna do now?'

'I have no idea.'

'How did that even happen?'

'I think–' said Max, touching his face and feeling a small bleeding cut on his right cheek, '– that he must have been touching me just as the gateway opened. Come to think of it, I think he grabbed my arm during the journey, but I thought it was you.'

'Well, we can't take him back,' said Anna groaning.

'I know, but it's not exactly fair to leave him here either, is it?'

The little warrior tribesman, however, saved them from any further discussion, as he jumped up, grabbed his little spear and after throwing them both a deeply mistrustful look, scampered off across the plateau, bones rattling and wobbling.

'Poor guy,' said Max. 'I bet he's wondering what just happened!'

'You wouldn't be saying that if we were still sitting there with six spears pointed at our heads! Anyway, are we safe here? Is anything else going to jump out at us at any moment?'

'No, I don't think so,' said Max. Then, seeing Anna's look of utter horror, he added, 'I mean, I don't think anything is going to jump out at us. Not that we aren't safe here... at least for now.'

'Finally!' said Anna flopping back exhaustedly onto the ground, 'Where do you think we are, anyway?'

Max stood up to get a better view; shading his eyes with the palm of his hand, he squinted across the landscape. They appeared to have landed on a wide, rocky, dry plain that stretched away from them in every direction. It seemed to be late afternoon and the sun was warm, but low in the sky. Some way away to the right were a series of bare sandy, rust-coloured hills, and to their left in the distance the stony plateau ended abruptly and a large area of trees and shrubs rose out of the rugged landscape, signifying the edge of a dense, green oasis. Running towards this, still to be seen jangling and wobbling as he scampered across the plain, was the little warrior.

'I have absolutely no idea,' said Max. They seemed, he felt, at least for the moment though, to be safe. The emptiness of the barren flat plain was strangely reassuring. At least, Max thought, there was nowhere nearby that anything could be lurking or hiding. Although, regrettably he also realised, that there was equally nowhere for them to hide. If they were to stay here, they would have to venture into the oasis. However, for now, just for the moment, it would do.

'That was close,' he said, sinking to the floor. His legs felt wobbly with relief.

'I didn't think we were going to get away, Max,' Anna's voice trembled with shock. She rolled onto her side to face Max; her face looked taut and pale. 'Did you see that thing? Those red eyes. That was the worst thing I've ever seen!'

'I know,' said Max, remembering with a shudder the Mothman's fiery hypnotic eyes. He'd never seen eyes like that before; they had burned with hatred and endless rage. He remembered the panic rising in his throat, as he'd watched the snake on the Key, desperately willing it to move more quickly.

'I didn't think the Key was working at first; it

just didn't seem to move. When I saw that thing burst through the door, I thought that was it.'

'I know. Me too.'

'Do you think that was Valac then?'

'Probably,' said Anna solemnly. She hesitated, 'I suppose that proves our theory right then — that Xegan and Valac still haven't found what they're looking for and they think you have it or know where it is. Max, if we're right and it is the map that they're after, they'll know you have it now and I guess that means they could still be looking for us, doesn't it?'

Max glanced down at the map in his hands. 'Yes, I guess it does.'

They sat in silence for a moment, lost in their thoughts. Max remembered the night that he had arrived back in the study at home and how thankful he was now that Imeda, Krake and Otty had been there; that he hadn't arrived back and had to face Valac on his own. He rubbed his chest, absently feeling the reassuring circular shape of the amulet against his skin. Then glancing up, he noticed that the sun had slipped a little further down in the sky.

'It's going to get dark soon. I think we need to find somewhere we can spend the night.'

'Okay,' said Anna, sitting up. 'Where should we go?'

'How about over there?' Max pointed in the

direction of the green line of trees and shrubs that marked the beginning of the oasis. 'I guess it'll be easier to hide in the trees if we need to...' Max's voice trailed away awkwardly.

Anna nodded grimly. 'OK.' She stood and scooped Lokie and the rucksack off the floor.

They set off in silence together, the orange sandy gravel crunched beneath their feet as they made their way across the rocky landscape towards the trees. The distance to the oasis, Max realised, was further than he had first thought, but he decided that they should probably make it before the sun went down and the light faded completely. What they would do then, he had no idea. They had no blankets and nothing to make a fire with and he remembered bleakly, how dark it had been when they landed in the middle of the tribe without any form of light. He felt oddly responsible for Anna now that they were here. He couldn't help feeling that if it wasn't for him and this stupid mysterious map, she wouldn't be in this mess and she would probably be getting ready to go to bed right now.

However, there was something else that was further preoccupying him. A nagging thought that he couldn't get out of his head. Max had remembered the conversation that he'd overheard between Elea and Templar earlier that day and how Templar had said that only the Elders had known that Max was staying at their house and that they'd be out that evening. Then, with a sinking feeling, he recalled the earlier conversation between Cade and

Maya where again Cade had said that it was only the Elders that had known of their location in Normington.

Max suddenly realised, sickeningly, that someone in the Elders had to have told Xegan. If nobody else had known, then it had to be the answer. Maya was right – they had been betrayed. Somebody in the Elders had betrayed them when Valac had killed his grandad and someone in the Elders had betrayed them again tonight. If the Uroboros Key hadn't happened to be in his bedroom, Anna and Max would have had no way of escaping from Valac and would probably be dead.

Max walked along in stunned silence, his mind a blur of questions, only dimly aware of the thin green line of trees that slowly advanced towards them.

As though sensing that something was troubling him, Anna gave him a quick sideways glance and frowned. 'What's up?'

Max hesitated, not quite sure where to start. 'Anna, there's something I have to tell you. Something I've just remembered from this afternoon. I overheard a conversation between your mum and dad, when they said they were going out tonight. Your dad said that nobody knew I was at your house. Nobody but the Elders.'

'So? We knew they were keeping it a secret.'

'Anna, the Elders were the only ones that

knew about me and the map being at your house and they were the only ones that knew your mum and dad were out at Krake's party tonight and that we'd be alone. Anna, I think that one of the Elders might be working with Xegan.'

Anna frowned deeply, 'I'm not sure...'

'Well, Cade said that where we lived on Earth was a secret, except among the Elders. It seems like it's the only explanation.'

'But, if you're right,' she said, her dark eyes suddenly very serious, 'Including Cade, there are only six Elders in Lucem. That means that it has to be either Cade, Krake, Imeda, Thebes, Malik or my dad. I find it hard to believe that it's Cade and it's definitely not my dad...'

'No, I know. But it does seem like it's the only explanation.'

'OK,' she said thoughtfully. 'We should tell my dad or Cade. They'll know what to do.'

'I'm not so sure,' said Max doubtfully. 'Don't you remember that day at the Ancient Council meeting, when I overheard Maya say to Cade that she thought that someone might have betrayed him from within the Elders? Cade didn't believe it. He said he would "personally vouch for every one of them." He said he "trusted them all implicitly". If he didn't believe Maya and she's one of the Ancient Council, why would he believe us?'

'OK. But what about my dad though? We can trust him.'

'I know, but your dad is an Elder and he works for Cade. If information from within the Elders is leaking out to Xegan somehow, how do we know it's safe to tell your dad?'

Anna's eyebrows met in a deep scowl, 'Are you saying you don't trust my dad?' She flared.

'No, I'm not saying that,' Max said quickly. 'But we don't know who it is that's working with Xegan or how they're leaking the information at the moment and Cade doesn't even believe that it's happening. If we go back now, how can we be sure it won't happen again?'

'I know. But we can trust my dad. I'm sure he'll know what to do. Maybe we could keep everything a secret, at least until we know what's going on and where the leak is.'

Max sighed. 'But Anna, all of this was already supposed to be a secret and look what happened: my grandad died. Look at what happened again tonight! It might be safer if nobody in the Elders knows where we are right now. At least, until we know what's going on.'

They walked along in silence for a moment, both lost in their thoughts. Lokie, who was perched in Anna's arms, was looking decidedly happier; Anna on the other hand looked much gloomier.

'We could dump the map!' she said loudly and suddenly, startling Lokie so that he yelped and nearly wobbled out of her arms, 'If it is the map that they're after, then surely once they know we don't have it anymore, we'll be safe!'

'Yeah, we could...' Max said slowly, pondering this idea for a moment, 'But would that stop them chasing us? How would they know? They would probably still think that we had the map anyway...'

Anna sighed then gave him a resigned nod of agreement. They both lapsed into silence again as they walked.

Max felt torn. Part of him wished that he hadn't picked up the map. He didn't even know why he had really. Maybe if he hadn't picked it up and left it on the bedroom floor instead, this would all be over. Valac and Xegan would have got what they wanted and he and Anna wouldn't be on the run right now.

But then the other part of him knew that there was no way he could ever have left the map behind. If they were right and it was the map that Xegan wanted, then Max had lost everything because of this map and there was a part of him, an angry awkwardness within him that just simply didn't want Xegan to get it. Xegan getting the map, somehow made everything that had happened even more pointless; his grandad's death even more futile.

But it was more than that even. If it was the map that Xegan was looking for, then the map was at the centre of everything. The map was the key. It was the reason his grandad had died, the reason he'd had to leave his home and the reason he and Anna had almost been killed tonight. Instead of getting ready to go to bed right now, they were standing on a deserted rocky plain in the middle of some unknown world. Looking at it in his hands, Max felt as though it held the answer to all his questions and the reason why everything had happened.

'So,' said Anna, cutting across his thoughts, 'In short – we've got the map. We think this is probably what Xegan and Valac are searching for. We think they're probably coming after us. And we don't think it's safe to go home.'

Max nodded grimly.

'So, if we're not going to go home Max,' she said thoughtfully, 'then what *are* we going to do?'

'I don't know.' Max shook his head, 'I'm just tired of people lying to me and I'm tired of not knowing what's going on. I need answers, Anna. Even Cade hasn't been straight with me. He said he would be, but he hasn't.' Max's voice rose angrily, 'I need to know why all this has happened and why this map's so important that my grandad would be killed over it!' A wave of anger and grief welled up inside Max, threatening to engulf him and he swallowed hard. Taking a deep breath, he glanced awkwardly towards Anna, 'All I know is no one seems to have given me a straight answer so far.

Now I've found this and for the first time I feel like I might actually be able to find out what's really going on. If this is really what Xegan's after, then this map is at the centre of everything. I need to find out the truth, Anna, and I'm not sure I'm going to unless I find out more about this map.'

Anna looked steadily at him, her dark eyes solemn. 'OK,' she said, nodding. 'OK. We'll see what we can find out about this map and what's really going on and then we'll decide what to do.'

Max hesitated, 'Anna, you could probably still go home, you know. It's me they're after really. They think I have the map, not you. And a few days ago, we hadn't even met. You've just been dragged into all this because of me!'

'Look,' said Anna, 'A few days ago, *you* didn't know any of this existed! You've been dragged into this too.'

Max shook his head, 'Look. I'm the one deciding to go after this and I'm the one who needs all the answers. It isn't your problem.'

'NO!' she said adamantly, her jaw set into a determined line. 'We stick together. This isn't just your problem; I was nearly killed tonight too, you know. You don't get to choose whether I stay or go home – I do. And if you will try to find out more about this map, then I'm coming too. We're in this together.' she paused and grinned, her face breaking into a smile for the first time since they'd made their escape. 'And anyway, you don't know anything about our worlds. You'd last about five minutes without me.'

Max felt his face redden; he was momentarily lost for words. It was a new feeling to have someone on his side. He glanced awkwardly at Anna and then nodded, a smile slowly spreading up to his eyes. 'OK, but I've got no idea where we should start, though.'

'Well, I guess it's probably got something to do with that writing we found on the map, hasn't it?' suggested Anna, 'this "Temple of Fangs" and "Uroborologs".'

Max nodded, 'I suppose something could be hidden in the Temple of Fangs,' he said thoughtfully, 'Something that Xegan wants and without the map, he can't find it.'

'Maybe it's this "Uroborologs"-thing that's hidden in the Temple of Fangs,' Anna agreed. 'I wonder what it is though. What could Xegan possibly want so badly?'

'And why would my grandad have the map?' said Max. 'It's strange, isn't it?'

'Your grandad was the Leader of the Elders for a long time, Max. From what my dad's told me, I'm sure he would know and have access to all kinds of things. He could have been given the map years ago. He might not have even known what it was.'

Yeah I guess,' said Max.

They had reached the edge of the trees and Max paused and looked back across the wide rocky expanse. The sun had crept lower into the sky and clung like a giant golden ball to the horizon; the sky was a blaze of hazy pink and red. The occasional boulders strewn across the landscape, cast long grey shadows that seemed to reach out towards them, like long shadowy fingers in the fading light. Max knew that they needed to move fast and find somewhere to settle down for the night; somewhere they could think and plan what to do next. Turning, he stepped onto the scrub and into the trees, hoping that this world, wherever they were, was really as quiet and unpopulated as it seemed. They wandered around for a few minutes in the fading light before eventually finding a small clearing where the trees thinned out and a few large boulders jutted out of the foliage and scrub.

'What about here? We could lie against these boulders,' said Max looking around. 'And we could get some leaves and branches to lie on and cover us to keep warm?'

'OK. Stay here Lokie,' said Anna, plonking Lokie down on top of one of the rocks and moving off to begin sweeping around the area in search of any dry fallen leaves.

They reconvened a few minutes later with a pile of leaves and branches and piled them up at the base of the rocks.

'If we can't go back home for a while Max, we seriously need to get some blankets or something – this is grim!' said Anna, as she grabbed Lokie and wriggled down into the leaves.

'Yeah I know, but we can manage for tonight, can't we?' said Max sitting down next to her and scooping the leaves towards them, so that they covered their legs, and the map and Key which he had placed in his lap.

They sat in silence next to one another, watching the last of the light fade away and the shadows steal out from under the trees. Night fell quickly, cloaking them in darkness.

As Max stared into the looming blackness, a new worry surfaced in his mind, 'Anna,' he whispered hesitantly, 'You don't think that it's actually me they're after do you – rather than the map?'

'No, you're forgetting what Lempo and Domovoi told my uncle and you're forgetting about the fact that your house was ransacked. If it was you, why would they go back to your house and search through everything like that? They were looking for something, Max; something they thought was at your house. Then, when they couldn't find it, they decided you must have it in Lucem with you which is why they turned up tonight and the only thing we've found is that map.'

'Yeah I guess so,' said Max feeling slightly better. He paused, 'I've been thinking about what we should do tomorrow as well and trying to come up with a plan.'

'Yeah, me too.'

'I suppose we could just set off and try to find the Temple of Fangs from the map.' He continued, 'But the problem is, if there is something hidden there, something that Xegan wants, we don't even know what we're looking for at the moment. How would we know, even if we found it? So I've been thinking that maybe we need to start by trying to find out more about what these Uroborologs are.'

'I've been thinking about that too,' Anna whispered. 'And I was thinking Uroborologs sounds quite a lot like Uroboros, doesn't it? I think I said to you before, the Uroboros is the symbol of the snake – the one in the centre of the Uroboros Key. The serpent curled around, eating its own tail. It's the ancient symbol of the Hidden People...'

'So do you think that maybe these Uroborologs are linked to the Hidden People then?'

'I don't know but it could be, couldn't it? It seems like a bit of a coincidence if not. It's not exactly a common word. And they are one of the most ancient civilisations; they're bound to have something that Xegan would find useful.'

'How could we find out?'

'Well, I've been thinking about that too and I think I might know a way. But it's a bit risky and it involves us going back to Lucem as soon as we can.'

'Go on...'

'Well, uncle Bron knows one of the Hidden People quite well. He trades with him. He's called "Irin" and I've met him at the shop a few times.' She hesitated before continuing. 'Max, I'm pretty sure that no one will know that we're missing at the moment. We know Mum didn't tell Uncle Bron about you and I doubt the Elders will want anyone to know what's going on. So, I'm pretty sure that at least for now, Irin won't know who you are and he won't know that we're both missing. I know where he lives, so I figured, we could just go to see him and ask him some questions about the Uroborologs. We'll pretend it's for a school project. He's bound to believe it, as he helped me once before and I'll just pretend you're a friend from school.'

'OK, great!' said Max, unable to hide the fact that he was impressed. 'Where does he live?'

'In Cassini, not that far from the centre. So, we could go back there tomorrow. We'll just have to make sure that no one we know sees us and hope that he's in and hasn't gone off exploring or something.'

'What do you mean?'

'Oh, you know, some of the Hidden People still like to disappear and go exploring and live in other worlds from time to time. Something to do with reconnecting with their heritage.'

'Oh, right, yeah,' said Max, remembering what Cade had said previously. 'Do you think it will work?'

'I don't know, but it's the only thing I've been able to come up with. So right now, I think it's the only plan we've got.'

Max thought about the plan. They would have to first make sure that they configured the Key correctly and safely got themselves back to Lucem without mistakenly landing themselves in some strange, scary world or tribe. Then they would have to find Irin's house in Cassini without anyone seeing them and then assuming that Irin was even there, see if they could convince him to tell them anything he knew about the Uroborologs. Max knew that the plan was far from straightforward, but at least it felt as though they were doing something positive and despite everything, his spirits lifted.

As soon as it was light enough, he decided, he would have a proper look at the Uroboros Key and see if he could figure out what all of the symbols meant and how it should work.

A low grunt rumbled softly in the darkness. Max looked around sharply, trying to identify the source of the noise, then realised that it was coming from the direction of Anna's knees. Lokie was curled up on Anna's lap, snoring gently. Max couldn't help feeling that Lokie's capacity to sleep even under the most stressful of circumstances was amazingly impressive. However, he found the normality of the sound strangely comforting in the thick blackness that enveloped them.

'Does he *ever* stop sleeping!?' Max whispered into the darkness.

Anna giggled, 'Well at least one of us will have a good night's sleep tonight. This ground is really hard and cold!'

'And damp!' Max whispered peering into the gloom, 'It's very dark, isn't it? There doesn't seem to be a lot of moonlight.'

'There might not be a moon here,' said Anna.

'You mean not all universes have them?'

'No, of course not,' she said simply and yawned.

Max lay silently in the darkness, listening to the low rumbling sound of Lokie's snores and the rhythm of Anna's breathing slowly changing, eventually becoming longer and deeper, until he knew that she had finally fallen asleep.

He would stay awake, he decided, and keep watch or rather 'keep listening' for a while, as it was impossible to see anything in the gloom. The darkness was so absolute; it seemed to hang in thick swathes around them. Everywhere Max looked, the shadows became giant, ragged, and moth-shaped. He wondered briefly if any glowing red eyes were watching them from the darkness, and then feeling the panic well up inside him again, he quickly pushed the thought away. The Mothmen hadn't found them yet. Maybe they wouldn't come.

An owl hooted in the trees above and a little while later something rustled softly in the leaves at the other side of the clearing. He tensed, straining to listen into the dense blackness, but heard nothing more.

Then sometime later, exhaustion finally overtook him, his body relaxed and he fell asleep, his hand gripping the Key.

SAM KINI

Chapter 16
The Journey Back

Max woke with a jolt early the next morning, unable to believe that he'd been asleep for so long. He rolled over and looked quickly around, relieved to see that the pale grey, blue light of dawn was slowly seeping through the trees, forcing the dark shadows to recede. His hands immediately went for the Key and the map and for a moment, he panicked, his fingers fumbling around in the leaves on his lap. Then he found them, they had slid off his legs during the night and were buried beneath a pile of leaves next to him on the floor. Max sighed deeply in relief; they hadn't been found. The Mothmen hadn't come.

He shifted and slowly sat up, not wanting to disturb Anna. She had rolled onto her side and was curled around Lokie.

He felt stiff, his bottom was numb and his body felt chilled, but they'd managed to sleep through the night and made it safely to dawn and for that, he was immensely grateful.

He sat quietly waiting for Anna to wake, watching the inky grey blurred shapes of the trees, undergrowth and rocks that surrounded the clearing slowly emerge from the dusky shadows, gaining shape and colour. Several birds (at least Max assumed they were birds) began to chirp loudly in the trees close by, greeting the dawn of the new day, but aside from that, the forest was remarkably still.

Pulling the Key and the map out from under the leaves, Max held the folded map between his fingers, considering it carefully. He frowned, wondering again, what could be so important about this map and the Uroborologs and what the day ahead would hold for them. Replacing the map, he picked up the Uroboros Key and began to slowly turn it over in his fingers. He realised suddenly, that the last time he had properly looked at the Key had been back in his grandad's study. Since then he had used the Key four times, all of which had been either accidental or in moments of blind panic. It felt strange he realised, to be planning where they were going now and to be using the Key intentionally. With this realisation came a sudden jolt of worry and doubt.

What if he couldn't work it out? What if they couldn't get back? The Key was essential to their plans. Turning his attention to the strange hieroglyphs and symbols that spanned the three dials, he realised that almost all of the symbols were completely alien to him and that hidden within these mysterious configurations, if they got it wrong, any number of strange worlds and dangerous monsters could be waiting.

The snake was now still and inert, the thin crest that came out of its head and flicked back over the dials appeared to have been lined up with, on the innermost ring, a symbol that consisted of a straight line and some kind of squiggly marking that Max couldn't decipher.

The middle dial, if Max remembered correctly (and he was not at all convinced that he did) appeared to have remained unchanged and was still aligned with some kind of spiky zigzag.

The outer symbol appeared to be pointing towards a straight line with two stars above it, which Max thought might have changed. But after scrutinising every symbol on the innermost dial, he was no closer to remembering what it had been pointing to previously.

He did, however, recognise two of the symbols on the innermost ring, a small symbol in the shape of a tower and the tiny, ridged spikes of what appeared to be a mountain range. Max knew that these had been the symbols that had changed when he had moved between Lucem and Earth.

Deciding that he needed to take much more notice of the symbols on all three rings from now on, Max looked at the symbols that were aligned with the snake's crest, making a mental note of where they were now.

Beside him, Anna rolled over and murmured something softly in her sleep. 'Ouch!' she said waking abruptly, as she rolled over and onto a rather sharp twig. She opened her eyes gingerly and peered at Max.

'Morning!' said Max.

'So, we made it to morning then, did we?' she said with a weak grin.

'Yes,' he said simply and grinned back.

'What time do you think it'll be back at home?' said Anna sitting up and rubbing her head.

'Well, I'm not sure, but I think it might be a few hours later than here. If I remember right, I looked at the clock just before Valac arrived last night and it was 8pm and dark, and then when we arrived here the sun still hadn't gone down. So, it's probably sometime earlier in the morning in Lucem right now. But I don't know, it's difficult to tell because we don't really know what time the sun sets here, do we? I think we should probably go as soon as we can though because anyway, I'm thirsty and hungry!'

'Yeah, me too,' said Anna. 'Whatever happens with Irin today and whatever we decide to do next, if we're not going home tonight, we need to get hold of some food and some clothes. We can't do this again. I'm frozen!'

They got up and began to move around the clearing, stretching stiffly and trying to warm up.

'I wonder what world we are in.'

'I was wondering that too,' said Max. 'The symbol on the Key is a straight line and a squiggly blob. You don't happen to recognise that symbol, do you?' He held out the Key for Anna to inspect.

'No, I don't know that one, which means we're definitely outside the Five Kingdoms. I wonder where we were when we landed in the middle of that tribe?'

'I have no idea. I changed the Key twice when we were trying to escape. I didn't think it was working, so I don't know which configuration the key worked for.'

'I bet that was outside the Five Kingdoms too,' Anna chirped cheerily.

Max looked at Anna with surprise, realising that he was far less impressed by this fact than she was and that despite everything – the uncertainty and danger – part of her couldn't help but be secretly thrilled to finally see something outside of the Five Kingdoms.

'If we're going to use this thing again, we need to work out what we're doing. How much do you know about these Uroboros Keys, Anna?'

'A bit. I've asked my dad about his, but he would never let me use it or anything. Like I said before, I know that the inner ring is the World ring, so all of those symbols represent a different world or universe. The middle ring is the Region ring and you change that for the region that you want to travel to within the world you've selected and the outer ring is the Location ring which is the actual specific place or area that you want to travel to within the region and world you've selected. Got it?'

Max nodded and frowned. He was trying to remember which rings he had changed but in the panic of what had happened, he was struggling to remember.

Anna pointed at the symbol on the outer Location ring. It depicted a straight line with two stars above it. 'You see that symbol there? When it's lined up with Lucem for the World and Cassini for the Region it might mean the woods near my house. But when it's lined up with a different World symbol, it might mean that clearing where we met the tribe last night and then when it's lined up with this World symbol that's being used now, it must mean this area where we landed last night.' she waved her hand in the direction of the rocky plain through the trees to their right.

'So, if the meaning for each of the symbols changes all of the time depending upon which World symbol has been selected, then there must be thousands of combinations that you can configure the Key for. How are you supposed to remember all of the configurations?' said Max sounding exasperated.

'Well, you're supposed to use a Travel Chart when you configure the Key,' said Anna.

'A what?'

'A Travel Chart. It's like a grid that tells you all of the symbol combinations and which worlds and locations they lead to. My uncle Bron sells them at the shop.'

'But I didn't see anything like that in my grandad's things; shouldn't there have been one there?'

'No, I didn't either. I don't know. Maybe it was accidentally left behind in his study.'

'So, this morning then, even if we recognise the symbol for Lucem and get that right, how can we be sure that we'll make it to Cassini and control where we are going to land back?'

'As long as the middle Region ring hasn't changed then we'll land back in Cassini rather than anywhere else in Lucem, and if the Location ring hasn't changed then I think we should probably land back in the woods near my house.

Max's spirits sank. He stared gloomily at the Key. He just wasn't sure.

'Why do you think they might have changed?' Anna asked uneasily.

Max swallowed. 'Maybe... I don't know. I'm pretty sure the Region ring is still the same,' he suggested helpfully.

Anna raised one suspicious eyebrow. 'Ummm, but what about the others?'

Max chewed his lower lip and stared at the Key thoughtfully, realising that no matter how long he looked at the Key, he wasn't going to be sure. 'To be honest, I don't know. I think I know which is the right World symbol to use to get to Lucem, but this–,' he said pointing at the outer Location ring, 'This might have moved too. I really can't remember.'

Anna shrugged. 'Okay, well at least if the Region ring's the same then we should get back to Cassini. But we could land back in a completely different part of the city. We'll just have to hope that we don't land somewhere really obvious and get seen.'

They decided to make their way out towards the flat rocky plain. A weak sun hung low in the early morning sky, lighting the area with a feeble watery yellow glow. A slight mist hung over the expanse between the forest and hills clinging to the ground like a wispy blanket.

'So, what do we do when we get there? Do we just make our way straight across to Irin's?'

'Yes,' Anna nodded, 'And then if he isn't there, at least we've got the rest of the day for him to come back. Then we'll go and find some food and things.'

'OK,' said Max, 'Here it goes then.' Max took the Key and twisted the innermost dial to the ridged mountainous symbol that he hoped he remembered correctly as being the symbol for Lucem.

They stood in a nervous huddle waiting, Anna clutching Lokie to her chest. The mist wafted around their legs, shrouding their ankles and feet. Then slowly the Key began to vibrate and the snake began its winding journey around the centre of the Key. Moments later Max felt the sharp jolt from deep inside his stomach and once again, their feet left the ground. Then, they were spiralling up into empty cold nothingness. The bitter icy wind howled past Max's ears, whipping his clothes and hair and stinging his eyes.

Suddenly they began to slow down and descend. Max felt Anna's hand tighten on his forearm in anticipation of the fall and moments later, they hit the ground with a dull thud.

They had landed, Max could tell, on a hard, stone-flagged surface, bright light and noise whirled around them. He blinked, squinting into the bright sunshine. Then to Max's utter dismay and alarm his eyes focused on the elaborate circular stone fountain that stood – which meant unfortunately that they did too – in the centre of the pyramid courtyard. The courtyard was busier than ever, with a steady throng of people rushing and bustling about their business.

'Anna!' he hissed, 'Get up – quick!'

'Where are... Oh no!' Anna gasped. She sat up sharply, her eyes wide.

Max glanced around quickly. For the moment at least, it appeared that in the clamour of the morning's activity, their sudden and unexpected arrival appeared to have gone unnoticed. But Max knew that they wouldn't go unnoticed for long.

Anna grabbed Lokie and leapt to her feet. 'We're doomed!' she whispered.

'I know! We need to get out of here, now!'

Max took a step backwards and then felt a sudden heavy jolt. Spinning around, he found himself staring straight into the dark, shadowy hood of a Wokulo that was making his way across the courtyard. Two empty blue eyes regarded him irritably from the darkness of the hood.

'Oh, sorry!' said Max startled.

'Watch out!' the Wokulo rasped sharply.

Max could just make out the shadowy outline of a strange, flat face with pale waxy skin that looked like it hadn't seen sunlight in a long time, slanted nostrils and a wide mouth just visible from beneath the dark beard. The empty blue eyes watched Max carefully from the shadowy depths of its hood.

'Sorry!' Max said again and grabbing Anna by the elbow, he quickly steered them both away from the Wokulo and towards one of the quieter narrow arched exits, set to one side of the courtyard. They reached the archway and Max glanced back but was grateful to see that the Wokulo had gone and that in the busy throng, nobody else appeared to be paying them any attention.

The archway led out onto the wide but quiet flagstone street that Max had walked along with

Imeda on the morning of his arrival. In the distance up ahead, the busy hubbub of the main street could be seen as it crossed the street on which they were standing. Three male Ebu Gogo's were delivering some boxes of food to one of the buildings close by. Max glanced at them cautiously but was grateful to see that they were busily unloading some food and paid little attention to them.

'That was close!' he whispered tensely.

'I know! Let's go this way,' said Anna turning right and quickly leading Max away from the Ebu Gogo's and in the opposite direction to the main street, 'It's quieter.'

They set off at a hurried walk, before turning down a narrower deserted street where they broke into a run. In the distance ahead of them, Max could see the ragged range of mountains that loomed above the city, jutting starkly against the bright blue sky. They scurried down the street without stopping, then down another, and another before they finally reached a narrow railing that led into a small, wooded parkland area.

It was only when they had passed through the small gateway into the parkland and found a secluded spot behind some shrubs, which could not be viewed from the street, that they finally lurched to a halt.

Anna doubled over, chest heaving.

'Well, I guess we can be sure that I moved the

Location ring then!' Max panted, slumping back against a nearby tree to catch his breath.

'Yeah, that was close!' Anna gasped. 'We haven't got the hang of this thing yet, have we?'

'No!' said Max looking at the key and making a mental note of the symbols again. 'We need one of those travel chart things. So how far is Irin's house from here, then?'

'It's not far away now. Rather than having to go back onto the street, we can get to it through these woods.' Anna straightened up and blew out a long breath, her face pink. 'We should probably keep moving.'

They set off walking through the woodland, Max carrying Lokie to give Anna's arms a rest. The woodland here was different to the forest in which they had spent the night. Birds chattered in the surrounding vegetation, the trees were less dense and the sun shimmered through gaps in the leafy canopy overhead, flooding patches of the forest floor in a dappled warmth and light.

After a few minutes of walking, Anna said, 'I've been thinking about what you said last night about someone in the Elders working with Xegan and,' she hesitated for a moment, 'Max, what about that conversation you overheard between Malik and Cade?'

Max thought for a moment. 'You could be right. Malik certainly didn't want me here, did he?

But just because he didn't agree with Cade's decision to bring me to Lucem doesn't mean he's working with Xegan, does it?'

'No, it doesn't,' Anna agreed. 'But if you hadn't come to Lucem, it would have made it a lot easier for Valac to find you and get the map, wouldn't it?'

'I hadn't really thought about that,' he said after a moment.

Max lapsed into a thoughtful silence. He realised that she was right. At least now, here in Lucem, he knew about the Mothmen. He knew that he must be on guard. But if he had stayed in Normington on his own and unaware of any of this, he would have been an easy target. Getting the map would have been easy for Valac. One thing was clear – Cade's decision to bring Max to Lucem had complicated things for Xegan.

The trees suddenly thinned, and they stepped out of the wood and onto a narrow pathway that meandered between the houses and trees. Irin's house stood on a small hillock surrounded and partially obscured by tall trees and shrubs and set away from the street and the other houses that were close by. A small wooden gate marked the entrance to the garden and beyond this a narrow path led away from the gate, winding up through the garden before disappearing behind shrubs and presumably in the direction of the house.

Max and Anna paused for a moment, surveying the garden and house before gently pushing the gate open and stepping onto the path.

'Lokie, you're going to have to stay here – sorry!' said Anna finding a few shrubs set off to one side. Indicating to Max where to put him down, she said, 'We'll be back for you as soon as we can. I promise.' Max and Anna set off up the path.

'Here goes,' said Anna in a tight nervous voice. 'I really hope I was right and that nobody knows we're missing, or this is all about to go horribly wrong.'

They rounded a bend in the path that curled around some large shrubs and bushes and the house suddenly came into view. It was a large imposing two-storey grey stone building with a grey slate roof that sloped up from all four sides to a pyramid-shaped peak. Large trees stood close to the house, partially obscuring some of the large windows that looked out onto the garden and affording the house yet more privacy. The path which wound up from the gate, eventually led to an intimidating huge dark oak door upon which hung a heavy door knocker crafted into the shape of the circular serpent, which Max now knew represented the Hidden People.

They hesitantly made their way up the path towards the front door. All was quiet and the windows were dark and unlit.

'Do you think anyone's in?' Max asked apprehensively.

'Doesn't look like it,' said Anna, taking hold of the huge serpent and heavily clunking the doorknocker so that it hit the door with a weighty thud and a resounding rap.

They waited, shuffling nervously back and forth on the doorstep. There was the muffled sound of a latch clicking, the door swung open and a tall slender man with blond, white flecked hair, a kind face and inquisitive, grey eyes reminiscent of Chandra's, stood looking questioningly down at them.

SAM KINI

Chapter 17
The Hidden People

'Hello Anna!' Irin said, with some surprise.

Although not enough surprise, Max registered with some relief, to imply that he knew that they were missing.

'Hi Irin,' said Anna in a voice that sounded to Max as though she was trying hard to make it seem bright and casual.

'Hi,' said Max. He gave Irin what he hoped was a winning smile.

'I'm doing another school project,' said Anna, 'And it's to do with the Hidden People and, well, I was wondering if you could help me again, please?'

'Fine, no problem,' Irin smiled. 'You know I'm always happy to help you. When would you like to come and discuss it?'

'Erm, could we do it now? It won't take long.'

'Now? To be honest Anna, it isn't exactly the best time for me right now.'

Max's heart sank.

'Oh, that's a shame,' Anna said in a voice that was heavy with disappointment. 'It has to be in byyy... tomorrow. The school has just given it to us at really short notice,' she rolled her eyes for effect. 'And Frederick and I are struggling.'

Irin hesitated and frowned. Max could tell that he was torn and didn't want to say no.

'Well, how long do you think it will take Anna?'

'Oh, not long,' Anna said hopefully, 'It's really only one question and it will really help. Last time you helped me, I got the highest grade and I don't usually.'

Max gave Anna a quick sideways glance, noting her earnest expression and bit back a smile.

'OK,' said Irin hesitantly. 'As long as it doesn't take long though Anna. I have to go out in half an hour and I really can't be late.'

'Oh, thanks Irin! It'll easily be less than that. Promise!' she said happily. She followed Irin into the house and beckoned Max to follow.

Breathing a sigh of relief, Max followed Anna over the doorstep and into the hallway. He was pleasantly surprised to find that the house; although austere and intimidating on the outside was very welcoming and homely once inside.

They followed Irin through to the back of the house and into a brightly lit kitchen, gesturing for them to sit at a large wooden carved table and two matching heavy wooden benches that were set to one side of the room. Sunshine beamed through the windows, flooding the room with warmth and light. A kettle bubbled and spat on a black range set into the wall at the far side of the room and a half-cut loaf of freshly baked bread sat on a wooden chopping board, filling the room with the warm, smell of breakfast. It was a welcome relief after the cold damp night in the woods and Max's stomach immediately rumbled.

'Would you like something to drink Anna? Frederick?' Irin said, moving over to the stove, 'I was just finishing up breakfast and there's some freshly brewed tea if you would like some.'

'Yes please,' said Anna.

'Please,' said Max perching down next to Anna on one of the benches and eyeing the bread hungrily. His stomach rumbled for a second time and he clenched his stomach muscles, trying to distract himself and focus instead on what they needed to do.

'So, tell me about this project then, Anna.' Irin poured three mugs of steaming tea and set them down on the table.

'Yes, sure,' said Anna.

He sat down on the bench across from them both and then looked at them both expectantly.

Max's stomach rumbled angrily again, louder this time and he quickly leant forward and crossed his arms over his chest in an attempt to stifle the sound.

Irin raised an eyebrow and smiled, 'Missed breakfast, have you? Would you like some fresh bread?'

Max felt his face immediately flush with embarrassment.

'Thanks, Irin, that would be nice,' said Anna cutting quickly across Max and aiming a swift kick at his legs under the table, 'We didn't get a chance to have anything this morning before we left. We just thought, you know, with the tight deadline and everything, that we'd come straight around to see you.'

Irin got up and went over to the side, where he began to slice and butter a couple of thick wedges of bread.

Anna turned and threw Max an exasperated glance.

'So, what's this project then?' said Irin, placing the bread down in front of them both and sitting back down on the bench.

'Well,' said Anna taking a deep breath, 'they haven't said much about it. The teachers have just asked us to go and find out whatever we can about the Uroborologs. All we know – well, all we think we know – is that it has to do with the Hidden People. It's a sort of fact-finding thing,' she explained earnestly.

Max nodded vigorously in agreement, his

mouth full of bread.

Irin slowly placed his mug back onto the table, a look of surprise registered across his face.

'Do you, erm, know anything about the Uroborologs, then?' Anna asked hopefully.

Max watched as the expectant smile slowly faded from Irin's lips and his eyes widened in shocked angry surprise.

'Who asked you to look into this?' he asked sharply.

Anna looked startled. 'Oh, erm, our teacher?' she said cautiously, sounding confused.

Irin's face had settled into an angry frown. 'What do you know of the Uroborologs?' he demanded.

'N-Nothing,' Anna stammered, her eyes widening in surprise, 'We don't know anything yet, and that's why we came to ask you.' she finished sweetly.

Irin suddenly became silent; he stared ahead, frowning into the distance.

Anna glanced uncertainly towards Max.

Max could see that things were clearly not going quite how they'd expected, even though Anna was doing her utmost to be charming. He flailed around trying to think of the next thing to say to fill the awkward silence.

'It is something to do with the Hidden People then, isn't it?' Max asked cautiously, after a moment.

Irin remained silent.

Max shifted uneasily in his seat, the remains of his bread forgotten. It was difficult to tell whether Irin had actually heard him or not. He glanced awkwardly towards Anna. Anna raised her eyebrows questioningly at Max; she shrugged slightly, looking nervous.

Then suddenly Irin turned towards them both. 'I can't help you, I'm sorry; I don't know anything about the Uroborologs,' he said with a forced smile.

'Oh, right,' said Anna, 'but you just—'

'Sorry,' he said more firmly this time, 'I do need to go out now Anna, but lovely to see you.' He abruptly pushed his chair back and stood.

'Oh, right,' said Anna again, sounding confused. She threw Max a puzzled glance and then hesitantly stood.

'Thanks for visiting Anna and nice to meet you, Frederick,' he said crisply. 'Say hello to your uncle Bron.'

Max stood up, not knowing quite what else to do but follow Irin, as he herded Anna through the kitchen. Then with one swift movement, they were through the hall, over the doorstep and the door had closed sharply behind them.

'Oh!' said Anna, in a startled voice.

They walked a little way down the path and then paused by a clump of shrubs and trees so that they were out of earshot and out of sight from the house.

'Well, that didn't exactly go well, did it!' said Anna, her voice heavy with disappointment, '*and* he knows something.'

'He knows something. Everything was going fine and then, did you see the way he reacted, the moment you mentioned the Uroborologs?'

'I know! I wonder why he wouldn't tell us about it though. I know Hidden People can sometimes be a bit secretive and suspicious, but Irin is usually really helpful. I wonder why he lied.'

'I have no idea,' Max paused. 'What are we going to do now?'

'I don't know,' Anna said glumly. 'Right now, that was our only plan.'

Max thought for a moment. 'I guess it does confirm one thing though, that it probably has something to do with the Hidden people. Even if we don't know what the Uroborologs are yet, at least we know that I suppose...'

'Well, no not really,' Anna said grumpily. 'We know it's something that he knows about and that he doesn't want to tell us about. But that's about it – he didn't confirm anything.'

'Yeah, but the way he reacted. It's got to be something to do with the Hidden People, hasn't it?'

'Ummm,' muttered Anna, sounding unconvinced.

'It has to do with the Hidden people.' A voice suddenly whispered from somewhere near them in the trees.

Startled, Max looked around sharply, wondering where the mysterious voice had come from. But there was no one in sight.

'You don't know that Max,' said Anna, irritably kicking a stone across the ground.

'I didn't say anything,' said Max looking around again.

'Yes, you did, you just–'

'No, I didn't,' Max whispered urgently, 'there's someone else here.'

There was a soft crunch as a twig snapped under someone's foot. Anna's eyes widened in surprise.

'Who's there?' said Anna, spinning around on the spot, 'This isn't very fair you know, just because you can be hidden!'

There was silence. For a moment, nothing moved. Then Max heard another twig snap. Looking down, he saw a small depression of grass that bounced up again moments later.

'Who's there?' Anna demanded again angrily, 'You shouldn't be listening in like that!'

'I know, I'm sorry,' said the voice again.

Then to Max's utter shock and surprise a faint grey, white, cloudy silhouette began to form in front of them. It quickly gained form and shape, turning pearly white and luminous, until suddenly what appeared to Max to be a teenage boy appeared right in front of their eyes. Max was aghast. He tried not to stare but couldn't help it; taking in the light blond hair, pale skin, high cheekbones, freckles and bright inquisitive silvery, grey eyes that suddenly appeared before him.

'I'm Bodhie. Irin is my uncle...'

'How long were you spying on us?' snapped Anna, cutting across him and looking far less shocked and impressed than Max.

'I'm sorry,' said Bodhie, 'I was just out here. I didn't mean to listen in on your conversation. You came right past me.'

Anna's eyes narrowed into a hard frown. 'You shouldn't have been listening,' she said defensively. 'What did you hear?'

'I wasn't following you, nor eavesdropping on purpose, you know! I'm living here – you came past me! Anyway, why did you come to see my uncle about the Uroborologs?'

Anna opened her mouth to speak, an

indignant expression on her face.

But before she could say anything further, Max quickly said, 'Why? Do you know about the Uroborologs too?'

'I – well, yes, I do. But we're not supposed to talk about it,' Bodhie hesitated.

They all stared curiously at each other for a moment.

'It would help,' pressed Max.

Bodhie frowned. 'OK... but first you need to tell me why you need to know and how you've heard about it, because outside of the Hidden People not that many people know about the Uroborologs.'

Max and Anna exchanged a glance; Anna shrugged and nodded. Max realised that they had nothing really to lose by telling Bodhie and everything to gain. The worst people who could know that they had the map – Xegan and Valac – already knew. So, in a way, it seemed pointless to worry about sharing it.

'OK,' Max said guardedly, 'Well, we've found this old map and there's a marking on it which we think marks the location of something and... well... we believe, that it might be something to do with these Uroborologs.'

Bodhie frowned and then said, 'And what makes you think that this map has the location of the Uroborologs on it?'

'Well, it has the word Uroborologs written on the map, that's why.' said Max.

There was a soft rustle of leaves in the trees close by, glancing up Max noticed that a sleek black bird had landed in the branches and was watching them inquisitively with dark curious eyes, through the leaves.

'OK,' Bodhie sounded dubious. 'So what's this location then? Which world is the map of?'

'Well, the Map is of Mimas actually.'

'Rightttt,' said Bodhie, eyes widened in disbelief, 'And where exactly did you find this map?'

Well, my grandad sort of had it,' said Max. He was starting to get irritated.

'Look, whatever it is you've got, I seriously doubt that you've got a map with the location of the Uroborologs on it.'

'But why is it so unlikely?' said Max defensively, 'What are these Uroborologs anyway?' He felt himself bristle with annoyance.

'What is the Uroborologs?' Bodhie corrected, 'It's one thing. It's a book. The Uroborologs was a book – an ancient and secret book of our people, the Hidden People. It contains maps and details of all the worlds that the Hidden People have ever travelled to and all of the worlds that our ancestors have ever lived in; to worlds that are rarely visited these days, even dangerous worlds. Because we're one of the oldest and well-travelled of all civilisations, the book is supposed to be the best record that exists about the worlds in which we live.'

Max and Anna exchanged a meaningful glance. It was immediately obvious why this book would be so valuable to Xegan.

There was the sound of a door slamming, followed by fast-approaching footsteps.

'It's my uncle,' whispered Bodhie, 'Quick!'

The three of them shrank behind a shrub that was close by, squashing together to ensure that they were hidden out of view from the path. Moments later Irin stalked past them and down the pathway, towards the gate. They watched him pass in silence.

He looked, Max thought, decidedly unhappy.

'Why did your uncle act so weird about it? Why wouldn't he tell us?' whispered Max, as they stepped out from behind the bush again.

'Well, outside of the Hidden People, the Uroborologs is not widely known about. It's an ancient and sacred book. We don't have a world that we came from; we didn't descend from Earth originally like you. This book was our heritage, the history of our ancestry.'

'Why do you keep saying "was"?' Max interjected.

'Well, that's the other thing, you see. The book is actually missing.'

Anna looked puzzled. 'How did it go missing?'

'Well, we don't really know. You see, the book is centuries old and each generation is given the responsibility to keep the book up to date and to keep it safe for future generations. I'm not exactly sure what happened, but what I do know, is that there were three secret Keepers of the book. These Three Keepers had sole responsibility for maintaining and keeping the book up to date and for keeping it safe and its location secret. Then about ten years ago, all three Book Keepers mysteriously disappeared and the book was lost forever.'

'What, they all went missing? At the same time?' said Max. He glanced quickly at Anna; their eyes locked in silent dialogue. They both knew that he and his grandad had moved to Earth at a similar time. The timings matched. It was entirely possible, Max realised, that the book could have gone missing and that a map marking the location of the book could have found its way into his grandad's hands before they had moved to Earth. But why? And how?

'Yes, they all mysteriously went missing,' Bodhie continued. 'There were all sorts of theories, but basically, they've never been seen since and neither has the book. Nobody but the Three Keepers knew of the book's secret location, so when they disappeared, it did too. It was searched for of course, but nothing was ever found. Most people think that the Keepers were probably kidnapped and forced to give up the secret location of the book, then killed and that the book was probably stolen. It was a huge scandal when it all happened.' Bodhie looked thoughtful for a moment.

The wind blew softly through the trees above them, rustling the branches and whispering in the leaves. A few leaves floated down settling near their feet on the grass.

'It's an embarrassment amongst my uncle's generation because, after centuries, *they* were the generation that lost the book. Actually, my uncle Irin knew one of the Keepers; they were very good friends. I think that's probably why he was so odd with you.'

'Oh, err, that makes sense, I guess,' said Max, slightly distracted.

There was a whisper of rushing air, the branches above them swished and swayed in the breeze. Max glanced up. The sleek, black bird gave a sudden squawk and flew off.

Something had startled it.

Anna nodded, seeming satisfied. 'Your uncle Irin does business sometimes with my uncle Bron, you know–'

A few birds in the nearby trees abruptly flew off, scattering and chattering in alarm.

'Oh yes, I went to his shop once, a long time ago.'

Max held his breath, only vaguely aware of the conversation now; he could hear a faint thrumming sound. The gentle rush and hiss of wind.

'Did you? It's great isn't it, my uncle's shop.'

The thrumming sound was joined by a low drone and the whoosh and hiss of something cutting through the air.

Suddenly, chillingly, Max realised, that he knew those sounds; that he'd heard them before. They'd been found.

SAM KINI

Chapter 18
The Rocky Start

Max put a warning hand on Anna's arm. 'Do you hear that?' he whispered frantically. 'We have to leave now.'

Anna turned quickly towards Max, her eyes were wide, horrified. She opened her mouth as if to say something, but no sound came out.

'What's going on?' said Bodhie.

'We have to leave now,' Max said in a panicky voice, 'They've found us.'

'Who's found you? What's going on?'

'The Mothmen – they're here.'

'What!' Bodhie's face lit up with horrified alarm.

There was a whoosh and the rushing sound of the wind as something cut swiftly through the morning air. The trees swung violently overhead. More birds scattered, chattering in alarm.

'We have to go now,' Max repeated, struggling not to panic as he groped for the Uroboros Key in his pocket, 'There's no time to explain.'

Something dark swooped overhead, momentarily blocking out the sun. The trees rocked above them.

'Hold on to me,' whispered Bodhie urgently.

'What?' Max wavered, confused.

'Hold on to me now, both of you,' Bodhie urged, 'Trust me. Do it!'

For a split second, Max looked into the serious silvery, grey eyes and then quickly reached out and gripped Bodhie's arm. Seconds later, Bodhie had disappeared.

But Max could still feel Bodhie. He could still feel the warm, round, firm shape of an arm beneath his hand. Then looking down, he realised that he could no longer actually see his hand. Or his arm or his feet. In fact, he could no longer see any part of his body or Anna's for that matter; they had all completely disappeared.

There was the thrumming sound of wings beating air, a rushing whoosh and suddenly out of the sky, an enormous black-winged creature swooped down, plunging to the grass, yards from where they were standing between the trees. It turned slowly on the spot and looked around with its red, bulbous insect-like eyes, as it folded its spiny, black, translucent wings against its body.

Max heard Anna gasp faintly from somewhere beside him.

'Don't let go,' came the sound of Bodhie's barely audible whisper.

The Mothman turned and began to slowly prowl around, making a faint clicking sound as it moved. It stretched and flexed its jagged claw-like hands menacingly. Then it slowly took a step towards them, hesitating feet away from them.

Max's breath caught in his chest; his body rigid, froze to the spot. He could feel Bodhie's arm stiffen beneath the clammy grip of his fingers.

The Mothman paused and drew in a deep rasping, rattling breath; its fiery eyes burned intensely with fierce hatred and rage.

It was so close now that Max could see the bristling fine, grey hairs that covered its body. He could smell the damp, clawing stench that lingered around its body. Then suddenly, it lifted its arm and slashed savagely at a shrub that was nearby, scattering leaves and branches.

Bodhie's arm trembled beneath Max's hand and he squeezed it reassuringly, swallowing down his own wave of panic.

The Mothman threw back his head and let out a haunting high-pitched shriek that echoed through the trees around them, and then it unfolded its huge filmy, black wings and shot vertically up into the air, disappearing straight through the trees.

Max felt Bodhie's arm drop away from his hand and two misty, translucent silhouettes immediately appeared in front of him that quickly developed into Anna and Bodhie. Bodhie immediately slumped to the floor, face very pale and clammy.

Max crouched down next to Bodhie on the floor, 'Are you okay? I-I think you just saved our lives.'

'I'm fine, it's just, very tiring to make other people invisible with you, that's all.'

'Thank you,' said Anna faintly. She slumped down next to Bodhie on the floor. Her face had gone grey.

'Was that a Mothman?' said Bodhie weakly.

Max gave a grim nod and then sat down with a bump, realising that his legs had suddenly turned to jelly. 'I think that was Valac. He's working for Xegan.'

A look of surprise registered on Bodhie's face, 'But why are they after you?'

'Well, we think it's the map,' began Max. 'You see, we're not imagining this.'

Bodhie nodded slowly, eyes widening with shock.

'They killed my grandad, Bodhie. They chased Anna and me away from her home last night, we only just escaped and now this.'

Anna suddenly leapt to her feet and stalked off. Max watched her disappear down the path, feeling dismal. He wondered if she was going to go home. He wouldn't blame her if she did.

'And you really think that this map has something to do with the Uroborologs then?' said Bodhie, looking rattled.

Max glanced hesitantly back towards Bodhie. 'Well, we don't know anything for sure yet, but the word "Uroborologs" is written on the map and you said the book disappeared about ten years ago. Well, up until last week I was living on Earth with my grandad and we'd been living on Earth for nearly the same length of time. Besides, Xegan and Valac are definitely chasing after us for something. And we haven't got anything else with us.'

They lapsed into a thoughtful silence.

'Have you told anyone, Max?' asked Bodhie, after a moment.

'No, we don't think we can; we think there might be someone within the Elders that's working with Xegan, but right now, we don't know who it is.'

Bodhie nodded and they eyed each other in companionable silence for a moment. Max noticed that Bodhie's skin looked less clammy now.

'There's something I need to ask you Bodhie,' Max said, slowly gathering his thoughts together. 'Cade told me that he thought Xegan was after power; he said that Xegan never agreed with the Ancient Council's ideas that universes should be allowed to evolve and live however they choose.

He said that Xegan thought the Ancient Council was weak and that he wanted to bring universes together; that he wanted power, and to create one way of living that every universe would follow, that they could rule and control. Bodhie, if we're right and it is the Uroborologs that Xegan's after, then wouldn't this book give him an awful lot of information about the different worlds that exist and the creatures that live within them – information that he needs?'

Bodhie frowned and nodded gravely. 'It's taken centuries of knowledge to create the Uroborologs.' Bodhie's voice was quiet, 'If Xegan got this book now Max, he would know more than anyone – anywhere – about what worlds and civilisations exist. It would give him unbelievable power.'

'That's got to be it. It's got to be what Xegan's after.' It was the sound of Anna's voice from behind them.

Max swivelled around. Anna was standing behind him holding Lokie; her face had resumed most of its usual colour and her jaw was set into a determined line.

'I think we should go and find the Uroborologs, Max,' she said, with sudden grim resolve. 'I think we have to. It's obviously still not safe for us to be here, and anyway, if we go back now we might never find out what's really going on and who within the Elders betrayed and killed your grandad.'

Max stared at Anna. He could see the conviction in her eyes. He knew she was right; he had to go on. He had to find out the truth. But he also knew that this was his problem. He appreciated what Anna had said the night before, about them both being in this together, but they were here now, near her home and Valac had come after them. Again.

Max swallowed. 'Anna,' he said slowly, 'You're right. I do want to see if I can find out what's really going on. I think I have to. But Xegan and Valac obviously want this map pretty badly. I really think they're going to keep coming after us now. They're going to keep trying to find us until they get it,' he hesitated. 'Are you *sure* you want to do this? I mean, it could get even more dangerous and you're not that far from home here. I'll understand if you want to go back.' He glanced down at the Uroboros Key in his hands, not really wanting to hear her answer.

Anna sighed, 'I've told you, Max, this isn't just your problem. Whatever we do right now could be dangerous. If we go back, we could be putting ourselves in danger; we still don't know if someone in the Elders is working with Xegan. I say we carry on and see where this map leads us; see if can find some answers.'

'OK,' Max nodded, feeling the tiny knot of worry inside him relax a little.

Bodhie threw them both a horrified look.

'What! You're going after the Uroborologs – on your own?!'

'Anna's right, what option do we have really?' said Max. 'We can't go back and besides, I have to find out what's going on.'

'Look,' said Bodhie, 'The book isn't going to just be sitting there, you know, waiting for you to go and collect it. Even if you do have a map which shows where the Uroborologs is, there's a reason why Xegan hasn't managed to find the book in the last ten years or even the Hidden People, for that matter. If it's in the original place, where the three Book Keepers left it and its location has just been lost and forgotten, then it will be really well hidden and really well guarded and even if it's not and it's been moved, it will probably still be really well hidden and really well guarded. This isn't going to be easy, you know.'

'OK, but like I said, what option do we have?' Max got up and dusted himself down. He placed the Uroboros Key back in his pocket. 'Look, thanks for your help Bodhie, but I have to do something.'

'We should get going,' said Anna, glancing around warily. 'I really don't think we should be hanging around here. What if Valac comes back?'

'I'll come with you,' said Bodhie suddenly.

There was a nonplussed pause. Max and Anna exchanged a startled glance.

'I'll come with you,' Bodhie repeated. 'Look, you're going to need my help, you obviously don't know much about the Hidden People and you've got absolutely no idea what you're looking for.'

Anna and Max looked at each other uncertainly. Max didn't know what to say. Bodhie was right – he was sure that they probably did need his help, but he also felt uneasy. He really didn't want any more people being dragged into this.

'Look, you do need my help. You stand a much better chance of being able to find the Uroborologs if I come with you and besides, to be honest, if it is the Uroborologs and we do find it, then my people stand more to gain from finding this than either of you two,' said Bodhie, with increased urgency. 'No offence, but five minutes ago, you two didn't even know what the Uroborologs was!'

Max wavered for a moment, uncertain of what to do. He glanced at Anna. She was chewing on her lower lip thoughtfully, but she glanced up and met Max's eyes, then gave him a shrug and nodded.

'Okay,' Max nodded. 'Come with us if you want to... thanks.'

'Right,' said Anna, 'Well, if we're going to try and find the Uroborologs and we're going into that forest, then we seriously need to get some things together, because I'm not spending another night on the floor freezing! So we'll need to get a couple of blankets, some food and water, and a book of Travel Charts so that we can get to Ridgefield... Oh, and some firelighters and things that might help us protect ourselves if Valac comes back and some water. Did I say that already?' She paused to take a breath and looked at them both expectantly.

Bodhie gave Max a bemused smile.

Max grinned, 'Okay, you're right, but where can we get all this from?'

'Well, I was thinking,' said Anna, 'We can get all of this from my uncle Bron's shop.'

'OK,' said Max cautiously, 'But we haven't got any money and even if your uncle doesn't know what's going on Anna, aren't we taking a bit of a risk going to see him? What if he sees your mum and dad?'

'He's not there today,' Anna said brightly. 'He has this dippy woman in to look after the shop because he goes off buying and trading with the Wokulo on Mondays to get more stock and anyway, we're not buying the things we need. We'll borrow them,' she added, with a gleam in her eye.

Max and Bodhie eyed Anna for a moment.

'Look, it's not stealing,' she said. 'Not really, anyway. He's my uncle. If I asked him for the things, he'd give them to me. We just can't ask him right now and anyway, we can always give them back to him later.'

'OK, fine,' said Max realising that they didn't have much of an option anyway. They needed to get some supplies and things from somewhere. Then, as an afterthought he added, 'But is there a way that we can get to the shop without going on the main streets? We don't want to risk being seen by anyone.'

Bodhie frowned, 'It's crossing the river that's the problem. The bridges are all busy and in the centre of town.'

'I know a route,' said Anna. 'There's a little bridge that crosses the river much further upstream, away from the city centre. It's on the edge of the forest and I think we can get to it by going back through the woodland.'

'OK,' said Max. 'Do you need to get anything from your uncle's before we leave Bodhie?'

Bodhie looked hesitantly back towards his uncle's house. 'No, I think we should just get going in case Valac comes back.'

'Come on then,' said Anna and they turned and set off back down the path.

Making a decision made Max feel a little better and as they stepped through the gate and made their way through the woodland that skirted the edge of the city, he felt a small, nervous leap of excitement.

'So, you've got a Uroboros Key then?' asked Bodhie as they walked.

'Yes, it was my grandad's. That's how we

escaped from Valac last night, but we don't really know how to configure it properly at the moment. Do you know how to work them?'

'A bit. I've used them before. But it's difficult to control without a Travel Chart. You could land anywhere.'

Anna grinned at Max. 'We know all about that!' she laughed, and she told him about how they had escaped from Valac and then landed in the middle of the tribe.

Bodhie laughed, 'You were lucky, you could've landed somewhere much worse, you know!'

'I know!' said Anna. 'But at least we managed to get away from Valac and hopefully, it won't be an issue for much longer if we can get a book of Travel Charts from my uncle's.'

'So, how did you do that, before? How did you make us invisible?' asked Max. He'd been desperate to ask ever since they left Irin's garden.

'We can make most things invisible with us. Small things are easy and just become invisible when we touch them, like the clothes we're wearing. It's just with big things like a person that it's more difficult and tiring. I probably couldn't have managed more than another couple of minutes today when Valac was there, without us appearing. It's incredibly draining on the body. Eventually, you just pass out.'

Max nodded, immensely grateful that they hadn't had to put that timeframe to the test. He couldn't imagine anything worse than suddenly materialising unexpectedly in front of Valac.

'It must be really good to be able to make yourself invisible,' said Max thoughtfully.

'It is,' said Bodhie hesitantly. 'But there are lots of rules that we have to follow. We can't just use it for anything. We get into trouble if we use it for things that we shouldn't. The Covenant says that we shouldn't use it to creep up on people as it breaks people's privacy,' Bodhie threw Anna a quick glance, cheeks pink. 'I didn't mean to do that before, you know.'

Max glanced at Anna but noticed that she wasn't listening anymore; she was frowning and examining the map of Mimas and Cassini.

'Don't worry about it,' Max shrugged.

'So you lived on Earth then, right up until this week?'

'Yes,' said Max. He paused for a moment, counting back over the days. It had been Tuesday night when he had woken and heard Imeda and Krake talking to his grandad. Today was Monday, and not even a week had passed. 'Six days' he said finally. 'It's hard to believe – it feels a lot longer.' And for nearly a quarter of an hour, he spoke. He told Bodhie everything: about how he had suspected that his grandad was keeping some secret from him; about the conversation he had overheard between Imeda, Krake and his grandad; how he had managed to find the Uroboros Key in his grandad's study and then unexpectedly landed in Anna's back garden and how he had arrived back to find his grandad dead. Then he told him about his conversations with Cade and the meeting with the Ancient Council, how he and Anna had then found the map and how Valac had arrived and they'd just managed to escape.

'I'm sorry about your grandad,' Bodhie said awkwardly when Max had finished. 'That's really terrible.'

Max nodded stiffly.

Glancing up, he realised that he had suddenly become aware of the steady rumble of fast-moving water. To his surprise, he found that they had reached the river.

The bridge was, as Anna had promised, located in a quiet area on the edge of a much denser part of the forest. The river here was narrower and deeper, slicing sharply through the gorge. The mountains much closer now, jutted up starkly into the sky to their right, sweeping the water down in huge torrents churning and rumbling over the boulders and splashing up the steep sides of the bank. Max could hear a faint faraway roar and in the distance through the gorge, he could just make out a huge waterfall cascading and rumbling down into the ravine. The bridge was rickety, wooden and forgotten. It looked like it hadn't been used for years.

'How – did you – know – about this thing?' said Max, standing on the edge of the bank and looking at the bridge cautiously.

'It looks a bit ancient,' Bodhie added uncertainly.

'I saw it on that map.'

'Which map? Do you mean that map of Mimas and Cassini with the Uroborologs markings on it? That really old map?'

Anna nodded.

'Umm, well that explains a lot,' Max muttered, eyeing its ancient worn frame suspiciously.

'Look we needed a quiet bridge to cross. This is a quiet bridge.'

'Yeah and I wonder why!'

A gentle breeze blew through the gorge shifting the bridge slightly so that it creaked suspiciously over the tumbling water below.

'If we fall into that, Anna, we're in trouble,' said Bodhie.

'Oh, stop moaning and let's get moving,' said Anna taking a step onto the bridge. The bridge immediately swung and groaned ominously. Lokie disappeared into the bottom of Anna's rucksack.

'I really don't think it's going to take all of us in one go Anna,' said Max. 'Why don't you let me test it out first?'

But Anna was already crossing the bridge and confidently striding ahead. The bridge moaned and bounced in her wake, rocking with every step that she took.

'Look, it's fine!' she called back to them.

Max thought that it looked anything but fine. The wooden slats that ran the length of the bridge were creaking ominously and the ropes that connected and held the bridge to the posts in the ground were taut, rigid and straining. Max doubted whether anybody had crossed the bridge in a very long time.

'We're probably quite a lot heavier than Anna, aren't we?' Bodhie's silver eyes studied the bridge with a grave expression.

Anna had reached the mid-point when the bridge began to rock violently. She faltered and turned to look back at them, a look of doubt suddenly flickering across her face.

'You're halfway. Just keep going,' shouted Max.

Anna gave him a jerky nod and gripping the rope on either side of her, restarted her faltering progress across the bridge.

The bridge continued to rock and sway,

quivering and trembling with every step.

'You're doing fine, you're nearly there,' said Max, trying to inject some confidence into his voice.

'I should probably tell you, I can't swim,' said Bodhie in a hollow, flat voice. The water swirled past and churned beneath them. The colour had completely drained from Bodhie's face.

Anna had reached the other side and she turned and smiled tensely across at them. Max could tell that, although she was unlikely to admit it, she was badly shaken.

'You should go next then,' said Max. 'Get it over with. You'll be OK.' He gave Bodhie an encouraging smile.

Bodhie swallowed and took a few halting steps towards the bridge.

'It's not as bad as it looks,' shouted Anna, from the other side of the river.

Max smiled and nodded but noticed that Lokie had still not reappeared from the depths of the rucksack, which was lying next to her on the floor.

'OK, here goes,' said Bodhie in a tight rather high voice, and taking a deep breath stepped onto the bridge. The bridge trembled and quivered with Bodhie's first step.

Panic zigzagged across Bodhie's face. 'Are

you sure about...?'

'Just keep moving,' Max interjected. 'Whatever happens, just keep going.'

Bodhie nodded tensely and turning, began to take slow, deliberate steps across the bridge. The bridge wobbled and swayed with every step; the ropes pulled taut, and began to creak and groan.

Max watched from the edge of the bridge, willing Bodhie forward with every step.

Then suddenly Bodhie halted abruptly about a third of the way across the bridge and stared down at the tumbling and churning water below. 'It's really moving!' Bodhie said, voice quavering.

'Don't look down; just look forward. Keep looking at Anna,' Max yelled across to him.

The ropes creaked again, straining against the wooden posts. Bodhie clung to the ropes that spanned both sides and slowly moved off and began taking hesitant, steady steps across the bridge.

Suddenly there was a resounding crack and the sound of splintering wood and the wooden slat that Bodhie was standing on snapped, plunging to the waters below. Bodhie's left foot and leg dropped through the gap, the bridge lurched and swung uncontrollably.

'Oh no!' Bodhie yelped sounding terrified, left leg dangling below the bridge.

Max watched in horror, as the wooden slat dropped into the river and was immediately swept away in the fast furious flow, before smashing into a rock and splintering into tiny pieces.

'Can you pull yourself up?' he shouted across to Bodhie, who was still half sitting on the bridge, leg dangling precariously below.

'I-I-I think so.' Bodhie attempted to heave at the ropes on either side.

The bridge lurched horribly. Max watched bleakly, as the frayed rope tightened and strained around the wooden posts in response. Bodhie standing again, began taking slow cautious steps towards Anna. The bridge swayed and trembled with every move. Then suddenly there was the sound of a faint twang. Max's heart sank. He looked at the wooden posts, realising to his dismay that one of the ropes was beginning to fray and snap.

'It might be good if you could move a bit faster,' he shouted to Bodhie who was still only two-thirds of the way across the bridge.

'Why?' shouted Bodhie, sounding panicked.

'It's fine,' Max lied, 'but – if – you – could just move a bit faster.'

Bodhie quickly hastened pace.

Max stared at the fraying rope, trying to glue it together with his gaze. The ropes groaned and whined, as they strained against the posts.

'Well done!' came the sound of Anna's cheering voice.

Looking up, Max noticed that Bodhie had reached the other side and was now sitting in a crumpled heap next to Anna.

The bridge was still again.

Max contemplated the frayed rope and the length of the bridge cautiously. He wondered what he should do.

'What's up?' Anna called across to him, 'It'll be okay. It's really not as bad as you think.'

Max gave her a tense nod, and then frowning, looked back at the bridge again, wondering if it would hold. There was absolutely no way of telling, he realised.

'Is there another way?' he shouted across to them over the splash and rumble of the water.

'I don't think so, why?'

'I think this is beginning to snap.'

Anna's eyes widened, and her mouth gaped slightly.

Max looked back at the bridge, the frayed rope and gaping hole where the wooden slat had fallen through and down into the torrent of water below. He was just going to have to go for it and if anything happened — if anything went wrong — make a hasty dash for it and hope for the best.

What else could he do?

Taking a deep breath, he stepped onto the bridge, gripping the rope to either side of him firmly with both hands. The bridge immediately groaned ominously, the rope creaked as it strained against the posts behind him. Turning he gave the posts a suspicious stare, and then set off at a quick but steady pace. The bridge stretched ahead of him in a long thin line, appearing longer somehow from this perspective. It lurched and trembled with every step, but Max gritted his teeth and pushed himself forward, trying to stay calm.

Looking ahead, he could see the missing slat and the middle of the bridge slowly coming into view and Anna holding onto the posts at the far end, her mouth clenched into a determined smile.

'You're doing great!' she shouted to him in a shaky voice.

But Max never got a chance to reply.

Suddenly, the bridge began to swing violently, the ropes quivered and vibrated taut beneath his hands. Then, without warning, the rope in his right hand suddenly went slack, the tension disappeared, his arm lunged forward and Max knew. He knew that one of the ropes had snapped.

Max felt as though his stomach had suddenly disappeared into the rushing torrent of water below. He grappled for the rope on his left with both hands, trying desperately to steady himself. The rope felt horribly taut beneath his fingers.

Wondering desperately, how long the left side of the bridge could take the strain, now that part of the right support had gone, Max set off running. The bridge lunged and swayed with every step that he took. He could hear the rumble and splash of the water, as it tumbled over boulders, churning and swirling below him. Heaving himself over the gap, Max pushed himself on, refusing to look down. He could see Anna and Bodhie clinging to the posts up ahead, their eyes wide in alarm, shouting things that he couldn't hear.

Then abruptly the bridge twisted sharply, suddenly tilting and twisting down to the right. Max's right foot slipped and shot towards the edge of the bridge.

Floundering, he lurched forwards grabbing the ropes to his left, just managing to swiftly pull his foot back before it slipped off the edge of the bridge and he lost his balance entirely. The ropes bristled and whined in response.

Glancing up, he saw Anna and Bodhie; arms outstretched, eyes popping, mouths wide in silent screams.

Panic rose in his throat. He pushed it down. Taking a deep breath, he set off running again. Stumbling, his feet slipping on the uneven surface, he dragged and hauled himself along. Blood roared in his ears. His lungs burned. He was almost there.

Suddenly, the bridge gave an appalling jerk and shuddered. In an instant, Max felt the base of the bridge tilt sickeningly sideways, the panels slipping away from him; hurtling forwards Max threw himself off the bridge, toppling into Anna and Bodhie.

Gasping for breath, Max turned and saw that a third rope had snapped and that the bridge was hanging perilously by one tenuous frayed rope. The wooden base of the bridge was hanging vertically downwards, groaning and creaking as it slowly came to a standstill.

Anna and Bodhie were staring at him, thunderstruck. The bridge was broken, impossible to cross. He'd made it.

But only just.

'Are you okay?' Anna said shakily.

'I-I think so,' Max wheezed, chest still heaving.

Bodhie breathed out heavily. 'I seriously didn't think you were going to make it then, Max!'

'Me neither,' said Max, immensely relieved. His body felt wobbly, as though all of the energy and tension had suddenly evaporated from his limbs. Legs trembling, he sank to the floor.

There was a pause, and then suddenly Anna gave way to nervous panicky laughter. 'That was far too close Max! Next time, can you try and move a bit faster?'

'Move a bit faster!' said Max. 'Next time why don't *you* find a better bridge! Like one that will actually hold a person's body weight!' He grinned. He could feel the laughter welling up inside him, his body relaxing with relief and happiness.

Then abruptly they all burst out laughing, collapsing into convulsions, the nervous tension and stress of the last few days suddenly unravelling and releasing into laughter.

The more they laughed the funnier it became, until they were clutching each other weakly. Max couldn't remember the last time he'd laughed that hard, like a huge weight had suddenly been lifted from his shoulders.

Lokie, curious about the noise, reappeared from the depths of Anna's rucksack and peered at them all quizzically.

Chapter 19
The Book of Travel Charts

'We should probably think about how we're going to do this,' said Anna, as they slipped down another deserted side street on their approach to the shop. 'It's not that far now.'

'OK,' said Max. 'So who is this woman that is managing the shop today?'

'She's called Flo. She's quite dippy and so I don't think that it will be that difficult to distract her. Now we need quite a lot of stuff and I'm not exactly sure where it's all going to be, so I was thinking that Bodhie, if you sneak in—'

'I don't know if that's such a good idea, Anna,' Bodhie said immediately. 'We aren't supposed to use our invisibility to do things like that. I'd get into huge trouble if anyone found out I'd been stealing. They get all funny about us using our invisibility for the wrong things. They reckon that it makes us no better than the Wokulo.'

'It's just borrowing,' said Anna rolling her eyes. 'Anyway, look, what I was going to say was, you sneak in and distract Flo. Just talk to her. And Max and I will get the things we need, because Max was in the shop the other day, and he knows roughly what the layout is.'

'OK,' said Bodhie, flushing slightly, but looking

relieved.

Max noticed the expression on Bodhie's face and was reminded not for the first time that day, how much there was that he needed to know about these worlds that he now found himself in.

'Look,' said Anna, 'I'll sneak into the office at the back of the shop where my uncle keeps his personal stuff and get some food, water, firelighters and a couple of blankets. I think he'll have most of that stuff there because he stays over and sleeps there sometimes. Max, you get the book of Travel Charts, which should be in the bookcase you saw the other day and anything else you can find that would be useful. I've been thinking that we could really do with something to defend ourselves with. So, if you find anything we could use, then grab that too. You'll just need to be careful that you stay out of sight of Flo.'

'OK, said Max, again impressed by Anna's crafty planning. Then as an afterthought, he added, 'Graul won't be around will he, with your uncle not being there?'

'No!' Anna laughed. 'He's only in the shop at night.'

Max grinned, feeling himself flush at the memory, 'I had a bit of a run-in with her uncle Bron's Watcher,' he explained to Bodhie. 'I expect you don't have that problem, do you? I bet you can just slip right past them without them noticing.'

'Actually, they can still see us when we're invisible!' said Bodhie, 'That's why people use them so much because they really can guard against everything.'

They rounded the corner and Bron's shop came into view. The small stone-flagged steps and railings that led down to the faded blue door, stood across the street; the faded blue sign that read 'Bron's Goods' creaked softly as it swung in the breeze.

'So, I'll just distract her by showing her something and pretending to want to buy something then?' questioned Bodhie.

Anna nodded, 'She never stops talking once you get her started anyway. It's getting away, that's going to be your problem. Try to take her over to the bottom left corner because that'll be away from the places we need to go.'

'Right,' said Bodhie nodding.

They lingered for a second on the corner and surveyed the deserted street. Then, after a final glance around, they hurriedly dashed across the street and down the stone steps before hesitating outside the door.

'OK,' whispered Anna, 'So you go in, Bodhie, and then as soon you get her talking, we'll sneak in after you and grab the things. When you see us leave, wrap up the conversation as quickly as you can.'

Bodhie nodded. Then taking a deep breath, Bodhie pushed the door open, disappearing into the subdued light of the shop. There was the soft tinkle of a bell from somewhere deep within.

Anna caught the door and holding it ajar slightly, pressed her ear to the gap, listening. She frowned; her lips pursed together. Moments later she nodded and gently pushed the door open, beckoning Max inside and into the dimly lit interior of the shop.

Bodhie was over in the corner of the room, pointing to a series of dead lizards that were hanging from the ceiling and nodding attentively at a woman with an electric shock of wild, frizzy black hair who Max presumed must be Flo. Bodhie eyed them as they entered and moved slightly to point at another strange yellow spotted lizard so that Flo shifted position and kept her back to them.

'Right,' whispered Anna, 'Travel Chart and something to defend ourselves with – OK?'

'Fine,' Max whispered back.

'Oh and try to avoid the brown wooden door this time!' Anna murmured under her breath and grinned, before sneaking off in the direction of a doorway at the back of the shop.

'Ha, ha,' Max muttered. He glanced ominously at the wooden door and then turned and looked quickly around the room. He immediately spotted the bookcase standing against a wall at the far side of the shop and taking care not to make a sound, he gingerly made his way around the heavily laden shelves and tables, easing his way towards the bookcase.

Like everything in the shop, the bookcase was crammed with books, manuscripts and papers of every shape and size. Max eyed the teetering shelves and his heart sank; he realised now that he should have asked Anna and Bodhie to describe exactly what the Travel Charts look like. He hoped it would be obvious.

He began to read some of the titles, his eyes scanning along the rows: 'The Covenant – A guide'; 'Earthe – A Study of the Human Race'; 'Great Sea Navigators – Vikings of the Ancient worlds'; 'Aether – What We Do Know'; I Win, You Win – Great Negotiating Tactics for Dealing With the Wokulo'; 'The Five Kingdoms – Working Together'; 'Uroboros Keys – A Guide'; 'Out and About in The Shadowlands', and 'The Four Cornerstones of the Five Kingdoms'.

His eyes hastily scanned back again, 'Uroboros Keys – A Guide'. Could this be it? He eased the book off the shelf, turning it over in his hands. It was a heavy dark leather-bound volume with the title inscribed on the front in gold. But as he flicked through the book, his eyes scanning across the pages, his heart sank slightly. He couldn't see anything that looked remotely like a chart, nor could he see any of the symbols that spanned the three dials on the Uroboros Key. The book was filled with writing and pages and pages of detail on the history of the Uroboros Key and how it had been discovered.

Disappointed, Max placed the book back on the shelf and then quickly glanced back over his shoulder. He was relieved to see that Flo still had her back to him. Bodhie caught his gaze and gave him a meaningful stare. Max immediately understood its meaning: Hurry up.

Cursing his stupidity for not asking more about exactly what he should be looking for; Max quickly resumed his search. His eyes scanned the shelves, the books and brochures danced before his eyes, but he couldn't see anything that looked remotely like a travel chart.

Worried that he was really beginning to run out of time, he crouched down and began to investigate the lower shelves. Here, there were lots of manuscripts and papers piled up, along with several smaller books and booklets. Missing the manuscripts altogether, as there wasn't time to check through them all, he quickly turned his attention to the small group of books that stood towards the end of the shelf. His eyes swiftly scanned across the titles. Then suddenly towards the end of the shelf, Max caught sight of a tiny circular gold serpent, engraved into the spine of a small, brown, leather-bound book. Easing the book carefully off the shelf, Max turned it over in his hands.

His heart leapt. There, on the front in gold leaf, was the familiar serpent motif and the words he had so wanted to find: 'Travel Charts'. Inside, he could see that there were pages and pages of grids filled with different symbols and words, laid out like a series of coordinates. With a sigh of relief, Max quickly tucked the book in his back pocket. Then he stood and looked cautiously back across the room.

'So, is this a lesser spotted variety?' Bodhie was asking Flo in an enthralled voice.

Max quickly gave Bodhie the thumbs-up sign and then wondered as an afterthought, if he would have any idea what that meant, or worse, if he would understand, but would take it to mean that he had got everything and that they could go.

Hastily, he looked away from Bodhie and glanced hurriedly around the room. 'Find something to defend ourselves with,' Anna had said. But like what?

He quickly spotted the table with the Buru gadgets and remembering the strange little robots and devices that he had seen on his previous visit, he slipped across the room towards the table. Looking down, he saw that the small, beetle-like, Tracker robots were yet again embroiled in a fight. One of the strange little robots had grabbed hold of another robot's leg and was swinging it around so that it rolled around the tabletop smashing into objects and scattering everything in range.

Max's eyes lingered over the Trackers for a

moment, undecided. Part of him wished he could take one. They looked fun, but as he watched them fight, a tiny antenna pinged off one of the robots; it shot through the air, narrowly missing Max's head and 'clinking' off a glass jar on the table behind him. Better not, he decided. If they happened to meet Valac again on their search to find the Uroborologs, he wasn't sure that he would want one of these bouncing around in his pocket.

Tearing his eyes away from the robots, Max looked swiftly around the table. His eyes fell on the box of metal disks labelled 'Poca Smoke Screens – Naburu' that he had seen on his previous visit. Smoke screens sounded useful, but as he leant forward, Max realised that there was only one of the shiny metal disks left in the box. His heart sank. When he had visited the shop just a few days before, the box had been full.

Glancing around, he spotted a Tracker robot idly kicking one of the smoke screens around the surface of the table, but when it saw Max, it quickly grabbed the shiny little disk and scuttled across the table to hide. Max leant forward and swiftly extracted the Poca from the tiny robot's clutches, but not before it aimed a sharp kick at Max's fingers. Definitely the right decision, he decided firmly, as he quickly pocketed the two shiny metal disks and watched the little robot charge across the table towards him. It skidded to a halt at the edge of the table and began jumping up and down, angrily thrusting one of its strange little electronic legs in the air.

There was a gentle click across the room, the sound of a door closing softly.

Glancing up, Max saw that Anna had emerged from the side room and was carefully picking her way across the shop towards him. Her rucksack was on her back and her arms were heavily laden with items.

He hurriedly scanned the surface of the table. He only had two Pocas, hardly a match for Valac. There must be something else. His eyes swept around the room, searching for something – anything – that might be of use. Then he remembered the small dagger with the intricately crafted handle that he had seen on his previous visit to the shop. Turning sharply, he looked quickly towards the end of the table. But it had gone.

Anna slipped past him. 'Come on,' she breathed, 'Let's go.'

Disappointed, Max turned and looked back across at Bodhie. Flo was still in full swing, jangling and waving a striped lizard about in the air. Bodhie, whose expression had now become very glazed, spotted Anna making her way across to the door and nodded almost imperceptibly.

Max hesitated; he didn't know what to do. Two Pocas didn't seem enough. It wasn't enough. But then, what would be?

Anna had reached the door and she turned, startled not to see him behind her. 'Come on!' she mouthed with exaggerated emphasis, jerking her head towards the door.

Max hesitated again. Then slowly, reluctantly, he turned away from the table and quietly slipped across the room towards the door. Anna was hovering by the door, her arms full. Max carefully turned the handle and eased the door open, before stepping aside to let Anna through. Suddenly the bell rang. They'd forgotten. Anna dived out of the door and bolted up the steps, dropping a blanket and a piece of fruit, as she went.

Max froze. Then glanced back swiftly over his shoulder. Bodhie had grabbed Flo by the arm and was leaning down to point at something on the floor. Bodhie glanced up and gave Max a meaningful stare.

Max blew out a long breath, and then turning, he quickly followed Anna out of the door, before carefully easing the door to a close, behind him. He could hear Bodhie's voice inside the shop desperately and unsuccessfully attempting to end the conversation with Flo.

Grabbing the blanket, he ran up the steps, hesitating at the top, but the street was deserted. Anna was hovering anxiously at the edge of a narrow side street. Her face relaxed into a grin when she saw Max appear at the top of the steps.

'Stupid bell! I completely forgot that it rings when the door opens. Did she see anything?' she asked, as Max slipped quickly across the street towards her.

'No, I don't think so,' Max shook his head. 'Bodhie managed to distract her.'

'What did you get then?' said Anna. She had dumped everything in her arms into a heap on the floor.

Max held out the little leather book of Travel Charts.

'You found one! That's great!'

'Yeah, I nearly didn't though! What an idiot! I only realised when I got to the bookcase that I hadn't actually asked you what it looked like! It took ages. Your uncle has a lot of stuff, doesn't he?!'

Anna nodded and grinned.

'...and I got these,' he said holding out the two Poca smoke screens. Max looked at the two small, shiny disks in the palm of his hand and couldn't help but feel that they looked pitifully small and ineffective.

'Sorry,' he said glumly, 'I didn't really know what else to get and I lost loads of time finding the book. I remembered that dagger that was there last time, but it was gone.'

'No, they're good,' said Anna shrugging her shoulders, 'I wasn't sure what you could bring either. If I'd have thought of something good, I'd have said.'

They looked up to see Bodhie, who was running across the street towards them.

'I now know nine million facts about lizards,' Bodhie said dryly. 'Seriously – anything you could ever not wish to know.'

'Oh, she's all right, really,' said Anna. 'She's harmless. She's just lonely and she seems to get really enthusiastic about the oddest things.'

'Hmmm, well you didn't just have to listen to the differences between lesser-spotted and striped lizards for fifteen minutes, did you? Seriously, she's completely batty!'

Max laughed, 'Oh, I don't know. You seemed really interested in all that lizard talk to me!'

'It's called acting!' Bodhie muttered. 'Anyway, was it worth it? Did we get everything we need?'

'Yes!' said Anna, sweeping her hands in the direction of the pile of food and blankets at her feet with a little flourish, 'My uncle stays over quite a lot, so I managed to get quite a lot of food and some blankets.'

'Great. And did you manage to find the Travel Chart?' Bodhie asked, looking at Max. 'You were at that bookcase for ages!'

'I know! I couldn't find it at first! But I got one.'

'Good. Well, we can use it now to get to Mimas to find this Temple of Fangs. Hopefully, there should be a landing point somewhere near the forest.'

'Of course!' said Anna excitedly. 'Max, you should check to see where the closest landing point is.'

Max flicked open the book of Travel Charts and quickly began to look through the pages, whilst Anna and Bodhie set about packing the blankets, food, water and firelighters into Anna's rucksack and a second bag that she had brought from the shop.

Max could see that each page in the book began with a World symbol and detailed an intricate little grid that contained a long list of symbol combinations and the specific location that each set of three symbols related to. He quickly found the Lucem World symbol. The Cassini landing points came first, he bypassed these, and then further down the same page was a list of landing points for Mimas. His eyes scanned down the grid.

'So, what's the name of that forest again – the one where the Temple of Fangs is?'

'Grigori,' said Anna glancing up at him. She was crouched next to the bags on the floor.

Max quickly scanned down the list. Sure enough, he immediately found an entry that read 'Grigori Forest'.

'I've found it!' he said, with a mixture of shock

and surprise.

'You sound very shocked!' laughed Bodhie.

'I know,' Max grinned. 'I just didn't expect it to be that easy.'

'Well, that is really the whole point of charts!' Bodhie laughed.

Max smiled and looked down at the two packed bags by their feet. With a start, he realised, that something was missing.

'Where's Lokie?' he asked suddenly.

'Oh, I left him behind.' Anna said calmly.

'What! Why?'

'Well, I figured that mum and dad would be worried about us and uncle Bron would think he'd been burgled, so this way when they find him at least they'll know that we've been to the shop and that we're OK and besides, I'm not so sure it's such a good idea for Lokie to come. We can't keep carrying him everywhere.'

Max nodded, 'That was a really good idea.'

'Right then,' said Bodhie anxiously, 'We should really go.'

They stood in a small huddle on the corner of the street. Anna and Bodhie gripped hold of his arms and Max quickly configured the three symbols on the Uroboros Key.

ANCIENT SECRETS

His stomach gave a nervous leap of excitement as he carefully held the Key and waited. Moments later the serpent began to slowly revolve, Max felt the familiar tug deep in the pit of his stomach and their feet abruptly left the ground.

SAM KINI

Chapter 20
The Search Begins

Moments later, they abruptly slammed into the ground. Max's legs buckled from underneath him and they landed in a crumpled heap on top of one another.

Max blinked and squinted into the bright sunshine. He quickly untangled his legs and then looked around, his eyes slowly adjusting to the light.

They were standing on the edge of a dense green forest. The forest here was more jungle-like than in Cassini, the air warmer and more humid. Behind them, the valley plunged away dramatically, affording them a spectacular vantage point across the vast flat patchwork-quilt expanse of fields and the stark range of mountains that jutted sharply into the sky in the distance. A city of pale stone buildings sat in the centre of the valley straddling both sides of a broad brown river. Max was guessing wildly, but he figured that it must be about ten miles away. A solitary pyramid loomed above the city, dwarfing the surrounding spires, buildings and turrets. The pale buildings gleamed in the early afternoon sunlight, giving the impression that the city glowed white.

'Is that also Mimas then?' said Max, standing and looking around.

'I think, so,' said Anna. She was once again inspecting the map.

'It is,' said Bodhie, 'I've been here before.'

Anna glanced towards Bodhie, and then quickly resumed her inspection of the map.

'So do you think this is where the trail starts?' asked Bodhie.

Max turned away from the valley and looked back towards the forest. The dense green jungle stood before them tangled and impenetrable, stretching away as far as they could see and reaching up the side of the mountains that loomed in the distance beyond. A rough track had been carved through the knotty vegetation to their right. Peering into the trees, Max could just make out a faint trail that wound away from them, disappearing into the undergrowth.

'Do you think that's the start of it then?' he asked.

Anna looked around, then frowned and returned her attention to the map. 'I think so. I mean, there are several trails on the map, but at this point, they all seem to go in the same direction; they all look like they curl around the base of the mountain, so I'm not sure we can go that far wrong. Not at this point anyway.'

Bodhie shrugged and nodded.

'Right,' said Max, 'Well, we better get going

then if we want to make any progress this afternoon.'

He turned and glanced back towards the valley and the white city that gleamed in the distance below them; then with a sense of trepidation, they stepped into the forest, and together they set off along the trail.

All afternoon they followed the trail through the forest, turning west as it curled around the base of the mountain and gradually climbing; slowly drawing them into the lower reaches of the mountains as the route traced the edge of the valley.

Sunlight shone through the canopy overhead, birds clamoured in the trees around them and there was the steady buzz of insects that whined, hidden from view somewhere in the surrounding vegetation.

Max almost felt happy as they pushed through the undergrowth on the sun-dappled forest path. They were on their way, towards what he wasn't sure, but at least he felt they were doing something.

They ate a lunch of bread, ham and cheese followed by a strange spiky purple fruit that tasted a bit like an apple that Anna had taken from Bron's fridge. They ate as they walked, unnerved by how much ground they had to cover, taking turns to read the map and carry the bags. At one point early in the afternoon, Bodhie had cautiously suggested that perhaps he and Max should always carry the bags, but Anna's indignant glance had immediately silenced him and they had quickly resumed their rotation.

By late afternoon, the trail had petered out and they were pushing through the jungle. The air was sticky and warm, thick with the steady clamour of birds and insects. Everywhere they turned was the same thick tangled, knotty vegetation, the same steady crunch and mulch of spongy decomposing branches and leaves beneath their feet.

On and on they walked, slowly climbing as the jungle ascended through the lower reaches of the mountain. Occasionally the trees would thin slightly, or they would reach a clearing and the jagged ridge of mountains would suddenly slip into view, before disappearing again as they passed through more thick vegetation.

It was late and the light was beginning to fade when they eventually stopped and made camp. They had reached a small clearing, the mountains, just visible above the forest line, jutted starkly into the sky behind them. The sun had slipped low in the sky and shone pink behind the ragged range of peaks throwing them into dark contrast.

'How far do you think we've got?' said Max as he gathered some wood for a fire and began piling it into a heap at the centre of the camp.

'It's difficult to say,' said Anna. She was

perched on a rock, frowning at the map. 'I think – well – we're definitely beyond the end of the trail, obviously, quite a long way and I'm pretty sure that we're still going in the right direction, but...'

'You don't know?' Max suggested.

'No not really, I don't,' she grinned, rubbing her feet. 'But if this map is drawn to scale, I don't see how it can be that much further in the morning. At least I hope not – my feet are killing me!'

'Let's hope so,' grinned Max. He glanced up at the sky. The sun was disappearing rapidly below the horizon, and as day yielded to night he noticed that the forest was awakening to the new sounds of tree frogs and insects.

They huddled around the fire as the shadows of the trees began to close around them, encasing them in a yellow flickering dome of light.

Max remembered the dense blackness and the cold dampness of the woodland floor the previous night and felt immensely grateful for the blankets and the warmth of the fire.

The sound of Anna's voice jogged him from his thoughts.

'So, where do you go to school?' Anna was asking Bodhie as she chewed some bread and ham.

'I don't go to school; I have a tutor that teaches me at home wherever I am staying. All the

Hidden people do that until they are seventeen years old,' Bodhie explained. 'Hidden People are very private and always tend to keep to themselves. I think it's something to do with the fact that they have always moved around and lived between worlds; they've never really lived in communities or anything.'

Anna nodded, 'Makes sense. I always wondered why I never had any Hidden People in my class at school. So, you're staying with your uncle Irin at the moment then?'

'I stay with him a lot. My parents travel almost all of the time.' Bodhie said simply and shrugged.

'So, what, they just leave you with your uncle?' said Anna between munches, 'Don't you get lonely?'

'They work in historical research for the Hidden People studying ancient artifacts of the Hidden People. It's a really important and responsible job. After the Uroborologs went missing, a lot of the documented history about our people disappeared with it. This work is to try to rebuild all of the lost knowledge of our people. So, I mostly just stay at my uncle Irin's or my grandze's. I don't see my parents much to be honest, maybe once or twice a year.'

'What's a grandze?' asked Max confused. 'Is that like your grandad?'

'Yes, but grandze isn't a man...'

'Oh, so it's your grandmother then?'

'No...' Anna cut across Bodhie and gave Max a meaningful stare.

Max opened his mouth to speak and then caught himself. He suddenly realised that he was missing something.

'Not everyone in the Hidden People is just male or female, Max,' Anna explained, 'The Hidden People have He's, She's and Ze's.'

'Oh,' said Max, so your grandze is someone in your family who is your grandparent... but not a man or a woman?'

'Exactly,' Bodhie nodded and shrugged. 'It's normal.'

Max fell silent for a moment; he was not sure what to say. He knew that it was silly to just assume that everything had to always be a certain way. He knew that there were lots of different genders, so why had he automatically assumed that there was just a male and a female? He glanced towards Bodhie who was hunched towards the fire poking the embers with a stick. The firelight flickered and danced across the profile of Bodhie's pale face lighting up the luminous skin, high cheekbones and silvery eyes. And then suddenly Max realised.

The prickly heat of embarrassment flushed up Max's neck. His thoughts skittered back over the things he had said since he had met Bodhie. How could he have been so stupid, he thought. He had just assumed...

As if realising what Max was thinking, Bodhie glanced back towards Max and almost as if answering the unsaid question that hung between them, Bodhie suddenly said, 'Yes, I'm a Ze too, Max.'

Max grinned and nodded. His cheeks still flushed. 'I just got that... Sorry, I just assumed...' his voice trailed away awkwardly.

Bodhie smiled. 'It's fine, you weren't to know. I suppose I should have told you, but it didn't even occur to me that you wouldn't know, until just now.'

Anna gave a bark of laughter.

'Did I say anything wrong?' Max asked sheepishly.

Anna laughed again, 'You mean apart from when you called Bodhie a big girl on the bridge? Yeah, that was really rude!' Then upon seeing the horror on Max's face, she said, 'I'm joking! You didn't say anything; that's why we didn't realise until just now.'

Max grinned and then laughed, feeling his embarrassment subside.

They fell into companionable silence for a moment.

'We should probably get some sleep, shouldn't we,' said Anna, rolling over and pulling the blanket around her shoulders, 'We've got a big day ahead of us tomorrow.'

Bodhie nodded, 'And the sun will rise really early here, too.' Ze paused before adding, 'I'm really glad I came along with you two...'

'We are too,' said Max. And he meant it.

Glancing up through the branches, Max saw the cold glint of stars above them. He pulled his blanket around his shoulders and snuggled down, trying to make himself comfortable.

It took Max a long time to fall asleep that night. He lay watching the brightly burning flames flicker, then fade. The last glowing embers slowly died away until there was only darkness and the gentle rhythmic sound of Bodhie and Anna breathing.

His eyes scratched with tiredness, but his mind was buzzing with thoughts. His mind quickly wandered back to his conversation with Bodhie earlier.

Six days.

The realisation shocked him to his core. In just six days, everything had changed. Everything. So many secrets. So many questions and things he didn't understand. Why hadn't his Grandad shared any of this with him? Why hadn't he prepared him for any of this?

The tiny knot of angry, resentment settled into

the pit of his stomach again and he rolled over, curling up on his side.

Sometime later, he finally drifted off to sleep.

Max woke. It was still dark. In the bright moonlight, the glade seemed empty. Except that, something had woken him. But, what?

Max lay rigid under his blanket, listening into the darkness, staring into the shadows that stretched between the trees, beyond the clearing. His hand crept to the Key. Then slowly, silently, he sat up.

He bit his lip and glanced about.

Everything seemed quiet. And yet, he had the unsettling feeling that something was watching them.

Max stared into the looming blackness of the trees and his heart began to pound. His eyes scanned the glade, the grey rocks and dark shadows between the trees. Nothing moved, yet still, his skin prickled and the unnerving feeling persisted.

Minutes passed and Max sat straight back, staring rigidly into the darkness. Then suddenly, inexplicably, the sensation was gone.

He glanced down; his knuckles shone white in the moonlight, as he clutched the Uroboros Key tightly in his hand. He quickly configured the Key back to the symbols for the deserted plateau; then slowly, hesitantly he lay back down. Beside him, Bodhie stirred in zer sleep.

He lay, watching and listening, staring rigidly into the darkness for a long time and then after a while his heartbeat slowed, tiredness finally overtook him and he fell into an uneasy sleep.

The next day dawned fine and bright, and as they set off again, Max's spirits rose. Sun streamed through the canopy casting mottled pools of bright sunlight across the forest floor. Snatches of clear blue sky were just visible through the gaps in the leaves above and the air smelt fresh and sweet.

He was tempted to tell Bodhie and Anna about what had happened the previous night. But what exactly had happened? What would he say? He wasn't completely sure. I woke up suddenly last night and didn't see or hear anything and then I fell back to sleep.

He'd sound ridiculous. Maybe he'd imagined it.

But then, by late morning he had twice heard a rustle of branches and seen a black bird flitting through the trees behind them and the strange, unsettling feeling returned.

The sun quickly rose high in the sky, the

jungle became thicker; the ground more boggy and soon they were sweating as they pushed their way through the dense tangle of foliage. The leafy dome of the jungle arced overhead, sometimes almost completely blocking out the light and enclosing them in its sticky embrace.

Now and then, Max would turn and see the black bird silently tracking their progress. Maybe he was imagining it.

Except that he knew, he wasn't.

He turned sharply.

Again, a flash of black silently tracked them between the trees.

Max swallowed, knowing how strange this was going to sound. 'I think there's a bird that might be following us,' he said finally.

They had reached an even denser part of the forest where the undergrowth was waist-deep in parts.

'What do you mean there's a bird following us?' said Anna, panting as she pushed her way through the foliage, 'There are birds all over the place, Max; we are in a jungle after all.'

'I know but I keep seeing this same bird, a big black bird; I'm sure it's the same one.'

'How can you possibly tell it's the same bird?'

'I don't know, but...' Max hesitated, 'I'm just

sure that it is.'

Bodhie gave Max a dubious glance, 'Anna's right, you know, Max. Black birds are not exactly unusual here.'

Max nodded but fell silent. I know, he wanted to say, but I can tell. It watches us like it's thinking; like it understands. But he could see that Anna and Bodhie were unconvinced, so he checked himself. He didn't want to sound silly. After all, they knew a lot more about this world than he did.

'Look!' said Bodhie suddenly cutting across him and saving them from any further conversation.

Max, who had been pushing his way through the thick tangle of undergrowth, looked up sharply and his heart skipped a beat.

SAM KINI

Chapter 21
The Temple of Fangs

The Temple loomed out of the vegetation ahead of them. From a distance, it was almost indistinguishable from the foliage and trees that surrounded and embraced it, having been long ago abandoned and reclaimed by the forest. Three crumbling stone turrets jutted out of the dense, sticky undergrowth reaching through the trees and towards the sky. Set into the front of each of the turrets, carved into the crumbling moss-covered stones, were three huge sleeping faces. An enormous tree grew out of a flatter section of the temple roof to one side, its giant roots cascading and tippling down the temple walls like fat twisted snakes. Grey, green moss and lichen covered the crumbling rock so that it was impossible to distinguish where the stone ended and the forest began.

They slowly pushed their way through the thick tangle of undergrowth towards the temple, casting aside creepers that dangled from the canopy of the surrounding trees like giant tendrils, curling and sweeping their way down to the forest floor. There was the constant clamour of birds chattering in the trees and the steady buzz of insects that whined and droned hidden from view somewhere in the surrounding vegetation.

Ahead of them, Max could just make out the shadowy entrance to the temple. Carved into the crumbling stone that surrounded the opening, were the giant jagged fangs of a huge snake, which jutted down sharply into the temple's shadowy mouth.

Max eyed the opening warily. The entire entrance, he realised, was a huge, gaping fanged mouth.

'Well, at least that's one mystery solved. We now know why it's called "The Temple of Fangs",' Bodhie muttered dryly.

Anna regarded the temple thoughtfully. 'It doesn't exactly look welcoming, does it?'

'It doesn't look particularly safe either...' added Max, as he eyed a pile of stones that had crumbled and collapsed around the entrance, becoming entangled in the forest's sticky, rambling embrace.

Pale dusty cobwebs clung around the temple's snarling mouth. Max doubted whether anyone had been here in a very long time. It was so concealed and entangled in the knotty vegetation, that you could pass within feet of it and not even know it was there. The temple was lost; completely forgotten.

Slowly, apprehensively, they began to make their way towards the mouth of the temple. Max felt as though they were carefully and quietly stepping towards some ancient sleeping beast. The forest had swallowed the temple and in turn, the temple's ferocious fanged mouth waited to swallow them.

They reached the entrance and Max hesitantly stepped forward and brushed aside the cobwebs. He peered into the darkness. A stale, musty odour immediately filled his nostrils. He couldn't see anything.

With a shiver of nervous excitement, his heart beginning to pound, Max slowly stepped over the fallen boulders and into the shadowy fanged mouth.

He blinked, his eyes adjusting to the gloom.

They were standing in a narrow dark stone passageway. The air inside immediately felt damp and cold, as though it hadn't been touched by the sun or wind in a very long time.

'Wow, it's chilly in here,' said Anna, as she stepped in beside him. 'And it smells.'

Max glanced around and spotted a heavy piece of wood that had obviously been used as a torch by a previous visitor, propped up against the wall.

'Can you pass me one of the firelighters?' he asked, picking it up.

The torch sparked and burnt immediately as though it had once been dowsed in some kind of fuel. Holding the torch aloft, Max looked around. The torch crackled and cast a yellow flickering light across the walls, revealing a series of intricate ancient carvings and inscriptions that covered every inch of the walls and ceiling and stretched away, disappearing into the gloomy shadows up ahead.

Bodhie's eyes were full of wonder. 'Wow, I think these engravings are about the Hidden People; about our past. My mum and dad would love these.'

Max regarded the engravings with interest. They seemed to depict scenes of an ancient history or legend, involving some kind of human-like race of people and a series of strange mysterious creatures.

'Come on,' Anna whispered impatiently, 'Now we're finally here, we should get moving.'

'OK,' Max muttered, reluctantly pulling his gaze away from the walls. Then, with a final glance over his shoulder at the fanged sunlit entrance, he turned and quickly followed Anna and Bodhie along the gloomy passageway.

The darkness quickly enclosed them, and the clamour of birds and insects, so intense outside, quickly faded away, leaving only a stale stillness in the air and the steady crunch of the gravel dirt floor beneath their feet.

Max shivered, feeling the goose bumps rise on his arms.

On and on they walked in a tight little huddle;

clustered together in their fragile sphere of light, slowly but steadily advancing deeper and deeper into the shadowy depths of the temple. Max had the vague notion that the passageway was gradually spiralling downwards and that they may well have dropped down below ground level, but he couldn't be sure as it was difficult to tell in the gloom.

'Where do you suppose this is going?' whispered Anna after a while, 'We seem to have come a long–'

A sound echoed suddenly through the passageway behind them cutting across her words; a dull scraping clatter, as though something had moved across the gravel stone floor.

They stopped abruptly. The torch flickered, the flame fading lower for a moment.

'What do you think that was?' whispered Max.

'I really don't know,' said Bodhie in a low murmur.

They stood together in silence waiting; staring back up the passageway into the solid wall of darkness that followed steadily in their wake, the torchlight flickering across their anxious faces. Max felt Anna's hand silently reach out and grip hold of his arm tightly. He felt as though his whole body was concentrating, as he held his breath and strained to listen into the thick blackness that stretched out beyond the reach of the torch. Everything was quiet; except for the occasional soft plink of dripping water.

'Hello? Is anybody there?' Max called, trying to keep the tremor from his voice.

His words fell into a pool of utter silence.

Then the sound came again, a low scratching scuttle echoing faintly through the passageway.

The stealthy rustle continued towards them, then stopped abruptly.

Max had the uneasy feeling that whatever it was could see the three of them huddled together in their shallow cocoon of precious light, but they couldn't see it; lurking somewhere in the darkness just beyond the reach of their torch.

He stared into the dense wall of darkness, his stomach clenching into a tight fist of fear. Then he took a hesitant step forward, and held the torch out, into the gloom.

Two small, bright, startled eyes immediately glittered close to the ground. It was a small, pale, frightened mouse.

Max took another half step forward and held the torch out, checking that there was nothing else hanging back in the shadows.

The mouse turned and scurried away into the darkness.

Max blew out a long breath. 'It's OK. There's nothing there,' he said, with more confidence than he actually felt.

'Phewww!' whispered Bodhie.

'This place gives me the creeps,' muttered Anna, 'It just seems to go on and on.'

'I know,' Max whispered. 'But let's keep going. At least for now.'

They set off again along the gloomy passageway, the rough stone floor with its broken foundations crunching softly beneath their feet. But no sooner had they walked another twenty paces, then a wall suddenly loomed out of the shadows ahead of them, cutting sharply across their path; the passageway suddenly diverged, splitting off to their left and right.

'Oh!' said Anna startled, 'which way do we go now?'

'I don't know,' said Max, looking hesitantly in both directions.

'Err, guys,' said Bodhie hesitantly. Ze was standing very still, staring transfixed at the wall. 'Look at this, it's — well, I think it's — some kind of map or maze.'

Max stepped forward. The torch crackled, illuminating a huge intricate square engraving that stretched across the wall in front of them. At first glance, it looked the same as all of the other carvings that adorned the walls and ceiling, but on closer inspection, Max could see that Bodhie was right. It appeared to detail a series of winding, twisting passageways that looped and cut across one another, diverging and weaving, crisscrossing and merging. However, unlike most other mazes, which led to one central point, this appeared to branch off in many directions, ending in many different places.

'But how can we work out our route, if we don't know where we need to get to?' said Max, puzzled.

'I don't know,' Bodhie hesitated. 'That's the problem. I'm not sure.'

Max looked around the map, his eyes searching the cryptic web of pathways and passages that led away from the two points where they stood. Only one passageway appeared to eventually lead to a large chamber; the rest appeared to finally conclude with some kind of wall that cut across their path, a dead-end.

'Look,' said Max, pointing towards the route that led to the chamber, 'It's got to be that one, hasn't it? It's the only one that actually looks like it leads to anything.'

'I think so,' Bodhie said uncertainly, his eyes still lingering on the map.

'Is there anything we can write on?' said Max, eyeing the labyrinth of winding twisting passageways and wondering how they could possibly remember the way.

'No, we didn't bring anything like that,' said Anna, eyeing the maze of passages grimly. 'I think we're going to have to try and remember it.'

'We'll have to do better than try,' said Max. 'If we get lost in there, we'll never find our way out again!'

'We could split the route up and each remembers a bit,' Anna suggested.

'There's something not quite right here,' interrupted Bodhie, eyes still fixed on the map.

Anna glanced towards Bodhie, 'Why? What do you mean?'

'Well, there are these two symbols,' Bodhie said, pointing at a passageway that appeared to end abruptly with a wall, somewhere near the centre of the map.

Max peered at the wall. Two strange spiky symbols had been neatly carved into the wall at the point where the passageway ended.

'But it's a dead-end,' said Anna.

'I know, but these symbols are the ancient language of the Hidden People. These two symbols here mean Ancient Heritage. Don't you see? That's what the Uroborologs are – that's what we call it. Our Ancient Heritage.'

Anna peered uncertainly at the wall and frowned. 'But it does look like a dead-end though,' she repeated.

'I know, but why would the symbols be there if it didn't mean anything?'

Anna looked doubtful, 'Isn't something as important as the Uroborologs more likely to be in a proper chamber or room though?' she said, pointing at the route that led to the large chamber.

'Maybe.' Bodhie hesitated, 'But those two symbols definitely mean "Ancient Heritage". I'm sure of it. My mum and dad made me study the ancient language as part of my schooling. And that's definitely what we call the Uroborologs. I know it seems odd, but if it doesn't mean anything then why is it on there?'

Max looked at the map thoughtfully. The two symbols were small and easy to miss in the complex labyrinth of winding passageways and tunnels, but Max felt sure that their existence on the map was not a mistake. Someone had very neatly and precisely carved the tiny symbols into the gap at the end of the passageway.

'Maybe it just looks like a dead-end,' he said tentatively. 'I mean if you wanted to hide something from everyone but the Hidden People, maybe you would hide it in the least obvious place and then leave some kind of sign that only a Hidden person would understand.'

Bodhie nodded, 'Exactly.'

'OK,' Anna shrugged. 'I suppose that makes sense.'

They spent a few minutes more in front of the map; each memorising a section of the winding route. Moments later, they set off through the temple's winding labyrinth of passageways, slowly but precisely moving through each bend and turn.

Deeper and deeper they travelled; the passageway twisted ahead of them disappearing into the gloom. The intricate hieroglyphs and carvings extended down the walls and ceiling, broken only occasionally by the coiled stone statues of fierce, fanged serpents, that would suddenly loom at them, out of the shadows.

'What is it with you guys and snakes anyway?' Max finally asked Bodhie, after another statue had lunged at them out of the darkness, making him jump.

Bodhie shrugged, 'It's just a symbol of our people. It means renewal and rebirth or something.'

Anna who was walking slightly ahead of them suddenly lurched to a halt.

A wall emerged from the shadows in front of them, cutting directly across their path.

'OH!' said Anna, 'So, it is a dead-end! I told you we should have gone the other way!'

Bodhie stared at the wall with a puzzled expression, 'I know, but that symbol, it just doesn't make any sense.'

Max looked around despondently. He reached out and touched the smooth carved surface of the wall. It felt solid and cool beneath his fingers.

'Wait. Look!' said Anna, suddenly pointing towards their feet.

Max stepped back from the wall and following the direction of Anna's gaze, shone the torchlight towards a dark shadowy patch at the base of the wall near their feet.

As the yellow crackling light swept down the wall illuminating the shadows, a gaping fanged mouth suddenly appeared before them. It was set into the base of the wall, the inside of the mouth had been carved away and there appeared to be a shadowy tunnel-like hole that disappeared into the throat.

Max leant down and held the torch close to the fanged mouth. A faint damp draft wafted up through the gap. The torch flickered. Max could see something stirring just inside the mouth. Hesitantly, he inched the torch closer. A dozen or so cockroaches and a giant centipede scuttled away into the shadows.

'Do you think that maybe we're supposed to climb into it?' Anna whispered.

'Maybe,' Max muttered, eyeing the gap

dubiously and thinking that she was probably right, but honestly, wishing that she wasn't.

'Would we fit?' said Bodhie, in a voice that sounded about as enthusiastic as Max felt.

'Unfortunately, yes,' said Max peering into the fanged gap. 'Do you think this could be it?'

'I don't know,' said Bodhie staring at the hole and frowning.

'We could go back and try the other route, I suppose,' said Anna.

'But this might be the right way,' said Max. 'I don't suppose the book was ever going to be just sitting here waiting for us to take it and besides, this tunnel must lead somewhere. It's got to be here for a reason.'

Anna nodded. 'You did say it wasn't going to be easy, Bodhie. Well, I guess there's no way of knowing unless we go down, is there?'

'OK,' said Max, looking up at them both from his crouched position on the floor next to the tunnel. 'I'll go first.'

'Are you sure?' said Bodhie. 'I'll go, you know,' ze hesitated. 'I know I couldn't swim, and I freaked out a bit on the bridge and everything, but I really don't mind doing this.'

'No, it's fine,' said Max, 'I'll shout up and let you know it's OK. Then you two can follow.'

Bodhie gave him a reluctant nod.

'Right,' Max said again, making sure that the Key and map were safely stowed away in his pockets. 'You better take this, then,' he said, handing Bodhie the torch. 'See you in a minute, I hope.'

Anna and Bodhie stood watching him pensively.

Then after flicking an unsuspecting cockroach out of the way, Max clambered through the gaping mouth on his hands and knees. The fangs scraped roughly across his back.

The passageway was damp, dark and narrow. His body filled almost all of the available space, blocking out virtually all of the light from the torch, which flickered and glowed faintly behind him.

Solid blackness loomed ahead. Dense and impenetrable.

Max twisted his head around and looked over his shoulder, scraping his head slightly on the roof as he did. He could see the reassuring glow of the torch illuminating Bodhie and Anna's apprehensive faces, framed between the fanged teeth that hung down from the entrance behind him.

Reluctantly, he turned away from the light and continued along the tight little tunnel, crawling and fumbling his way along. The stone felt cold, damp and rough beneath his hands and scraped at his knees, through the fabric of his trousers. A damp draft wafted up again from somewhere in the darkness up ahead.

'Are you OK? What can you see?' Anna's muffled voice called through the tunnel behind him.

'I'm fine, but I can't see anything, it's just black. Pitch black.' The tremble in his voice echoed back towards him in the darkness. Max swallowed hard, trying to remain calm.

Something scuttled away, brushing past his fingers and a brief image of the giant tarantula at the market, flitted through Max's mind. He tried to ignore it, refusing to think about what could be sharing the dark, confined space of the tunnel with him.

Then without warning, the rough hard floor suddenly ran out. His hands grappled emptiness, the tunnel disappeared, and he was falling, slipping and sliding down through dense empty blackness.

SAM KINI

Chapter 22
The Room with No Exit

'Aaaaaaaarrrrrrrrggggggghhh!' The scream was in his ears almost before it was out of his mouth.

Down and down Max spiralled and slid. Cold damp air rushed past him in the darkness.

Panicking, he thought of the Key, Travel Charts and map, and pictured them flying out of his pockets and bouncing off into the shadows. He grabbed hold of his pockets and tried desperately to clamp them shut, his elbows bumping and scraping against the sides of the tunnel as he hurtled by. Then as quickly as it had begun, the slide came to an abrupt finish and Max felt himself flying briefly through the air, only to land unceremoniously in a heap on a hard stone floor, a few feet from the tunnel's entrance.

Gathering himself, Max looked around, his eyes slowly adjusting to the light. It took a moment for him to register the significance of the fact that there was actually light in the room.

Daylight.

He was lying in a square stone room. Faint daylight was seeping down through two long stone shafts which fed into the ceiling to either side above him, casting a subdued grey light through the room.

The daylight was weak and looked to be some distance away, which meant, Max assumed, that they must be in some kind of underground chamber deep beneath the temple. Ornate hieroglyphs and carvings adorned the walls and a huge, engraved stone disk was set into the wall at the far side. The tunnel exit jutted sharply out from the wall behind him and was carved yet again, into the open shape of a serpent's fanged mouth, poised as if ready to strike.

Max heard a muffled yelp, followed moments later by a stifled scream, which meant, he thought, that Bodhie and Anna had probably followed him into the tunnel.

Moments later, they both crashed through the fanged mouth and landed in a heap on top of one another. They were followed seconds later by Anna's rucksack which shot through the mouth of the tunnel and bounced across the floor, before finally spinning to a halt halfway across the room near the wall.

'Uggghh,' said Anna picking herself up off the ground and rubbing her elbow, 'That was pretty grim.'

'So, you came then?' Max grinned. 'I thought you were supposed to be waiting for me to check things out first?'

'We heard you scream, so we thought we'd better come and rescue you,' said Bodhie, grinning. He looked around, 'Where do you think we are?'

'I have no idea, but at least there's light,' said Max, pointing to the ceiling. It was certainly an improvement he felt, on the endless shadowy passageway and the dark insect-infested tunnel.

'Just as well, cause I left the torch.' Bodhie shrugged and grinned, 'I had to leave it behind. I nearly killed myself trying to crawl along with it.'

'We'll manage,' said Max looking around. 'I can't see any sign of the book though.'

'Never mind the book. What about a door!' exclaimed Anna. She had retrieved the rucksack and was standing in the centre of the room, a mystified expression on her face.

There was a pause as the three of them surveyed the room in utter silence.

'Oh,' said Bodhie quietly.

It was true. Max couldn't understand why he hadn't noticed it before. He had been so relieved to be out of the cockroach-infested tunnel and the pitch black, that he hadn't spotted the most obvious thing – that there didn't appear to be a door or, in fact, any kind of exit from the room.

The room was comprised of four ornately carved stone walls, but it was completely empty, except for the serpent-fanged tunnel exit that protruded into the room behind him and a large circular stone disk that was engraved and set into a wall at the far side of the room.

Max looked around despondently. Moments ago, this place had seemed like a welcome relief from the dark, claustrophobic passageways and tunnels. Now, it seemed more like an elaborately designed cell.

'Well, we can't crawl back up that slide. It's too steep,' said Bodhie, peering back up into the gloomy tunnel.

'What about this circular disk thing?' said Max, wandering over to the far wall to inspect the strange, engraved stone that was carved into the wall.

Upon closer inspection, it looked remarkably like a Uroboros Key. At its centre was a snake that was curled around, its tail in its mouth and surrounding the snake were three rings or dials that were covered in symbols.

'It looks a bit like a Uroboros Key,' said Anna slowly. 'I wonder if it moves like one?' Reaching up, she stretched her hand out and touched the outermost ring, dragging at it gently with her fingertips. It clunked gently and then with a dull scraping sound, the outermost dial shifted down and to the right. 'I guess it is like a—'

She didn't get to finish. A dull grinding sound suddenly filled the room, as though some kind of ancient mechanism had slowly whirred into life.

Startled, Max and Anna looked at each other. Bodhie who had been walking towards them, suddenly stopped dead.

'I don't like the sound of this,' Bodhie said quietly. 'What did you just do?'

'I just turned the Key,' said Anna.

The dull grinding rumble was abruptly joined by a heavy scraping sound as though huge heavy stones were being slowly dragged across one another.

Panic swam to the surface of Anna's face. 'What is it? What's happening?' she asked, voice raised.

'I don't know,' said Bodhie, eyes sweeping about the room.

Max looked helplessly around them. There was nothing, just the tunnel exit and a series of patches on the floor where the heavy dust had been disturbed when they'd landed. He cast his eyes up to the faint circular tubes of light and then down again to the dusty floor. But something was different. The smudged dusty patches on the floor had changed – or rather, they'd moved. One of them was now partially covered by the wall. But then, that couldn't be right. Maybe he'd been mistaken.

The ancient grinding and scraping sound rumbled on.

Max looked around again and then back at the floor. But he wasn't mistaken. The patches looked different again. Suddenly, Max realised to his horror, that either the dusty patches were moving or–

'Oh, no!' he yelped, 'The walls are moving!'

'What!' said Anna and Bodhie in unison, their eyes widening with panic.

'The walls are moving – look!' said Max, pointing at the floor across the room and towards the first dusty patch, which was now almost entirely concealed by the wall.

Anna's jaw dropped. 'We're doomed!' she whispered.

Looking around, Max could now see that the wall that stood closest to them that housed the strange Uroboros Key and the tunnel wall appeared to be stationary. However, the two side walls were slowly, but very definitely drawing steadily towards them.

'Why? Why did you have to turn it?' said Bodhie, crossing the remaining expanse of the floor in two brisk strides and joining them in front of the Key.

'I just wanted to see if it moved, that's all. I didn't know anything was going to happen,' said Anna indignantly.

'When did you ever turn something on a Uroboros Key and nothing happened?' muttered Bodhie angrily.

'Well, to be fair, you don't generally expect the walls to start moving!' she snapped, looking flushed, 'And anyway, I didn't see you coming up with any bright ideas to get us out of here!'

'Arguing about this isn't helping!' Max cut in. 'We need to try and work out how to use this thing. If the Key started this, then maybe we can stop it.'

'Okay, you're right,' said Bodhie, hurriedly leaning forward to inspect the huge stone Key.

'They don't look like the same type of symbols that are on my grandad's Key,' Max said quickly.

'No, they're not the same. It's like before – this is our ancient language.'

'Can you read it?' urged Max, shooting a furtive glance over his shoulder at the rapidly encroaching walls.

'Sort of, but it just seems to be a lot of random words,' Bodhie said in a panicked voice. 'And I don't know which words we're supposed to select. I need to work it out.'

Max glanced quickly around the room again. He could see the walls moving steadily towards the two faint tubes of light in the ceiling, when that happened, they would be plunged into total darkness.

'Maybe if we just turn the Key back to where it was before, that will stop it?' he hurriedly suggested.

'Okay,' said Bodhie quickly. 'Which symbol was at the top before, Anna?'

'I-I think that it was this symbol,' Anna said in a small voice. She hesitantly pointed at a strange swirling symbol three spaces to the right on the outermost ring.

'You think or you're sure?' said Bodhie, hand hovering over the ring.

'I think... I'm sure. I-I don't know. I can't really remember, I'm sorry!'

'Okay, let's give it a go,' said Bodhie and ze twisted the dial sharply to the left, so that the swirling symbol lined up with the top.

Max held his breath and stared at the walls, willing them to stop.

There was a momentary pause, then the grinding rumble suddenly increased in intensity.

'Oh no!' cried Anna. She looked horrified.

Max looked desperately around the shrinking room, at the two walls that were steadily advancing towards them and then with a sinking feeling, up towards the two pale tubes of daylight.

'OK,' he said, turning back towards Bodhie and trying to remain calm. 'What else can it be, then?'

'I don't know,' Bodhie said, rubbing the symbols desperately for greater clarity, 'It's just a lot of random words.'

The dull grinding and scraping rumbled relentlessly around them.

'Okay, well what does it say? What are they?' said Max, shooting another hasty glance over his shoulder and noticing with dismay that one wall had almost reached the first tunnel of light now.

'Okay, well, temple, tree... err... bird, ancient, forest, fangs...'

'Temple of Fangs!' said Anna quickly. 'Could you configure it to say "Temple of Fangs"?'

'No, there's no "of",' said Bodhie, hurriedly scanning around the rings.

'OK, carry on,' said Max.

The light was beginning to dwindle in the room now, which meant Max knew that one of the walls was beginning to block out the first tube of light.

'Moon, serpent, aether, council.'

There was a sudden heavy thud, followed by a terrible scraping sound. Max turned sharply and saw that one of the walls had reached the protruding stone tunnel and was grinding and gnashing as it scraped and strained against the serpent's head. A huge fracture had appeared where the snake's head jutted out from the wall. It would hold the wall back, but not for long.

'Clock, hidden—'

'Hidden People!' shouted Max. 'Can you do that?'

'Erm... no, there's no People symbol and—'

'OK, carry on,' Anna interrupted.

There was a deafening crash and the sound of crunching stone.

Turning, Max saw that the snake's head had caved in, collapsing into the tunnel's entrance. The wall — still moving forward — had partially covered the blocked tunnel.

'Max!' Anna cried suddenly, 'The Key! We can use the Key to get out of here!'

'Of course!' yelped Max, grappling for the Key. How could he be so stupid as to forget?

He yanked the Key free from his pocket, fumbling to configure it in the fading light. There was no time to consider the Travel Charts, so he swiftly ran his finger around the edge, searching for a symbol that he recognised. The symbol for the world he and Anna had left yesterday morning when they had first set off to find the Book.

The Book.

Max's hand faltered on the Key.

'Hurry!' Anna said desperately.

Max hesitated. 'But if we go now, that's it. The tunnel's blocked, so we won't be able to come back. It'll be over.'

Anna glanced fearfully over her shoulder. 'Yes, but at least we won't get crushed to death, Max, and we don't even know if the book is definitely down here!'

'All this is down here for a reason, Anna. It's got to be here to protect something.'

'If the book is down here and we can't get to it, at least now Xegan won't be able to reach it either.'

'We don't know that for sure. He might. This could be our only chance.'

Anna and Bodhie looked at each other.

'Hurry up!' said Max glancing anxiously towards the second tube of light, 'We have to decide; we don't have much time!'

Anna gave Max a quick nod of agreement.

'OK,' said Bodhie in a panicked voice, 'But get the Key ready because I'm really not sure I'm going to be able to do this.' Ze turned swiftly back towards the Key, 'Right. Council, clock.'

'You've already said that,' Anna said urgently. 'What's next?'

'Shadows, covenant... err... key, secret,'

The light in the room was fading fast, casting a grey gloom throughout the room.

'History, book, heritage,' said Bodhie, squinting at the Key.

Max gave a start. 'Heritage!' he said suddenly. 'Ancient Heritage was the symbol before. Didn't you say that's what the Uroborologs are?'

'Of course!' yelped Anna. 'Try that, Bodhie.'

'That's not enough symbols,' Bodhie said desperately. 'I need three.'

The light in the room had almost completely extinguished. The wall which had not been hampered by the entrance to the tunnel stood just feet away from them now and was continuing relentlessly forward at its steady grinding pace.

Max gripped the Key tightly in his hands, his fingers lingering over the outermost dial. He knew that in a minute it would all be over. They would have to leave.

Bodhie leant forwards and peered at the Key. 'Wait!' ze yelped, 'There's a strange blank disk on the outside dial. It might be right after all!' Squinting in the fading light, ze rapidly turned the rings. The last dial swung around and slowly clunked into place.

'Max, we'll have to go in a second,' Anna

urged. 'We have to allow enough time for the Key to work.'

'Just a few more seconds,' said Max, 'Just so we're sure. Then we'll go.'

Bodhie took a hesitant step away from the Key and peered at them both through the gloom. Moments later, the room was plunged into complete darkness. There was a momentary pause, then the grinding rumble and sounds of scraping stone, commenced again. The blackness was absolute.

'I don't think it's worked,' Bodhie's voice faltered in the darkness. 'I'm really sorry Max. I think it's over.'

Max's heart sank. The light had extinguished and along with it, any chance of finding the Book and the truth. He felt as though all his hopes of answers had suddenly slipped away from him, disappearing into the darkness.

'It's OK,' he said quietly. 'You tried. We'd have stood no chance at all without you.'

'It's not your fault anyway, it's mine,' Anna said in a hollow whisper. 'I twisted the stupid thing...'

The grinding rumble echoed around them. The darkness was complete.

Max clutched the Key tightly in his hands, his fingers lingering hesitantly over the dial. He could feel the vibration of the walls. Almost sense them edging ever closer. Any moment now, he would have to use the Key.

'Come on, Max,' Anna urged.

But suddenly he became aware of a faint greyness. The blackness somehow seemed less thick. Max looked around numbly and blinked. A tiny crescent of pale light had appeared in the ceiling.

A small sliver of hope. His heart leapt.

He watched the faint chink of light for a moment, hardly daring to breath. The tiny crescent grew bigger, the chink of pale light brighter.

'It worked! Bodhie, you did it!' he yelled. 'Look – there's light. It's working!'

'What?'

'The walls are moving back!'

The crescent grew, allowing a faint grey light to slowly seep into the room. Then just as the walls had revealed the second tunnel of light, a second heavy scraping sound filled the room and a huge stone slab to the right of the giant Uroboros Key slowly depressed through the wall, before it slid sideways, disappearing out of sight. A pale window of light spilled into the room.

Diving towards the exit, they collapsed in a heap outside the door.

Max felt relief, warm, glorious, giddy relief, flood every cell and nerve in his body.

Bodhie crumpled into a heap, next to him on the floor, a huge grin on zer face. 'It worked! We did it! We actually did it!' ze mumbled, looking dazed.

'Not we; you did it, Bodhie.' Max gave Bodhie a relieved grin. 'We'd never have got out of there without you.'

Anna lunged towards them both, pulling them all into a clumsy embrace, 'I thought we were stuck in there! Bodhie, you were great!'

Bodhie reddened and grinned sheepishly.

Max lay still for a moment and blew out a long breath, his heart rate slowly returning to normal. Then he placed the Key back in his pocket, stood up and looked around. A dim light was seeping in from somewhere because he could just make out a vast shadowy cavern that opened up around them.

Rummaging through her rucksack, Anna retrieved a firelighter and quickly lit a torch that had been propped against the wall to their right. It sparked and burnt immediately with a strong bright flame, revealing a deep, rocky chasm.

They were standing on a rugged stone platform in a huge underground rocky cavity. In front of them, the platform dropped away sharply, disappearing down to shadowy hidden depths. A narrow stone bridge led away from the platform, stretching out across the jagged cavernous drop and towards a second stone platform which stood in the dim reaches at the far side of the cave.

The bridge had no rail or sidebars of any kind, consisting only of a narrow flat strip of stone that stretched out precariously across the vast shadowy chasm.

'Do you think that the Book's over there then?' whispered Max, pointing towards the far side of the cave.

'I guess so,' said Anna. She held the torch aloft and peered over the edge of the platform and down into the gloom below. The torch crackled, casting a yellow, flickering light across the rough cave walls.

'Well, we definitely can't go back,' said Bodhie, 'So, it looks like it might be the only way out of here.'

'Come on then,' said Anna, taking a step towards the bridge. 'Let's go see if it's there.'

'Hang on a second,' said Max, thinking of their experience on the rope bridge the previous day. 'Not so fast. Let's just check it out first.'

He took a hesitant step towards the bridge and stepped on it cautiously with one foot. The bridge didn't budge. 'It feels safe enough,' he said uncertainly, prodding it again, more firmly this time.

Anna crouched down on the platform next to Max and peered at the side of the bridge, 'It looks okay; it's really thick stone.'

'But what about the middle?' said Bodhie

eyeing the bridge mistrustfully, 'It was when we got to the middle last time that it all went horribly wrong.'

'We can't really see the middle from here,' said Anna. 'And to be honest, I don't think we've really got another option.'

They all lapsed into silence for a moment as they surveyed the bridge.

'We should cross together,' said Max firmly, 'That way, if anything happens, no one is going to be left behind.' It was one thing he decided, to be stuck on the bank of a river, but an entirely different level of problem being stuck down here in this vast shadowy underground cave on your own.

He shivered and then took several halting steps along the bridge. A stone rattled underfoot, then dropped into silence. From far, far below, came the echoing 'plink' of water.

Warily, Max peered over the edge and stared into the blackness below. 'We'd better be careful,' he whispered hoarsely. 'If we slip... well, put it this way... it looks really deep.'

They carefully stepped out in single file and began to shuffle their way slowly across the narrow strip of the bridge. Nobody spoke. To either side of them, the cave plunged away sharply, disappearing down into the shadows and broken only occasionally by jagged rocks that jutted sharply out of the darkness.

At the far side of the chasm, the stone platform gradually came into view; it was set into an alcove, carved out of the rough-hewn walls. As they gradually drew closer, Max could see that a raised stone step stood at the centre of the platform. Sitting on top of this step was something huge.

Max cautiously inched his way forward along the last stretch of the bridge. He stared at the enormous, hunched shape, his heart hammering in his chest. It looked like a huge stone statue, carved into the shape of a crouching man.

Max eyed the stooped figure from the edge of the bridge and felt his pulse begin to quicken. The statue was sitting cross-legged, its back hunched forward, hands on knees, as though it carried the burden of some great weight which pressed down heavily upon its shoulders. In fact, Max was certain, something large and square was pressing down heavily upon its shoulders.

Max's stomach squeezed with nervous excitement. 'Look!' he whispered hoarsely. 'There's something on its back.'

'I know!' Anna said breathlessly.

They reached the platform and eagerly crossed the expanse in three brisk strides, skidding to a halt directly in front of the statue.

Max stared at the statue and blinked. Something large and square was resting on its shoulders. But it wasn't a book.

ANCIENT SECRETS

SAM KINI

Chapter 23
The Second Key

They stood together in silence together, momentarily lost for words.

Max blew out a long breath and frowned. He stared at the engraved stone tablet, trying hard to fight his disappointment.

A snake had been carved into the surface of the tablet. It looped around the edge of the stone in a thick circular coil. Inscribed into the centre, were a series of strange spiky symbols. Max recognised them immediately as being the same as those that had covered the Key in the previous room. The symbols were the ancient language of the Hidden People.

'Oh!' said Anna sounding deflated. 'Wha-? Where's the Uroborologs then?'

Bodhie fell silent for a moment.

'Were – we – wrong? It is about the Book, isn't it?' Max asked cautiously. He was trying hard to fight his disappointment. Bodhie had said that it wouldn't be easy, that there was a chance that it might not be here.

'Oh no,' Bodhie said slowly, still staring at the tablet. 'We were right. We were definitely right. This whole thing is definitely about the Uroborologs. But it isn't here.'

'I can see that!' Anna exclaimed gloomily, 'So, where is it? What does it say?'

'Well, it doesn't really make any sense. It's a sort of riddle.'

'A riddle?!' Max repeated, 'Well what does it say? What kind of riddle?'

Bodhie shrugged and then hesitantly, ze read:

You seek our Ancient Heritage,

But your journey is not yet complete.

A gate guards the key to our secret,

Where shadows and light pyramid meet.

'That's it? So, what does that mean?' said Anna, flatly.

Bodhie frowned thoughtfully, 'I really don't know.' Ze paused. 'I guess it does confirm something, though.'

'Like what?' said Anna.

'That we're on the right track and that we now know for sure that Xegan is searching for the Uroborologs.'

Bodhie's words hung in the air between them

for a moment.

Max nodded slowly, feeling his heart lift a little. Bodhie was right. They had made it this far. Maybe it wasn't the book yet, but it did prove that at least they were on the right path to finding it.

A sudden heavy thud echoed through the cave directly behind them jolting Max from his thoughts. Max spun around and to his utter horror, found himself looking straight into two huge red unblinking eyes. In an instant, a huge, clawed hand reached out, gripping his shoulder savagely. Max felt sharp talons dig into his shoulder, piercing the skin. Seconds later, he was yanked off his feet and he felt himself being thrown across the cave. He hit the wall with a dull thud that knocked the breath from his chest, and he slumped to the floor. Pain seared up his right arm and shoulder and his hip ached agonisingly. He gasped, winded. A wave of blackness threatened to engulf him.

They were here. Valac and another Mothman had entered the cave. Where and how, he didn't know.

Horror washed over him.

Gulping down air, Max fought off another wave of blackness. He couldn't lose consciousness; couldn't go under. If he fainted now, the thought was terrifying.

Pain seared up his right arm again. He could taste a metallic trickle of blood in his mouth. He blinked hard and took another deep breath, willing himself to focus.

From his crumpled position on the floor, he looked out across the platform. Anna and Bodhie were facing Valac, their faces frozen in silent terror. Max could see that they had taken a step away from Valac, but the raised step and statue were behind them and they had nowhere to go. They were stuck between Valac and the stone tablet.

Valac stepped forward menacingly and let out a deep rasping, rattling breath.

Then in an instant, raising his clawed hand, he lunged towards them.

Bodhie dived towards Anna, his arm shot out and ze grabbed her arm. Max had a brief glimpse of them diving sideways towards the edge of the platform before they vanished in mid-air.

Valac let out a deep, shuddering scream, filled with loathing and contempt and lunged forwards savagely, slashing at the place where Bodhie and Anna had just disappeared.

There was a stifled scream that sounded like Anna.

Valac lunged towards the sound of the scream, slashing at the air ferociously again.

Terror washed over Max. He knew if any of those swipes found their mark, it would kill them, invisible or not, they could all easily die here.

He tried to think. They needed to leave now. They needed a plan.

Glancing up, he could see from his slumped position on the floor that both Mothmen seemed to have momentarily forgotten about him. Valac was studying the stone tablet, whilst the second Mothman was prowling around the cave, clicking faintly as he searched for Anna and Bodhie. He could feel the heavy round shape of the Key lying beneath him, in his pocket.

His heart hammering in his chest, Max managed to shift very slightly and slowly slip his hand under his leg. He eased his hand into his pocket; his fingers felt the hard round shape of the Key.

But something was wrong. Very wrong.

A sharp edge ran down the centre of the Key. He ran his finger over the hard ridge, tracing its shape. Confused. The Key shifted apart slightly.

Max swallowed hard, feeling a cold dread settle inside him. No wonder his leg ached so horribly. The Key was cracked.

They were trapped.

Max felt a hand silently reach out and touch his arm. He knew that it would be Anna or Bodhie. He knew what they expected. This was their perfect moment.

Except that it wasn't.

Max felt sick.

Two misty white forms slowly faded back into view. Bodhie and Anna were crouched next to him on the floor. Bodhie's tired eyes searched Max's expectantly.

Max looked away, he didn't know what to say. He felt as though he had let them down. The Key was his responsibility, their only means of escape; he should have taken better care of it.

He glanced quickly towards Valac. Valac was standing in the centre of the platform and had lifted the stone tablet into the air; his fiery bulbous eyes were studying the tablet carefully. With a sinking feeling, Max realised suddenly that they'd leave, they'd take the tablet with them and they'd work out the clue. The three of them would be left stuck in the cave, Xegan would get the book and everything would have been a waste, all their efforts, his grandad's death. Everything. Anger and frustration boiled inside him. His fingers touched his pocket, lingering over the fractured shape of the broken Key. There had to be something he could do. There had to be a way out.

He glanced quickly around the platform again. But there was nothing. Just the jagged cave walls that arched around them and the sheer drop where the edge of the platform plunged away sharply, disappearing into the darkness below.

Then a thought occurred to him. His eyes fell on Valac again. There was something, he realised suddenly, that didn't quite make sense. If there really was no way out of the chasm, then how was Valac here? His heart hammering in his chest, Max glanced quickly around the cave again. Valac was studying the stone tablet and was momentarily distracted. The second Mothmen was still on the bridge, his back towards them. The three of them would go unnoticed, but not for long. He cast his eyes desperately around the chasm, ignoring the confused expressions on both Anna and Bodhie's faces.

Then suddenly he saw it and Max's heart skipped a beat. Valac's Key was balanced on the edge of the step furthest away from them. Next to his feet.

Max swallowed; to get to the Key, he would have to first get past Valac. The beginnings of an idea quickly began to form in his mind. Looking back towards Anna and Bodhie, Max noiselessly rose to his feet. Pain seared up his arm again and he gritted his teeth, wincing with pain. His eyes never leaving Valac, his hand slowly crept to his pocket. Easing the two halves of the Key out, he silently held them towards Anna and Bodhie.

Bodhie's jaw dropped. Anna looked at him in horror.

Putting his finger to his lips, he silently pointed towards the Key resting on the platform at Valac's feet.

The blood drained from Anna's face. She

stared at Max in shocked disbelief.

Reaching back into his pocket, Max slowly pulled out one of the Poca smoke screens that they had taken from Bron's shop.

'Stay here,' he mouthed silently to them both.

Anna shook her head slowly, her eyes widening in horror.

Ignoring the fear in their eyes, Max turned away and looked back towards Valac. He knew it was risky. But what option did they have? If he didn't do it, then Valac would get the tablet, Xegan would get the Book and they'd probably die here.

Taking a deep breath, Max quickly pressed the release valve and tossed the smoke screen across the floor in the direction of Valac's feet. He hoped that the smoke screen worked properly on Mothmen and that those enormous red bulbous eyes didn't somehow have extra capabilities which meant they could see through fog. The thought of them still being able to see, whilst he couldn't...

The Poca skittered across the floor, hitting the platform with a gentle clink. There was a soft bang and a burst of thick grey smoke shot from the shiny disc filling the chasm. Valac screamed angrily.

Pushing the thoughts from his mind, Max dived into the rapidly expanding wall of smoke without looking back, leaving Anna and Bodhie standing horrified behind him.

The smoke swirled thickly around him. But Max knew that whilst the fog should give him some protection, it also brought him danger. It would be all too easy to lose his sense of direction and not find the Key or to find the Key but not be able to find his way back to Anna and Bodhie. He could easily overshoot the edge of the platform plunging to the rocks below or even worse he could stumble straight into Valac.

Forcing himself to ignore his fears, Max tried to focus on what he needed to do. He had to find the Key and get back to Anna and Bodhie before the smoke started to disperse. The problem was, the Key was behind Valac and he didn't know exactly how long the smoke would last.

Max stepped forward. A darker solidness loomed ahead of him and crouching low, he threw himself towards it, at what he hoped was Valac's legs. It was. Catching him unexpectedly, Max felt Valac's huge frame stumble back, then overbalance, toppling backwards.

An ear-piercing shriek rang out through the cave. Something heavy and solid, which Max assumed must be the tablet, landed with a dull thud nearby.

His heart hammering in his chest, Max fumbled blindly along the edge of the step, his hands reaching out desperately into the mist. He could hear Valac lumbering around blindly behind him, screeching with anger. He flinched, recoiling from the sounds and expecting the sharp retaliation of Valac's claws to reach him at any moment.

His fingers brushed against something, nudging it slightly along the step. He snatched it up quickly, his fingers closing triumphantly around its welcome circular shape. Then, clutching the Key and wincing with pain, Max staggered to his feet, desperate now to find Anna and Bodhie.

The smoke was beginning to thin, and he could make out the vague shape of the huge stone statue in front of him.

Stepping forward, his foot hit something hard. Looking down, Max could see the faint shadowed outline of the tablet on the floor. He hesitated. He could hear the sound of Valac lumbering around somewhere to his right. He probably only had moments now to make it back to where Anna and Bodhie were before the smoke dispersed and Valac would be able to see him.

Wincing with pain, Max bent down, and then quickly and deliberately shoved the stone tablet towards where he hoped the edge of the platform would be. He knew that he was taking a risk, that it would only make Valac even angrier. But with the tablet, Xegan might still be able to find the Book.

The tablet dragged and scraped as he desperately urged it forward across the hard stone surface. Then, suddenly the tension released, and he felt it topple forward, disappearing down through the swaths of mist and into the giant shadowy cavity below. Sounds of splintering and shattering stone as it tumbled and crashed over the jagged rocks, sounded through the cave.

Valac roared.

Turning around, Max could see that the smoke was quickly dissipating and losing its denseness. To his right he could see the dark solid mass of Valac's huge frame. Max knew that if he could now see Valac, Valac could probably also see him. His heart in his mouth, Max charged across the platform and in the direction of what he hoped was Anna, Bodhie and the wall. His hands found rough cold stone. He fumbled his way along, afraid that he wouldn't be able to find them, but too scared of alerting Valac to call out to them through the mist.

Suddenly a hand reached out, grabbing his arm. Max jumped, his head jerking around. Anna and Bodhie's frightened faces suddenly appeared through the mist towards him. Their eyes searched his, scared and expectant. But there was no time to explain. Lifting the Key close to his face, he quickly scanned around the dials, frantically searching each symbol for a combination he recognised.

Max stared at the Key for a moment and swallowed. A fresh wave of panic washed over him. The Key looked different. He hadn't even considered this. A fourth dial ran around the outer edge of this Key covered in a strange series of numbers. Numbers he could read but had no idea how he should configure. Frantically he thought back to the book of Travel Charts. He couldn't remember there being any numbers on any of the World locations. He had only ever seen symbols.

There was a loud thud from somewhere close by. Swallowing down a fresh wave of panic, Max thought fast and speedily began to line up the first three dials.

A haunting high-pitched scream pierced the cave.

Turning, Max saw Valac looming towards them out of the mist. 'Hold on to me,' he whispered hoarsely, clutching the Key firmly between his hands.

Valac took a second step towards them, clicking gently. Tendrils of mist lingered around him, curling and wafting around his huge frame and spiny wings. His eyes focused on them triumphantly, blazing savagely with contempt and pure rage.

Max felt the grip of Anna and Bodhie's hands tighten around his arm. Anna gasped.

Max's stomach lurched with fear. Panic rose in his throat. He swallowed it down and clutched the Key tightly, willing it to move.

The second Mothmen suddenly loomed out of the mist to Valac's right.

The snake moved and slowly began to wind its way around the inside of the Key.

As though suddenly comprehending what was about to happen, Valac shrieked with rage.

The snake continued to slowly revolve. Max felt the stirrings of the familiar tug deep inside his stomach.

In a heartbeat, Valac flew at them, fury and hatred boiling in his eyes. Razor-sharp claws outstretched. Reaching.

'No!' screamed Anna.

Max felt his feet abruptly leave the floor. Then they were swirling up into the ice-cold nothingness, a raging high-pitched shriek echoing after them in the darkness.

SAM KINI

Chapter 24
The Clue

They landed, moments later on a hard rocky surface.

Max lay on his back for a moment, dazed. He blinked, watching the bright white lights dissolve around them, his heartbeat gradually slowing. Then suddenly he remembered the strange Key and sat up with a start. He groaned; his arm throbbed, and his hip ached.

Blinking and squinting in the bright sunlight, he peered apprehensively around the landscape but was relieved to see that they were once again sitting on the wide, rocky, dry plain where he and Anna had spent the night when they'd first escaped from Valac.

The deserted rocky expanse stretched away from them in every direction, leading to the sandy, rust-coloured hills located in the distance off to their right and the dense green line of trees, which signified the edge of the oasis where they had camped, off to their left.

'H-he's – not – here, is he?' stammered Anna. She sat bolt upright and looked very pale.

Max met her eyes and swallowed, 'No, I don't think so.'

'I was so scared when he flew at us like that... I thought he'd make it through with us... like the little tribesman did.'

Max nodded weakly. His legs and arms trembled, and he felt sick with relief.

Bodhie also sat bolt upright, rubbing his head absently and looking completely dazed. 'I didn't think we were going to make it, then. That was far too close!'

Max nodded, 'I know. When I felt in my pocket and the Key had broken...'

'I know. I didn't know what we were going to do. I wanted to make us invisible again, but I couldn't. I just didn't have the strength.'

They all fell silent for a moment, whilst the enormity of what could have just happened settled on them.

'How did you get it? The Key?' Bodhie stared at him in disbelief.

Max shrugged, 'I was just lucky, that we had the Pocas and that it worked and Valac couldn't see me...'

'But what happened? How did you actually get the Key? I mean it was behind Valac!'

Max shrugged for a second time, 'I sort of ran into his legs and managed to catch him off guard. He fell over, so I was able to grab the Key...' His voice trailed away.

'You knocked Valac over!' said Bodhie incredulously, eyes wide.

'We kept hearing all of these terrible crashes,' exclaimed Anna. 'We didn't know what was happening... We thought that maybe Valac had got you!'

Max gave a stiff nod, 'I thought Valac might have got me too, and then I didn't know whether I was going to be able to find my way back to you both again.'

'I can't believe we made it out of there alive,' said Anna, shaking her head again in disbelief. 'And we got the clue.' She paused, a concerned look suddenly passing across her face. 'We can remember it all, can't we?'

Bodhie nodded.

Max sighed and breathed out deeply, feeling every muscle in his body slowly unravel and relax. They'd made it.

The sun was high in the sky and Max looked up blinking for a moment, suddenly aware of the sun's bright intensity after the endless, dark underground passageways and chambers that they had just left behind. He closed his eyes and tilted his face towards the sun, basking in the comforting warmth.

'How did you know to come here?' asked

Bodhie after a moment. 'I was really scared with it being Valac's Key that we were going to end up in the Forbidden Lands or something worse.'

'This is the place we accidentally came to, when we escaped from Valac the other day,' said Max opening his eyes. 'We camped over there.' He pointed towards the dense green line of forest that marked the beginning of the oasis. As he did, pain shot up his arm again and he winced.

'Are you OK?' Anna said frowning.

Max moved his arm tentatively again and grimaced. He could feel each of the tiny puncture holes where Valac's claws had dug into his skin. They smarted and stung, every time his T-shirt moved over the tiny wounds and there was a dull ache in his hip, where he had fallen on the Key.

'I'm all right,' Max lied. He knew that telling them anything different would only worry them and besides, everything seemed to be moving OK, so he decided that it couldn't be too bad.

'Mmmm,' said Anna, looking thoroughly unconvinced. 'Well, you don't look it. Your lips have gone grey. Is that what happened when Valac grabbed you? Let me see.'

'I think so,' said Max. 'But honestly, it'll be fine.'

'Let me see,' Anna repeated in a firm voice.

Max hesitated then peeled back his T-shirt. A series of bloody puncture marks where the talons had dug into his skin and an ugly dark purple bruise stretched around both sides of his shoulder.

Anna sucked in her breath sharply and frowned, 'They look quite deep you know, Max.'

Bodhie frowned, 'Anna's right. That doesn't look great Max. We need to treat that with something.'

'I know, but we haven't got anything, have we? Look, it'll be fine. I don't think anything's broken. It just aches and stings a bit. Anyway, we should probably go and set up camp, you know if we're going to stay here for the night,' he added.

Anna's eyes narrowed suspiciously. 'Mmmm,' she said again, clearly not at all convinced.

They set off walking across the rocky plateau towards the forest.

'Do you think there's a chance they might still be trapped in there?' Anna said hopefully as they walked. 'You know, now that we've got their Key?'

'You mean Valac?' said Bodhie thoughtfully. 'I don't know... maybe... Who knows what Valac is capable of though... Maybe they still managed to get out.'

'Do you think Valac managed to read the clue?' said Anna.

Bodhie frowned, 'No, they wouldn't understand the ancient language. Their only hope would be if they manage to get the tablet out of the cave and then somehow work it out later.'

'Well, they definitely didn't manage to do that,' said Max.

'How do you know that?' questioned Bodhie.

'I forgot to tell you both. I pushed the tablet off the platform and down to the rocks below. It smashed into bits... well at least, I think it did... It certainly made a lot of noise.'

Bodhie's jaw dropped.

Anna grinned, 'Brilliant!' So, there should be no way of Valac and Xegan working out the clue and finding the Book then.'

'I'm not so sure,' said Max shaking his head. 'Something just doesn't quite make sense in all of this.'

'Why? What do you mean?' said Anna frowning.

'Well, how did they find us today? How did they even get in there? They didn't follow us down all of those passageways and they certainly didn't come through that blocked tunnel and into that room with the moving walls. So they must have used the Key to get in there – but I thought you could only configure Keys to take you to the places listed on the Travel Charts. I thought you said that because of the Covenant, all of the Keys could only be configured for pre-agreed locations. I'm certain,' said Max tugging the small book of Travel Charts free from his pocket, '...that there isn't going to be a location in here that says, "secret underground cave beneath the Temple of Fangs". So how did they get in?'

Bodhie nodded slowly and frowned, 'I've been wondering about that too. Let me see that Key.'

Max handed it to him. 'And that's the other thing: that Key doesn't look anything like my grandad's.'

Bodhie stopped abruptly on the plateau. Frowning deeply, ze slowly turned the Key over and stared at it.

'No, it isn't the same,' ze said quietly. 'This is not good. Not good at all.'

'Why?' said Anna.

'Well, I think this explains why the Key Maker disappeared,' Bodhie said hesitantly. 'They must be using him to change the Keys, so that you can use them to travel anywhere, to any location, in any universe.'

'But I thought that wasn't allowed. I thought the Covenant didn't allow it,' said Max.

'It doesn't. The Ancient Council strictly forbids it. Keys are only allowed to be configured to travel to the list of pre-agreed locations listed in the Travel Charts. They must've got the Key Maker to attach this extra dial so that they can put in extra coordinates; not just the pre-agreed ones that take you to the proper agreed landing locations. This is really, really, bad.'

Anna shuddered, 'So, if Xegan and the Mothmen have these, then that means they could just turn up – everywhere and anywhere at any time?'

'Yes,' Bodhie said nodding, 'I think that's exactly what this means. Xegan and Valac can travel anywhere, to any location, in any universe instantly.'

The three of them stared at the Key warily.

'It doesn't have one of those return home switches, does it?' Max asked suddenly. He couldn't imagine anything worse than suddenly finding that they had unexpectedly returned to Valac's home or cave or wherever it was that Mothmen lived.

Anna's head shot up and she gave Max a horrified look.

Bodhie quickly flicked over the Key. 'No,' ze said, sounding immensely relieved.

'Well, that's something I suppose,' muttered Anna.

Max turned this news over in his mind. 'Well, at least that explains how they got into the temple then. What it doesn't explain is how they found it... and found us.'

'Why? What do you mean?' said Anna.

'Well, even if they found a way of being able to configure the Key to travel to any location, how did they know where we were? How did they know the temple was even there?'

Anna and Bodhie stared at Max.

'Look, they couldn't have already known where the temple was,' Max continued. 'If they did, they would have gone after the Uroborologs years ago, wouldn't they? And anyway, why chase after us for the map, if they already knew where it was? It would be pointless.'

Anna's eyebrows raised in alarm. 'So, how do you think they found us? Do you think they're following us now?' she added, looking around suddenly anxious.

'I don't know,' said Max, 'It does seem like the only explanation.'

Bodhie frowned and nodded. 'I suppose they have to be, otherwise, how do they keep appearing all of the time and finding us?'

But that wasn't right, Max thought suddenly. They weren't appearing all of the time – just some of the time.

'Actually, that doesn't make sense,' he corrected himself. 'If Valac was following us all of the time, I think we'd know. I mean if they knew where we were right now, wouldn't they be here?

It's almost like they know exactly where we are some of the time, but then, when we shift worlds, it's like we throw them off or something.'

Bodhie's silvery eyes locked on Max and he frowned, 'Maybe we do. Maybe that's exactly what happens. But if we manage to keep losing them, then how do they keep finding us again?'

'I don't know,' Max shook his head. 'That's what I don't get. There's something we're missing. Something we don't understand yet.'

They walked along in silence for a few moments, lost in their thoughts. The dense green line of forest drew steadily closer.

'I really think that bird might have something to do with it,' Max said carefully after a while. The thought had been turning over in his mind. 'I know you think I'm crazy, but it does keep appearing all over the place, as though it's watching us.'

'Not that black bird again!' said Anna rolling her eyes. 'Max, I don't think you realise how many black birds there are out there.'

'It's not like that,' said Max, throwing Anna an indignant glance, 'It's different. I can tell it's the same one.'

'Mmmm,' muttered Anna dubiously.

'I'm not even sure that birds could be trained to follow and track you like that, Max.' Bodhie added tentatively.

'It might not be from here,' said Max bristling slightly, 'And anyway, I thought that you said we didn't know what Xegan and Valac were capable of...'

Anna and Bodhie fell silent, but Max could tell that they weren't convinced. He knew it sounded crazy, but he could tell that it was the same bird and he didn't like the way it kept suddenly reappearing and in completely different places. He couldn't explain it, but he just knew that the bird was somehow linked to all this.

'Your eyes went really silver today, Max,' Bodhie said later. They had set up camp in the same clearing that Max and Anna had stayed in two nights earlier and were sitting around the campfire huddled under their blankets. They had eaten a supper of some of the bread, a pale crumbly cheese, nuts, some sweet purple spiky plums and a green banana-like fruit that Anna had stolen from her uncle Bron's shop. Behind them, the sun was fading fast, casting long thin shadows through the trees.

'Did they?' said Max thoughtfully.

'When we were in the cave and Valac arrived...'

Max nodded slowly, 'I guess I was really angry. Maybe that's why,' he said, after a moment.

'Well, I don't think I've ever heard of anyone, who wasn't a Hidden Person, whose eyes changed so much before.'

Anna nodded, 'They were a lot more silver than when they changed last time, Max. They were sort of greyer before.'

'I think that might mean that your abilities with aether are growing Max.'

Max hesitated, 'Or maybe it just means I was a lot more scared than last time.' He threw another branch onto the fire and started prodding it with a stick.

'That's how it starts with Hidden People, Max. The eyes change and then it develops from there.'

'But what develops? I mean, I understand that the Nix can shapeshift and Hidden People can make themselves invisible and stuff, but what can humans do?'

'Well,' Bodhie continued haltingly, 'I don't really know. The only other human that I've heard of that has this kind of skill with aether, is Xegan.'

'I have heard of other humans having it, but you're right, it is really rare.' said Anna.

'Well, my grandad's eyes changed and my dad's did too.'

'So, what could they do?' said Bodhie.

Max fell silent for a moment, 'I have absolutely

no idea. My dad died when I was really young and my grandad — well — he never told me about any of this.' He broke off, feeling the familiar knot of sadness, anger and resentment settle in his stomach again.

'But do you remember your grandad being able to do anything strange or unusual?' added Anna.

'No, nothing whatsoever. I expect he just kept it hidden from me like everything else,' Max said bitterly. He couldn't believe how much his grandad had kept from him and in doing so, how little he had prepared him for all of this.

An awkward silence fell between them. Bodhie and Anna exchanged a glance.

The fire crackled and spat, casting flickering shapes around the camp.

Max stared gloomily ahead. He felt oddly cut off; his mind full of an endless stream of questions; questions that seemed to have no answer.

'So, what do you think we should do next then?' Bodhie's voice was full of false brightness.

'Well, we're going to solve that clue, of course,' said Anna. 'What was it again?'

'Well, I think it went like this,' Bodhie's eyes were shut as he recited,

You seek our Ancient heritage,

But your journey is not yet complete.

A gate guards the key to our secret,

Where the shadows and light pyramid meet.

'What do you think it means?' said Max, tugging his thoughts back to the conversation.

'I have absolutely no idea,' said Anna, shaking her head and stifling a yawn.

They lapsed into a thoughtful silence together.

Anna stifled a second yawn and then flopped back exhaustedly onto the ground. She put her hands behind her head and stared at the night sky just visible through the branches of the trees. 'It's no use,' she said after a moment, 'My brain's just not working! I'm sooo tired; I'm just too exhausted to think! Maybe we should just sleep on it.'

Bodhie nodded and stifled a yawn, 'I agree.' Ze lay down and tugged the blanket around zer shoulders, 'Not exactly a normal day, was it Max?'

'No, not exactly,' said Max, shaking his head and staring into the fire.

He sat in silence for a long time, feeling the warmth and light of the fire gently flicker across his face, mesmerised by the bright dancing shapes of the flames and listening to the rhythm of Anna and Bodhie's breathing slowly become longer and deeper.

He rubbed his T-shirt feeling the reassuring round shape of the amulet resting against his chest. Today had been their third narrow escape from Valac in as many days and he still couldn't quite believe that they'd managed to get out of the underground cave. Anna was right; Valac had been seconds from reaching them and if he had...

Max shivered; maybe there was something protective about this amulet after all.

He watched Anna and Bodhie sleeping contentedly under their blankets. The firelight gently danced across their peaceful faces.

It was only then that he realised with a sudden, sickening jolt that today had been his grandad's funeral.

SAM KINI

Chapter 25
The Near Miss

Max woke at dawn, feeling stiff and sore. He had a huge purple-blue bruise on his hip and another on his shoulder that seemed to have grown overnight and now stretched right down his arm, reaching his elbow. But nothing felt broken, so he decided that he was still okay.

He rolled over and eased himself up into a seating position, making sure that he didn't put too much weight on his arm and being careful not to wake Anna and Bodhie.

The soft pink glow of dawn was just visible on the horizon through the trees and a couple of strange-sounding birds were chirruping happily in the trees close by, greeting the light of the new day. The fire had gone out during the night, leaving a small heap of charred blackened wood that was still smoking faintly.

Max sat looking at the fading wisps of smoke for a moment, wondering whether he should start to make the fire again, when suddenly Bodhie's eyes flickered open.

Ze looked at Max sleepily and smiled.

'Did I wake you?' whispered Max.

'No, just a light sleeper,' Bodhie said simply as

ze sat up slowly and yawned.

Max eyed Bodhie's pale blonde hair that was stuck up in all directions, creased face and pale grey eyes and wondered for a moment how tired and scruffy they must all be looking after sleeping rough. He rubbed his hands through his own hair realising that it felt matted and dirty and tried to flatten the tufts.

'I was thinking during the night,' Bodhie whispered, interrupting Max's thoughts, 'That now that we have the Travel Charts, we can check where we are. We can see what world this is.'

'Of course!' Max grinned. He quickly pulled the small brown leather-bound book out of his pocket and began flicking through the pages. Each page in the book began with a World symbol and detailed an intricate little grid that contained a series of symbol combinations and the locations that they related to. It took him a moment of flicking back and forth through the book to find the World symbol that matched the one he had configured on the Key the previous day.

There, neatly inscribed were the words 'Barren Lands'.

Then scanning down the little grid of Region and Location symbols for the Barren Lands he found the two symbols that he knew matched the ones he had configured on the middle and outer rings of the Key.

There, neatly inscribed into the table were the words,

Great Rift Plateau

(For travel to the Grimbald Forest and Van Geld Crystal mines)

Max held the open book excitedly towards Bodhie, indicating the symbols and location on the intricate little grid. 'Look!' he whispered, trying not to wake Anna. He knew that he had heard of the Barren Lands before, but he couldn't remember when and, more troubling, he couldn't remember whether it had meant something good or bad.

Bodhie's serious grey eyes studied the page for a moment, then ze nodded. 'There's not much in the Barren Lands. I've read a bit about this place. There's some mining here for crystals and precious stones but there are very few creatures that live here. I suppose that's why it's called the Barren Lands. I think that means we're pretty safe here.'

Max nodded, then closed the little leather book of charts, safely stowing it back in his pocket. He felt oddly relieved. He didn't think that he'd actually been expecting to find that they'd be staying in the Forbidden Lands, but he still felt relieved to have it confirmed all the same.

'I've got it!' said Anna, her eyes suddenly

flickering open, 'I think I know where it is!'

'Wha-? Weren't you just asleep?' said Bodhie, startled.

'Yes, but anyway – look,' she said, sitting up and leaning forward excitedly.

'Wow! When you said sleep on it, you really meant sleep on it!' said Bodhie, sounding bemused.

Ignoring his comment Anna continued, 'Right, so anyway, I've been thinking about the clue and... well... I've got an idea...' Her eyes gleamed.

'Go on,' said Max, 'What is it?'

'Well...' She shut her eyes and recited, '"You seek our Ancient Heritage, but your journey is not yet complete." OK, so that bit is pretty straightforward. "A gate guards the key to our secret, where the shadows and light pyramid meet." So, I was thinking about the light pyramid part and obviously, the pyramids that immediately come to mind are the buildings of the Elders and Ancient Council in Lucem and at first, I dismissed that as I thought that it was too obvious. But then I was thinking about what the gate part meant and I remembered that as well as the main archway into the pyramid courtyard, several smaller gated archways lead out of the courtyard and into the side streets. Do you remember Max? We went through one of them the other day when we travelled back to go to Irin's and we accidentally landed in the middle of the courtyard. Anyway, I remembered that they have various engravings and things carved into the stone around each archway. I think they're meant to represent the different groups within the Five Kingdoms. So, there's a gateway for each group: the Yeti's, the Buru, the Nix etc. It's supposed to represent the meeting together of the Five Kingdoms or Ancient Council or something... I forget exactly. But anyway, there is clearly an archway for the Hidden People too and I think engraved into the top of it, if I'm not mistaken, is a Key, like a Uroboros Key – like the one yesterday in that room. Sooo–' she said, pausing for a second to take a deep breath, 'We've got the gate, the key and the pyramids. What do you think? How far did you two get?'

She stopped and looked expectantly at them both, looking decidedly pleased with herself.

Max and Bodhie looked at each other and laughed.

'Well, we er – well, we hadn't really started yet to be honest,' said Max grinning. 'Did you seriously think of all that while you were asleep?' he added incredulously.

'No, I woke up in the night and I couldn't get it out of my head. It took me ages to doze back off again.' She shrugged, 'So, anyway, what do you think?'

Max thought about it for a moment. It certainly sounded believable enough.

'I don't know,' said Bodhie thoughtfully. 'I mean, if it is there, it would have been right under our noses all this time. But then again, I suppose the last place the Book was meant to have been located before it was lost was somewhere in the Five Kingdoms. So I guess, it could be right.'

'Maybe they thought that that the Book would be safer if it was hidden really close to where the Ancient Council and Elders are based?' Anna suggested tentatively.

'Maybe... What about the shadows part though?' said Bodhie thoughtfully.

'I don't know. That was the only part that didn't really make sense. I thought that maybe it might mean in the shadows of the pyramids, which I suppose the archway is really when you think about it.'

'I definitely think we should go and check it out,' said Max. 'I can't think of anywhere else. But then I suppose I wouldn't be able to really, would I? Can you think of anywhere Bodhie?'

Bodhie looked thoughtful for a moment, 'No I can't, I think we should check it out too.'

Anna smiled at them both happily.

'The only thing is, it's not exactly the quietest place for us to investigate, is it?' said Max, 'And I imagine that by now there might be quite a few people that will know we're missing.'

'That's OK,' said Bodhie. 'You said that there was a location that you configured for the Key before, that took you right into the centre of the courtyard. Well if you can configure the Key for the Courtyard, then I'll make us invisible. We can have a quick look and once we've checked it out, we'll come straight back here. Now that we know we are fairly safe here.'

Max looked at Anna's enquiring expression and added, 'We checked out the Travel Charts and we now know where we are. We're in the Barren Lands and Bodhie thinks that there's not much that goes on here apart from Crystal–'

'Mining! Of course!' said Anna, 'Crystal Dust. My uncle sells it, remember?'

So that was where Max had heard of the Barren Lands previously, he thought, remembering the jar filled with twinkling sand-coloured dust that he'd seen on his visit to Bron's shop.

'So, when should we go, then?' said Anna flattening her hair and extracting some twigs that had become entwined in it during the night.

'Well...' said Max, 'If you remember, Lucem is a few hours ahead of here, so I'm guessing if we went soon, then it would probably be late morning there and hopefully a bit quieter in the courtyard, as everybody would have already got to work.'

Then a sudden thought occurred to him. Remembering his experience with the Wokulo that they had bumped into on their last trip to the courtyard, he added, 'What would happen if we arrived in the courtyard in the exact spot where someone else was standing? What happens then? We wouldn't squash them, would we?' Max had a fleeting but horrifying vision of them landing directly on top of someone's head.

Anna looked at Max blankly and shrugged, 'I never even thought about that before.'

But Bodhie grinned and said, 'No, the Bridge opens up in an approximate area, they're designed that way to avoid just that. Otherwise, two people could decide to travel to the same place at the same time and they could crash into each other. The Bridge will move you slightly and open up the gateway in a different place if that were to happen. So today, we might not land in exactly the same spot in the courtyard as you and Anna did last time.

They ate breakfast of the strange spiky purple fruits, nuts, cheese and bread and prepared to leave shortly after. Having already decided that they would return to their camp in the forest, as soon as they had investigated the archway and gate, they decided to leave most of their belongings behind. However, just in case, they rolled up their blankets and belongings and hid them under a pile of leaves and branches.

The Key, Travel Charts and last remaining Poca were safely stowed in Max's pockets. The Map which had led them on their journey to the Temple of Fangs, Max decided was probably now no longer of much use to them, so he left it behind, buried in the bottom of Anna's rucksack. Max couldn't bring himself to discard his grandad's broken Uroboros Key, but it was too heavy to carry along with the other Key and Travel chart, so he carefully wrapped the two fractured halves of the Key in Anna's jumper and buried that in the bottom of Anna's rucksack too, which he then hid under a pile of leaves and branches.

Then they stood in a small tight huddle at the edge of the camp, whilst Max slowly selected the three symbols that he had checked and double-checked in the Travel Chart. Despite having done this numerous times now and having the Travel Chart to confirm the symbols he should select, he still felt nervous. The combination of the additional mysterious ring that they knew very little about and the fact that this was Valac's Key, troubled him. He knew it was probably silly, but he couldn't help but have this fear that the Key might just suddenly decide to transport itself – and them – back to its owner.

'So, you're definitely sure that we don't need to worry about this extra dial then?' said Max, glancing at Bodhie and feeling as though some tiny creature was doing backward flips in his stomach.

'Well no – not definitely. But you didn't change it when we left the temple and came here, did you? You just changed the usual three dials and it worked. So I'm thinking that maybe that new dial of Valac's only kicks in when you actually do something with it and that the Key just works like normal otherwise. Well, that's the theory anyway...'

Well, let's hope you're right,' said Max tensely. 'Otherwise we'll have to be ready for a speedy escape.'

Bodhie nodded stiffly, 'We should be OK as long as we're invisible. So, when I feel that we are coming down and about to go through the gateway, I'm going to make us invisible. We'll just have to make sure that we don't split apart when we land; that we're still touching each other. Otherwise, someone is going to suddenly pop into view. I can only keep it up if we're touching.'

'How long do you think you can keep us invisible for?' said Anna.

'I don't know. Maybe five minutes or something?'

'OK,' said Anna. 'Come on, we might as well get going then...'

Max clicked the last dial slowly into place and then they stood in a tense huddle, silently watching the snake.

The journey was swift, filled with blasts of swirling ice-cold air and harsh howling winds that whistled in their ears and whipped at their face and hair.

Max kept his eyes shut throughout but clung stubbornly onto Anna and Bodhie determined that they wouldn't be separated by the fall. There must be something that they weren't doing quite right, he realised, thinking of the neat little landing that had taken place when he had travelled back with Imeda, Krake and Otty that night.

Then suddenly they were slowing down and Max could feel them spiralling downwards before they abruptly thudded into the ground. Max felt Anna veering away to their right and he yanked her back towards them, clutching her wrist tightly.

'Ouch!' she yelped. 'That hurt!'

'Sorry – had to,' whispered Max.

They sat still for a moment in an uncomfortable clump of intertwined legs and arms and looked around.

His heart racing, Max blinked quickly in the bright sunlight and looked around. His eyes focused on the elaborate circular marble water fountain that stood directly in the centre of the pyramid courtyard. He breathed out heavily, watching the water sparkle in the bright morning sunshine as it tumbled and cascaded over the marble circles and spheres. Across the courtyard, Max could see a steady flow of people moving to and from the pyramid buildings. They were here.

'Phew!' whispered Anna next to him, 'We made it!'

Suddenly out of the corner of his eye, Max noticed a tall man striding towards them, completely unaware of the invisible clump of bodies that were sprawled in his path.

'Move!' Max breathed, scrambling to extract himself from the awkward tangle of limbs and get out of the man's way.

But it was too late. The man's foot caught Max's and he stumbled, then fell, landing a few feet from where they lay in a tense sprawled heap. He stood up sharply and looked around, his expression at first startled and perplexed — then narrow-eyed and suspicious.

Max held his breath, his heart hammering in his chest. He could feel Anna and Bodhie lying rigidly next to him, Bodhie's hand clutching his arm.

The dark-haired man cast a second suspicious glance around the square, which lingered momentarily on the spot where he had tripped over Max's foot and then after dusting down his trousers, he stalked off in the direction of the pyramids.

'Phew!' whispered Anna, sighing heavily. 'Watch your big feet, will you Max!'

'Sorry,' breathed Max.

'Anna, we need to hurry, where do we go?'

whispered Bodhie urgently.

'Erm, it's over here,' muttered Anna quietly.

She quickly guided them to the far side of the courtyard, weaving through the steady flow of people that bustled about, as they went about their business.

The narrow stone archway stood at the opposite side of the courtyard to the archway that Max had used on his previous visits to the pyramid buildings. Like the other archways, it was built into the high stone wall that surrounded and encompassed the courtyard. An elaborate wrought iron gate made of interwoven snakes that weaved and twisted around one another, stood open to one side, enabling a steady flow of people to pass through the archway, between the courtyard and the busy street beyond. The archway itself consisted of two simple stone pillars that rose to a single arched peak. Looking up, Max could see that set into the top of this was a large circular, carved stone. It was, exactly as Anna had remembered, a Uroboros Key. Max smiled to himself. Anna had been right.

'It's there,' whispered Anna.

'Okay, let's stand here,' murmured Bodhie, leading them carefully to one side and away from the main bustle of people. 'Can someone keep watch whilst I have a look at it? We don't want someone coming up from behind and banging into us.'

'I'll do it,' said Max. Making sure that he didn't let go of Bodhie's arm, he turned and looked back across the courtyard at the steady throng of people that were milling around between the two pyramid buildings.

'Imeda!' A deep voice called out across the courtyard.

Max's head jerked around.

A tall lean man with brown hair and dark brooding eyes strode quickly past him and walked briskly towards the pyramids.

Turning, Max saw that Imeda had emerged from one of the buildings. She gave the man a strained smile and stepped away from the throng, meeting him halfway across the courtyard. She looked tired, her face was strained, her bright blue eyes unusually grave.

Taking care to keep hold of Bodhie's shoulder, Max took a step towards them, straining to listen.

'Is there any news?' Max heard the man say as he reached her.

Imeda shook her head solemnly, her eyes serious and pensive. 'No, still nothing.'

'When is the next search going ahead?' said the man.

'Tonight. Krake is leading it. He's taking this whole thing very badly, you know. He blames himself. If everyone hadn't been at the party, then he thinks they might not be missing...'

The man nodded stiffly but said nothing.

'Listen, I'm sorry Malik, but I must go. I've actually got a meeting about the next search now with Cade and Krake. Can we talk later?'

The man nodded.

Then turning, Imeda swept off in the direction of the first pyramid building and presumably in the direction of Cade's office.

Malik turned, his dark brown eyes searched the busy courtyard. Then he hesitated a moment, his eyes narrowed.

Max watched Malik and then following the direction of his gaze, found the heavy figure of Krake striding across the courtyard. He was heading towards the imposing entrance of the first pyramid building, into which Imeda had just disappeared.

Krake looked strained. His jaw was set in a worried, rigid line; he was unshaven and he had dark shadows under both eyes. He looked, Max thought, as though he hadn't slept properly in days.

Looking back, Max watched Malik's unwavering gaze track Krake's steady progress, as he walked across the courtyard and disappeared into the first building.

Then suddenly out of the corner of his eye,

Max saw something black flash past.

Looking up, he saw a large raven-like bird with sleek black feathers swoop by, landing on the nearby wall.

The bird tilted its head to one side, and looked inquisitively around the courtyard, with dark watchful eyes.

The same dark, watchful eyes. It was, Max was absolutely certain, the same bird. Again.

Looking back at Malik for a moment, Max saw to his surprise, that Malik too was looking at the bird.

Malik's dark eyes narrowed on the bird for a moment, then to Max's utter shock, he gave the bird a very slight, but very definite, nod of acknowledgement.

The bird watched Malik with dark enquiring eyes and squawked.

Then turning sharply on his heel, Malik marched across the courtyard and in the direction of the second pyramid.

Max watched Malik quickly disappear into the throng, in stunned disbelief.

The nod had been so slight – could he have imagined it? He didn't think so. But then, what did it mean? Glancing back towards the wall, Max saw that the bird was still perched, surveying the courtyard with dark watchful eyes.

With a start, Max realised that someone was tugging, sharply on his arm.

'Max!' whispered Bodhie urgently, 'What are you doing? We've got to go!'

'Sorry,' whispered Max, startled, 'I'm sorry, I–'

'Hurry,' breathed Anna.

The bird glanced around. Its dark inquisitive gaze hesitated in their direction.

Max's breath caught in his chest. He felt certain that the bird had heard and understood them.

Gathering himself, Max quickly lifted the Key and then confident that Anna and Bodhie, were both holding onto his arms, he twisted the innermost dial back to the position that he knew should take them back to their camp.

Glancing up again, Max saw that the bird was still sitting on the wall, staring directly at the spot, where they invisibly stood, with its black unblinking eyes.

Moments later, they were swirled up into the ice-cold void.

SAM KINI

Chapter 26
The Standing Stones

'What were you doing?' said Bodhie when they landed back in camp a few minutes later.

Bodhie looked pale and clammy. Knees sagging, ze had slumped to the floor.

'I'm sorry,' said Max. 'I'm really sorry. I just didn't hear you! Malik and Imeda were there and I just got distracted.'

'Why? What were they doing?' said Anna, turning quickly towards Max.

'Well, it sounds like they're searching for us.' said Max, thinking back to the exact words he had overheard them say and remembering that Imeda and Malik hadn't once actually mentioned their names. Although they had mentioned the night of Krake's party as being the night when they had gone missing.

Max hesitated, 'I think that they've got searches going on to try and find us. Imeda said that there's another search tonight. She was talking to Malik, and she said that Krake has taken our disappearance really badly because if everyone hadn't been at his party... then maybe we wouldn't have gone missing...' He looked at Anna.

'Did they mention my mum and dad?'

Max shook his head.

'I wonder if they think I'm missing too and if they know that we're all together?' said Bodhie thoughtfully.

'I don't know,' said Max shaking his head, 'I would have thought that they must know, once they realise that we were at your uncle's place and that you went missing straight afterwards. It would be obvious, wouldn't it?'

Anna nodded. 'What else happened?'

'Well, to be honest, Malik was acting a bit weird.'

'What do you mean "weird"?' said Anna.

Max shrugged, 'I don't really know how to explain it, but the way he acted, it was kind of strange.' He paused, searching for the right words, then added, 'Suspicious. He was acting kind of suspicious.'

Anna raised her eyebrows and gave Max a meaningful stare, 'What did Malik do this time?'

Max hesitated. He thought about Malik nodding at the bird and knew what Anna's reaction would be. He knew how ridiculous it sounded, even before the words left his lips, but he also knew what he'd seen. The bird had definitely been the same bird and Malik had definitely nodded at it.

Taking a deep breath and bracing himself for

their reaction he said, 'Well, Malik hung around after Imeda had gone and that black bird arrived again and he, well look, I know what you're going to say – but he nodded at it.'

'Not this again Max!' said Anna rolling her eyes. 'Why are you so sure that it's even the same bird?'

'I don't know. I can just tell. Why are you so sure that I'm not right?' said Max determinedly not looking at Anna's raised eye brows and exasperated expression.

'Because it's a black bird Max. Because there are loads of them and because I just don't get how you can be so certain that it's always the same one. That's why.'

'You've got a ball of orange fluff for a pet. Why do you think it's so strange for there to be smart birds? Anyway, I think it's the same bird and what's more, I think Malik recognised it too.'

'Hmm,' Anna muttered dubiously, clearly unconvinced. Then turning to Bodhie she added, 'Anyway, so what did you think then? Do you think the archway is linked with the Book?'

Bodhie's expression was gloomy, 'No, I really think it's just a gate.'

'No! What, really?' said Anna looking startled. She looked crestfallen.

'Yeah, I know. I'm sorry. But I really, honestly,

don't think there's anything there.'

'But how can you be so sure?' said Max.

'Well, it really does just look like a carved stone Key. I looked for any clues or anything that might be written in our ancient language, but there was nothing.'

'But how can it not be right? It seemed so perfect,' said Anna kicking a stone across the floor angrily.

'I know, I thought so too, but I really do think that it's just an archway decorated with a carving of a Uroboros Key,' said Bodhie.

Max sighed heavily. He realised now that he really hadn't expected this at all. He felt utterly dismal.

'So what are we going to do now, then?' said Anna, looking totally deflated.

'I don't know,' said Bodhie sighing, 'I really don't know...'

They spent the rest of the afternoon around the camp, unpacking their few possessions, eating the little food they had left and gathering more wood to make a fire.

The mood in the camp was flat. Max knew that they had all secretly believed that they would find what they were looking for in the courtyard that morning and now nobody quite knew what to do. They had completely run out of ideas about what this light pyramid could be and so everyone was busying themselves around camp, in order to avoid the looming question over what they should do next.

Max's thoughts kept drifting back to the conversation that he had overheard that morning between Imeda and Malik. Thinking back, Max realised that Malik had actually spoken very little during the conversation with Imeda, but there had been something about the way he had acted that had been odd. The way he had watched Krake cross the courtyard had definitely been strange. Then there was the bird; that sleek mysterious black bird with its intelligent, watchful eyes. Despite what Anna had said, Max was certain that he had recognised that bird, and what's more, he was equally certain that Malik had recognised it too.

But what did it mean? How was Malik linked to the bird? Was Malik working with Valac and Xegan? And how did the bird, like the Mothmen, keep appearing wherever they went?

Then of course, there was the missing Uroborologs. Max realised grimly, that he had absolutely no idea what they should do now. He sighed and tugged the little leather-bound book of Travel Charts free from his pocket, then began absently flicking through the pages. The symbols and words danced before him, as the pages fluttered before his eyes. So many secret worlds, so many places that seven days ago he hadn't even known existed. Was the location of the Uroborologs contained somewhere within these pages? he wondered. Was Xegan secretly hiding in one of these worlds? Suddenly a word flitted into view, catching Max's attention and he quickly flicked back through the pages until he found it again. His eyes focused on the word and he stared at it for a moment, frowning.

The Shadowlands

Max swallowed. Could they have been so stupid?

Hardly daring to breathe, he quickly scanned down the list of locations, looking for anything, any location or word that they could possibly link back to the clue. He blinked, his finger wavering over a line.

City Central Square, Tyria

(For access to buildings near City Central Square, World Transportation Bridge, and Prism Fountain)

The glimmerings of an idea began to take shape in Max's mind. Once again, he ran through the lines of the clue. Where the shadows and light pyramid meet... Wasn't a prism something like a pyramid or triangle? Max wasn't sure, but he did seem to remember learning something about prisms at school, and he was certain that they had something to do with light.

He stared at the words and read them again, remembering the third line of the clue. A gate guards the key to our secret. Didn't Bodhie say Bridges and Uroboros Keys both opened up gateways to different locations and worlds? What if the word 'gate', rather than meaning an actual gate, really meant a gateway or Bridge? What if the gate that guarded the Key to the secret was actually a Bridge in the Shadowlands?

Max's heart skipped a beat. Could it be possible? Could this actually be it? 'Guys...' he said slowly, 'I-I think — that I might've just found something...'

Bodhie and Anna, who had been busy kindling the fire, looked up immediately.

'Why? What have you found?' asked Anna eagerly.

'Well, I might be completely wrong... but... I was just flicking through this book with the Travel Charts in and... well—' he held the book out towards them, 'You don't think... It's not the Shadowlands, is it?'

Anna's eyes widened.

'What if the "shadows" part of the clue is actually the Shadowlands?' Max continued, 'And, Bodhie, yesterday you said that Keys and Bridges open up Gateways to different worlds. What if the "gate" part of the clue is actually a Bridge? There's a location in here for the Main Bridge in a place called

Tyria in the Shadowlands.'

'Tyria is the capital of the Shadowlands,' Bodhie said, nodding.

'And there's another thing. What's a Prism?'

Anna shook her head blankly.

'Isn't it something made from glass that light goes through? Usually a triangle type shape?' said Bodhie, hesitantly.

'Well, there's a Prism Fountain listed in exactly the same location as the Main Bridge for Tyria in the Shadowlands. So, maybe that is the Light Pyramid... What do you think?'

'It could be,' said Anna eagerly, her face suddenly brightening. 'It really could be. I guess the "shadows" part of the clue never really made sense before. Everything else did, but that didn't.'

'I just don't know why we didn't think of the Shadowlands before,' said Bodhie eagerly. 'It seems so obvious now.'

'I know! This could really be it. We should definitely go and check it out,' said Anna excitedly.

'OK, so what do you think we should be looking for when we get there?' said Max.

'Well,' said Bodhie slowly, 'If, like the clue says, a gate guards the key to our secret and if it is the main Bridge in the central square that is the gate, then I think we should start by checking out the stone circle that surrounds it. Some of the standing stones that surround Bridges have engravings on them. Maybe there will be a clue there.'

'Sounds like a good plan,' said Max. 'And we could check it out invisibly, like we did this morning.'

'Yeesss,' said Bodhie hesitantly. 'But I think that it's going to be a lot trickier this time. I mean, there could be arrivals and departures through the Bridge all of the time. People will be coming and going; we could easily be seen. Not to mention the risk of one of us accidentally getting transported through the Bridge to some other world or location.'

'But as long as we're together and we've got the Uroboros Key, if it does happen, we should at least be able to get back again,' said Anna excitedly.

'And we should go at the quietest possible time,' said Max, 'When there are less people around and less Bridge departures and arrivals. We should go at nighttime. That would be less risky, wouldn't it?'

Bodhie nodded and grinned.

'That's decided then,' Anna's eye's gleamed. 'We go tonight.'

It was almost dusk, when they slowly began to gather themselves together in readiness for their departure to the Shadowlands. The sun, just visible through the trees, had slowly sunk below the horizon of the plateau, leaving an inky velvet blue sky and the dark mounds of the sandy rust-coloured hills silhouetted starkly against the sky in the distance.

Anna and Bodhie had both remembered the time difference in the capital of the Shadowlands: Tyria was three hours later than Lucem. Having already decided that Lucem seemed to be a few hours later than here, they reckoned that dusk at camp should in theory mean the middle of the night there. Well, that was the theory anyway.

'So, we're agreed that if we get there and we've got it wrong and it's still day time, then we come straight back,' said Anna tensely, as they gathered in a tight little group at the edge of camp and prepared themselves to leave.

'Agreed,' said Bodhie, 'And don't forget, just like last time, whatever you do we can't let go of each other when we land in the Square. Otherwise, you'll suddenly be visible and we might get seen.'

'Okay, got it,' said Max as he carefully twisted the three dials on the Key. Then clutching the Key tightly, he gently clicked the last symbol into place.

'Right then, hold on,' he said tightly, his stomach fluttering nervously.

Moments later the snake slowly began to revolve.

Within minutes, it seemed that they were

swirling downwards through the raw freezing air and harsh howling winds and they hit the ground with a soft thud, landing together in a crumpled but compact heap.

Max sat still for a moment and breathed out heavily, grateful for the reassuring feel of Anna and Bodhie seated next to him on the floor. He realised, remembering back to the elegant-all-standing arrival with Imeda, Krake and Otty, that their landings, although vastly improved on his early face-slamming-into-the-floor attempts, were still missing some elusive but clearly vital part of the landing technique. So, he made a mental note for himself, that if they ever got out of this, that he would find out what it was.

Blinking, he looked around, his eyes adjusting to the dark. Faint, pearly white beads of light were twinkling and slowly dissipating above them in the darkness.

They were sitting on a hard stone flagged surface, somewhere near the centre of a large plaza or square. Tall stone buildings ran around the edge of the square, their dark empty-eyed windows looked blankly out, lit only occasionally by the warm glow of an inside light. A series of ornate streetlamps ran through the square illuminating it with yellow narrow pools of light. The square was deserted. Everything was quiet.

At the centre of the square stood an imposing glass pyramid shaped fountain. Water cascaded down over tiny undulating steps in the pyramids four angled walls, glistening and twinkling as it glided and bounced over the glass. A series of tiny lights set into the base, shimmered over the fountain creating miniature rainbows of colour as the glass and water reflected and refracted the light.

Max hesitated for a moment, marvelling at the fountain.

Where the shadows and light pyramid meet. It was – quite clearly – a pyramid of lights. This had to be it. They were here.

'Over here,' whispered Bodhie, gently tugging at his arm.

Turning, Max saw a huge series of standing stones standing off to one side of the square.

'We need to be quick,' said Bodhie, as they hurriedly made their way across.

Max realised that it was far bigger than the Bridge in Lucem. At least twenty stones rose out of the square in giant thick slabs circling the area of the Bridge – many of which, Max could already see, were covered in intricate carvings and engravings.

'It's no good,' whispered Bodhie, 'Look at this thing – it's absolutely huge. We aren't going to be able to check all of these and manage to stay invisible. I can't make all of us invisible for that long.'

'OK,' said Max, glancing around the square

and spotting a large stone statue of three distinguished gentlemen that stood in front of a wall, to one side of the Bridge. 'We'll go over there. Me and Anna can hide, while you check it out. You take the Key and that way if something happens, you can get back to us.'

'Are you sure?' whispered Bodhie's voice. 'But what if you need it?'

'Take it,' Max urged. 'In case there's a Bridge departure or something and you accidentally get taken through somewhere... If we need you, we'll shout out.'

Max glanced quickly around the deserted square, and then let go of Bodhie's arm. Looking down, he saw his feet and body suddenly materialise in front of his eyes, then moments later Anna suddenly appeared next to him.

'Here, take it,' he said, holding the Key out to empty space. He let go of the Key, which promptly disappeared into thin air.

They quickly made their way across to the statue and then crouched down, squashing themselves into the narrow gap between the statue and wall, so that they were hidden out of view from the main square, but could peer out between the stone figures towards the fountain and Bridge. With a sinking feeling, Max realised that he could feel the chunky square shape of the Travel Charts, pressing tightly against his leg, in his trouser pocket. He'd given Bodhie the Key, but not the Travel Charts.

A door slammed, distracting him from his thoughts and glancing up, Max saw a Yeti in a heavy black cape walk quickly down some stone steps that led away from a large building across the square, before disappearing down a side street. The square became still again.

They crouched together in silence, waiting.

Max shivered. It was cold here; much colder than in Lucem or their little makeshift camp in the Barren Lands.

'Do you think we'll actually see one?' whispered Max, as he stared out across the square.

'See what?'

'You know, now that we are in the Shadowlands, one of their shadows wandering around on its own.'

'I don't know,' whispered Anna shivering. 'I guess we might. It's chilly, isn't it? I forgot it was so cold here.'

'Is it always this cold?'

'Well, I've only been here a couple of times before, but it was then.'

Max nodded and rubbed his hands together, trying to keep warm.

'How long do you think it will take Bodhie to check them all?' whispered Anna, her eyes were bright, and her cheeks glowed in the cold air.

'I really don't know. There's a lot of stones.'

Anna nodded and looked back across the square. 'Look, it's Krake!' she whispered suddenly, pointing across the plaza in the direction of a spot, close to where they had landed ten minutes earlier.

Turning, Max saw Krake standing at the opposite side of the square. He was wearing a long dark cloak, similar to the one he had worn on the night he had rescued Max with Imeda and had a Uroboros Key clutched in his left hand.

'He must be searching for us,' breathed Max. 'Imeda said there was a search going ahead tonight.'

They crouched together in silence, watching Krake as he slowly moved around the square searching for them, his jaw set in a grim line.

Watching the strain in Krake's expression, Max realised guiltily, that their disappearance must be causing people a great deal of worry.

Krake's heavy frame moved slowly across the square, momentarily appearing in the shallow yellow pools of light before fading into the shadows again, as he passed beneath the ornate street lamps set around the square. Then he disappeared around the corner of a building and out of view.

Max watched Krake disappear and felt oddly flat and ashamed. Could he have got it wrong? Maybe nobody within the Elders had betrayed them to Xegan after all. He'd thought someone had betrayed them because it was only the Elders that had ever known their location – with his grandad and at Anna's on the night of Krake's party. But then, none of the Elders knew where they were now and Valac had still been able to find them. He'd been so sure... so convinced... What if he had got it all wrong?

A faint rustling sound overhead suddenly distracted him from his thoughts.

Looking around sharply, Max saw disconcertingly, that a large black bird had landed on the wall behind them.

It was, he was absolutely certain now, the same black bird.

The bird looked around and then down at Max and Anna crouched behind the statue with dark watchful eyes, its head cocked slightly to one side.

Max looked quickly back across the square, but Krake had vanished. His heart began to pound. He realised that they had never seen the bird outside Lucem before, but then apart from their little makeshift camp in the Barren Lands, they themselves had never actually travelled outside of Lucem before. All they had ever really done was travel between the Barren Lands and Lucem. Now they were here – and the bird was too. But why was it here? And how had it found them?

He quickly glanced up at the wall behind them. The bird was sitting very still and staring fixedly down at them. It looked, Max thought, almost as though it was thinking. Max felt his stomach clench with fear. He glanced nervously back towards Anna. She was staring at the stone circle, watching for any sign of Bodhie's reappearance. He couldn't put it off any longer. He had to tell her.

'Anna...' he began in reluctant voice.

'Can you see Bodhie?' she whispered, glancing back quickly towards Max.

Max took a deep breath. 'Err, no...' he paused, 'But I can see that bird. It's sitting right above us. It's watching us.' He indicated the wall behind them.

'Max!' exclaimed Anna, her dark eyes narrowing into a deep frown.

'Before you say it,' Max cut in, 'It is the same bird. I know it's the same bird and it's staring at us. Birds don't stare.'

'Maybe it's asleep.'

'What, with its eyelids open?' he snapped.

'Do birds even have eyelids?' she hissed. 'You know what, Max, you're getting totally paranoid about this bird business.' And with an angry huff she turned and stared determinedly back towards the stone circle.

Clenching his teeth angrily, Max turned and

stared out across the square. Neither Bodhie nor Krake were anywhere in sight.

There was a sudden swish as something moved stealthily above them. Startled, Max looked up sharply.

Fleetingly, he saw that the bird had swooped down and towards him. In a flash, there was a down rush of air and a flurry of dark beating wings. Then suddenly, there were wings beating and thrashing at his head; claws grappling at the skin on his neck.

Max recoiled. His arms flailing out in terror.

A confusion of black wings flashed before his eyes, beating his face and head. Wind hissed past his ears.

He couldn't see. He shut his eyes.

'No!' cried Anna frantically.

Max forgot to breathe. A blur of frantic thoughts flitted through his mind. Claws scratched at his skin and then suddenly he felt something being yanked upwards from around his neck. It snagged on his t-shirt. In a heartbeat, he could feel his father's chain being dragged up and over his head.

And it was gone.

The bird squawked and swooped off, the heavy amulet and chain swinging gently from its clawed feet, as it flew over a nearby building and disappeared into the night.

'Max!' yelped Anna, the blood draining from her face. 'Are you OK? I'm so sorry!'

Max staggered to his feet and the world tilted sickeningly; he gripped hold of the statue and took a gulp of air.

That bird – I'm sorry I–' her voice trembled, then broke off.

A misty white shape appeared next to them, quickly becoming denser and more solid, until suddenly Bodhie was standing in front of them. Ze was holding a rolled piece of old parchment and an odd shaped shiny metal object and wearing a triumphant smile. The smile quickly faded and Bodhie's jaw dropped.

'Let's just get back, let's go...' Max answered thickly.

'Yes, let's go,' said Anna. Her eyes were wide with shock and fear.

'Err... OK,' said Bodhie, hesitantly, looking from one to the other and back again, with an anxious, baffled expression. Ze lifted the Key and quickly configured the dials.

They huddled together in a solemn silent circle and moments later, they vanished into the swirling icy void.

SAM KINI

Chapter 27
The Veiled Woman

Max's knees sagged and he slid to the ground, his head in his hands.

The light had faded completely now, and the camp was pitch black.

'Oh Max, I'm so sorry,' Anna's voice faltered in the darkness.

Max said nothing. Shakily, he rubbed his head, wincing slightly as his fingers brushed across a series of cuts on the back of his neck. His fingers felt sticky and he realised numbly, that he must be bleeding.

The fire slowly crackled into life, illuminating the shape of Bodhie's body hunched over the fire as he gently prodded it, feeding it branches and leaves. The fire grew, casting warm dancing shapes around the camp. Anna's face flickered into view – wide-eyed and fearful.

'What happened?' said Bodhie. Ze stared at them both with serious grey eyes, taking in Anna's shocked expression and Max's dishevelled bloody appearance.

'The bird–' began Anna, 'That black bird. It was there and it attacked Max. It stole the amulet–' her voice broke off. 'I didn't believe you Max, I'm so sorry...'

Max nodded stiffly but said nothing. He didn't trust himself to speak.

He knew that it wasn't really Anna's fault. She hadn't made the bird follow them and she hadn't made it attack him and steal the chain. But he had known it was the same bird – he had been absolutely certain that it was the same bird – and she hadn't believed him. Maybe if she had believed him, they'd have been more prepared and then maybe they could have stopped the bird from stealing the amulet. But she hadn't and they weren't and now the amulet was gone. And he wasn't ready, even though he knew that he probably should, to say that it was OK. They'd been caught off guard, because he'd been too busy arguing with Anna about whether the stupid bird was awake or asleep. And he was still too angry to trust himself to speak.

He gingerly felt the back of his neck again. The pain had subsided and the tiny cuts and scratches seemed to have stopped bleeding. He was OK.

Except that he wasn't.

They'd lost the amulet. His father's amulet. The amulet his father had found on his world travels with Krake that was supposed to provide them with some kind of protection. Maybe it actually did. They had certainly got out of enough scrapes in the last few days. But now it had gone and along with it, their protection probably too.

A disturbing thought slowly began to take form in his mind. Maybe that was exactly why the bird had wanted it; to take away whatever protection it had given them.

'You can't carry on ignoring me,' Anna said stubbornly. 'Look – I'm sorry Max. I'm sorry I didn't believe you, but I didn't make it happen. I didn't make the bird attack you!'

Max slowly raised his head and met her eyes. He noticed that her eyes were red and her cheeks glistened slightly, but her expression was defiant.

'All I know,' he said with sudden fierceness, 'Is that if you'd believed me and stopped telling me that I was imagining things, then maybe we'd have been able to stop it. I said it was the same bird. I said that I didn't like the way it kept showing up and that maybe it was linked somehow to all of this, to Xegan or Valac or Malik or something. But you wouldn't believe me and now it's attacked me and the chain has gone.'

'Max, I know we should have believed you, but we didn't make the bird attack you and take the chain. We didn't know this was going to happen. Even if I had believed you, how would that have stopped this from happening tonight?'

'But we could have been more ready for it. We could have been more prepared, instead of arguing over whether the stupid thing was awake or asleep. And what about the protection it was giving us? What about that? Now that's gone too.' He said fiercely, stabbing a stick into the fire.

The fire crackled and sparked, spitting burning embers out of the fire.

'But Max, we don't even know if it was actually giving us any protection. Not really. It was probably just some strange object that Krake found on his travels somewhere. Just because there was some tale about it giving you protection, doesn't mean it's true. There are always objects like that, which crop up in my uncle's shop. Most of the time, they don't do what the Wokulo say they do. Krake probably just said that to make you feel better.'

'It wasn't just a chain. That was my dad's chain. Krake and my dad found it on their world travels. Do you know how many things I've got that belonged to my dad? None!' he shouted angrily.

Anna fell silent.

'And anyway,' Max continued, 'If it was just any old chain, then why did the bird steal it? Doesn't that prove something? Doesn't that prove that there must be something about it? There must be a reason why the bird took it.'

Anna stared at her hands.

'Look,' said Bodhie, 'I don't know why the bird took the amulet. Maybe it did steal it, to take away some kind of protection it thought it was giving us. And I'm sorry I didn't really believe you about the bird either Max. It just seemed really unlikely that a bird would be following us around like that. And I'm really sorry that you lost your dad's chain,' ze hesitated awkwardly. 'But look – I've got something to tell you both. I think I know where the book is.' Bodhie hesitated and glanced at them both, face flushed with suppressed excitement.

'Why? What happened?' said Anna, turning quickly towards Bodhie, her face brightening and looking as though she was sincerely grateful for the change of subject.

'Well at first, I couldn't find anything. But then, after I'd checked about five of the stones, I found something. It was sort of hidden in amongst one of the patterns engraved onto the stones and it was in our ancient language again.'

'Go on. What was it?' said Anna.

'Well, it told me to go to the sixth standing stone where there were these dimples and holes that covered the surface of the stone, in this huge pattern and I sort of had to press my fingers into these dimples, in a certain order. The problem was, I kept forgetting which order I was supposed to press them in. Anyway, after I'd checked the first stone about three times, I got the pattern right and this little stone drawer-thing popped out of nowhere – right in the middle of the standing stone! And this was inside it!'

Ze held a hand out proudly towards them to reveal the rolled piece of parchment and the strange metal object that Max vaguely recalled seeing earlier.

Max could now see that the strange metal object was in fact a small shiny key. It was like no other key that Max had ever seen before. It had been twisted into an ornate geometric design that finished with a key at both ends. The little double ended key sat in the palm of Bodhie's hand, glinting softly in the fire light.

'Wow, it's like two keys in one!' said Anna.

'And look, there's this,' said Bodhie nodding excitedly and unrolling the small piece of cream parchment.

'What is it?' said Max breathing out and feeling the tight coil of anger inside him relax a little.

'Well, it's the next – and final – clue,' Bodhie paused, and gave them a wide expectant grin. Then reading from the parchment, ze said,

You will finally get to know your fate,

In a changing world we cannot state.

A veiled woman knows where our heritage rests,

But you must pass through our final series of tests.

Choose wisely lest you may regret,

A leap of faith may be the answer yet.

A second door hides a chamber and terrors not yet known,

ANCIENT SECRETS

The final hurdle to the secret tome.

'And you actually know what this means?' said Anna with a baffled expression.

Bodhie's face was full of suppressed triumph. Ze gave them a confident nod.

'You know how my mum and dad are into all of this stuff and they study ancient Hidden People artefacts and things? Well, there's this statue in Hyperborea of a beautiful, veiled woman. It's very old. It's probably one of the oldest remaining statues by the Hidden People in Hyperborea. The woman is covered in this veil. I guess the veil is meant to represent her invisibility, secrecy and knowledge – "see but not be seen" – like the Hidden People. Anyway, I think that's what the line – "A veiled woman knows where our heritage rests" – really means. And then when you see the line before it – "In a changing world we cannot state". Well, of course Hyperborea is the place where the Nix live and the Nix are shapeshifters. People form. So, I really think that's what that part of the poem – "You will finally get to know your fate, in a changing world we cannot state. A veiled woman knows where our heritage rests, but you must pass through our final series of tests" – means.'

'And what about the rest of the clue?' said Max.

'Well I think we'll only be able to understand

the rest of it, when we actually get there.'

'And you're absolutely certain about this veiled woman?' said Max, thinking of the mistake they had made in going to the pyramid courtyard.

Bodhie shrugged, 'No, of course I'm not absolutely certain. But I know that statue exists and it is in Hyperborea – which is the changing world. I know that it is an ancient statue of the Hidden People. It would totally make sense that there could be some kind of hidden passage or chamber beneath it. It could have been built years ago before most of the buildings in that area were built. Nobody would even know it was there and, outside of the Hidden People, the statue isn't really anything special.'

'But inside the Hidden People it is. If the Book was really there, wouldn't it have already been found by now?'

'Not necessarily. The only reason I've really heard of it, Max, is because my mum and dad research this stuff. There's loads of stuff around our house about ancient Hidden People relics and over the years, they've dragged me on lots of trips to see this stuff. You've got to remember that it's their job, that's why they're away all the time. Secondly, the Hidden People have travelled around worlds for thousands of years. There were lots of places to check, in lots of worlds, Max. If you don't know what you're supposed to be looking for and you have no clue to work from, once the Three Keepers disappeared, it would have been impossible to find. I mean, that was the idea really – they didn't want anyone to find the Book outside of the Three Keepers. It had been secretly moved around for centuries.'

Anna nodded; her eyes gleaming excitedly.

'I think Xegan killed the Three Keepers and then somehow he lost the map marking the location of the Temple of Fangs. Then, I don't know how, Max, but it somehow ended up in your grandad's possession when he was the Leader of the Elders and then when you went to Earth, your location was a secret and Xegan couldn't find you to get the map back. I bet he's been trying to find you to get that map, so he could finally get hold of the Book for years.'

'And then he found us and he killed my grandad and now he's chased us away from your home and we've nearly been killed, I don't know how many times in the last few days.' Max said darkly.

'Listen Max,' said Bodhie, 'I really think that this is it. We've got a chance here, a chance to stop Xegan from getting what he wants and to get the book back. When you asked me last time and we got it wrong, and landed near the pyramids in Cassini, I said before we went that I wasn't sure. Something about it didn't seem quite right. But this time, I really do think this is it. I think we've found the Uroborologs, where the ancient Book of our

People has been hidden all this time.'

Max hesitated and looked at the flushed expression on Bodhie's usually pale face. He could tell how much Bodhie would love to be able to find this Book and take it back to the Hidden People. And he wanted to find the Book too, more than anything. He needed to find the Book. In a way, he'd lost everything over it. If he could stop Xegan from getting the Book, and somehow give it back to the Hidden People, then maybe, in some small way, it would make everything a bit better; make everything he'd lost less futile.

But there was something else. He still couldn't help feeling that they were missing something. There was something that still just didn't quite make sense in all of this.

'We're so nearly there now, Max. We've managed to get so far. I agree with Bodhie, I really think we might be able to do this,' said Anna, mistaking Max's silence for doubt.

Max nodded, 'I think we should go too. Of course, I want to go and see if we can find the Book. I just think...' he paused and tried to recollect his thoughts, 'I get this feeling that there's something we're missing here. Something still doesn't add up.'

'Like the bird?' said Anna slowly.

Max glanced quickly at Anna.

But her eyes were serious and she gave him a cautious smile.

Max bit his lip in hesitation. 'Yes, like the bird. Like, how do Valac and the Mothmen keep finding us? Like how and why did my grandad have the map in the first place? Like why did my grandad keep so much from me?'

'Look Max, I was wrong. The bird attacked you and maybe it *has* been tracking us for Xegan and Valac all along. There are some strange worlds out there and we don't know where Xegan has been or what he's found over the last few years. And maybe Malik is working with Xegan. You said that he seemed to recognise the bird and we know that he's been acting strangely. And maybe your grandad just thought he was protecting you. Maybe he thought that he'd tell you about all this one day, but then he never got the chance...' she reached out and touched his arm softly. 'Until we find the Uroborologs, maybe we won't know.'

Max nodded uncertainly. He wished that he felt as confident that his grandad was planning to tell him about this. The trouble was, he didn't. And every time he thought about his grandad, every time he remembered all of the lies that there had been between them, the same tight little knot of anger would settle heavily in his stomach.

'Did you manage to get the Key and the clue without getting caught by the Bridge?' said Anna turning to Bodhie. 'I was really worried that there was going to be a scheduled departure and that you were going to get dragged through somewhere.'

'Yes, but only just!' said Bodhie, 'Luckily there didn't seem to be many Bridge arrivals and departures at that time of night. There was just one departure that happened, just as the secret drawer was opening. But I managed to grab the clue and the Key and get out of the way just in time.'

'Wow that was lucky!'

Bodhie nodded and grinned, 'So, when do we go then?'

'Where is the statue of the veiled woman?' asked Max, trying to tug his thoughts back to the present.

'It's in the capital. In the old part of town, called "Rineferth".'

'Is it going to be difficult to get to?' asked Anna, her expression had brightened considerably.

'Well, I've only been once. My parents dragged me to see it when we were on holiday in Hyperborea a long time ago. But I think that it's right near the centre; near all of the main Hyperborean Government buildings. So, the good news is that there's bound to be a coordinate in the Travel Charts that we can configure the Key for and that will get us pretty close to the statue. But the bad news is, because it's near those buildings, I think it's going to be a really busy area again. We'll need to go at night like last time.'

'OK. I wonder what the time difference between Rineferth and here is, then?' said Max, tugging the little book of Travel Charts out of his pocket and quickly thumbing through the pages until he found the grid of time zones.

'So,' he said hesitantly, scanning across the grid until his eyes found the point where their current location, the Great Rift Plateau, Barren Lands met Rineferth, Hyperborea. 'According to this, Rineferth is two hours ahead of here. It'll be night time there now...'

'What do you think then?' said Bodhie. 'Should we go now or get some rest first?'

Max hesitated, 'Look. That bird. Before tonight, we had only ever seen it in Lucem and we'd only ever seen Valac in Lucem. Every time we escaped to another world using the Key, every time we came here, we seemed to be safe. I thought that we were managing to lose them somehow when we shifted worlds. But tonight we saw that bird in the Shadowlands. It managed to find us and we were only there for ten minutes. What if we've just been lucky so far and they can find us here?'

Fear flickered in Anna's eyes. 'I think we should go now. Maybe we're harder to track if we are on the move.'

Max glanced at Bodhie, 'Are you OK to go

now though? What about you getting tired with making us invisible? Do you need a rest after everything you've just done in the Shadowlands?'

'No, I'm fine. It's not tiring when it's just me. If it's night-time there now, I think we should go.' Bodhie's expression was firm.

'OK, let's do it,' said Max. He paused for a moment, collecting his thoughts. 'If we find the Book tonight – if we can actually get it – then what happens then?'

'If we find the Book tonight,' said Anna decisively taking charge, 'We'll take it to Cade and we'll tell him everything. Look Max, you were right all along that that bird was following us and it stole the necklace. You saw the bird communicating with Malik, so, I think we can be pretty sure now that Malik is the one that's involved with this now, can't we? Why else would he be communicating with that bird that attacked you? I bet it was him that told Valac where you were in Wiltshire with your grandad and it was him that told Valac that you were staying at my house and that we'd be on our own that night. So, we'll go to Cade and we'll tell him everything. We'll tell him about the map and the Temple of Fangs and how Xegan tracked you and your grandad for the map. We'll tell him about the Mothmen, about Malik and the bird, we'll tell him about everything that's happened and how we've managed to find the Book. Then hopefully, everything will get sorted out.'

Max nodded but said nothing, a lurking doubt resurfacing in his mind.

Could this really be it, he wondered. Could this be the final resting place of the lost Uroborologs? Would they really find the Book tonight? And if they did find the Book – if they did manage it – then would it really be the answer to everything he didn't know? Would all the secrets finally be revealed?

'Max? Are you ready to go?'

Max looked up, startled from his thoughts.

It was Anna. She was standing by the fire; her brows were set into a concerned frown.

'Are you OK?'

'What? Yes, I'm fine,' said Max standing and quickly scooping up the Key and Travel Charts.

'You're not in any pain, are you... after that bird?'

'No, I'm fine. They're just scratches.'

'I think we should leave everything here again – except for the things we absolutely need,' said Bodhie, 'And we should go just like we did before. We can land invisibly, check it out and then decide what we're going to do.'

Max nodded and began to flick through the Travel Charts checking for the listed locations in Hyperborea. There was, as Bodhie had predicted, a location for Rineferth, listed under the Hyperborea World symbol. But there was just one, and he had no idea how large the old town was or where they would land in relation to the statue. He thought about the clue, remembering the line, 'A second door hides a chamber and terrors not yet known.' One thing was for certain – even if they were on the right track, even if they had got the right place – getting that Book tonight wasn't going to be easy and that was without including Xegan and Valac who were almost certainly still after the Book; almost certainly still after them.

'Right then,' he said, 'I've got the Location symbols for Rineferth.'

'OK,' said Anna, nervously rubbing her hands together. 'Let's go, then.'

Bodhie nodded and reaching out, ze gripped hold of both their shoulders.

Moments later, they were invisibly swirling into ice cold nothingness.

Chapter 28
The Secret Chamber

'I think it's just a few streets from here,' whispered Bodhie a few minutes later, as they stood hesitantly on the corner of two narrow dimly lit streets.

Tall grey stone buildings rose up on either side of them, disappearing into the shadows as they reached up towards the black, star-strewn sky. A string of old-fashioned streetlamps similar to those that they had seen in the square in the Shadowlands, stretched away from them, casting shallow yellow pools of light across the stone cobbled floor.

Max bit his lip and glanced about. Everything seemed quiet.

'It doesn't seem like there's anyone about,' whispered Bodhie. 'I think that maybe we should become visible again. I'm not going to be able to hide us all for very long and we might really need me to do it later.'

'OK,' said Max, letting go of Bodhie's forearm, which he had been clutching ever since they had landed.

Looking down, Max held his hands out in front of him. For a second, there was nothing, just the stone cobbles of the street, then suddenly a misty whiteness began to form. He could see his hands again. He wiggled his fingers. It really was the weirdest thing, he thought to himself. Cool – but weird.

Moments later, two white cloudy outlines appeared in front of him, which quickly materialized into Anna and Bodhie.

Max breathed out, then he turned and looked quickly around. He peered down the deserted gloomy streets that led away from the corner where they stood. Everything was silent. Nothing stirred. It was almost as if the streets themselves held their breath.

'We should stick close together,' he said quietly.

Bodhie nodded tensely.

'Which way is it, then?' whispered Anna, glancing around warily.

'I think it's this way,' said Bodhie, turning quickly and leading them off down the street to their right.

They hurriedly made their way down the street. Max looked around at the shadowy concealed doorways and dark empty windows. Not a single light glowed from behind any of them. He reminded himself of what Bodhie had said earlier about the statue being near the Hyperborean Government buildings and decided that they were probably mostly offices, which he supposed would be empty at night. But even so, he couldn't help but find the shadowy empty streets eerie.

'There should be a left turn around here somewhere,' said Bodhie, peering ahead at the long string of buildings.

'There!' whispered Anna, pointing in the distance to their left. 'There's a little side street leading off over there.'

'That's it!' breathed Bodhie. 'I think it's down there somewhere.'

They hurriedly approached the dimly lit side street and turned sharply, heading straight down it.

'This is right, I'm sure this is it,' Bodhie whispered eagerly, as ze moved speedily down the gloomy side street with Max and Anna following closely in his wake.

Suddenly Bodhie halted. The street ended abruptly and they found themselves on the verge of a large deserted cobbled square.

They hesitated a moment, hanging back in the shadows and stared nervously out across the square.

It was dark, quiet and deserted. A series of imposing ornate buildings looked out onto the square, their windows shrouded in darkness. Heavy stone steps with baroque balustrades were set at intervals, leading up towards grand entrances and huge shadowy recessed doorways. A number of statues stood around the edge of the square.

'There it is,' breathed Bodhie, 'It's over there.'

Following Bodhie's gaze, Max could just make out the elegantly carved stone shape of a woman sitting, her hands clasped in her lap. The statue was set against the wall of a building at the far side of the square.

Max glanced around. The square was wide open and there was nowhere to hide. Once they crossed over towards the statue, they would be totally exposed; unseen eyes could be watching them hidden from view, everywhere.

'Do you think that maybe we should be invisible?' said Anna quietly, her eyes fixed on the statue.

'Yes, but what if we really need it later?' whispered Bodhie. 'I'm not sure I can do it so many times in one day.'

Anna nodded stiffly but said nothing.

They gazed at the statue in wary silence, knowing that they were each thinking the same thing. They all knew that the sensible thing to do was to preserve Bodhie's energy in case they needed it later, but stepping out into the square would immediately leave them exposed. Anything could be lurking in the shadowy doorways.

They had lingered for a second longer in the safety of the shadows, then together they moved out across the square. Max's hand crept to his pocket, his fingers closing around the reassuring shape of the Uroboros Key. He glanced around again and back over his shoulder; at the blank shadowy windows and doorways shrouded in darkness. Everywhere he looked he saw shadows that could easily become giant, ragged and moth-shaped.

He blinked and breathed out deeply.

Everything was still.

The statue stood against the wall of one of the grand old buildings that bordered the square. As they approached, Max could see that the statue was of an elegant, seated lady, facing towards the square with her hands clasped delicately in her lap. Her back was proud and straight and she had a quiet dignified expression that was just visible behind the delicately carved veil that hung elegantly around her head and shoulders.

Max looked at the statue. His eyes traced the shape and the folds of the carved veil that flowed softly around her, gently shrouding her face and cascading down over her body. It was most certainly a veiled woman. He recalled the first line of the rhyme again: 'A veiled woman knows where our heritage rests.' What secrets was she hiding? he wondered. Could the book really be here?

'OK, so we're here. Now what?' whispered Anna, glancing at the statue and then back over her shoulder at the buildings around the square.

'Well, I guess she's got to be hiding something...' said Max, hesitantly reaching out and touching the folds of the carved veil as they flowed gently over the statue's arm.

'Like what?'

'I don't know.'

'What do you think, Bodhie?' whispered Anna.

I'm not sure,' said Bodhie. Ze crouched down and began inspecting the heavy slabs of stone that sat beneath the statue.

Max crouched down next to Bodhie and began to do the same. The stone felt smooth, solid and cool to touch.

'Maybe there's some ancient writing?' suggested Max.

Bodhie nodded. 'That's what I'm looking for.'

'I can't see any writing anywhere,' whispered Anna, impatiently leaning forward to peer at the statue.

'No,' Bodhie sighed and stepped back from the statue. 'I can't see anything either.'

'This is taking too long,' said Anna nervously, glancing back warily over her shoulder.

'I know,' said Max, 'But there's got to be something we're missing.'

A soft clatter suddenly rang out across the square and they turned sharply, their eyes darting towards the shadowy doorways and dark windows. A dark grey cat slipped out from the shadows. It paused and glanced across at them. Then with a flick of its tail, it turned and slinked away, melting back into the shadows.

Max blew out a long breath and then quickly returned his attention to the statue. There had to be something here; something that they weren't seeing.

'What about the Key?' he whispered suddenly. 'The Key's got to be for something.'

'But this is a statue, not a door. You don't unlock a statue,' said Anna.

'No, I know, but...' Max's eyes swept over the statue looking for anything – a tiny nick or indentation that might fit the little Key. His eyes fell on the woman's hands clasped tightly in her lap. He frowned and swallowed. There where her forefingers and thumbs intertwined together was a small, dark, shadowy gap.

'Bodhie,' he whispered hesitantly, 'Let me see that Key.'

Bodhie pulled the Key out from zer pocket and handed it to Max. Leaning forward, Max held the small shiny Key out towards the gap and then carefully inserted it between the lady's intertwined fingers. It slipped positively into place. The Key clicked home.

Shocked, he turned and glanced back towards Anna and Bodhie. Their eyes widened in surprise. Then slowly, carefully, he turned the Key. The Key clicked for a second time. It was followed a second later by a dull scraping sound that echoed faintly through the square. Max looked up startled. The sound seemed unnervingly loud in the quiet, stillness of the night. But there was something else about the sound, it was almost... familiar.

Glancing around, Max saw to his surprise, that a tall narrow stone set into the wall directly behind the statue, was slowly moving backwards and to the side, revealing a narrow shadowy opening.

'I guess a key can open a statue,' whispered Anna, her eyes glinting with anticipation in the darkness.

The opening revealed a narrow spiral stone staircase that curled away from them, descending below the ground.

'It looks like it takes us beneath the square,' Bodhie said, hesitantly stepping towards the shadowy opening.

A wooden torch was propped up against the wall, just inside the opening. Picking it up, Anna quickly lit the torch with one of the firelighters they'd brought with them and they stepped inside the shadowy entrance and onto the first step.

Max looked around in the flickering torchlight. A carved stone snake had been crafted into the wall in place of a handrail. It curled away from them, as the staircase wound downwards, disappearing around the corner and into the shadows.

'Here goes,' Bodhie whispered hoarsely, and they slowly began their descent into the winding darkness.

Down and down the staircase spiralled, curling away from them, as they slowly descended deeper and deeper beneath the square. The torchlight crackled and flickered off the smooth curved stone walls. Then abruptly the staircase opened out and they found themselves in a dark stone passageway.

Max shivered, feeling the goose bumps rise on his arms. There was something unnervingly familiar about all of this, he thought, remembering with a shudder their experience at the Temple of Fangs.

They hurriedly made their way along the passage in silence; the smooth stone walls and stone flagged floor stretched away from them, disappearing into the darkness. Then suddenly something loomed into view up ahead.

'Look!' Anna gasped suddenly, 'It's a door!'

Squinting ahead in the darkness, they could

just make out the shape of a large heavy wooden door that stood at the end of the passageway from the light of the flickering torch.

Max stopped abruptly, 'Wait,' he said suddenly, not even really knowing why.

Cautiously, he peered around the passageway in the gloom. Instinctively Max felt as though he was looking for something, but he didn't really understand why. He just knew he felt really uneasy.

He stepped forward again uncertainly and held the torch aloft. In the darkness, a large gaping hole suddenly appeared in the ground directly in front of them.

Beside him in the darkness, Bodhie gave a sudden sharp intake of breath, 'Look at that! There's a huge hole!'

'Geez, that was close!' muttered Anna shakily, 'I didn't see that!'

The hole was enormous and square and spanned almost the entire width of the passageway, leaving only a narrow stone strip on either side of the gap. Beyond the hole, standing in the shadows was the huge, arched, wooden door.

Max peered down into the hole. Large slabs of smooth stone were set into the sides of the hole, creating an almost perfect square that dropped away from them, disappearing down into the darkness. It looked deep. But there was something else – it looked built. Very precisely built.

'I think we can get across, by walking across those narrow stone strips on each side. They look just about wide enough,' said Anna.

Bodhie bent down and began examining the lengths of stone at one edge.

Max was silent. He looked at the door and then stared down into the hole again. Something just didn't feel quite right, but he wasn't exactly sure why.

'I'm not sure about this,' he said quietly.

'Why? What do you mean?' said Bodhie, glancing up from where ze was positioned on the floor.

'I don't really know,' Max paused, feeling his way through his thoughts. 'Can we just quickly read the clue again? The whole thing.'

'Sure,' said Bodhie, tugging the little scroll of parchment out of zer pocket.

You will finally get to know your fate,

In a changing world we cannot state.

A veiled woman knows where our heritage rests,

But you must pass through our final series of tests.

Choose wisely lest you may regret,

A leap of faith may be the answer yet.

A second door hides a chamber and terrors not yet known,

The final hurdle to the secret tome.

Max hesitated, 'I think...' he said slowly, 'that we're not meant to go through that door.'

Bodhie frowned, 'But surely that's the second door, isn't it?'

'Maybe. But what about, "Choose wisely lest you may regret, a leap of faith may be the answer yet". What about that?'

Bodhie shook his head blankly, 'I don't know. I was thinking that maybe that bit comes next, after we go through the door?'

'Maybe,' said Max, 'or maybe not. Maybe that's the choice we'll come to regret. I think we're being tested here.'

Bodhie's brows knitted into a deep frown. Ze nodded slowly.

'But I don't see a choice. I see one door,' exclaimed Anna. 'Surely we have no option but to go through there?'

'Not necessarily...' Max said slowly, 'We could go down...'

'Down! What, down there?' said Anna, pointing at the black hole incredulously.

Max nodded, 'Look, we're being tested here. Look at what happened the last time, when we went to the pyramid courtyard and we ignored one part of the clue, the bit about the shadows. We ended up being wrong. A gate guards the key to our secret, where the shadows and light pyramid meet. The Clue had to be followed exactly and I think we should now. "Choose wisely lest you may regret." We're being asked to make a choice.'

'If we go down that hole, we might regret it!' Anna said flatly, 'We can't see how deep it is Max...'

'I know, but the leap of faith... If it's not going down that hole, then what is it?'

Bodhie looked thoughtful. 'But what about the second door? That's in the clue too.'

'But the door bit comes afterwards in the clue – after the choice and the leap of faith. Maybe this is actually the first door and the second door is down that hole. We don't know what's down there.'

'No we don't know what's down there. That's the point. It could be really dangerous!' said Anna.

'All I know,' said Max, 'Is that this feels far too straight forward. It's too obvious. The clue says that we're being tested. It says we have a choice to make or we'll regret it. The only choice here is through that door or down that hole and it tells us we have to take a leap of faith. Look at what happened in the temple when we were at that maze. It was the least obvious path – the dead-end – that we needed to take then. And that turned out to be right.'

Bodhie peered into the hole and frowned. 'I hate to say it, but I think you might be right, Max.'

Max looked at Anna's stubborn expression. 'The hole has got to be here for a reason, hasn't it?'

'Yes, maybe so people can fall in and plunge to their deaths! Look Max, I know what you're saying, but it could also be a trick. When we were in the temple, we nearly got crushed to death. This could be exactly like that; it looks really deep.'

'I know. I'm worried about that too. But if you think about the clue, I don't think just going through that door is right either. It's just...' Max hesitated, 'It's just too straight forward. Look I'll go down and I'll take the Key. If it's right and it's OK, I'll shout up to you and you can jump down and join me. If it's wrong, then I'll have to use the Uroboros Key to transport myself out.'

'But couldn't we just try the door first and see what happens – see what's in there – and then if we're wrong, we go down the hole?'

'I'm not sure it works like that, Anna. If we go through that door and I am right, and we do need to follow the clue exactly – if we're supposed to take a leap of faith or we'll regret it – we might lose our chance to get the Book. Anyway, there could be something worse behind that door. It could be a trap.'

'And if it's really deep?' said Anna glancing down at the hole, her eyebrows raised.

'If it's really deep, then hopefully I can configure the Key in time before I hit the floor,' he grinned at her. 'Look, if I am right, I don't think we have an option.'

Bodhie was still peering into the hole and frowning thoughtfully. Ze was looking, Max realised, for some kind of clue that would support Max's theory. 'OK,' ze said after a moment, nodding, 'I can't find any other messages around the hole, but I do know what you mean. Compared to everything else so far, this does seem far too straightforward and so far, the clues have always had to be followed exactly. But look Max, it doesn't always have to be you. I'll go.'

'It's not about who goes and who doesn't,' snapped Anna, 'I'll go. It's about whether it's a stupid idea or not.'

'And it's my stupid idea, so I'll do it,' said Max. 'if I'm right, you can jump down and join me. If I'm wrong... then it's my mistake. I've got the Key. I'll have to meet you outside again.'

They stood in silence at the edge of the hole. It looked deep and very, very dark.

'Well, you'll need a light when you get down there...' said Anna, handing him one of the firelighters. 'Sorry, there's only one. It's all we've got left.'

'Thanks,' said Max, taking the fire lighter and peering down into the gloom. After making such a convincing argument, he now wondered if he'd totally lost his mind. What was he doing? Could there really be anything down this hole? He could break his leg. Or much worse...

He glanced at the door again, standing in the shadows at the end of the passage. But if he was wrong and they were supposed to go through that door, then half the clue just didn't make any sense. It had to be right. He was sure of it. His heart beginning to pound, he placed the firelighter in the pocket of his trousers.

'If you need help, shout... and you've got the key of course...' Bodhie's voice trailed away awkwardly.

Max glanced at Bodhie and for a moment, their matching silvery grey eyes met. They both knew that he would struggle to use the Key on his way down. Something was either going to catch him or he was going to hit the ground.

'Well, good luck,' Anna muttered quietly. But she reached out and gave Max's arm a tight squeeze.

Max nodded. Then, clutching the Uroboros

Key firmly in his hand, he took a deep breath and jumped.

Max felt himself falling through dark nothingness. Cold damp air rushed past him. The wind whistled past his ears.

Down and down, deeper and deeper he fell through the blackness.

Then flop, he hit something, it gave way around him and then sprang back taut. He bounced back up. He fell. It caught him again and he lay there sprawled; bouncing and wobbling as the thing slowly came to a rest, beneath him in the darkness.

Max lay still, breathing out deeply, his eyes focused on a small flickering square of light, somewhere in the distance above him. He blinked. He could just make out two faint dark blobs at the edge of the square hole, which must have been Anna and Bodhie's heads peering down into the darkness. He'd made it.

'Max?' Bodhie's voice floated down to him.

'I'm alright!' he yelled.

'Are you sure?' shouted Anna.

'I'm fine; I've landed on...' he hesitated, 'Hang on.'

What had he landed on? he wondered. He rubbed his hands across the surface around him.

Something flexed and moved beneath his fingers. His fingers found tiny gaps. It felt like rope. It felt like a net.

He wriggled himself forward in the darkness. The net wobbled and quivered. His foot found an edge and he heaved himself forward.

Something twanged faintly in the darkness. The net jerked beneath him, and then suddenly gave way.

'Aaaargh!'

Max felt himself drop sharply. He hit the ground with a dull thud, landing in a sprawled heap across the floor. Whatever it was that had caught him, appeared to have just snapped.

'Max?! What's going on? Are you okay?' Anna shouted.

'I'm-I'm fine. Hang on!' he yelped, tugging the firelighter out of his pocket.

It sparked and burnt brightly. Max blinked for a second, unaccustomed to the light. Smooth stone walls suddenly appeared around him in the gloom. He was standing at the bottom of a very long square vertical shaft that stretched above him reaching up towards the faint square of light and Anna and Bodhie's heads in the distance. A torn rope net that had been attached to the wall, hung down loosely and was strewn across the floor. A wooden torch was propped against the wall.

Bending down, Max picked up the torch and lit it. The tunnel shaft was suddenly flooded with light.

'I'm fine,' he shouted, 'there was a net – it caught me, but it's snapped.'

Turning, Max looked around the tunnel and his heart skipped a beat. Behind him, there was a door. A heavy wooden, arched door. He swallowed.

'There's a door,' he shouted hoarsely.

'Great! We'll come down,' called Bodhie.

Max turned and looked back at the net on the floor, it had snapped and torn, where it had attached to the wall. He picked up the piece of net, stretching it back towards the wall. It didn't reach.

'I don't think you can. The net's broken!'

'Can't you fix it?' yelled Anna.

'No, I don't think so,' he called to them, doubtfully.

There was a long pause.

'What do you want to do?' shouted Bodhie.

Turning, Max looked back at the door. The door was made from a heavy dark wood. A piece of twisted metal, looped in the shape of a serpent, hung down in place of a handle. Next to the handle was a small shiny keyhole.

Max hesitated for a moment. If he used the Uroboros Key and left now, they might not be able to get down here again. This could be their only chance to get the Book before Xegan. On his own or not, there was no way he was leaving. Not when they had come this far. Max knew there was only one thing to do.

His heart hammering in his chest, he took a step towards the door and pulled the strange little double-ended key out of his pocket. Holding the key out, he carefully placed one end of the key in the lock and twisted it.

The lock clicked and Max's breath caught in his chest.

'It's worked! The key's worked!' he shouted hoarsely, 'I'm going through. I'm going to see if I can find the Book.'

'What, on your own?' Anna shouted anxiously.

'What other option do we have? We might not be able to get back down here again.' Max shouted up to them. 'I've got to try. If it's not here or if I can't get it, I'll use the Uroboros Key and meet you back outside in the square in a few minutes.'

'But maybe we could get some help and come back, instead of you going in alone?' shouted Bodhie.

'You're forgetting about Xegan. There isn't time. If the Book's still here, we've got to try and get it,' said Max, trying to inject some confidence into his voice.

Max turned and faced the door. His heart pounding in his chest, he reached out and gripped hold of the serpent shaped handle.

A second door hides a chamber and terrors not yet known. He glanced back up towards the faint square of light far above. The light flickered, and then faded as Bodhie and Anna slowly disappeared back along the passageway. The light extinguished. The pale square of light disappeared.

He was alone.

He hesitated, wishing for a moment, that he'd asked them to stay, instead of telling them to meet him back outside in the square. But then, what would they be able to do anyway? They couldn't get down here. No matter what happened, they wouldn't be able to help him. He was on his own.

Max swallowed hard. Then slowly, apprehensively, he turned the handle.

SAM KINI

Chapter 29
The Uroborologs

He was standing at the end of a large dimly lit chamber. Towering stone pillars rose out of the floor arcing and arching as they disappeared into the distant shadowy reaches of the ceiling, and casting long black shadows through the gloomy chamber. Ahead of him, Max could just make out a large alter-like carved stone table.

Max blinked. Something was sitting on top of the table. It was thick and square and looked, unless Max was deeply mistaken, like a book. His heart skipped a beat.

He hesitated in the doorway and peered around the chamber. The room stretched away from him in every direction, disappearing in the dark spaces between distant pillars and beyond. He couldn't see how far the room reached. He couldn't see what lurked in the unseen corners and shadowy spaces beyond the reach of his torch.

Fighting down a tiny wave of panic, Max held his breathed and listened. Everything was still. There was just the sound of his torch crackling in the chilly silence of the chamber. His eyes fixed on the line of pillars that stretched away from him and the stone table and book up ahead. A second door hides a chamber and terrors not yet known. Could he be wrong? Was there nothing down here after all?

Max slowly stepped forward into the chamber. Then he hesitated again, straining to listen into the dark reaches of the room. Nothing stirred.

Clutching the Uroboros Key tightly in his hand, Max took a deep breath and then set off quickly across the chamber. His footsteps echoed sharply off the shadowy stone walls and he stopped abruptly, unnerved by how loud his footsteps sounded in the chilly silence of the room.

He glanced around the chamber again, at the gloomy shadows lingering between the pillars. Everything seemed still.

He stepped forward again, his eyes darting around the chamber. Then suddenly, out of the corner of his eye, Max glimpsed a movement up ahead, something was shifting slowly in the darkness.

Max froze. Between the pillars, no more than ten paces away up ahead, something black had stirred in the shadows. Something was watching him. Something huge.

Max felt the sweat start out on his forehead.

A scraping sound echoed faintly through the chamber, as though a sharp object were being gently dragged across the hard stone floor. It was followed by a low rumbling growl that reverberated softy around the room. Fear immediately flooded

Max's body. He knew that sound. He'd heard it before.

Max turned and ran in the opposite direction, throwing himself behind a nearby pillar.

A deep rumbling snarl immediately rang out across the chamber behind him.

Fighting a rising tide of panic, Max inched towards the edge of the pillar and quickly looked around. A huge black Watcher had stepped out of the shadows. Max couldn't even see its full length, as it was still partially hidden in the shadows, but it stood at least twenty feet high. It was quite possibly the biggest creature that he had ever seen.

The Watcher's yellow slanted eyes narrowed as it looked slowly around the chamber, taking in the open doorway. It snorted menacingly and grey smoke shot from its nostrils. The yellow gaze slowly scanned back again, then stopped. Its eyes fixed on the pillar where Max was hiding.

It knew where he was.

Max's heart began to pound. He quickly drew back behind the pillar, his fingers clutching the Uroboros Key tightly in his sweating palm. What should he do? He guessed that maybe five pillars stood between him and the Book. The stone altar was solid. If only he could get to it, he could hide behind it and use the Uroboros Key to get out of there. But to reach it meant moving out into the open and that meant moving out in front of the

Watcher. With dismay, Max realised that for him to be able to get to the Book, the Watcher would also be able to get to him.

A deep guttural growl reverberated around the chamber. It was followed immediately afterwards by the sound of claws scraping across the hard stone floor. Max froze behind the pillar, his stomach twisting into a tight knot of fear. It was moving towards him. He had to think fast. What was it that Templar had said about Watchers? It was all in the confidence and tone of voice. But would it work? Wasn't the whole point that Watchers were supposed to guard things? That they should attack? He hesitated. But then, it must work sometimes. Otherwise no one would ever be able to tell a Watcher to do anything and the Keepers must have been able to get past it to get to the Book. Bodhie had said that Watchers could see Hidden People even when they were invisible, so the Keepers must have done something to get past it.

A soft scraping sound echoed again through the chamber.

Max knew that he had to do something before the Watcher reached him. Filled with misgiving, and hardly able to believe what he was actually about to do, Max took a deep breath and stepped out from behind the pillar.

'I'm a friend of the Hidden People and I'm here to get the Book,' he said in a voice that was as confident and commanding as he could muster.

Even as the words left his lips, Max knew that it was a huge mistake.

The Watcher blinked, almost as if it could hardly believe that Max had stepped out in front of it; a thick curl of dark grey smoke seeping dangerously from its slanted nostrils. Then its yellow eyes narrowed and it roared.

Max dived across the room and threw himself behind the next pillar, just as a blast of smouldering heat shot across the chamber, narrowly missing him.

The air smelt acrid. The Watcher snarled.

Max could hear the snap of its ferocious teeth, stood just feet away from him on the other side of the column. He could feel the heat of its breath.

Forcing down a wave of panic, Max struggled to think. He needed to do something. If he stayed, he would be scorched, but if he moved...

Dropping the torch, Max dived across the chamber floor, just as the Watcher roared and a bout of flames shot from its mouth. He lunged towards the next pillar, scrambling quickly behind it. Flames seared past him, barely missing his legs and scorching the air. Glancing back, he could see that the pillar he had just left, was blackened and smoking.

This wasn't working. He had to do something. He was about to become dinner. His hand slipped quickly to his pocket and he pulled out the last remaining Poca. Would smoke work? he wondered. Watchers could see Hidden People even when they were invisible. What if they could also see through smoke? But then, besides the Uroboros Key and Travel Charts, the Poca was the only thing he had.

A deep rumbling growl reverberated around the chamber again.

Max thought fast. He knew that this could totally backfire on him. He swallowed and looked down. The Uroboros Key was clutched in one hand; the Poca glinted in the palm of the other. With fear flooding every cell and nerve in his body, Max stepped out in front of the Watcher for a second time.

Fighting every impulse in his body to run, Max squared his shoulders and met the Watchers furious, yellow-eyed gaze. He stared up into the huge snarling face and for a moment he forgot to breath.

The Watcher let out a deep guttural growl that ended with a snarl, blasting Max with its hot pungent breath. Then it took a step towards Max and lunged at him.

This had been the moment that Max had been waiting for. Diving sideways, he skidded across the floor.

The Watcher let out an ear-splitting roar that rumbled around the chamber. Its head swung back towards Max. In an instant, Max threw the Poca into the Watchers wide-open mouth. Then leaping to his feet, he threw himself across the chamber and in the direction of the stone altar.

A second roar erupted behind him, rocking the chamber.

Max ran and ran. He didn't look back.

A blast of heat surged towards him that ended abruptly, with a muffled bang.

His heart racing and blood pounding in his ears, Max charged towards the stone altar. He lunged at it, knocking the book to the floor as he dived across the hard stone surface. Glancing back fleetingly, Max saw to his astonishment that the Watcher was engulfed in a swirling cloud of thick grey smoke. He hadn't expected it to work.

Crouching down behind the altar, Max's eyes scanned frantically around. To his relief, the Book was there, sitting beside him on the dusty floor. It was huge, ancient and bound in a rich, dark leather, with the faded gold emblem of the serpent, inscribed into the front. Down the side were seven gold clasps that folded over the edge of the book, each pressed shut with a red wax seal. Max's heart skipped a beat; he stared at it for a moment, hardly able to believe his eyes. Then heaving the Book towards him, he quickly began to configure the Key.

The Watcher roared from somewhere behind him. But it wasn't close. Max knew that it couldn't see him; the Watcher was still struggling in the smoke. Max paused for a moment, confused. How did he know the Watcher was still in the smoke? Turning slightly, Max stretched up and looked quickly back across the chamber.

The Watcher was still standing by the pillar, enveloped in a thick swirling plume of grey smoke. But then, he'd already known that.

Max faltered. He was looking at it. But he was also looking from within it. He was inside the swirling mass of thick fog too. He could see the thick tendrils of smoke curling around his eyes. He could sense the Watcher. He could feel its confusion.

This isn't possible, he thought.

Shaking himself and clutching the Book to his chest, he quickly finished configuring the Key.

The Watcher shuddered. Max felt the erupted Poca deep inside. He could feel the Watcher's surprised discomfort.

Doubt flickered through his mind. What was happening?

The Key began to slowly vibrate in his hands. The snake began to revolve. Looking down, Max clasped the Book tightly to his chest, gripping the Key firmly in his hands. Then he felt the sudden, familiar sharp jolt deep in his stomach and his feet abruptly left the stone-tiled floor.

Moments later, Max landed with a gentle thud, back on the corner of the two narrow, dimly lit streets. He glanced around quickly, noticing vaguely that for once he'd landed on his feet. Nothing stirred in the tall grey stone buildings that rose up on either side of him; the windows were still shrouded in darkness.

Looking down, Max gazed at the ancient Book resting in his hands. The faded gold serpent imprinted into the front, glinted faintly in the gloomy light of the street. He squeezed it, feeling its weighty solidness filled with the promise of secrets and knowledge, the smell of its ancient musty pages. Then, clutching it triumphantly to his chest, he set off quickly down the street to his right.

The Book was here. They'd actually done it. Max felt a gentle thrill of delight, a bubble of warmth slowly began to expand in his chest. He couldn't wait to find Anna and Bodhie. He couldn't wait to see their faces.

He set off running down the street, keeping to the shadows. He glanced around at the concealed doorways and dark empty windows but nothing stirred. He ran on, his eyes scanning the long row of buildings to his left, searching for the narrow dimly lit side street that he knew would take him back to the square. Then he saw it, tucked neatly between two buildings and turning sharply, he hurried down the side street, clutching the book tightly to his chest. The street ended and Max stopped abruptly, breathless and excited. He looked out across the square, his eyes searching for Anna and Bodhie.

Breathing in sharply, Max hastily drew himself back into the shadows, flattening himself against the wall. Two men wearing long dark travelling cloaks were standing in the middle of the square. They were leaning towards one another and talking in low, gruff voices.

Cursing himself for being so stupid, Max held his breath as their brisk, urgent voices drifted towards him over the square.

The men were standing close to one another in the centre of the square. One of the men wore a long dark full-length cloak; his face was almost entirely concealed by his hood. The other man had his back towards Max and was taller with dark hair. There was something about his rigid stance and the way that he moved, that made Max certain that he was angry about something.

Crouching down to make himself as inconspicuous as possible, Max leaned forward as far as he dared, straining to listen to their voices. His eyes searched the square. He couldn't see Anna or Bodhie anywhere.

'You said it would work...' came the sound of one of the voices.

There was the sound of a second deeper voice, but Max couldn't quite catch the words. He glanced back towards the men again. The hooded man appeared to be gesturing towards the statue of the veiled lady and the shadowy gap of the secret passageway, just visible behind her.

Max felt his stomach clench with fear. There was no sign of Anna and Bodhie. He couldn't see them anywhere. He glanced back towards the passageway and a terrible wave of dread rushed through him. Had they already been caught?

A soft thrumming sound suddenly filled the air. Max looked around. The thrumming sound grew steadily louder. Seconds later, it was joined by a rushing sound of wind as something cut swiftly through the night air and two Mothmen swooped down, plunging to the ground near the two men. The Mothmen folded their spiny black translucent wings against their bodies and turned to face the man with dark hair. It was, Max was absolutely certain, Valac and the other Mothman from the giant, underground chasm beneath the temple.

A thin trickle of sweat slowly slid down Max's back.

He looked quickly around the square again, at the statues and the doorways. If he could just find them — if he could just meet up with them somehow — then they could get away from here.

The voices became louder, clearer. Max could hear the strange clicking sound of the Mothmen drifting faintly towards him.

'They could have already got it,' said the man

with dark hair, he sounded agitated.

'If they have, they've got to be around here somewhere. They can't have gone far,' the hooded man said gruffly, glancing around the square.

Max shrank back, clutching the Book and Key to his chest. So, they hadn't been caught. At least, not yet.

Leaning forward again slightly, Max looked back across the square – and froze.

The man with dark hair had turned towards him now. His face was gaunt, his cheeks sunken and hollowed. His steely silver eyes scanned the square, searching.

'I want that Book. You know how important this is to our plans,' he said angrily. Something very dangerous glinted behind the hard silvery eyes.

Max stared back from his crouched position in the shadows. Every fibre of his being told him that this was Xegan.

Xegan. The man who had caused all of this. The man who had killed his grandad. Chased them. Nearly killed them. Max felt anger flood his body; fists clenched, his nails dug deep into his palms.

'Let's finish this. You know where to find me,' said Xegan turning back towards the hooded man and Valac.

'What about them?' said the hooded man.

'If you find them, do whatever you need to do. Just bring me the book,' said Xegan. His voice was cool, hard. 'And don't let me down.'

Max watched with gritted teeth; a silent rage boiling inside him.

The hooded man murmured something to Xegan that Max couldn't quite catch, then turned to the second Mothman. The Mothman unfolded his huge black wings and shot vertically up in to the air, disappearing into the darkness.

Xegan turned and glanced quickly around the square again; his silvery, hard, grey eyes flashed. Then he lifted his hand, the sleeve of his cloak fell back and Max saw that he was holding a Uroboros Key. He twisted a dial on the Key, nodded at the hooded man and seconds later he vanished, leaving the hooded man and Valac alone in the square.

Max crouched in rigid silence; fists still clenched. He stared at the spot where Xegan had just disappeared with a strange mixture of relief and dismay. He'd gone.

Max bit his lip. He felt like a coward. He'd sat there and watched the person who had killed his grandad leave and done absolutely nothing. Why hadn't he done something? He should have done something. But what? said another tiny part of his brain. What could he have done? It would have been four against one. He'd have got himself killed.

Hating himself for doing nothing, Max looked back across the square. The hooded man had turned back towards Valac and was talking in a low, urgent voice. Max couldn't hear the words, but the rhythm of his voice sounded angry, agitated. He pointed over towards the statue of the veiled lady.

Beginning to panic, Max looked around the square again. He needed to find Anna and Bodhie. They needed to leave now. Surely, they couldn't still be invisible. Not after all this time...

A sudden, abrupt clatter echoed across the deserted square. Valac and the hooded man turned sharply, their heads swung around.

Max froze.

The man's hood had fallen back and suddenly Max found himself staring into a pair of dark brooding eyes. A pair of eyes he recognised. Max gasped and recoiled, sinking back into the shadows. With a sickening jolt, he realised that those dark eyes belonged to someone he knew. But they weren't Malik's. They belonged to Krake.

Chapter 30
The Hooded Man

Max shrank back and crouched against the wall. He clutched his knees, feeling sick and confused.

Krake. But how could it be Krake?

Krake that come to his rescue with Imeda, that had saved him from the Mothmen. Krake that had blamed himself and taken their disappearance so badly. Krake that had been searching for them. They'd *seen* him searching for them. He'd looked so upset.

All lies.

Max remembered with some revulsion that it was only the Elders who had known their location on Earth. Krake had only just become an Elder – he had only just gained access to their location. It was his first visit to see his grandad. He remembered his grandad congratulating him, as he'd sat on the stairs that night. The night when all this had started.

The night after, Valac had arrived for the map. But the plan hadn't worked, they hadn't got the map, it had come to Lucem with Max. But of course, Krake hadn't known that. He hadn't known what Imeda and Otty had packed with Max's things. He'd been outside saving them. No wonder Krake had worried so much about finding them. He'd wanted the map. He wanted to find them for Xegan.

Max felt sick. Slowly, numbly, he knelt forward and looked back across the square. He had to find Anna and Bodhie. They had to leave now.

Valac and Krake had turned away and were moving quickly towards the statue of the veiled lady.

Slowly, cautiously, Max inched forward. He glanced around the square, searching the gaps behind the statues, the gloomy corners and dark doorways. He couldn't see them anywhere.

Then out of the corner of his vision, Max caught a furtive movement, over near the statue of the veiled lady. With a sickening sense of foreboding, Max looked quickly across the square. It had been fleeting, but he was sure that something had moved, it had definitely been there, just beyond Valac and Krake.

Valac and Krake had seen it too, as they fanned out and began moving hurriedly towards the statue, arms outstretched, Valac's vicious talons clawing the air.

Seconds ticked by. Max stared desperately towards the statue and fought a rising tide of panic.

Then a pale, translucent, mist suddenly appeared across the square.

Max watched in horror as the white mist quickly moved away from the secret passageway and away from Krake and Valac.

Krake saw it and turned. Valac roared.

The mist vanished.

Max's heart tightened with dread. He could see the expanse of open space in the square. There was nowhere to hide.

In a heartbeat, Valac lunged forwards, grappling savagely at the place where Bodhie and Anna had just disappeared.

Valac's hands found air; he turned and let out a deep shuddering scream.

Just beyond, something moved again. A glimmer of white.

A chill of horror swept through Max.

Two misty white shapes appeared across the square. The pale hazy forms quickly gained shape and substance, before materialising into the startled figures of Anna and Bodhie.

Max could see the shock and terror etched across their faces.

Lunging forwards, Valac seized them, gripping them both fiercely by the shoulders.

Anna screamed. Bodhie gasped with pain; ze looked exhausted.

Valac screeched triumphantly.

Krake turned; a gloating sneer on his twisted,

unrecognisable face.

They were caught.

'Finally! Now, where is the Book? What have you done with it?' Krake said coldly, grabbing Anna and shaking her roughly by the shoulders.

Max could see the fear in her eyes. But her expression was defiant, and she didn't reply.

'Tell me!' Krake roared, his face contorted, 'What have you done with it? Where is Max?'

Anna looked terrified. But she stayed stubbornly silent, instead she kicked out, narrowly missing Krake's chest.

Krake grabbed her roughly by the top and leaning in close to her face, hissed something that Max couldn't hear. Then he turned and grabbed Bodhie by the neck.

Horror rose inside Max. He had to do something. He had to save his friends.

His mind racing, he looked desperately around the square; for any sign of movement, for any kind of help. There was nothing.

Thinking fast, Max rose silently to his feet. Then he edged away from the square and backwards into the darkness of the street. He turned and looked quickly around; a shadowy recessed doorway stood off to the right. Three heavy stone steps led up to the door, flanked on either side by an ornate railing. Max eyed it for a moment, thinking. Then he quickly stepped forward and tucked the Book into the shadows, behind the railing.

He knew that anybody really looking, would easily be able to see the Book and by daylight, it would be obvious. But he had no time. It would just have to do.

Panic rose inside him. He pushed it down, then taking a deep breath, Max turned and walked quickly back towards the square. 'Leave them alone! If it's me you want, I'm here!' he shouted gruffly.

Krake turned to stare at Max. His face twisted with smug satisfaction.

Max walked steadily across the square towards them. His heart was hammering in his chest so hard, that he was sure that they could probably hear it. He tried to swallow but his mouth had suddenly gone dry. He could see Krake eagerly watching his approach. There was a hungry look in his dark eyes.

Valac turned, still restraining a struggling Anna and Bodhie. Two fiery red unblinking eyes focused on Max. The silent glare followed him as he steadily made his way across the square.

Gulping down a wave of panic, Max thrust his hands into his pockets. He could feel the shape of the Uroboros Key in one pocket and the strange little double-ended key in the other. Slowly, tensely, he breathed out. He could do this.

He glanced quickly towards Anna and Bodhie as he approached. Anna immediately met his eyes and opened her mouth as if to speak, but Max frowned and silenced her with a quick, indiscernible shake of his head.

'Where is it?' said Krake angrily. 'You've opened up the chamber. Now where is it?'

'I-I couldn't get it,' said Max, trying to inject some confidence into his shaking voice.

Krake frowned at Max, his dark eyes full of suspicion.

'I wasn't able to get it. But I know where it is.'

Krake's eyes narrowed.

Max swallowed but said nothing.

'You'd better hope that you're telling me the truth,' he said, his voice dangerously quiet.

He grabbed Max and tugged the collar of his shirt down.

'So, I see you worked out about the tracking device then?' A smile curled the corners of his mouth, 'I thought that the tale about your father and I finding it, would have made sure you took better care of it...' He tutted softly under his breath.

Max frowned, uncomprehending. He touched

his collar. So the chain had been tracking them all this time. The amulet hadn't been his father's after all. He'd lied. Again.

'Quite clever of you to dump it at the other side of the town, like that, to throw us off track. I underestimated you. Although maybe you should have dumped the chain in another world altogether. We still found you!' he laughed, his twisted smile widening.

Max felt sick. All this time, whilst he had been treasuring his father's chain, he'd actually been helping Krake and Valac to track them down. How he and Xegan must have laughed about that!

His fists clenched in his pockets angrily.

He remembered Krake searching for them in the Shadowlands; how quickly he had arrived, just minutes after they had reached the stone circle. How obvious it seemed now.

'So, the bird...' began Max.

'What bird?' said Krake, his eyes narrowed.

Max fell silent. So, the bird had actually helped them.

Max looked into Krake's dark brooding eyes, the eyes that days before, he had believed held friendship. He felt a deep, boiling rage.

'Why? Why have you done this?'

'Why, what?' said Krake shrugging, an ugly

look on his face, 'We wanted the map; we need it for our plans. Xegan has wanted it for years, but no one was allowed to know your location.' Krake gave a hollow laugh. 'It was only when I finally became an Elder that my precious father allowed me to know where you were. I didn't want people getting suspicious, so I made up a story about Xegan being recently sighted, so that the protocol of us coming to inform your grandad would kick in. I came to visit your grandad with Imeda so that I knew for sure where you were. Then, I sent Valac.' He paused.

Max looked steadily into his eyes, a furious pounding in his ears.

'Unfortunately, Valac didn't get it in time. The fact that you had chosen that night to go poking around in your grandad's study, stopped Valac from getting the map, because *you,* with your blundering around, alerted everyone to the fact that something was wrong. If you hadn't gone snooping and ended up accidentally using the Key that night, then this whole situation would have been dealt with, and we would have got the Book by now.'

Max stared at Krake, his teeth gritted. This whole situation would have been dealt with. Krake meant that he would have been dealt with. He would probably have been killed, just like his grandad.

'We thought that the map might still be at the house, of course,' Krake continued coolly, 'But it was only when Valac returned and searched the place, that we realised that either it had gone and your grandad had got rid of it or you must actually have it; that it must somehow have been packed with your things. So I began tracking you and we've been chasing you ever since. Unfortunately, we could only track you inside the Five Kingdoms. We kept losing you. You've been leaving the Five Kingdoms, haven't you?'

Max ignored the question. He glared into the dark eyes. Anger coursed through him.

'But my grandad – you killed him. You nearly killed us. You're supposed to be an Elder! Why?!' he said, shaking with suppressed rage.

'Casualties of a greater cause, Max. My father doesn't know how to lead Lucem forward; he doesn't know what the Five Kingdoms need. Neither do the other leaders in Five Kingdoms or the Ancient Council. Your grandad was the same: just as bad, just as weak. They're all weak! Xegan knows better. He has the strength to take us forward.'

So, his grandad's death, his home, everything, just discarded; casualties of some supposedly greater cause, Max thought bitterly.

Krake's expression grew hungrier. 'All this talk of tolerance and understanding the cornerstones of the Five Kingdoms – it's just an excuse to be passive, to do nothing. To let worlds continue in blissful ignorance. How can we know all that we do and sit back whilst world after world makes the same mistakes? We can help them, we can improve things, we can unify all of the worlds. We can lead them; guide them forward in a better direction.'

'You mean you can rule them,' Max said under his breath.

'You know nothing!' Krake snapped, his face darkening, 'Now, take me to the Book.'

For a moment, Max didn't move. He gritted his teeth; a silent fury boiling inside him.

'But why?' he said quietly, his voice full of hatred, 'I thought you were my dad's friend! I thought you served together. Why would you do this?'

Something flickered behind the dark gaze.

'We did serve together in WEAM. However, your father had the same deluded ideas as your grandad and my father.'

Max stared at him. He didn't think that he had ever felt so much disgust for anyone before in his life.

Krake looked at Max, his eyes narrowed.

'Your eyes,' he regarded him narrowly, 'So, you do have it too. He wondered if you did.'

Max said nothing.

'You were bound to, I suppose...' his voice trailed away, a smirk crossed his face, 'It was a waste on your father and grandad. They didn't know what to do with Aether. They didn't understand its power...' he shook his head, 'Not like your uncle...'

Uncle?

Max felt a flicker of unease.

He glanced nervously over at Bodhie and Anna, but they were both staring at Krake, transfixed.

Krake laughed loudly, unable to conceal his pleasure.

Max's stomach tightened with a sick sense of dread.

'Didn't you ever wonder why your grandad left like that?' he sneered, 'Why you were living on Earth in the first place? Why you had the map? It was *Xegan's* map. Why would your grandad have it? Didn't you ever wonder why Imeda and I would bother coming to tell your grandad that Xegan had been sighted? After ten years – why would he even care?'

Max stared at Krake. His mind filled with dreadful certainty.

Bodhie and Anna were frowning at Krake. A look of shocked comprehension slowly registered on their faces.

'The reason why your grandad had that map–' said Krake his eyes gleaming maliciously, '–was because Xegan was his son. Xegan is your uncle.'

The full horrible truth kicked in and suddenly Max was flailing in empty space. He felt as though he were falling from a great height.

Krake looked at Max and smirked, his face full of contempt.

'The map accidentally ended up in your grandad's possession. I doubt he ever knew what it was. Then after the death of your parents, your grandad suddenly decided to leave. You went to Earth. Unfortunately, he took everything – including the map. Xegan's map; before he had a chance to retrieve it. That Map – that Book – is the key to Xegan's plans.'

Max said nothing. He could hear Krake still talking, he could see his lips moving, but he was no longer listening. He stared numbly ahead, the words crashing over him.

He felt sick.

'Now!' Krake hissed, jabbing his finger into Max's chest, 'Enough! Take me to the Book!'

Anna and Bodhie were watching Max warily; their expressions were shocked, awkward. He didn't move.

'You'd better not try anything, Max,' said Krake softly, his dark eyes full of suspicion.

Max tried to swallow. A heaviness settled

inside him. He knew Krake was right. For the first time, Max realised sickeningly that everything in his life had suddenly and very sharply come into focus. Everything finally made sense.

'Where is it, then?' Krake snapped.

Max shook himself. He couldn't think about this right now. He had to focus.

'It's down the passageway, behind the veiled lady,' he said hoarsely.

Krake's brows lowered suspiciously.

Max tried to compose his face. He stared steadily back at him, aware of Krake's scrutiny as he spoke.

'There's a passageway, I think the Book's down there,' he said, louder this time.

Krake's eyes narrowed, 'And how do you know it's down there?'

'There was a clue, that's how we knew to find the statue.'

'And where is this clue?'

'It wasn't written down,' said Max quickly, 'We had to remember it – like the tablet.'

Valac made an ominous, angry rasping sound.

Krake regarded Max for a moment.

'And what did it say – this clue?' said Krake

suspiciously.

'I-I don't remember all of it, but the first bit talked about a changing world and then it said something like, "A veiled woman knows where our heritage rests". So, it led us to this statue, and there was a key which opened this secret passageway and then it said something about a door hiding a chamber and the Book...'

Krake's eyes narrowed, 'What key?'

'This one—' said Max, holding the strange little metal key out towards Krake.

Krake took the key and regarded it, slowly twisting it between his fingers. 'So, you opened up the passageway and just left? You haven't actually been down there?' His heavy eyebrows rose sceptically.

Max swallowed, 'We-we got separated. I didn't want to go down on my own. I was looking for them. That's why we're all here.'

Krake stared shrewdly at Max. His expression was hard.

'OK,' he said in a dangerously quiet voice, 'Let's go and see if you're right. But I'm warning you Max, if you lie to me, if you try anything – I promise you – I will kill you.'

Turning, he shoved Max towards the statue.

'Bring them,' he hissed, glancing back towards

Valac.

Krake's hand clamped down firmly on Max's shoulder and he felt himself being quickly propelled forward across the square, before being thrust past the statue, through the shadowy entrance and onto the spiral stone staircase.

A second later, Anna and Bodhie suddenly appeared next to him.

He glanced sideways, trying to catch their eye, but no sooner had he moved than he was shoved roughly in the back.

A light sparked up from somewhere behind him and the spiral stone staircase suddenly loomed into view, curling away from them, as it wound downwards, disappearing around the corner and into the shadows.

'Go on, then,' said Krake fiercely.

Max set off, tensely, down the stairs. He could hear the gentle clatter of footsteps descending behind him and the sound of Valac's soft, rasping breath.

Down and down they descended, the spiral staircase curled away from them, disappearing into the gloom.

The staircase suddenly opened up and Max saw that they had reached the beginning of the stone passageway. He shivered and set off down the passage. He knew that in a matter of minutes they would be there. In a matter of minutes one way or the other, this would all be over.

Fear welled up inside him. His hand crept to his pocket and he felt the comforting solid round shape of the Uroboros Key. If only he could put just enough distance between them, then maybe, just maybe, he could somehow configure the key without them noticing and the three of them could escape.

Glancing back quickly over his shoulder, Max looked back towards the group. With a jolt, he realised that Valac had moved forward and was walking directly behind him; his red eyes gleamed softly in the darkness. Max turned back sharply. Then felt a swift jab between his shoulder blades, reminding him to keep moving. Trying to control his panicky thoughts, he looked down at the floor, his eyes searching for the hole.

The torch light flickered, casting long moving shadows over the stone floor. He could hear the soft click of Valac moving along the passageway behind him.

Suddenly the floor opened out, dropping away sharply and Max stopped abruptly. The large heavy wooden door loomed just beyond the hole, shrouded in darkness.

'There's a hole!' said Max trying to sound surprised, 'And a door...'

'Good,' said Krake coolly, 'Perhaps you were

telling the truth after all.'

In an instant, Max felt something sharp grab his shoulder and he was dragged backwards. A huge, clawed hand gripped his shoulder savagely, spinning him around and Max found himself suddenly facing back towards Krake and Valac.

Sharp talons dug into his shoulder. Pain seared through his arm. He could feel each of the tiny puncture wounds that had only just begun to heal.

Max gasped, wincing with the pain. White lights winked before his eyes.

Valac squeezed Max's bruised shoulder again, his red eyes gleaming maliciously.

Pain tore through Max's arm. Tears stung in his eyes. He blinked hard and took a deep breath. Then gritting his teeth, he looked up and stared angrily back into Valac's fiery, red eyes.

Krake leaned over him and tugged something roughly from his pocket.

'Aaahhh! We almost forgot,' he said in a quiet, gloating voice.

Max's heart sank.

He held the Uroboros Key out towards Max. 'Now, I think it's time you returned something to us, don't you? This isn't yours.'

Max swallowed but said nothing.

'I hope you didn't think this was your way out of here...'

Max glared at Krake. He could feel the blood pounding in his ears.

Krake snorted, 'I hope this wasn't your big heroic plan to save your friends... because if it was, you've failed.'

Valac's eyes burned triumphantly. He let out a deep rasping, rattling breath. The warm, stale air wafted gently across Max's face, making his skin crawl.

'Now,' said Krake turning towards the gap, 'To business.'

Valac shoved them towards the hole.

'All of you across,' Krake barked, eyeing the door hungrily.

Max's heart began to pound. Reluctantly, he followed Anna and Bodhie across the narrow stone strip on either side of the gap. His stomach clenched nervously. He'd lost the Uroboros Key. What if this didn't work and they couldn't now get out? What if he'd judged this all wrong?

Valac unfolded his huge filmy black wings and swooped across the gap with Krake, landing directly in front of the door.

Standing slightly to one side, Max watched on anxiously with Anna and Bodhie, as Krake eagerly leant forward and placed the shiny little key in the lock, his breath caught in his chest.

There was a soft click. The key turned. Krake and Valac exchanged a glance, and then the door swung open to reveal another large, dimly lit chamber.

Shifting slightly, Max peered cautiously past Krake and Valac and through the open doorway. A large stone altar-like table, similar to the one that Max had seen earlier, stood a little distance away, towards the back of the room. An enormous stone statue of a coiled serpent stood to one side in the shadows.

Krake pointed over towards the stone altar and muttered something excitedly to Valac. Valac stepped forward into the chamber. He paused for a moment and looked cautiously around, then seeming satisfied that there was nothing lurking in the corners, he began to move quickly through the chamber in the direction of the altar.

Edging forward slightly, Max held his breath and peered further into the room. His eyes darted around. What if he had judged this all wrong?

Krake was hovering excitedly in the doorway. He stepped forward, eager to join Valac, then glanced back warily towards them. Max knew Krake was torn, uncertain how far he dared to step away from them in case they tried to make their escape. Avoiding Krake's narrowed, suspicious stare, Max gazed passively past him into the room and tried to fix what he hoped would look like a resigned, obedient expression on his face.

A faint sound, emanated softly through the doorway.

Max held his breath, straining to listen.

The sound came again. Soft, barely audible. A low hiss.

Max's heart began to hammer in his chest. His eyes darted back to Valac.

Valac was moving quickly through the chamber, heading directly towards the table.

Krake was still hovering in the doorway; he turned and glanced suspiciously towards them.

Something hissed again softly in the shadows. Krake's head jerked back sharply towards the doorway.

Max's eyes darted around the chamber. With a jolt, he noticed that the huge stone statue was stirring in the corner of the room. It was slowly unravelling and uncoiling; slithering, stealthily across the floor. Max blinked. It wasn't a statue; the giant serpent was real.

Valac didn't appear to have noticed, he was moving eagerly forwards, the table almost within reach.

The serpent slithered through the shadows, silently tracking Valac's steady progress through the room.

Krake opened his mouth, then froze.

The enormous serpent had suddenly slithered out into the open. Its thick grey body glided, scales gleaming, across the stone floor. It slid to a halt in front of the altar, blocking Valac's path.

Valac stopped abruptly and shrieked angrily.

The serpent eyed him beadily. It hissed. It's long forked tongue flicked.

Valac opened his huge spiny black wings threateningly, savage claws outstretched.

The serpent reared up, arching and spitting. It loomed over Valac, rising higher and higher; long, venomous, fangs glistening...

Valac froze.

In a heartbeat, Valac let out an ear-piercing shriek and flew at the serpent.

The serpent lunged towards Valac, striking. Its mouth stretched wide – wide enough to swallow him whole.

Valac veered sideways, narrowly missing the serpent's fierce glinting fangs.

The serpent drew back, hissing and spitting, then lunged again.

Valac shrieked, and then launched himself

forwards, savagely slashing at the serpent's head. But the serpent was too quick; it weaved, twisting out of the way, then lunged again. Striking.

Suddenly, the great serpent was coiling around; coiling in upon itself. Slithering round and round until it held Valac; crushing him in a vice like grip.

Valac screamed, red eyes bulging. His arms flailed, talons thrashing as he desperately tried to claw his way out. But it was no use. The crushing coils only tightened. It slowly squeezed and constricted; strangled and choked.

Max watched chillingly as Valac was slowly dragged downwards, disappearing down into the huge contracting coils. Peeling his eyes away, he glanced quickly towards Krake. Krake was staring at Valac, his face quite expressionless.

Valac let out a spine-tingling shriek.

Krake took a reluctant step forward, and then stopped again, uncertain what to do.

Max turned. This was their chance. Bodhie and Anna were frozen, staring aghast as Valac was slowly sucked down into the thick, twisting coils. Max gingerly prodded them both, then silently pointed back up the passageway. Anna looked around sharply at Max, her eyes wide in terror.

Glancing quickly back towards Krake, Max saw that he was still staring, transfixed in horrified, grim fascination.

Slowly, carefully, they edged away from the door. Then turning, they began to silently inch their way across the narrow stone strips on either side of the gap. Anna had just reached the other side and Bodhie and Max were part way across, when suddenly Krake turned.

'Stop!' he roared.

Max lunged towards the solid floor of the passageway, then pausing for a second, he glanced back.

'Where is the book?!' Krake demanded, his face twisted with anger.

'It's gone,' said Max simply.

'You tricked me!' Krake roared his face contorted.

Something snapped inside Max. He couldn't remember ever having felt so angry. 'I tricked you?' he bellowed, fists clenched, 'You tricked me. You lied to me about that stupid chain. You killed my grandad and you've betrayed everyone!' He stared defiantly at Krake, his mind ablaze. A fierce exultation surged through him. Finally, after everything that had happened, they were fighting back.

'Max!' said Bodhie from somewhere beside him, 'Let's go.'

Krake lunged towards them, then stopped abruptly at the edge of the hole, 'You!' he roared.

'What?' Max yelled, fists still clenched.

Behind him through the open doorway, Max could see the serpent and one black clawed hand reaching out of the thick twisting coils, grasping desperately at the air.

Krake glared at Max, his face a deep crimson, 'You'll regret this!' he spat. Behind him, the hand vanished.

Max turned and ran.

The pitch-black passageway swallowed them, plunging them into darkness. Down and down the corridor they hurtled. A spine-chilling shriek echoed through the passageway behind them. Then it stopped abruptly. Max didn't look back.

The passageway bent, and they hit a wall, then fumbling their way along, they stumbled off again. On and on they ran, stumbling blindly in the dense, musty blackness.

Footsteps echoed along the passageway behind them. Panicking, Max glanced back over his shoulder; a faint light was bobbing in the distance. He could hear Bodhie breathing heavily beside him. Grabbing Bodhie's arm, he dragged him forward.

All of a sudden Max tripped, then stumbled. His knees hit stone. He fumbled his way along. His fingers found a thick stone ledge. They had reached the staircase.

Bodhie was drawing breath in sharp, painful gasps.

Max pushed Anna up the staircase before him, and then launched himself up, heaving Bodhie up the thick stone steps. His shoulder seared with pain.

Behind them, he could hear the sound of Krake's approaching footsteps.

'Did – you – get – it?' panted Anna, as she charged ahead of them up the stairs.

'Yes,' gasped Max, 'I got it!'

A pale light suddenly illuminated the staircase ahead of them. Then abruptly they burst out of the passageway and they were back in the square. The pale grey, blue light of dawn was slowly seeping across the sky. The darkness was fading.

Max lurched to a halt; doubled over, chest heaving. He could feel the blood pounding in his ears.

It took a moment for Max to realise that a huddle of people was standing in the square. Amongst the group, was an elegant dark-haired woman. She stood with her back to them, addressing the group.

Then suddenly everything happened at once.

A man in the group saw them and pointed.

The woman turned. With a start, Max saw that it was Maya – the woman that he had met in the meeting with the Ancient Council, the leader of the Nix.

'Max!' she exclaimed, her face relaxing with relief, 'We've been so worried!'

Max could hear the sound of fast approaching footsteps echoing through the passageway behind them.

Maya smiled and stepped towards them. Max hesitated, then glanced nervously towards Anna and Bodhie.

Then suddenly, out of the corner of his vision, Max saw something black swoop past. With a start, he noticed that a black bird was flying low over the square. It was the same black bird.

The bird swooped down, landing next to Maya. But before the bird had even reached the ground, something was happening...

Max frowned, confused.

Where moments before there had been a bird, it was quickly blurring and growing, rapidly changing and morphing, until suddenly it had transformed into a woman – a woman with long blond hair. She stood next to Maya and looked across at them.

'Of course!' Anna gasped next to him, 'You're a shapeshifter!'

A sound behind them jolted Max to his senses. Footsteps thundered up the staircase behind them.

Grabbing Anna and Bodhie, Max quickly stepped sideways and away from the entrance.

Moments later Krake burst forth, out of the passageway. He was holding a burning torch aloft in one hand and clutching the Uroboros Key in the other. He stood at the edge of the passageway and frowned, eyeing the group with narrow eyed distaste.

'Krake!' said Maya, 'You did this! How could you do this?'

Krake ignored Maya. His gaze fell to Max; the hard, dark eyes regarded him for a moment.

'You will regret this,' he whispered.

A second later, he had lifted the Key and was gone.

SAM KINI

Chapter 31
The Return

Half an hour later, Max found himself sitting in a spacious office. They had been quickly led away from the square and guided into one of the imposing grand old buildings situated close by. Various people had bustled in and out and then a lady with soft, grey hair and a kind smile had brought them hot cups of sweet tea and told them, in a gentle but efficient tone, that someone had gone to retrieve the Book from the doorway, that Cade was being contacted and that Maya would be along shortly. Nobody had spoken.

'Do you think this is OK, then?' said Max after a few moments. He was perched rigidly on the edge of his chair, a blanket draped around his shoulders, watching the steam rise from his cup.

Anna gave Max a tense nod. 'I think it's all over now,' she said simply.

Max sipped his tea. It tasted sweet and sugary and burnt his tongue slightly, but it was good. Sitting back in his chair, Max blew out a long breath. He became aware that his arms and legs suddenly felt heavy with tiredness and that the dull throb was back in his shoulder.

'So you got it, then?' Anna said quietly, her tired eyes were eager. 'You actually got the book!'

Max nodded and gave them both a weak grin. He watched Anna and Bodhie's expressions relax with relief and joy.

Anna gave a sudden laugh of relief. A triumphant smile slowly lit her face.

Bodhie's pale face split into an exhausted grin. 'That's amazing, Max. I can't believe you got it! So, what was down there in the chamber?'

'A Watcher,' Max smiled ruefully. 'It was absolutely enormous.'

'What did you do?' exclaimed Anna.

'Well, at first, I thought I was going to become dinner. But then I managed to throw that Poca in its mouth. It didn't like it much!'

'Why? What happened?' Bodhie's silvery eyes were wide with admiration.

'I think the smoke erupted inside it, it got really confused and I managed to grab the Book and use the Key to get out.'

Max paused, his thoughts wandered for a moment, returning to the strange feelings he had felt in the chamber. He decided not to mention it for the moment – maybe he'd imagined it.

'Wow, that was lucky,' Anna beamed.

'I wouldn't describe it as lucky exactly,' laughed Bodhie. 'He nearly got roasted – again!'

Max gave them both a grin. 'So, what happened in the square then, when you were waiting for me?'

'Oh!' said Anna rolling her eyes. 'What a nightmare! When we got out, Xegan and Krake were already there. We started walking across the square and then realised that we couldn't stay invisible for long enough to get past them. There's nothing really in the square – no cover – so, we went back to the tunnel but then we were trapped in there. When they started walking towards us, and they were going to come down the passageway, we had no choice: we either had to go further into the tunnel (but then we'd be trapped in there with them) or we had to try and get out across the square and then... well, we couldn't quite make it...'

'You saw what happened, I suppose,' said Bodhie reddening.

Max nodded. 'I couldn't believe it when Valac and Krake came towards you...' He shuddered. 'How long had you been invisible for?'

'About fifteen minutes... on top of everything today, it was just too much. I'd tried to do it too many times with you both. I've only ever done it once or twice before with other people,' ze hesitated. 'I'm so sorry, Anna.' Bodhie's pale cheeks flushed; ze looked angry with himself.

'Don't be stupid!' exclaimed Anna. 'They'd have found me in about five seconds if I hadn't been with you. Anyway,' she said, turning to Max,

'How did you know that that snake thing was going to be down there?'

'I didn't really. It's just that when I figured that the rest of the rhyme had turned out right, I sort of guessed that there must be something behind the second door, a trap or something... The rhyme had said that we had to choose wisely or we'd regret it and if we'd regret it, there had to be something in there. I was just hoping I guess... I didn't know what else to do.'

'Well, that was a bit risky, wasn't it!' Anna's eyebrows shot up in alarm. 'What if we'd got down there and the chamber was empty? Blimey, when you came striding across the square to save us, I thought you had a better plan than that!'

'Grateful, isn't she!' Bodhie laughed, head shaking in mock disbelief. 'Thanks, Max. You really saved our skin there,' ze added with exaggerated emphasis.

'You seem more perky, all of a sudden,' grinned Anna.

Max glanced at Bodhie and noticed too that some of the colour was finally returning to Bodhie's cheeks. As he glanced back at Anna, she caught and held his gaze.

'Max...?' she started hesitantly. She looked uncomfortable.

Max knew what Anna was thinking, but he

wasn't ready to discuss what Krake had said. Not now. Not yet.

'The Book!' he said suddenly, floundering around for something else to say, 'I hope it's still where I left it. I had to hide it behind a railing in a doorway. It wasn't very well hidden.'

Anna frowned but said nothing.

There was a light knock on the door and Max was relieved when the door opened and Maya came in.

'I'm sorry you've had to wait,' she said gently. 'I've been to see Cade. He's on his way. There was a lot to discuss. Your parents...' she said gesturing to Anna and Bodhie, 'They are also on their way.'

'What, my mum and dad too?' said Bodhie reddening. 'But I thought they were away...'

Maya slipped across the room and sat in a chair close to the three of them. 'You've all been through so much,' she paused and looked at them all. Her dark eyes held a deep warmth and kindness, 'And I would very much like you to tell me about it. But I think perhaps we should wait for Cade to arrive, and I also realise that perhaps I owe you something of an explanation.'

There was a light knock on the door.

'Come in!' Maya called.

The lady with grey hair that had brought them

the tea, reappeared in the doorway. She was carrying the Book which she handed to Maya and then quietly retreated from the room.

'So, it is true,' she said quietly, 'You found the Book. After all this time.' She placed the Book on the table in front of her and touched the cover gently, her eyes lingering over the gold clasps and seals. Your people will be very glad to have this returned to them, Bodhie. The three of you have done very well. You have been incredibly brave.'

Max felt a tiny shiver of pride. He glanced towards Bodhie and Anna and noticed that they were beaming.

Maya gave a light cough. 'I didn't realise that this was what Xegan was after at first. Not until Lorelei overheard the three of you discussing it.' She sighed. 'I had suspected Krake was involved, but it was impossible to prove and we kept losing you. Lorelei was there that day at Irin's, but then Valac arrived and you disappeared and by the time she came back with help, you'd already gone. We struggled to find you again after that and then when we did, we kept immediately losing you. We also couldn't understand how Krake kept finding you. Then we remembered that day at Anna's house, when Lorelei had seen Krake give Max the amulet and we wondered if that was how he was tracking you, so we changed tack: we decided to follow Krake. Sure enough, Krake brought us back to you. We tried to help you by taking it from you,' Maya gave Max an apologetic smile, 'The problem is that

Lorelei brought the amulet here to the government buildings to be assessed and investigated and that would have been fine had you also not been coming here to find the Book. The problem was, it brought Xegan and Valac straight back to you.'

Max felt more tiny pieces of a gigantic puzzle slowly fall into place in his mind.

There was an urgent knock at the door; Maya rose from her seat and disappeared from the room.

Max gazed blankly out of the window. Dawn was breaking through the window outside and the light was growing in the square; he could see the statue of the veiled lady in the distance and the shadowy outline of the passageway behind. His mind wandered back to what had happened in the square. There was so much to think about. So Valac had gone. Krake had betrayed them and disappeared. And Xegan – Xegan was his uncle. Even now the shock of the realisation hit him like a bus.

There was the sound of talking out in the hallway and moments later, Maya reappeared with Cade. Cade looked strained, his skin was grey and he looked as though he had aged considerably in the last few days. He pulled up a chair and sat down next to Max.

For a moment, nobody spoke.

'Right,' said Maya re-joining the group, 'I think we should probably start at the beginning. Can you start by telling us what happened the night of Krake's party?'

They talked for almost an hour after that. Anna spoke first describing how they had found the map, how the Mothman had arrived and how they'd fled with the Uroboros Key. They explained how they had hidden in the Barren Lands and then gone to find Irin where they had first met Bodhie. They told them about how they had found the Temple of Fangs and then the clue and how Valac had found them again and that the Uroboros Key had been broken. Then Max explained how he had used the Poca and stolen Valac's Uroboros Key. At this point both Maya and Cade had become very concerned and the conversation was halted whilst they discussed the implications of the extra dial on the Uroboros Key. Then Bodhie took over the story and told them about the clue and how it had eventually led them back to the Veiled Lady and the square and... Xegan.

Nobody had discussed what Krake had said. Anna and Bodhie gave Max an awkward glance. A long pause stretched between them.

Max felt his stomach tighten, he stared at his trousers and tugged at a loose thread in the seam.

It took Max a moment before he could speak. 'Why didn't you tell me that Xegan was my uncle?' he said heavily. A wave of weariness washed over him. It was unsettling to hear the words spoken aloud.

Maya's bright blue eyes flicked quickly towards Cade in alarm.

Several emotions fought on Cade's face. 'I'd like a moment alone with Max,' he said quietly.

Maya gave Cade an understanding nod and rose gracefully from her seat, 'Anna, Bodhie. I'll take you to see your parents now. They'll be waiting.'

Anna caught Max's eye and gave him an anxious frown. Max gave them both a nod to show he was OK. Then, they followed Maya out of the room. The door clicked quietly shut behind them.

For a moment neither of them spoke.

'It doesn't change who you are, you know,' Cade's voice was heavy with sadness.

'How can you say that? I don't even know who I am anymore!' Max said bleakly.

'You do, Max. You are still the person that you always were. Don't let this news about Xegan change all of that. This was exactly why I was scared of telling you...' Cade gave a long weary sigh.

'But you said that you'd be truthful with me!' Max exclaimed.

'Yes, Max, and I was. I just didn't answer all of your questions fully. What would you have me do, Max? It was only a few days ago that you didn't know about any of this. There are limits as to how much one person can absorb in such a short space of time! After your parents died and Xegan became... how he is now, your grandad... he just wanted to look after you. You must understand Max; you were being protected.'

Max opened his mouth to disagree but he checked himself. When he thought about how he had felt, the shock of everything he had learned about himself over the last few days, he knew that Cade was right. He looked into Cade's face filled with nothing but concern for him, and there was nothing he could say. He also realised suddenly that he wasn't the only person who had just received a major shock. Krake was his son.

For a moment, neither of them spoke.

Max shifted awkwardly in his seat. 'I'm sorry about Krake,' he said uneasily. 'Where do you think he's gone?'

A shadow fell across Cade's face. 'I have no idea. Wherever Xegan is, presumably.' He hesitated, his face taut with sadness. 'I should have suspected. What with Krake only just having been made an Elder.' Cade let out a bitter laugh. 'I guess there's a reason why every world has the same saying – love is blind.'

A companiable silence fell between them both for a moment.

'Is Xegan really my uncle then?' Even now, Max was still finding it hard to believe.

'Yes,' Cade said solemnly. 'I'm sorry to say that he is.'

'But what happened?'

'Xegan was always... different to your grandad and your father. He always had different ideas. When he came back from his travels with WEAM I'm sorry to say, he became worse. His ideas about how we should handle the truth about our universe ran so contrary to everything that the Five Kingdoms believed.'

'What do you think they will do now?'

Cade shook his head wearily. 'I really don't know, Max. The Ancient Council will meet today and we will review everything that has happened and then make an assessment about the level of threat we face and what the Five Kingdoms should do next to protect themselves.' Cade paused, collecting himself, 'Thanks to you three though, whatever Xegan was planning to do, whatever his plans were until now, they have taken a significant step back today. You should be deeply proud of what you have achieved, Max. You have all been exceptionally brave – exceptionally stupid –' Cade smiled and for the first time, the smile reached his eyes, 'But exceptionally brave.'

Max felt a tiny flush of warmth spread through his chest.

'There's something else I need to explain to you, Max.' Cade paused, his blue eyes held Max's for a moment, 'It's about Aether.'

'That I have some kind of ability with it?' Max questioned. 'I know. That's why my eyes go silver sometimes, isn't it?'

A flicker of surprise registered on Cade's face. 'You already know?'

Max shifted uncomfortably in his seat. 'I overheard Chandra talking about it that day when I came to see the Ancient Council.'

'Ahhh,' Cade gave a soft chuckle. 'I'm sorry you had to learn about it that way. It's true. Your grandad, your father and Xegan all had the ability and now it looks as though you do too.'

'But what does it mean? Why can't I tell I have it?'

'It doesn't usually manifest until you reach your teens properly. Other than your eyes changing colour, you might not have really known anything until now. Have you experienced anything unusual, Max?'

Max hesitated for a moment. His thoughts wandered back to the underground chamber and the experience he had with the Watcher. 'I'm not sure,' he began. 'I think I might have felt something weird last night in the chamber. When I was in there with the Watcher, I felt like I knew things...' His voice trailed away, he felt embarrassed.

'What sort of things?' Cade's expression was

questioning, but kind.

'It's strange...' Max said, feeling his way through his thoughts. He thought back to how exactly it had felt in the chamber, trying to make sense of what had happened. 'It's like I was inside the Watcher's head,' he said finally. 'Also when we were in the underground corridor, it's like I knew something was wrong. I knew something wasn't right but I just couldn't understand the feeling and then there was this huge hole in the ground that we hadn't seen...' His voice trailed away for a second time.

Cade nodded thoughtfully. 'It was like that with your grandad. I never really understood it fully, but I think that's one of the things that made him such a good leader.'

Max turned this over in his mind. He'd often felt like his grandad had known what he was thinking. 'And what about my dad?'

'Your father was the same, but even stronger perhaps... We didn't really know how it manifested with Xegan. We never really thought that he was particularly skilful compared to your father but with everything that he has done, everything that he has seen over the last few years... who knows what he can do now...' Cade paused. 'Did you see anything last night, Max, when you saw Xegan in the square or did Krake mention anything about what Xegan could do?'

Max thought back to when he had seen

Xegan in the square but it had all gone so fast. Apart from the steely grey eyes, he couldn't remember very much. Then a horrible thought struck him.

'His eyes were very silver, grey,' he said thoughtfully. 'The whole time I saw him. I only saw him for a short time, but they seemed to be constantly silver.'

A deep frown creased Cade's forehead.

'Do you think that means that he can use Aether all of the time or that he has become really powerful with it?' Max said worriedly.

'I don't know; I sincerely hope not. What you have to understand, Max, is that we still don't really understand Aether. It manifests in so many different ways: with the Nix, Aether allows them to shapeshift, in the Shadowlands the Shadow People can release their shadows, the Hidden People can become invisible. We still don't really understand it properly.'

'And what about with me? What do you think will happen?' A million questions surfaced in Max's mind.

'It's hard to say... but there will be something, Max. We will just have to watch how it develops with you and help you to try and understand it when you start to notice things happening.'

Max paused, understanding the significance

of what Cade had just said. 'So I'm going to stay here, then? You're not going to send me back to Normington?'

Cade smiled, but his expression was confused. 'No, of course not. What could ever make you think that, Max? How could I ever do that?' Then a look of embarrassed recognition slowly spread across his face. 'Oh...! You're referring to that conversation you overheard with myself and Malik.' He smiled wearily, 'Yes, Malik wasn't happy about the fact that we brought you back. But he was trying to protect you,' Cade said earnestly. 'He knew how little we knew about what was going on, and he knew it wasn't safe here...'

Cade paused. 'Listen Max, I know it's a lot to take in right now but Anna's parents have said that they would like it very much if you would like to live there with them. If you want to, that is.'

Max gave a jerky nod; a hard lump had formed in his throat. 'That would be great,' he managed. He sat back in his chair. He blinked and stared out of the window across the square. The sun was getting higher in the sky now and the daily morning hubbub and traffic of people were starting to bustle through the streets. A new day was beginning. Max felt himself slowly relax, the tiny knot of grief and anger in his stomach loosen. Finally getting all of his worries and questions off his chest, felt good.

At long last, Max felt like he understood

everything. Ever since his grandad had died, he had felt adrift. Ever since that night, there had been a tightness in his chest, a hard, shard of anger that he had been carrying around inside him. Suddenly, the pain in his chest broke loose and lifted free.

Two days later, Max was sitting out in the garden with Anna and Bodhie, watching Lokie trying to tug an enormous purple striped sticky slug off his bright orange fur.

'We're all going to get an award, you know,' Bodhie was saying happily. 'My mum and dad are sure that the Hidden People are going to give it to us because we found and returned the Uroborologs.'

'Good to see someone is happy with us,' Anna grumbled. 'My uncle Bron still hasn't spoken to me yet after all of the things we took from the shop. Apparently Lokie fell asleep in the back of the shop and so he didn't realise for two days that it was us that had been there and taken his things. He accused Flo of stealing from him! It was only when he found Lokie snoring on the sofa in his office and the fridge in the office raided of food that he realised what must have happened and twigged it was us. He's had to apologise to her and give her a salary raise to make it up to her – she isn't even very good!' Anna rolled her eyes, then grinned at them both.

Max laughed and sat back on his arms, his

face tilted towards the sun, basking in the warmth of the late afternoon sunshine. Ever since he had returned home to Anna's house he had felt... different. The heavy grief that had been pressing down on him for days about his grandad had finally gone, the angry disappointment had slipped away and behind it there had been a different wave of emotion. He finally felt able to think about his grandad. But there was something else, something new had crept over Max: a new sense of understanding about who he really was and with that, came a sense of determination and resolve.

Max didn't yet understand what all of these new things he had learnt about himself meant; only that he still felt better for knowing the truth about himself and all of the ancient secrets he had discovered.

Every now and then his thoughts would drift back to what had happened and he would remember that Xegan and Krake were still out there plotting something. He knew that this was only the beginning of the journey. Now that he had learnt the truth about Xegan, he knew that their paths would cross again in future; that somehow there must be more to come. He just didn't know what. Yet.

But right now, today, sitting in the sunshine with his friends, his worries faded away along with Krake's threat towards him.

A few days later, a small package arrived at Anna's house addressed to Max. The package contained his grandad's Uroboros Key that had been carefully and meticulously mended and contained a small hand written note –

Max,

I took the liberty of collecting your things from the Barren Lands and mending your grandad's Key. I thought that you would appreciate having something of your grandad's returned to you, but I return this on the understanding that you will promise not to go running off again...

By way of my apology and my thanks to you,

Cade

ANCIENT SECRETS

SAM KINI

About the Author

Sam Kini is based in the UK in London and Manchester with her family. She works in Technology for global organisations. She has always had a passion for travel and became interested in the myth and history of countries where she was struck by how many things we still don't really understand about the universe around us, the mysteries of our past and the huge gaps that there are in our understanding of things.

She decided that she wanted to write a book that was about just that: many of the secrets and mysteries of our universe in a fast-paced action packed plot; a book that would be about growing up and trying to make sense of the world, in a very real sense.

The result was Ancient Secrets: a story set in the present day about a fourteen-year-old boy named Max who discovers a series of startling secrets. The story takes place over nine days – nine days that change Max's life forever and force him to question everything that he knows about his life, his past and the very fabric of the universe.

SAM KINI

Printed in Great Britain
by Amazon